The Bounce in the Captain's Boots

Ladies Most Unlikely,
Book Three

Jayne Fresina

A TWISTED E PUBLISHING BOOK

The Bounce in the Captain's Boots
Ladies Most Unlikely, Book Three
Copyright © 2017 by Jayne Fresina

Cover design by K Designs
All cover art and logo copyright © 2017, Twisted E-Publishing, LLC

ISBN-13: 978-1976327162
ISBN-10: 1976327164

When Emma Chance met her best friend's elder brother, she knew instantly that he needed somebody to put the bounce back in his boots.

But it couldn't be her, of course. She wouldn't know where to start.

Against the odds, Emma Chance survived a childhood of cruelty and neglect. She's never had time for fairytales or Prince Charming and, as a young woman with a logical mind, her preference is for tidy facts over messy feelings. But with one glance from his dark eyes, Captain Guy Hathaway causes poor Emma a bundle of the latter and turns her cautious world on its head.

To him she is nothing more than his little sister's shy, awkward friend, and she wouldn't know what to do with herself, in any case, if he ever looked at her as anything more than that.

But there's something about Captain Hathaway...

* * * *

The charismatic captain has a reputation for trouble. Brawls, duels and dangerous women litter his past. With a mischievous sense of humor, a hot temper and a reckless impulse to leap in with both feet, he has always sailed along at a steady clip, determined never to be anchored too long in one place and never risking his heart. But lately he's felt a strange emptiness, a yearning for something he cannot identify. It began a few years ago, about the time he escorted his younger sister and two of her friends to a ball. Did he lose something there, or did he find it?

Until he gets to the bottom of this mystery, he knows he won't be whole again.

In the meantime, while he seeks out the source of this discontent, he can make himself useful, initiate some changes in his life and do a few good deeds for once. Why not? For instance—timid, plain little Miss Chance, his sister's droopy best friend, could surely benefit from a helping hand.

The first time he met her she was a mess of nerves, covered in a red rash and itching as if riddled with fleas. But he can't help feeling there is more to the strange creature than meets the eye.

Yes, indeed, there is something about Emma Chance...

To All Those Who Generally Finish Last

Jayne Fresina

Sehnsucht: (n.) The inconsolable longing in the human heart for "we know not what"; a yearning for a far, familiar, non-earthly land one can identify as one's home.

Prologue
Hamberton,
Norfolk Coast of England
November, 1822

"Sometimes the wind do puff and blow up 'ere," a whiskered fellow had once remarked, his ruddy, weathered face cheerful as he tipped his hat to her. "Mind you don't go too near the edge, miss. A slight thing like you could blow right o'er."

She, on her first journey along these cliffs, had nodded and smiled in reply, then walked on, heading up the slope as he passed down it. The kindly concern of strangers still surprised her back then. But the merciless tug of the wind at the highest point of the cliffs had shocked her even more, despite his warning.

Each subsequent time she walked this path, Emma remembered that fellow and murmured to herself, "Sometimes the wind do puff and blow," in his accent.

The wind did indeed billow, gust, and belch like an old man's belly after a cask of cider. It was strong enough to pull on a woman's skirts and drag her to the edge.

And a person standing on these cliffs might imagine they hear voices wailing, a malevolent tune caught up and twisted around with every gust. Some hear mournful weeping.

A few hear screams.

On a particularly blustery day, like this one, when

a brooding sky of livid clouds brought about that sinister, jaundiced light, not many would bravely venture closer to the edge and investigate the source of that sound.

Emma, however, was a rarity. And she wouldn't miss this for the world.

As she stepped closer to the cliff edge, she looked down. Below her, a woman clung desperately to a few dry tufts of scrappy grass, while that harsh, salty wind blew hard off the sea, screaming and howling across the ancient layers of cliff face, alternately buffeting and tugging on her skirt, trying to pry her free. Those beefy fingers, now clawing at crumbling chalk, were capable of delivering many hefty slaps and beatings, but even they would not keep her from falling forever, and she must have known it. Or perhaps not; she was a survivor, a scrapper who always found a trick out of any tough corner, looked at any tragedy for how it might benefit her.

Of course, one should never look down when so high above safe ground. Any logical person knew that. But this fallen woman watched to where her black bonnet had tumbled down the reddish limestone to the savage rocks below. It lay there for a moment, ribbons clawing at the air, until two frothy waves of high tide converged upon it— the first leaving it drowned and limp, the second carrying the bonnet corpse away on a victorious crest of white. All this the stranded woman watched, having no idea at that moment that she herself was calmly observed from above.

No more than a dark shadow against the heaving, bruised sky, the witness stood upon the cliffs and looked out over the storm-whipped sea. Her gaze drifted slowly downward to the scuff marks in the ground, to the crumbled edge and then, once more, to where those fingers clung.

"The wind do puff and blow," she muttered. Apparently nobody had warned the other woman, although it was doubtful she would have listened, in any case.

For a moment the standing woman considered her own hands.

She might have reached down, she supposed, and offered assistance. There was still time. But everybody said she wasn't strong. They would understand. Nobody would blame her.

Salted rain drops touched her face.

One more hearty gust of wind should do it.

Suddenly the woman dangling from the cliff edge glanced up and saw her standing there, holding fate in her hands. At first there was a look of relief, then confusion, for it took a moment for the dangling woman to recognize the other. Perhaps it was the angle that tricked her, for the world had turned on its head.

This was finally the end. For one of them it was sublime victory; for the other it was a deadly blow— worse than any she herself had ever dealt with those thick, hard palms.

Funny how things turn out.

Well, not so droll for one of them.

* * * *

For so many years this is how the pleasant dream proceeded for Emma Chance, who saw herself standing on the cliff edge, calmly surveying the desperate scene. Today, however, there was a difference.

This time she was wide, wide awake.

Child

Chapter One
A dozen years earlier, in the midst of a London Particular

You are about to be properly introduced to the strange, unlikely heroine of this story.

It is not usual, I know, for the reader to be warned in advance, but I fear you might miss her entirely if not sufficiently alerted. Your fancy could be taken with one of the lovely, rosy-cheeked, shining-eyed girls gathered in a knot upon the third floor landing of this tall, narrow house on the end of a row, and you could be lured in by their tale instead. They all have one, of course.

But tonight it's finally her turn. About time too. And I won't let her be overlooked.

Because I know somebody who needs her.

Even more importantly at this moment in time, she requires a champion, for she is so small and slight a thing that few folk notice her. They hear her even less. As we join her story she has lived twelve years on this earth and in this house, without ever stepping out into the street, except to scrub the front step. Only two living souls are fully conscious of her sorry existence and how she came into being, and in their minds she is naught but a nuisance. To other folk she is a shadow.

But she is not a ghost like me, even if she sometimes imagines she must be, and she knows she is not because—

"*Chance*! Come here at once, you ungrateful chit of a girl. *Chance*!"

Ah, there you have it. The one voice that shouts for her is the reason she knows that she is, in fact, alive. The bruises and welt marks left on her skin by the owner of that voice would never be felt by an otherworldly spirit. But she feels them. Every one.

So you are advised to look hard and you might see our unlikely heroine shifting against the wallpaper, her shape slowly forming out of the pattern. You might hear her footsteps shuffling along the floorboards. Do not mistake her sigh of effort for the lonely drip of damp within the rafters.

Here she comes now.

No, not that one. Or that one. Or that one! Rub the sleep from your eyes, dear reader.

The crowd of pretty young girls, standing about in nightgowns, curling papers and morbid curiosity, slowly divides, allowing to emerge from their midst... a shadow.

* * * *

"Don't make me come and find you, girl!"

God forbid Mrs. Julia Lightbody, headmistress of the Particular Establishment for the Advancement of Respectable Ladies, should have to bestir her stumps, leave her gin and depart her cozy study on such a grim night. Fortunately she had, at her disposal, a charity pupil. And while "charity" has another definition for most people, for Julia Lightbody it meant "free labor".

"I come forthwith, madam," Emma Chance shouted breathlessly, struggling down the stairs with a mop taller than she and a bucket that weighed considerably more.

"Bran and water for my corns and flea-powder for my hair. Make haste, wretched creature. Where have you been?" The lady had her door ajar and a wedge of brighter amber firelight cut across the cold, dimly lit passage at the bottom of the stairs, her angry face protruding out into it like a turtle's head from its shell. Already dressed for her bed, she wore a lacy night cap perched atop the handful of grey strands yet remaining across her scalp; the wig she wore in daylight abandoned to its faceless wooden stand. Without her wig, Mrs. Lightbody would never want to be seen outside her study. And indeed nobody would want to see her, for the woman's head was bulbous and generally angry in appearance, folded in upon itself like a boxing glove, not of a dainty shape that might lend itself to the exotic state of semi-hairlessness.

"I've called for you these past ten minutes, Chance! My throat is sore!"

No such luck that it might render her mute, however.

"I suppose you dilly-dally again, falling idle the moment I can't see what you're up to."

"No, madam. I was cleaning the landing carpet where Miss Harding was sick, madam."

The headmistress twitched her head, like a dog attentive to the distant scent of burnt sausages and the sound of a spoon scraping against an iron pot. "Sick again was she? The Harding girl?"

"Yes, madam. She's abed now, like all the others. I shall take her something to settle her stomach."

"Not before you deal with my corns, Chance!"

"No, madam. Of course, madam."

"But for pity's sake empty that stinking bucket in the back yard and wash your hands before you come back here."

Emma hurried onward along the passage, gradually feeling her edges evaporate into shadow and dust as the candle sconces that hung upon the wall became more frugally spaced in this portion of the house— the part never exhibited to visitors and parents. As the distance between each comforting glow grew longer, the candles themselves became smaller and narrower. Their sad, nervous flames ducked and sputtered in the draft, some of them left without covers where broken glass had never been replaced. It was a good thing Emma knew her way in the dark, having walked up and down this passage so many times at all hours of the day and night, often in a hurry and with Mrs. Lightbody's voice shouting for her, or at her.

Just before she descended the narrow steps to the kitchen, Emma heard the headmistress shut her door with a thud, but she knew the lady must have stood there a while, pondering this news about one of her charges. It was not sympathy or concern for Miss Harding's health that bothered the lady, of course. Instead, she dwelt upon the likely consequence to herself, specifically to her accounts. If Miss Harding's illness continued, a physician must be called and his services would cost money, but sending the girl home to her family would create another expense, and the possibility of a lost tuition fee always caused Mrs. Lightbody to itch worse than the hardy colony of insects she imagined residing in her wig.

The students at her academy paid thirty guineas a year for lessons, food, and board, but she squeezed every little bit she could out of comfort and provisions to save most of that money for herself. And the "lessons" amounted to nothing more than a smattering of French, a little sewing, art appreciation, music, and some dancing. There was more to learn if one had the will, but most girls who came through that door and found themselves trapped in Mrs. Lightbody's web had no inclination to open a book unless it was forced into their soft, well-tended hands. They were not likely to seek out an education for themselves. In fact, sent there by families who hoped they might catch a titled, wealthy husband, these girls would have found any enlightening education to be a detriment.

But whatever Miss Harding had or had not learned at the school, this was the third consecutive day that she'd been sick and Emma Chance had cleaned it up. Something would have to be done, it seemed. The poor dear was off her food and very ill-tempered, which was most unlike her. She'd even suffered a fainting spell during the minuet last week in dance class, although Mrs. Lightbody revived her speedily with smelling salts and a slap to the cheek.

Emma thought the former would have been sufficient and the latter was merely over-excitement. But Mrs. Lightbody did like to administer her slaps. Usually they fell upon little Emma's "worthless" head and shoulders, and those whacks were much harder than the single paw print delivered to the elegant Miss Harding's porcelain cheek.

Collecting a lantern as she went, Emma carried the bucket through the kitchen and outside to the water pump. The pigs that Mrs. Lightbody raised for bacon and sausage, snorted and grunted contentedly from their sty in the far corner of the yard, but, as usual, one of them was out and rootling around the cobbles, trying to trip her up as she struggled along with her heavy burden. Although fearful of the pigs, she wouldn't give them the satisfaction of seeing it, so she was always very brisk and stern when they turned their mean little eyes toward her and came after her ankles.

"Be gone, Apollo, or I shall take the axe to you myself when the time comes."

Mrs. Lightbody, fonder of the pigs she raised than the girls in her care, liked to name them after Greek gods. They were certainly treated like deities, fed only the very best scraps and given the softest straw for their bed. It had, naturally, given them an inflated sense of importance and since they didn't like the fence of their sty they often broke out of it with nonchalance to explore the rest of the yard. Whenever poor Emma Chance had to cross the cobbles to the water pump, it was their greatest pleasure to chase her and push her about, toying with her as cats would with a mouse.

It was a cool and clammy night, the air dank, pinpricks of rain shimmering across the cobbles wherever her lantern's light shone. She didn't mind the rain, especially when she was alone in it, as she was tonight— apart from Apollo and the other pigs. Nobody else was out of bed at that hour. Often Emma was the last one to bed and the first to awake, for there were chores to be done and, as the headmistress frequently reminded her, who should do them other than the girl taken in out of charity? The foundling with no family to pay for her board. The bastard child abandoned to Mrs. Lightbody's care when she was a newly weaned babe.

Her father, so she was told, desired to remain anonymous, never wanted to know her or be known to her.

"Is it any wonder at that?" Mrs. Lightbody would exclaim. "Look at you. A sorry piece of flotsam with a face as cheerful as the third consecutive wet Wednesday in October!"

Emma puzzled over how to have a more pleasing face. It seemed to her a matter of family likeness and the degree of happiness in one's life. Since she had no control over either it seemed to her quite unfair that she be blamed for the unsightly state of her features.

Besides, she rather liked October, especially when it rained.

But she kept that to herself. Her opinions were as welcomed in that school as unexpected parental visits.

"I wouldn't want to know you either," the lady continued, "but alas somebody had to take you in and out of the generosity of my heart I gave you a bed under my roof. Now you repay my kindness and forbearance with scowls, snivelings and mutterings, always hovering about in corners like the grim reaper!"

In truth, Emma was often found in the corner because she was too shy to stand in the light, too afraid of being examined and found, inevitably, wanting. She muttered under her breath because she disliked the sound of her own voice and knew that anything she said would only be criticized and ridiculed. She much preferred to keep her thoughts in the corner too, out of poking reach. And she scowled because on the few occasions she'd been caught smiling, Mrs. Lightbody had wanted to know why she thought she was so special and what could she possibly have to smile at? Or else she would assume the luckless girl to be laughing spitefully at her and then she'd put her heavy, vicious hands around Emma's throat and choke the laughter out of it.

Frequently Emma considered how fortunate it was that her guardian did not see what truly went on in her mind— all the many colorful and spectacular ways that woman had been murdered by the hands of her wicked charity pupil in a dream universe. Over and over again.

Well, a girl had to have some entertainment.

But thankfully Mrs. Lightbody had no idea; she thought this shadowy wisp of a creature was quiet because she was cowed. Not because she plotted dramatic death scenes for her own pleasure.

So, all things considered, "Chance" went through her life keeping her thoughts to herself and trying not to be noticed at all. Now, at twelve years of age, she had seen many girls come and go from the academy. Most of them had probably never noticed the small, plain, colorless creature running up and down the stairs all day, but Emma remembered the detail of every pretty face and fine dress. In the beginning she had wished she might leave with them when they finally departed the place. But, of course, she had nowhere else to go, nobody to shelter her, and, as she was reminded often, she would one day be old enough to make recompense for these years under Mrs. Lightbody's roof, by becoming a governess, sent wherever the headmistress thought to put her and forfeiting her fee directly into that lady's greedy hands. There was no other reason for the foundling to read books and be allowed to study, was there, unless to make money from her one day? And money certainly could not be made through a marriage in her case, for who but the devil, as Mrs. Lightbody said, would want her?

These days Emma no longer yearned to leave through the front door of that house, slipping away by hiding inside the trunk of a graduating pupil. Never having ventured beyond the wall that enclosed the back yard and the water pump, she had begun to shrink further into the dimly lit passages she knew so well, taking her comfort from the familiar. After all, a creature that must live in the dark soon adapts its senses to survive, until, eventually, living in the sun would cause it pain. So it was for Emma Chance who, despite the dreariness of her days and nights under Mrs. Lightbody's command, now feared the prospect of having to leave that behind and go out into the world.

While she pumped water into the bucket, a thick, reasty vapor descended upon the yard, as if the rain had extinguished an angry dragon's fiery breath, reducing its power to smoke and ashes. Soon she would not be able to see her hand before her face. It was a curious, wet, dun-colored cloud that contained odorous remnants of every industry in town: the tannery; gas pipes; soap boilers; bakeries and breweries; fish guts from the docks; choked, overflowing gutters, cabbages and coal smoke. This was the kind of fog they called a "London Particular". Emma sometimes thought of herself as being of a similar creation, concocted from a mixture of the town's effluvia, and appearing as a mist to inconvenience folk. Something to be cursed at and railed against, but impossible to be rid of.

The only light currently piercing this hovering menace came from the lantern at her feet, but muffled sounds crept through the fog all around her— a mizzle of slow rain tickling the puddles and dripping against the high brick wall that surrounded the back yard, drunkards singing as they came along the street on the other side, guard dogs barking in the brewery yard across the square, and an old lady shouting out from her salop still on the corner.

People said the country was cleaner and quieter. Emma had never seen it for herself, could barely even imagine it. Open space with nobody living in it for miles, just grass, trees, barley fields and cows? She would be afraid of falling off the edge with no walls to keep her in.

She'd seen a cow once in a painting. Whether it was the fault of the artist's perspective, she could not say, but the beast seemed as big as the house painted next to it. The thought of encountering one in actuality was quite terrifying. She'd heard they made a noise far worse than the whinnying of horses, barking of dogs, or the grunting of pigs. Worse even than the braying of Mrs. Lightbody, her "kindly benefactor".

The latter sound she heard again now, as a window creaked open above her head in the fog.

"Hurry up, girl! What are you doing out there? Waiting for Prince bloody Charming?"

"Just getting Apollo back in the sty, madam."

No, Emma did not wait for a prince, charming or otherwise. Princes were too busy saving pretty girls, who carelessly left their shoes behind or were at leisure to sleep for a hundred years with nobody shaking them awake. Must be nice. Emma always took very great care of her few possessions; she would never leave them behind, even in a fire. As for sleeping, she was lucky to get a few hours of peace if Mrs. Lightbody had a heavy night with her gin. And to be honest, she would rather not be noticed by any man— prince or pauper. They were just as horrifying as those bovine beasts with four belching stomachs, rampaging across the countryside, biting people and rumbling with horrific noises.

She left the handsome men and romantic dreams to girls like Miss Harding, who slipped out at night sometimes to visit one such "prince". Emma was not supposed to know, of course, but she was too observant for her own good. Not only had she seen the young lady going out and coming back to the house in the small hours, but she knew a few other things too: Miss Harding was the only daughter of a very wealthy gentleman— a northern mill owner— and in possession of a vast dowry, while her secret amour was an indolent rake, all surface and no substance, and in debt up to his jaundiced eyeballs. Finally, Emma knew that not only was Mrs. Lightbody complicit in these nighttime trysts, but she had introduced the couple and encouraged them from the beginning.

It was not the first time such an affair had been conducted thus between a pupil of the academy and some young buck about town, who was in need of a rich bride to help settle his debts and fund his do-naught life. Among Julia Lightbody's acquaintance there were a great many such men and she maintained a house full of naive, romantically-inclined young ladies— several of them from families of the upwardly striving, new-money class, anxious to squeeze themselves, with a little "polishing" into a higher status.

The headmistress was always well compensated for her assistance in these illicit affairs, not only by favors from the rake, but by the unfortunate young lady's family when she offered to help them "hush up" the incident and initiate a hasty marriage before the result of the affair became evident. Naturally, the parents' first consideration was discretion and even when some of them might have made a ruckus, accusing Lightbody of not keeping her charges better guarded, the headmistress was accomplished at ducking the blame.

"These young girls! What can I do short of tying them to their beds? Your daughter would not be told. Such a trial she was on my spleen. A rotten, shameless girl."

Or "This wounds me, as much as it does you. I swear it has never happened here before."

Or "I am shocked, horrified. I cannot conceive

of such treachery committed under my roof. I must ask that you take your daughter away at once before she disrupts my house and infects the other girls with her scandalous, wanton behavior. After all, I have young ladies here from some of the finest families in the country."

She had to know her audience well, of course, and chose her excuses and accusations according to the temperament of the parents and the level of their social standing. Julia Lightbody was no genius, but she knew how to read people, specifically how to find their fears and feed upon them.

Inevitably, rather than risk exposing their daughter's downfall, destroying their own chance of ascension to a higher class, or jeopardize the place to which they had already scrambled, these ambitious families chose silence. Expensive silence.

They could have no idea that their case was not isolated.

Julia Lightbody was everybody's savior, everybody's keeper of secrets, playing both sides of the coin with the ease and sly cunning wrought of practice and experience. And with no conscience to trouble her, only the desire to feather her own nest.

All of this was supposed to go over Emma Chance's mousy, inconsequential head. Nobody — if they ever thought of her at all— believed that unbecoming smudge of a girl understood much of anything, beyond scrubbing, laundry and sewing. Well, her world might be a very narrow one, her life experiences confined to what happened within the walls of that house, but nothing went on there that she did not know about. And a lot went on.

Again the window above her exhaled a rusty squeal. "Chance! I still hear you at that blasted squeaking pump! Get up here at once, girl. I don't keep you fed and in health, so you can waste time playing with the pigs and dancing in the rain when my corns are playing up."

Sometimes Emma wondered if the lady's aches and pains, including the constant itching she experienced under her wig, were merely the remnants of a conscience gnawing at her flesh. After all, any real fleas must have been eradicated, long since, from that hairpiece. But there was no telling Mrs. Lightbody that they were gone. There was no telling her anything.

Better get back to work. There was much to do yet before Emma could lay her own head on that lumpy straw mattress in a corner of the kitchen.

"And mind you don't trip pig shit and rainwater all over my floors or you'll get the willow switch, ingrate!"

Lantern in one hand, bucket in the other, she made her way back across the yard. On the other side of the wall, the street was quiet at that moment, but her ever alert ears caught a slight sound shivering through the air, parting the moist froth. A sigh. Deep with sorrow. An impatient foot scuffed against the brick and the soft trace of cigar smoke wafted under her nose.

Definitely a male presence and, tonight, as spectral as her own.

Chapter Two

She would not usually stop for a man, but something about that unhappy sound prevented Emma from walking on into the house.

He must have heard her bucket on the cobbles as she set it down, or perhaps the shuffle of her footsteps stumbling to a halt apprised the fellow of another life behind the wall.

"Who's there?" he called out in the brusque voice of a young man afraid they might have been caught committing a shamefully tender act.

She held her tongue and went very still. The dragon exhaled another breath around her, thickening the cloud.

Again the foot scuffed impatiently over brick and she heard a low, terse huff. "Nobody, eh? Just a damned cat, I suppose. Who else but me would be out at this time of night in a London Particular?" Then followed the sound of a nose blown into a handkerchief.

On the other side of the wall, where the mournful fellow stood, there was a street lamp lit. Emma could just see it above the top edge of the brick. By then it gave off a soft, undefined blob of yellow, as if the wick had been swaddled in cotton bombast. The clogged air was very still now, heavy and pregnant with expectation. Distant sounds, of course, would be lost as the fog thickened, and only up close would one hear clear voices or the sudden flap of a startled crow's wing.

It made Emma feel as if she and the young man on the other side of the wall were all alone in the world.

Closing her eyes, she pictured him leaning there, the sole of one foot pressed to the wall, likewise the shoulders of his coat, marked with damp. Later he would find green moss staining the fabric, but just then he did not care apparently. His voice was youthful, but not boyish. There was a weary resignation to the "damned cat", as if he was destined to be plagued by those creatures.

Did he whisper to himself now? She moved closer to the brick and listened.

Crisp paper fluttered and flapped.

"New, fur-lined Italian riding gloves for the lady, two pounds, eight shillings." Another hearty sigh. "Seems extortionate. Were they really so much? Bonnet the lady could not live without, seven pounds and seven shillings. Flowers to match her eyes— fifteen shillings a day for ten days. That's...seven pounds five shillings in addition." He paused. "Seats in a box at the theatre, two nights in a row, ten shillings. Admission to Vauxhall gardens, two shillings. Steakhouse dinner for two, shillings two." Another pause. Foot tapping irritably. "Barrel of oysters, three shillings and thruppence. Three bottles of good claret, fifteen shillings total. One pound of Fry's drinking chocolate, five shillings." Soft groan. "This seduction business takes its a toll on a lieutenant's pay. I can hear my father's lectures already."

Emma strained to hear more, her ear to the damp wall, her breath merging with the lowering fog.

"So that's a grand total of eighteen pounds, ten shillings and thruppence," he muttered. "For a ten-day affair."

Oh, she shouldn't speak. She didn't want him to think she was anything more than a cat, because he would be embarrassed to know she'd heard his sadness in that sigh which was very nearly a sob. But Emma Chance could never stand a careless miscalculation.

"Nineteen pounds, sir, two shillings and thruppence," she whispered through the wall.

His foot stopped tapping.

"Flowers at fifteen shillings a day, for ten days, sir, is seven pounds *ten* shillings. Not seven pounds five shillings. But I don't know where you went wrong with the rest of it." She could not see the columns that would show his sums, of course. Otherwise she could have found where he made the error and corrected it for him.

"Who the blazes are you?" he demanded.

"Nobody, sir." She stepped away from the wall, her heart skipping erratically, like a drunkard across the cobbles after midnight.

"Nobody? Obviously you're somebody."

"No, sir. I'm not. I'm not anybody."

Horses' hooves approached through the thick

pea-soup, so he raised his voice. "Well, you're a clever chit. And a nosy one. Shouldn't poke your nose into a man's business."

That was vastly unfair, Emma thought, but no doubt he found it necessary to be harsh, just in case she'd heard his sadness before. She did not know much about men, except that they were prideful and sometimes cruel. The boy who cleaned their chimneys tried to put spiders in her hair. This one couldn't, of course; he was on the other side of a wall. A safe distance. And in need of advice, which she, on this strange occasion, decided to give.

"You should take better care of your coin, sir. Young men are ruined every day through poor judgment with their finances. Flowers at fifteen shillings a day? Whoever heard of such a thing?"

There was a brief pause and then curt laughter sputtered out of him. "How do you know the lady wasn't worth it?"

"You wouldn't take such resentful note of the cost if she was."

A huff, but half-hearted, more irritated and impatient with himself than anything or anyone else.

"Have you not heard the saying that less is more, sir?" she added. "It is not quantity but quality that counts. So many flowers sent every day would surely lessen the effect."

He grunted. "Is that so?"

"Besides, flowers are loveliest when they're picked wild and don't cost a penny. Flowers what grow accidentally between stones, or wherever their seeds fall, are often overlooked. But they can add a spot of color just as well as an armful of expensive hothouse blooms." Was that her voice, spouting all these opinions out loud? Yes, apparently. It seemed as if once one thought was let out, others followed it, like drips of water through an invisible fissure in a clay jug.

"Flowers that grow between stones? Aren't they called weeds?" He sounded amused. Ah, at least she had succeeded in making him forget his sorrows for a while.

"That's just a name, sir. A rose by any other name would smell as sweet."

"Shakespeare too, eh? As well as your sums. And French?"

"Je connais beaucoup de choses. Plus que ce qui est enseigne dans cette ecole. Je m'apprends moi-meme."

"Ah yes." His feet shuffled. "That's right. I know this place. It's a ladies' academy. I didn't know they turned out young ladies with any intelligence though."

"They don't."

"Except you."

Emma couldn't answer that.

"You *are* a pupil here, aren't you?" he demanded.

"Not...not like the others," she managed, the words fighting their way out as she inhaled a startled breath and tasted the fog.

"No. You have a quick brain, clearly. I'm sure

you're a rarity." His foot stamped— crushing ash from his cigar perhaps, or else trying to keep his toes from going numb with cold— and then, before she could say anything else, those horses, pulling a rattling carriage behind them, came to a halt under the damply glistening, ghostly lamplight. Emma heard the beasts snorting, their iron shoes scraping the cobbles in urgency to be off again.

Another man's voice bellowed genially, "Well, if it isn't Lieutenant Guy Hathaway! There you are. Barely saw you in this dratted fog. Should have taken shelter while you waited, man. I suppose you stood out here in the rain too."

"I don't mind the rain at all. Never did. Like to be out in it. And it suited my mood tonight, to be sure."

"Not still pining over that Phoebe hussy, I hope!"

"Good lord, no. Just relieved to get away before she caused me to spend my entire year's wages. In fact, my frivolous spending on that lady's behalf has just been pointed out to me, and I am duly chastised."

"Best not stand there dripping, Hathaway! Took me the devil of a time to find a carriage and driver for hire. You want to be in Norfolk in time for your mama's funeral, don't you?"

And her bad mathematician replied, "Help me with the trunk, will you?"

From the sounds she now identified on the other side of the wall, he was leaving. But suddenly he said,

"Goodbye then, Clever Puss. Thank you for the advice. I shall keep a tighter grip on my finances from now on and seek out those wild flowers... *what* grow accidentally... to save the wear and tear on my pockets."

"My condolences on your loss, sir."

"Oh." His voice caught on a hitch of breath. "Thank you. Clever Puss."

Emma placed her hand against the cold brick, drawn again to the sadness in his voice. It must be dreadful to have family and lose parts of it. Hers at least was gone before she knew it. She'd never had the chance, or the misfortune, to love anybody, including a mother.

As she stood there listening to his carriage depart, a hand suddenly formed out of the curls of fog, hard fingers seizing her by the ear.

"I knew it! Slacking off! Deliberately making me wait! Wretched, fiendish girl! Well, I warned you."

For an old woman, Mrs. Lightbody had considerable strength in her arms. Of course, nobody knew how old she truly was. She confessed to thirty and nobody disbelieved that; they only had difficulty believing there were not at least twenty more years added to the sum.

While those blows and curses knocked her back and forth around the back yard, Emma thought only of the young lieutenant on his way to his mother's funeral. Like him, she didn't mind the rain or the fog at all. Which was a good thing, since there was plenty of it in her life, and inevitably she was outside in it.

But she had never known any other soul who stood out in it willingly when they might have sought shelter. She sometimes did, simply because she knew nobody would come to bother her while she was out in it. For Emma, foul weather meant a moment of respite. But what did it mean to him?

Lieutenant Guy Hathaway. It was a name she would never forget. How could she forget it now? He'd called her Clever Puss.

Obviously you're somebody.

He was adamant about it, as if he would brook no argument.

She'd been rather bold with him, Emma thought in some amazement. That was not like her at all. But with a wall and a foggy evening between them, she was braver. If he could have seen her— if she ran into him on a sunny street— she would have been too tongue-tied to speak, even if he did have a sum to set straight. She would have kept her gaze on the ground and not dared stop to exchange words.

Obviously you're somebody.

For the first time in her twelve years, she felt as if this was true. She did exist. She *was* somebody. A voice on the other side of the wall had assured her it was so.

Even with Lightbody's firm fingers squeezed around her throat, the living breath shaken out of her and her world going black as she faded into unconsciousness, Emma felt herself smile inside with a new strength.

Obviously you're somebody.

His firm statement blew a hole in the fog, and she saw through it at last to blue skies.

And hope.

Girl

Chapter Three
Six years later

Emma had sewn her own ball gown, copying a pattern from *La Belle Assemblee*, but with the omission of any touches she found too gaudy and showy. Made up in a very soft, ivory muslin, it was the nicest frock she'd ever owned, so lovely, that packing it safely into a trunk seemed an impossible task. And herself doing justice to it later seemed even less likely.

"What the devil are you doing, Em?" exclaimed Melinda Goodheart, dashing into the room they shared, having launched her own tattered luggage down the stairs with a hearty shove. Packed with little care at all and nothing more than a bemused glance at the frayed ball gown she'd bundled into it, Miss Goodheart's trunk could be heard now, descending bumpily and landing with a resounding bang upon the hall tiles, possibly leaving a dent in the floor. "I swear you were standing in the exact same spot, looking at that lovely frock with an identical, silly expression on your face a quarter of an hour ago. Georgie's carriage should be here any moment!"

"I just cannot seem to move." She thought her bones might be stuck. Her brain was too preoccupied, unable to communicate any instructions to her limbs. All it could do was calculate and worry about the time, as well as all the things that might possibly go awry on their journey. "The muslin for this gown must have cost Lady Bramley more than *three pounds*, and these white evening gloves another four shillings at least. She has gone to such trouble and expense for me. How am I ever to repay her?"

"That, my dear, is easy! You simply do as she says and agree with everything she utters— at least, in her presence. That will more than satisfy the lady. You know you are her favorite little pet project now that Georgie has returned to her father's house. Lady Bramley means to train you like her lap dog, because she knows you'll be far more obedient than Georgie."

"Oh, don't say that. Now I am all fingers and thumbs, worse than before!"

"Well, good heavens! Let me help you fold the gown."

"But it will be creased when we get there. No, no! Let me do it. It must be folded in the proper way, and I have researched exactly how it must be done." Emma didn't want to be rude, and she understood the need for haste, but Melinda's hands, while enthusiastic in any task they undertook, were not the most delicate.

"You're a bundle of nerves, Miss Chance," the other girl exclaimed, dropping to the bed with all the grace of a sack of potatoes. "What's the matter with you?"

Emma slowly and cautiously arranged her precious ball gown in the small trunk she'd borrowed for this occasion— her first overnight foray into the world outside. "I've never been to a ball before, have I?" she muttered, the tension mounting inside her even worse now that she spoke the words aloud. "I've seldom been outside these walls, except for the occasional errand, lessons on deportment at Lady Bramley's house and her garden party last spring. Naturally, I'm apprehensive." Wide-eyed, she looked at her friend and added solemnly, "It is logical to be so, surely."

But Melinda knew little of logic, feared nothing and barreled through life like a wolf-hound chasing a bumble bee. Frequently the young lady received a sting for her troubles, but it didn't stop her. That, Emma supposed, was one of the reasons why she loved Melinda dearly, for the girl was everything she wished she could be: bold, self-confident, and utterly unmoved by what anybody else thought of her. Now her friend sprawled across Emma's bed in her customary, unladylike pose, arms folded beneath her head— this inelegant motion straining the seam under her sleeve, where the dress had already been repaired several times as evidenced by the uneven stitches in a different color thread.

"A ball is nothing to make a fuss about," Melinda said calmly. "Folk stand around for several hours with nothing to do but complain about the music and gossip about ugly dresses and who fills out a good pair of silk knee breeches. It's really only enjoyable if somebody starts a fight, a scandal, or a fire. Preferably all three."

Emma, now kneeling by her open trunk, looked over the lid of it and eyed her friend with consternation. "I hope that doesn't mean you plan to start any of those, Melinda Goodheart."

"Perhaps I shall." The other girl grinned. "Not intentionally, of course. I never, in the whole course of my life, meant to cause any trouble. And pray do not cast me one of those looks, Miss Chance! Although you pretend not to enjoy the mischief which is *occasionally* and quite accidentally caused by my company and Georgie's, you know very well that you secretly adore the excitement. You never had any adventures until we came along, as you said yourself not too long ago."

"I only join you to save you both from a hanging. Somebody has to be the voice of reason."

In their little trio of friends— named by Mrs. Lightbody, in one of her temper tantrums, as "The Ladies Most Unlikely"— Emma was the one with the patience and a respect for caution that her two companions severely lacked, despite both being a year older than she.

"What would we do without you," said Melinda in a rare moment of sober reflection.

But Emma felt the same about her friends. Almost as soon as Melinda Goodheart and Georgiana Hathaway first arrived at the Particular Establishment for the Advantage of Respectable Ladies, a little under three years ago, they had taken her under their wing, protected her and defended her from the wrath of Lightbody.

Somehow Georgiana had discovered— probably

while tidying the woman's study as punishment for some misdemeanor— that Emma's father still paid a nominal fee for his illegitimate daughter's needs at the school. She had seen, in the ledger, that payments were made under Emma's name every quarter, on time and in full.

"Is this young lady's father not paying her fee just like the rest of us?" Georgiana had demanded one day, standing proudly before the headmistress with her chin up and hands on her waist. "Then she is not here on your charity alone, madam, whatever you tell her. She is entitled to the same as the rest of us. You will stop treating her like a slave."

"The girl was left here by a gentleman who wanted naught to do with her."

"Just because he doesn't come here to make certain she receives even the basic necessities for which he pays, does not mean that you can—"

"I need not explain myself to you, girl, and next time I find you snooping through my books you'll get the willow switch along with Chance."

But Georgiana was adamant. "Miss Chance will have a bed with Melinda Goodheart and myself, she will attend lessons with us, meals with us, and have new frocks whenever needed— even if I must pay for the material myself. She will not spend her days being worked ragged as a scullery maid for you. You have no right to make her labor day and night, when she is a paid student of this academy."

"Rights? What do you know of rights?" The

woman had never heard of such a word, of course, unless used in reference to her own, and then it was shouted from the pigeon-clad rooftops.

"I know *this*, madam. Anybody who treats that poor girl as you have done deserves to be exposed. And as *you* know, my father runs a very successful and prominent newspaper. I'm quite certain he would be appalled by this girl's fate. The parents of your pupils deserve to know how you treat a girl left in your care."

From then on Georgiana was referred to as "Miss Sharp Mouth", amongst other things— some far less pleasant— by the headmistress of that school. But Lightbody did not seem to know exactly what to do about this particular troublesome pupil. Georgiana's father was ambitious new wealth, who had moved to London from Norfolk to expand his printing business. As a man with the columns of a popular newspaper at his disposal he could be dangerous to the reputation of her school, and imperil the sly, wicked business she maintained behind that facade. Georgiana was certainly more outspoken, canny, and determined than any other girl who had ever come through her front door. So Lightbody had needed time to think how best to manage Georgiana and her threats. Once Melinda Goodheart added her own hard-headed, fearless brand of defiance to the argument, the headmistress had decided simply to lump the three of them together as a lost cause and get on with saving herself.

Emma had still often been shouted at and ridiculed, but her two new friends certainly improved life for her at that school and she, eternally grateful to them both, always looked for ways to repay their kindness.

In recent weeks, further improvements had taken place. Mrs. Lightbody, finally deposed as school headmistress, was temporarily replaced by a generous patron and member of the school's board— Lady Bramley. Emma had been called upon to assist her ladyship in planning an improved curriculum for the other pupils, and she often taught classes for the younger ones.

Slowly she emerged from her shell, but it would be a long struggle. She did not have Georgie's beauty, or her proudly mutinous fortitude. Nor did she have Melinda's open, undaunted heart. Their gregariousness, their rebellious attitude and, occasionally, their boundless optimism was something she could only aspire to copy. Emma was too cautious, too diffident about her own abilities, still the girl who preferred a shadowy corner and a walk in the rain with her own thoughts, to crowds, sunny days, and being the center of any attention.

But today, she and Melinda were traveling into the county of Surrey with Georgie, for the three of them had been invited to attend a ball at Woodbyne Abbey, the home of Lady Bramley's nephew. Now she must force herself to be sociable when it was the very furthest thing from her nature. With all these good, kind folk looking to help her come out from behind her walls, it would be ungrateful to hide herself away again. She wanted to please them, repay them for their faith in her. It was just such a daunting task for a girl who spent so many years being beaten down.

At first she tried declining the invitation, using the excuse that she had no ball gown. Never had one. But then generous Lady Bramley had bought her eight yards of that lovely angelic muslin as a gift for graduating from pupil to teaching assistant at the school. Thus her excuse to stay behind was wrenched away.

For Emma, this trip into Surrey might as well be an expedition to the Himalayas. Which was, incidentally, somewhere her two friends had decided they would all go one day. After they had ridden camels around the pyramids of Egypt and visited Mount Etna. Nobody conferred with Emma, naturally; they simply assumed she'd come along. Why not? Somebody would have to arrange rescue for the other two when they fell down into the volcano.

"I wonder what Lady Bramley's nephew is like," Melinda mused, still stretched out across the bed, pondering the roof beams. "Although Georgie spent those weeks with her ladyship this summer at his mansion, she has been miserly with her information. I cannot tell from her letters what she thinks of him at all. He's supposedly quite eccentric and a recluse, yet now he holds a ball in his house. Mark my words, our friend, Georgie, is behind this change somehow."

Emma replied gravely, "We must bear in mind that our host spent several years alone, shipwrecked on an unchartered island. I am sure that has made Commander Sir Henry Thrasher somewhat reserved, folded into himself." She thought of her own years abandoned to Mrs. Lightbody's "care" and compared her situation to the commander's. Of course, there had been other folk on her island, but she was invisible to them until Melinda and Georgiana came along.

Only one other person had ever paid attention to Emma Chance and suggested she existed for something more in life than drudgery and pig-herding.

She had never told anybody about the young lieutenant in the fog, not even her two friends, because, not long after Emma met Georgiana, she came to realize — as perhaps you have by now—that the young lady's beloved and frequently mentioned elder brother, a young man most often away at sea with the navy, was actually none other than Lieutenant Guy Hathaway.

And then, of course, she could say nothing about their strange encounter. Instead she tucked her dragon prince even deeper down inside her secrets.

Whenever Georgiana received a letter from her brother, Emma had tried to behave herself and not be curious, but her friend was too proud not to show them off. His handwriting was messy, written on a

steep slant and covered in ink blots, as if he always
wrote in haste during a bad storm at sea. Didn't think
to wait for calm waters and a quiet moment. His news
was shot out at the beginning of every letter, like gun
fire, in list form with a dark dot to mark its place—
Emma thought of them as the cannon balls
discharged from his ship. But when the letter was
longer and he had cause to describe one of the men
on his ship, or a prank that had been played, then his
sentences flowed one into the other with mischievous
wit, the cannon balls forgotten. Occasionally, at the
end of the letter, he remembered some other point
he'd neglected to mention and then the list resumed
briefly, because he had run out of time and space,
thus leaving tantalizing headlines with no further
explanation.

- Almost eaten by cannibals last Monday.
- Tuesday met beautiful native girl.
- Wednesday Joe lost a finger. One found in the
rigging. Alas, not his.
- Ate octopus in ink Thursday. Cannot
recommend.
- Native girl stole my boots while I slept on
Friday.
- Bought parrot.

Lieutenant Hathaway's letters and their lively
snippets of life at sea had cheered their spirits and
made them all laugh. Often he sent his sister gifts

from his travels— fine silk scarves, bracelets made of shells, and ribbon that smelled of some far away marketplace, spice and adventure.

Other girls envied Georgie for those gifts, but Emma thought only of the young man who sent them and yearned, in secret, for the brother she'd never had. But at least she had him in her thoughts and sometimes she'd made pretend that he was *her* brother.

Well, she used to. Of course, at the grand age of eighteen, she was too old for those fanciful thoughts. Now she was a teacher's assistant, all grown up. She even had a ball gown and gloves of her own to prove it.

"There!" She closed the lid of her trunk. "Everything is packed." In its place. For now.

Oh, but her heart was beating far too hard. It seemed to vibrate throughout her body, wanting to escape her rib cage, to run away on little thrusting feet. Where would it run to? More than likely it would run in circles, too indecisive and afraid, even if somebody opened the gate for it.

She glanced over her shoulder, feeling the sudden prickle of a warning against her spine. But no. There was no Mrs. Lightbody standing there, waiting to slap her for being too slow, or mock her for thinking she might attend a ball with the other girls.

Reaching for her leather traveling gloves, she fumbled, her fingers trembling.

It was only a ball, and other young women

attended such occasions all the time. As Melinda assured her, this was nothing to make a fuss about. If only she knew how to gossip and talk about other girls' dresses, but she knew nothing of how to simply "be" like a normal person— a woman in particular. Skills that other girls picked up from their mothers, by lesson or example, were, of course, absent for Emma Chance. Etiquette and relationships— the things that other girls took for granted and which, in her eyes, made them feminine— were a mystery to her. Even with Georgiana and Melinda she often felt self-conscious and inept, not certain whether she had clutched onto them too tightly, wondering what they really thought of her, feeling still the outsider, a ghostly mixture of vapors not properly formed into anything solid, neither man nor woman.

Sometimes she sat and listened to her friends chatter away so merrily, wondering how they did it. Both girls had lost their mothers too when they were young, but they were more fortunate than Emma in that they had *some* warm and tender memories of the women who shaped their earliest years. They also had families who took an interest in their lives, siblings to quarrel with and learn from, and other folk who cared what became of them. They had both been able to grieve for their mothers. Emma had never felt it right to speak of hers and, in any case, growing up she had only Mrs. Lightbody with whom to discuss anything of that sort. Better off not speaking at all.

Her friends, on the other hand, could talk for an

hour or more, about nothing in particular. And they seemed to enjoy the pastime. When Emma tried to join in she felt as if it spoiled the flow, because she invariably said something too dull and practical. Generally, she stayed quiet until she was called upon to speak.

She hoped nobody would try to talk to her at the ball.

"At least *you* can dance, Emma," her friend exclaimed, sprawled on her side now, head resting on one hand, elbow stabbed into the previously neat and fluffed pillow. "You are much better than the rest of us."

"Only because you decline to practice and Georgiana prefers to make up her own steps. I have applied careful study to the pastime in order to perform properly and I do not veer off the pattern just to confuse everybody and amuse myself."

"And thus you have quite taken the fun out of it, my dear Em."

Fun? Was it meant to be fun? Emma's idea of a pleasurable interlude was sitting alone in a corner and solving a complex mathematical puzzle. Or sheltering under a tree while it rained and everybody else ran for stouter cover. In fact, put those two things together and she'd be happier than a piglet in mud.

Unless, of course, there was lightning, in which case a tree would be an extremely risky place to shelter. Emma Chance, despite her name, did not take risks.

"Oh, I hear a carriage outside!" Melinda leapt up from the bed and ran to the window. "It must be Georgie! Come on, Em, let's—ooh, wait just a damnable moment! What's this? There's a man with her. Handsome too. And it's not the commander, for we saw him from a distance at Lady Bramley's garden party last May." She opened the window, leaned out and began to wave down to their friend with her usual violent passion, not in the least concerned for the unladylike impression she left upon anybody passing in the street below. Or for the much-abused stitches of her seam. "Georgiana Hathaway, you're late! Where the devil have you been?"

Emma barely paid heed. The presence of a handsome man was just one more pebble weighing down her bucket of troubles, but he was not likely to take any interest in her. Thankfully. Rather than go to the window, she studied the list she held in her hand again— "Items Not To Be Forgotten"— then thrice checking the stout lock of her trunk.

At the risk of being as dramatic as her friends, Emma knew, with absolute certainty, that this would either be the Very Best, or the Very Worst day of her life. Oddly, she hoped it would be the latter. She could manage *The Worst*. After everything she'd put up with, how much worse could The Worst be?

If it was the Very Best day, however...well, "best" was an idea of which she could hardly conceive. And it suggested that everything after that would be dreary and mundane again.

So either way there was not much to look forward to.

Perhaps she should simply hope they were not kidnapped, or held up by highwaymen, their bones broken by an overturned carriage, or chased into exhaustion and crushed by a ferocious herd of rioting cows. They were, after all, heading into the countryside where the wild beasts roamed.

From all that she'd heard and imagined of this traveling lark, it would be a miracle if they survived the journey with all their limbs intact and maidenly parts unmolested.

Chapter Four

"Brother, do cheer up," Georgiana chided him under her breath. "I know you're not fond of balls, or entertaining young ladies, but it will all be over by this time tomorrow and then you can rest content in the knowledge that you did your gallant duty by safely escorting your dear younger sister and her two best-loved friends to their very first ball."

"Cheer up?" He scowled. "What the deuce is that supposed to mean?" It was not in his nature to share his problems with anybody and he thought he did a good job of hiding any sadness he felt over the latest debacle in his life. But his little sister could be surprisingly and annoyingly perceptive. Only when she wanted to be.

"For a beginning, brother dear," she arched an eyebrow, "unfold your arms. It makes you look stuffed and annoyed."

"*Stuffed?*"

"As if your straw stuffing might fall out if you don't hold it in."

Sighing heavily, he let his arms fall, relaxed to his sides. Georgiana could be a bossy little madam. "And what, sister, makes you think I do not care to entertain ladies? It is, in fact, one of my greatest talents."

"Ah, but these ladies are different to those with which *you* are familiar," she replied, nose in the air. "My friends are not your standard variety hussy. Like me, they are destined for grand adventures, and in such cases men are merely in the way." Pausing, she looked him up and down, brushed a hand over his coat shoulder and adjusted his lapel. "We are all decided against waiting for a handsome knight on a white steed. I love you dearly, brother, but any amusement you might provide for them, I fear, will be slight and probably at your own expense."

"In short then, these are giggling girls, not women, and just as full of addle-pated ideas as you." He readjusted his lapel to his own satisfaction as soon as she'd finished with it.

"Nevertheless." She grinned broadly. "I expect you to dance with them both, Captain Hathaway. For at least two sets each. It would be rude of you not to. Furthermore, you will converse merrily and smile the entire time. If you do not, I shall prick you with a hat pin, as Lady Bramley advises for the treatment of all inattentive and obstreperous men."

"But you just said it's impossible for me to entertain your silly little friends, unless they find something about me at which to laugh. Therefore I need make no effort. It seems the matter is out of my hands."

"As our escort, it is incumbent upon you to *try* and please, however hopeless." She stepped back to look him over again and then sighed heavily. "Men. What is to be done with you? As Lady Bramley says, you're either an obstruction to progress, or nowhere to be found when required."

He shook his head. "I'm not entirely assured of any beneficial education you received from this establishment and this Bramley person, Georgie. If I was home when father first thought to send you here, I would have advised him strongly against it."

"And I very much doubt you could have dissuaded our papa from the idea, especially with stepmama whispering loudly in his other ear to make it proceed. He seems not to hear any of us when that lady speaks, and she wanted me out of the house. In any case, if I had never been sent here, I would never have met the two lovely young ladies you have so kindly and heroically agreed to accompany into the Surrey wilderness this afternoon, would I?"

He gave only a sullen grunt in reply. Already he regretted this journey, but what could he do? Their father had asked him to escort his sister and her friends to the ball at Woodbyne Abbey and since Guy was on leave, at a loose end, he had no immediate excuse. Indeed, he'd thought it might even take his mind off his troubles. He could hardly sit about the house moping, could he? Especially not with the endless squawking of their stepmother's latest offspring shaking the walls. And he was not the sort to drown his sorrows in drink, or turn to gambling. Just needed to set his thoughts elsewhere, keep them occupied a while, so they would not return again and again to linger over the scene of his lover in a compromising position with—

No, don't think of it. Erase it from your mind, man.

"But it is very good of you to volunteer your services," his sister exclaimed suddenly, briefly setting their customary teasing aside and patting his arm. "Don't look so glum. I did not mean to sound ungrateful. It's just that I find myself rather anxious that everything should go well tonight."

"I didn't volunteer. Father petitioned me and I had nothing else to do." And since his father had found out about the latest duel over a woman, he was even more irritated than usual with his eldest son, making it necessary that Guy remove himself from the house as much as possible.

His sister looked askance. "Pray don't spoil my illusions. Allow me to imagine, just for a little while longer, that my brave, sea-faring brother actually wanted to escort me to a ball. That he is not doing this solely to mend a rift with our father and get himself put back in The Will."

Guy had joined the navy, thirteen years ago, against Mr. Hathaway's wishes. Since then a definite chill had existed between father and son, but there was never any grand gesture such as the re-writing of a will or the threat of disownment. Georgiana, as usual, chose to be theatrical about what was really nothing more than a rather dull, commonplace chafing of personalities.

Glancing at his sister, as she hummed merrily and waited for her friends to come down, he wondered again at how she could have grown into this deceptively normal and harmless-looking young lady while he was away at sea. The last time he was home, she had been a little girl still, in trouble for getting mud on her elder sister's slippers when she borrowed them to run out into the rhubarb patch and rescue the family cat. Georgiana, one of many siblings and lost in the midst of the pack, had always striven for their father's distracted attention by creating as much havoc as possible. After their mother died and their father remarried, his sister's rebellion reached new heights, culminating in the theft and burning of a gentleman's wig at a party to which she was not invited. Hence her removal to the Particular Establishment for the Advantage of Respectable Ladies.

Now, here she was, a well-dressed, pretty, smiling young lady with all her curls in place and considerable self-confidence. Whether or not she had stopped causing havoc and setting wigs alight remained to be seen. It would be up to him tonight to keep her away from naked flame.

If only somebody could do the same for him, he mused. He seemed to walk into it too often, even when he knew it would hurt. Somehow he couldn't stop himself from seeking the danger. Or was it the danger that sought him? He never seemed to meet a good, honest sort of woman and that, he supposed, was where most of his troubles began. His best friend, Joe Tidings, used to say he wouldn't know what to do with a proper young lady.

His *former* best friend.

Ah, at last, here they came!

Guy moved forward swiftly to take one end of the first trunk as it emerged through the front door of the house. Good god! They were only going away for one night, but she must have packed for a fortnight, he mused. The trunk was tattered and beaten about, tied together, it seemed, with inadequate knots of string. A puff of lace stuck out from under the lid, but when he suggested the owner of the trunk might want to open it and amend the situation, the young lady to whom the luggage belonged gave a careless laugh and said it was "only" her ball-gown.

"Trust me, sir," she added with a wry smile, "it is such an ugly thing and I look so ill in it, that a smattering of dirt on the lace might even improve matters. One cannot stuff a turkey into swan's feathers, and mostly it's best not to try."

As Guy looked up from the trunk, the early afternoon sun painfully bright in his eyes, he foundered over a suitable reply, but his sister stepped in swiftly to make the introductions.

"This is Miss Melinda Goodheart. Melinda, at last you meet my brother, Captain Guy Hathaway. I know you've heard so much about him, of course. He is on leave at present and so has kindly agreed to be our escort."

Just as his name was mentioned, he thought he heard the distant mewl of a kitten, but from whence it came he had no idea. There was no sign of any four-legged creature on the steps— only his sister and the other girl beside her in an extravagantly decorated bonnet. The proper bow and curtsey were given, as well as the necessary exclamations of "Delighted" and "How d'you do?"

Miss Goodheart was a tall, robust young lady, but he could see nothing of her face, for her features were eclipsed by the shadow of that extraordinary array of striped ribbon bows, feather and fruit orbiting her head.

As he helped her up into the vehicle, she managed to bang her shoulder, her knee and her elbow, before poking him in the eye with a finger while trying to direct the tying of her trunk, which kept falling open.

Once her luggage was tied firmly to the back of the vehicle— various shoes and lacy unmentionables saved from the grimy pavement each time an effort was made to hoist the burden upward— Guy turned for the next piece of luggage. Thankfully this one was lighter, neater, and tied with a good lock.

He looked around. "Where is she then?" he exclaimed somewhat impatiently to his sister. "The other one?"

Again he thought he heard that kittenish squeak. He looked down at his boots, worried he might have stepped on a paw. Georgiana also appeared confused for a moment and then, with a small cry, stepped aside to reveal the faint tracing of a girl in a wilted bonnet. She must have sidled out of the house and lurked behind his sister on the steps.

"Oh, here she is! This is Miss Emma Chance."

Parts of her had apparently been lost in the shadow of Miss Goodheart's enormous head apparatus, while the rest of the young miss was hidden by his sister's more substantial form, wedged between that and the fence railings which seemed to be holding the lurker upright. It was lucky indeed that she had not fallen through the bars, down the servants' steps and into the coal bunker below.

Guy had to look twice before she fully emerged into the light as a person of sorts. He bowed. "Miss Chance."

In reply the girl opened her lips and whispered a very unhappy-sounding, "Lieutenant Hathaway."

"Not Lieutenant any longer," his sister proudly corrected her friend. "He is now Captain Hathaway."

Nothing this time. The girl leaned precariously to one side, her eyes downcast. She breathed rather heavily and her fingers wound so tightly around the embroidered purse in her hands that he could almost hear the bones cracking.

"Is she...alright?" he muttered to his sister. The last thing he needed was one of his charges being ill on their journey. "She's not a swooner, is she? Or somebody who gets sickened by the motion of a carriage? She's white as a ghost."

"Oh, she's alright, aren't you, Em?" Miss Goodheart cheerily bellowed from inside the carriage. "She just doesn't get out much. I don't suppose she's ever ridden in a private carriage. And she's dreadfully shy."

In response to this assessment, the poor girl's cheeks flushed scarlet and her gaze remained on the pavement. A single strand of wispy, pale hair fluttered in dejected surrender against the brim of her bonnet.

"Don't fret, Miss Chance," he said, as brightly as he could, considering his own apathy for the event ahead of them. "You're in safe hands with me." Guy had often been told— despite his little sister's doubts— that he had a talent for putting folk at their ease, a genial ability that buoyed his smile and the spirits of others, even on days when he felt himself sinking.

But it seemed to have no good affect on this small, droopy creature. "Anyone might think you are on your way to the gallows, not a ball, Miss Chance," he added, teasing amiably. "Surely, all young ladies live for balls?"

Silence met this remark as both his sister and Miss Goodheart, who now leaned out of the carriage, looked at their pale friend.

Finally her lips parted and she exhaled a tortured sigh that stretched across the silence like a washing line, her words the limp but carefully spaced, wet shirts and stockings strung upon it. "It's a quarter past the hour of one, and we were meant to leave promptly at noon."

Suddenly she lost that bony grip on her purse and it fell. Guy's instincts were swift enough to save it in mid-air, but when he held it out to her, she wouldn't take it. In fact, she moved a timid step backward, tripping over an uneven crack in the pavement, leaving his sister to snatch the purse and pass it to her friend.

"It's my fault, Em," Georgiana explained. "My brother did try to drag me away, but I was in the midst of writing."

The wisp of a girl now seemed preoccupied with the cracks by her feet, looking down at them as if they might suddenly expand and leave her nothing upon which to stand.

"Well, let's advance, shall we?" Guy said, forcing another smile. "Since, as Miss Chance pointed out, we're already late."

When he put out his hand to help the trembling girl up into the carriage, she finally moved forward, stepping carefully to avoid the cracks. Her touch was so light, her fingers resting so briefly against his knuckles that he barely felt the pressure and had to look twice to make certain she had not actually taken flight back inside the house. But no, there she was, as far from him as she could put herself, and seated on Miss Goodheart's left side. Apparently on the verge of tears, she squeezed her knees together, bowed her head, and held her shoulders in a rigid fashion, as if she feared taking up too much room. The material of her spencer actually appeared to match the seat cover, making her disappear further into the upholstery.

"I was about to suggest that you sit facing the horses, Miss Chance, and lessen the possibility of feeling nauseated. But I see you thought of that for yourself already." He smiled. "If you need air, open the — ah, I see you already opened the sash window too."

She merely looked puzzled by his attempts to make her comfortable. Two wide eyes, the color of faded ink, peered out from the shadow of her coal-scuttle bonnet.

His sister poked him in the side. "Don't startle Miss Chance."

How the devil could he be accused of that?

"Stop staring at her," she whispered harshly.

The subject of Georgiana's remark turned her limp head away and shrank another few inches into her corner.

"I can assure you I am not staring at Miss Chance," he whispered, the words squeezed out between teeth still gritted in a smile. "There is nothing whatsoever to stare at." His sister stepped up into the carriage, and he followed, muttering. "Let's hope the journey is short."

Abruptly the grim creature on the opposite seat exclaimed, "On the map, it is twelve and three quarter miles to Little Flaxhill and well-shod horses, on average, can manage four miles an hour." While her small hands throttled the life out of her reticule, she did not look at anybody. "We should arrive in just under four hours, allowing time for the refreshment of horses."

Guy closed the carriage door firmly and said,

"Well, I wouldn't make wager on it. Anything can happen on a journey into the unpredictable countryside, Miss Chance. Accidents caused by man and beast, lost horse shoes, flooded roads, trees blown asunder, highway robbers." He rubbed his hands together and grinned. "Who knows what excitement lurks in wait for us?"

Familiar with his sister's desire for adventure, he expected this comment to please her friends too. But Miss Chance stared, unmoving. Her eyes filled with silent panic, tempered with annoyance.

He thought of that tidy trunk and her careful steps to avoid cracks in the pavement. He looked at her plain, but neat clothes— the spencer hooked all the way up to her throat where it surely choked her; the bonnet ribbon tied directly under her chin in a severe, joyless knot; the sharply ironed cuffs of her sleeves, already smoothed down thrice as she sat there, and her knees clenched together like the teeth of a horse with lockjaw.

"Emma Chance does not much care for unpredictable," his sister confirmed. "She likes to be prepared for any eventuality and, although she has never traveled herself, she is a great studier of maps."

So what else could a man do but tease? Had to fill these painful hours somehow.

Stretching out one leg, he sighed and shook his head. "Maps, in my experience, have a tendency to suggest one's route rather than give factual information. On land, one is better off not conferring with them at all."

Bounced about by their progress over some particularly uneven cobbles, the girl across the carriage squashed her lips together and stared out of her open window.

He continued, "It once took me six hours to travel six miles when a flock of sheep surrounded the carriage, a bull got loose from a field, and the coachman consumed some bad ham for his luncheon, requiring frequent pauses along our route. I believe one of our number had expired before we reached our destination. The coach was so malodorous by then that it was difficult to separate the dead and rotting flesh from the living. Alas, the horrors of a journey into Kent. I cannot recommend it. I daresay Surrey will be no safer."

His sister and the colorful one both laughed. "I must apologize for my brother," Georgiana exclaimed. "He is quite insufferable, particularly when bored, at one of his loose ends and forced to be a dutiful gentleman."

"I beg your pardon, sister?" he demanded. "'Tis all quite true. Every word of it."

Miss Chance's lips parted in mute horror, but she kept her gaze on the passing scenery.

"At least you have me to protect you on this journey," he added solemnly.

But this did not appear to bring the girl any cheer. Neither his playful teasing nor his reassurance made her relax those rigid shoulders.

Georgiana commanded him to "stop telling ghastly fibs", which he found remarkably amusing since she was so fond of spinning outrageous yarns herself. Seated beside his sprawled form, she now ignored her brother and chattered away to her friends. Apparently they had much news to share. Or two of them did.

"The Ladies Most Unlikely," his sister cried, glassy-eyed with excitement, as if she might have been at their father's sherry before they left the house, "here we are all together again at last!"

Guy exhaled a heavy sigh, aware that similar melodramatic and girlish exclamations were bound to fill the next few hours. His sister tended to live her life as if she and everybody around her were desperate characters in a novel.

Since he'd already been accused of staring at the shy, plain one— as if he did it with deliberate malice— and his attempt to make her smile had failed, Guy looked peevishly out of his window, determined to pay no great attention to any of them. He'd be polite, play his part as their escort to this wretched ball, but he would take no further interest.

The sooner this torturous excursion was completed the better. At least, that was clearly the case for him and for the odd little smudge in the sad bonnet.

Chapter Five

It took half an hour at least before Emma felt the warmth return to her shocked bones.

Guy Hathaway — the man who had possessed her dreams for the past six years— was there before her. In the flesh. A real man with limbs and a head and all his parts. No longer was he the mere memory of a voice floating through the moist breath of a sorrowful dragon.

Obviously you're somebody. Clever Puss.

Georgiana had said nothing of her brother being in London. They'd all assumed her father would escort them to the ball. In a sense, Emma was glad she had not known, for then she would have been even more anxious before the event. Earlier today she was nervous only about a ball among strangers and a lengthy carriage ride away from everything familiar. *I don't suppose she's ever ridden in a private carriage*, Melinda had said. But Emma had never ridden in any carriage before, not even a public coach. So many new experiences all in one day.

Now here was another, worse than any of her previous worries.

She heard every sigh, every grunt, every tap of his fingers. Her senses were alert again, as they had been on the night of the fog, all those years ago, when she first felt his presence on the other side of a brick wall. He was sad again today, despite that smile with which he decorated his face occasionally. It didn't fool

Emma. When the Captain thought he was unobserved, he sank within himself, despondent as an autumn leaf soon to fall.

Perhaps he suffered the effects of too much drink the night before. It was a common problem for young gentlemen, so she'd read. And although the navy was a heroic body of men, it did tend to produce a great many hard drinkers— according to Lady Bramley.

Seated diagonally across from her in the small carriage interior, he stared out of the window, watching the London streets flutter by as the horses carried him backward at a steady clip. Captain Hathaway did not look at her again. Why would he? She was nothing to look at, just as she had heard him whisper to his sister.

People often talked about her as if she wasn't there, but Emma had excellent hearing. All her senses worked perfectly, especially when something caught her attention and her curiosity. As he did. As he had from the first sound.

Captain Guy Hathaway had the same unruly curls and dark, attractive features as his sister. He dressed smartly— not in his uniform, of course, at present— and looked very much a gentleman. Handsome enough to turn heads. His hand, when offered to help her up into the carriage, had looked enormous, but now she saw it resting on his knee and it was of normal size, not nearly as fearsome as it first seemed when it loomed out at her. His gloves looked and smelled like new leather. One of her favorite scents.

Her heartbeat slowed as she realized how foolishly timid she'd behaved, not even thanking him for retrieving her reticule before it landed on the pavement. If only she could have been daring and witty like Melinda. At the very least, she should have smiled and said "*Thank You*" when he saved her reticule. Instead she could only recite her dull, organized facts— those things that had crowded in upon her mind for days now as the event drew near.

What must he think of her? Nothing much, in all probability.

It was an inauspicious beginning, and the encounter would end tomorrow. In less than twenty-four hours he would return them to the door through which they'd just left and all this would be over. She had missed her opportunity to make a dazzling first impression with the man about whom she'd cherished silly notions for six years. The urgency of the situation, the moments ticking by, only added to her fumbling awkwardness.

Suddenly he turned, caught her eye, and hastily looked away again.

Well, Emma knew she was nothing pleasant to look at. She'd started out as an ugly, grizzled, tiny baby and not much had changed in the years since. Born too early, so she'd been told, nobody had expected her to live long at all— hence the last name given to her. It must have been an unpleasant surprise to Mrs. Lightbody when the premature baby put into her neglectful hands managed to thrive against all odds. But here she was at the age of eighteen, still alive. Since Emma had constantly been assured that each year was likely to be her last, a lack of something as superficial as beauty never seemed to matter much. Not in the great scheme of things.

Until now.

If only she had dewy skin and mahogany or auburn waves of hair; a little, upturned nose and rosebud lips; midnight blue eyes with long, ebony lashes; small ears and a willowy neck.

She was ashamed of herself for wanting those shallow things. It was illogical. Statistically, great beauty seldom did anybody any good, not in the long term. History books and plays were full of tragic beauties. But there was no stopping the lament in her heart at that moment. To have a little handsomeness for just these few hours would have been enough for her.

Alas she was a girl with sallow skin, lank hair and big ears. A girl who melted into the grey background, all her colors merging dully together, leaving only a faint and somewhat irritating, unsightly outline. Like a stain on plaster where the rain leaked through.

"Miss Emma Chance!" Georgiana's voice abruptly shattered her self-pitying thoughts in all directions, like a rubber ball landing among jacks. "You never wrote to tell me!"

Emma frowned, for she had no idea what the others had been talking about. Aware now of the captain looking at her again, she felt her cheeks warm. Fortunately, Melinda filled her in with a nudge and a whisper, "The teaching assistant post you've taken since old Lightbody heaved ho."

Ah. "It has not long happened," she replied apologetically to her friend across the carriage. "And I have been very busy. Lady Bramley is a hard taskmaster. I have barely had time to write a letter."

"But everything must be markedly improved now that she is in charge and the heinous Lightbody is gone."

"Yes. Although I suppose I might still be sent away as a governess eventually." She tried to ignore the inquisitive, dark gaze of her dragon prince. "For now I am reprieved and can stay at the school."

"Reprieved?" exclaimed Melinda with a snort. "I would have imagined you couldn't wait to get away from that place."

She swallowed and clasped her reticule tighter in her lap. "But it is all I have ever known."

Georgiana leaned forward, reached for her hand and squeezed it lightly. "You look very pretty with your hair in that new style."

Emma knew this was said merely to make her feel better and boost her confidence. Yes, Melinda had tried to curl and knot her hair in a new, "more fashionable" style, but their other friend could not have seen it since Emma had yet to remove her old bonnet. Perhaps the two of them had conferred in their letters about what to do with her, how to improve her looks. Nobody else had ever bothered about Emma as they did. Unaccustomed to the concern, sometimes theirs was a little too overwhelming for her, but she daren't appear ungrateful. After all, one could hardly feel sorry for oneself about having nobody who cared, and then protest when somebody did.

If only there was some middle ground. Then she might have a better chance to try her own wings and learn how to manage the world her way, to emerge slowly from her corner, rather than be dragged out by two well-meaning hellions.

"To think," exclaimed Melinda, "we have been friends now for four years. How the time has flown."

"Not quite three years," Georgiana corrected.

"It is four. I remember it distinctly."

"Then you remember wrongly, dear. It is three."

"It was winter in the year 1813."

"1814. I wonder that you can be so confused. Perhaps your hat crushes your brain."

The two girls bickered and then applied to Emma for final judgment, as they often did in these cases. Those years of their acquaintance, however, had taught her a valuable lesson.

"Although I could give you the exact number of days, down to the very hour, I prefer not to take sides," she said carefully. "You are, neither of you, pleasant company in a sulk, and we have precisely two hours and twelve minutes yet to travel— barring unforeseen circumstances, which could only lengthen our journey. Besides, it is generally wiser for the third person in any group to remain neutral in an argument, so I respectfully withdraw from this one."

The captain's gaze sought her out again, his eyes full of little sparks— the sort that shot out of the fire when it was stirred anew. He looked as if he might like to laugh, but he kept it to himself and turned away again.

"Oh, Emma," his sister exclaimed, "you can be so dreadfully aggravating!"

"Yes, indeed," Melinda added. "Must you always be right?"

She sighed. "That is exactly the accusation I attempted to avoid in this case." But she had slyly succeeded in ending the quarrel, for her two friends were now united in their despair of her.

Emma stole another glance at Captain Hathaway and was relieved to find him intently studying the view through his window, his thoughts apparently far away.

It was one of those in-between days, with summer making its last glorious effort to show off before autumn advanced crisply. A subtle change in the air had already daubed the trees with a gilt brush and soon, perhaps within days, they would be splashed all over with copper and gold that shimmered in a bolder, sharper breeze. For now, summer clung on, too stubborn to retire and yet weary of its work. The afternoon sun had a lazy, mellow amber tint to its edge, the light bending like cider about to overflow a cup.

In that gilded glow, Captain Hathaway's stern profile could have belonged to an Egyptian Pharaoh. Or a desert Sheikh. Enigmatic, commanding and possibly dangerous.

Riding on a camel, or a golden chariot, he would not look out of place. Just put him in different clothes.

And now she amused herself by doing so with her mind, trying him in various garments and guises.

Emma had often thought Georgiana Hathaway's looks rather exotic, but while that young lady's features only hinted at mysterious, foreign sap running through the family tree, her brother's eyes unabashedly, proudly proclaimed the fact. Naturally, the tropical sun endured on his journeys had colored his skin a darker shade too, adding to the air of mystery. Captain Hathaway might dress and act like a proper English gentleman, but there was something not quite right about it. Something out of the ordinary. *Too* striking, perhaps. Even wickedly so.

For Emma, who liked everything in order, neatly explained, numbered and cataloged in her mind, he was a puzzling beast, one moment teasing and the next somber. A strong man who spoke with laughter in his voice, even when he was sad. A man who kept looking at her, despite the fact that he said she was nothing worth looking at.

Lady Bramley had taught her little about men, except that they usually took up too much room.

Physically Captain Hathaway certainly filled his corner of the carriage, and his masculine presence overflowed into the remaining space, dominating her senses. Is that what the lady meant?

Emma's had always found her comfort in education. If she could amass as much knowledge about the world as possible she need never be afraid or unpleasantly surprised. Everything could be explained with careful and thorough study.

But today she ran up against something she could not learn about in books.

There was only one person in the world she might have gone to with these questions and not been teased. But it was impossible.

Today, more than ever in her life before, she yearned for her mother.

* * * *

Guy saw her small, questioning face reflected in the carriage window.

All well and good for her to stare at him, apparently, but he was not allowed to return the curiosity for fear of "startling" the creature. Didn't seem very just.

If his gaze met hers directly again, would she open the door and bolt while the carriage rumbled along? There was a rather desperate, skinny rabbit look about her, as if she stood up on her hind legs in the long grass and might dart away at the first scent of a hound dog.

His sister and the noisy, colorful one did most of the chattering on their journey. Every so often they paused to fuss over Miss Chance, as if suddenly remembering her there and trying to poke her out of her shell. But the attention seemed to make her more nervous and awkward; she was clearly at greater ease listening to them and not forced into making a contribution until she was ready. When she did venture a comment it was done so in a manner that suggested she carefully chose her words and checked them over before she let them out. Like a nanny buttoning the coats of her charges before they ran out into snow.

Now his sister pointed out some pretty pink flowers along the grassy verge, and Miss Chance was asked to identify them.

"Cranesbill," she said. "And that one there is Red Campion, I believe."

"How clever you are to know all their names," Miss Goodheart exclaimed. "I grew up in the countryside and the only names I know are daisies, buttercups, shepherd's purse and stinging nettles. The latter because I invariably ended up falling into them as a child. At least, my brother says I fell. I'm sure he pushed me."

"Emma has a passion for wildflowers," he heard his sister remark. "She prefers them to the fancier cultivated flower."

"I would not say it is a *passion*," the meek young lady objected timidly. "But I have made a study of the common flowers to be found in hedgerows and meadows, as well as the wild plants that spring up in unlikely places...between the cracks in a wall or a pavement. Anything that grows where it was not meant to be and thrives all by itself, is of interest to me."

"Yet you have never travelled into the country until now, Em."

"No. My study has been confined to books and pictures."

"And today you are out in the world," his sister said, hands clapped together as if she might burst into song. "Miss Emma Chance is *out* at last. What will become of her? It is very like the beginning of a romance, don't you think?"

Romance? He snorted softly to himself. They could keep Romance. He was thoroughly done with it.

"Emma dear, we shall find you a handsome suitor this evening," Georgiana continued excitedly. "I am quite resolved upon it."

"I thought you and your friends were above the idea of gallant knights on white steeds, sister," he grumbled, unable to stay silent now. "I thought you said you were all adventurers and men would get in the way?"

"Of course men get in the way if one tries to take them along with the luggage— they slow a woman down— but that doesn't mean we can't enjoy ourselves along the way. We are agreed that a little

78

flirting and dancing is admissible *en route*."

"We are?" Miss Goodheart frowned. "I thought men were out of the question. What's changed your mind?"

Guy saw his sister's cheeks color slightly. "One has to have some entertainment indoors on a stormy evening."

Miss Chance ventured shyly, "There is always chess."

"Chess? I refer to entertainment of a different sort, dear Emma."

"Besides," said Miss Goodheart. "You always win, Em. Where is the fun in that? I'd rather be poked in the eye with a stick than sit down at a chessboard with you again."

"What of books?" the small creature replied hesitantly. "Books are always most beneficial company, whatever the weather outdoors."

Georgiana laughed softly and shook her head. "Poor Emma, you do not understand quite what I mean by entertainment, I fear."

Clearly this conversation ventured off into realms Guy had better not follow, so he tried to get more comfortable and hopefully drift off for a discreet nap while his sister chattered onward. With his head still turned away from the ladies, he yawned discreetly into his curled fist and tried stretching out both his legs, first one and then the other. He had not slept last night, still too outraged by the recent discovery of his best friend's betrayal and his latest paramour's infidelity. The friend hurt most. Women were devious, flighty, easily distracted creatures who usually wounded him in the end, let him down and left him resolved never to embark upon another affair. At least for a while.

Women were an inevitable pain, a danger that ought to arrive on one's doorstep in crates burned with a skull and crossbones, just as a reminder. Although, he mused with chagrin, that would probably only entice him in. He couldn't imagine why he set himself up for it again and again. He had only himself to blame for *that* portion of the tragedy.

But he'd known Joseph Tidings for years and they'd been through a great deal together. Surely a bond between men ought to be stronger, more dependable than the connection between a man and a woman. Apparently the decade-long friendship had meant far less to Tidings than it did to him. Now it was in ruins. As the saying went among seamen, they had "parted brass rags."

He rubbed his brow with thumb and forefinger, eyes closed, trying to erase the picture that instantly formed in his mind— of Joe and Marianne, his best friend and his lover, the two of them on the sofa together, their embrace of the sort that could not be misconstrued in any way. Wished he could stop thinking of the scene and their surprised, guilty faces turning to see him there in the doorway, but his thoughts picked at it like fingernails at a scab, making it bleed anew so that it could not heal.

He'd called for a duel, naturally. It was a matter of honor. Both bullets missed their targets— Guy's deliberately. Joe, however, had never been a very steady shot and managed to take off one of his own toes.

As far as Guy knew the couple were still together— Joe Tidings hobbling around on crutches and complaining as if it was everybody's fault but his own. The romance would never last, and Marianne was probably already looking for her next gentleman. One with two working feet. Damn them both to hell.

"When will you grow out of this impulsiveness?" his father had exclaimed wearily. "There are other ways to settle a quarrel. Have you not entrusted your life to fate enough times?"

But when Guy lost his temper there was no discussion. It was the same when he embarked upon an affair; he gave all of himself, leapt in with both boots. Usually came out of it barefoot, because the wench would fleece him of everything he had before it was over.

If only he didn't feel as much. If only he *could* be like his father and guard his emotions so well that they were rarely ruffled.

"So now a man is shot in the foot, is he not? Crippled for life and all because of a loose woman."

"He shot *himself* in the foot, father. I aimed at the nearest tree."

"Foolishness! Utter stupidity. When will you learn?"

Thus his father tut-tutted and turned away from him, disappointed as ever. When Guy considered it, he realized that the back of Frederick Hathaway's shoulder was a more common sight than his face. At least, it was for *him*— the son who, since he could do nothing to please his father, had long since given up trying.

With grim thoughts such as these, and true sleep evading him, he sank into his seat and glowered at the passing scenery as the carriage trundled farther into countryside.

"Ooh look," Miss Goodheart cried, "the cows repose most comfortably in the field. That means rain."

"C...cows?"

In his peripheral vision he saw Miss Chance grip the edge of her seat and turn a vivid shade of white.

The other two laughed. "Worry not, Emma dear, they are not likely to get up and chase the carriage. Unless, of course, they are due for milking and betaken with a sudden desire to run after us."

After that, each time the carriage passed in sight of cattle, Miss Chance was teased until she began to look annoyed. He wondered if she would ever lose her temper and shout at his sister and her other friend. After all, a jest was only amusing for so long, especially on a three-hour journey. *He,* at least, knew when to stop— when a joke had outstayed its welcome. But the frayed little creature stoically bore their mockery with only a thin line between her brows and a slight downward tug upon the left corner of her lips.

Guy began to be sorry that he had teased her. While he had meant to put her at her ease, she must have thought it was simply the same as she usually suffered at the hands of his sister and her friend.

Chapter Six

At last, after a change of horses and two stops along the route, they arrived at the Black Bull Inn just outside Little Flaxhill.

Resuming his task as affable escort, shaking off the melancholy as best he could, Guy refreshed his smile to help the ladies out of the carriage and untie the trunks. The occupation helped. It was only when he must sit and could not move about that he found his mind dwelling on the thoughts that pained him.

"Miss Hathaway! You are late, young lady! I had begun to think I must send out a search party, that you would be recovered, turned upside down in a ditch. And, I'll have you know, young lady, this lingering summer weather is far too warm for mourning black."

He looked over his shoulder and saw a stout, fast-moving lady coming to greet them across the inn yard, other folk stumbling hastily aside out of fear or reverence; he couldn't be sure which. The tenor of her voice certainly inspired the former. Dragging his feet across the muddy yard, a young boy followed in her wake.

"Lady Bramley, I did not expect you to meet us here," his sister exclaimed. "Is anything amiss?"

"Not at all, my dear. Of course, I must meet you here and see that all is as it should be, that you are well tended during your stay at the inn. Surely you did not think I would abandon you to this wild place? It is my duty to ensure that you are safe, comfortable and well guarded. I only wish my nephew might have accommodated you all at Woodbyne, but you know how few bed chambers are suitable for the habitation of young ladies at present. And Henry is rather keen to have the place decorated to surprise you, so he informs me." She shook her head, although it was more of a tremble of irritation than a full shake. "Henry who has never been ornamental, nor decorated anything in his life before except with a dirty footprint, now thinks he can dress a house for a ball without my help."

"Oh, I quite understand the matter of rooms at Woodbyne, your ladyship. Besides, we will have fun together here at the inn."

"I do hope not *too much* fun," the elderly lady replied, stopping before them with one hand pressed to her side as if she had a stitch. "I have considerable experience of your misadventures, young lady."

"Really, Lady Bramley, I strongly object to this idea of yours that my friends and I cannot be trusted to behave."

Guy had lifted the last trunk from the carriage when he felt the sharp point of a parasol prodded into his shoulder. "And you, young man? You must be Miss Hathaway's brother. Skulking about there with the luggage. What do you have to say for yourself?"

He turned cautiously, brushing a hand over his shoulder.

"For making these ladies so late," she added,

raising a lorgnette on a chain to study him through it. "Doubtless it will be your fault. Men never do anything quite so well as thwart or complicate progress wherever they can." She prodded him again, this time in the ribs, as if he were a hanging tapestry and she suspected an enemy eavesdropper of hiding behind it.

Georgiana hurried to his side. "Guy, this is Lady Bramley, a patroness of our school. I have spent this summer as her companion, and she's worked very hard to improve me."

"Then she must be a very brave and determined lady," he muttered. "Now I understand the necessity of a that sharp parasol and the brutally adept wielding of it." She'd surely bruised him with the damn thing.

"*Captain* Hathaway, is it not? Oh yes, I have heard of *you*, young man." By her tone it was nothing favorable that she'd heard. Again the piercing eye, enlarged through that glass lens, gave him a thorough appraisal from boots to hat, which he removed for a hasty bow.

"I hope you will not believe all the gossip, madam." He smiled broadly. "I am quite harmless, in truth."

"Nonsense. No young man is harmless. Even one in monk's robes. And *you*, from all I've been told, are certainly not fit for holy orders. What excuse do you have for this lateness? I expect better punctuality from a captain in his majesty's navy."

"Your ladyship. I'm afraid our late arrival is

indeed my fault. I failed to herd my sister out of our father's house in a timely fashion and—"

"*I* am to blame," Georgiana intervened. "I was so caught up in my writing that poor Guy could not drag me away before noon. He's too much of a gentleman," she added proudly, "to confess the truth."

"Hmm. Well do I know how absorbed you can become with your writing, Miss Hathaway," the lady replied, shaking her head again. "But now make haste inside for I have arranged a cold, late luncheon for all of you in the private dining room. It is a small, cramped place, but clean and adequate, I suppose. The landlord is a truculent fellow who complained when I insisted upon the inspection of his kitchens, but I certainly would not have friends of mine eat here until I had assessed the place and the cook's abilities to my satisfaction. His wife is an equally ill-tempered creature who made slovenly protest to my inspection of the rooms above, but fleas are all too common in these places. One can never be too careful."

"Thank goodness you are here for us, Lady Bramley," said his sister with a sly grin for her friends.

"Indeed you are fortunate, for I am— Miss Chase, you are ghostly pale." They all now turned to observe that young lady as she held her arms tight to her sides and bowed her head. "There is never much to you, of course, but you look more transparent even than usual. Come closer and stop hovering in that fashion. It gives you the appearance of a nervous pickpocket, or somebody charged with giving bad news and overcome by the task."

The timid ghost ventured forward, clutching her purse.

"You're breathing too hard, girl, in that distressing way. I'm quite certain it is not necessary to take in the air with so much frenzied performance." Before the girl could mutter any reply, the lady added crossly, "Captain Hathaway, make use of yourself. Give Miss Chance your arm and take her indoors before somebody trips over her or she falls down and frightens the horses into a stampede. Leave those trunks. For a shilling this boy, the cook's son, can bring them in." But as the scrawny lad dashed forward, she grabbed him by the collar. "*When* he's finished exploring his nostrils with a finger and washed his hands to my standards."

Thus, prodded and shouted at, organized and reorganized, their small party advanced across the yard with Miss Chance, looking exceedingly wretched, forced to take his arm. Again Guy barely felt her touch and had to put his hand over hers to be sure it was there.

"Don't fret, Miss Chance," he whispered. "I shan't mind how hard you breathe. *I* shall only be distressed if you stop completely."

She looked up at him, her eyes wide and the color of sky heavy with raincloud.

He smiled.

There was, very nearly, a smile in return, but it was too uncertain to hold up under the bright sun and then her gaze dropped to his sleeve, where his hand rested lightly over hers.

"Go directly ahead to the private dining room, Captain Hathaway," Lady Bramley shouted behind them as he once again felt the prick of her parasol between his shoulder blades. "And then I have much to test you with, before I leave these young ladies in your company, sir."

So he quickened and lengthened his stride, as eager to get away from her stabbing parasol as he was to save Miss Chance from the sun's heat. In his haste he almost tripped over the step and banged his brow on the low lintel over the ancient door.

The pain, combined with the effort of not cursing out loud in the company of ladies was enough to make him hot-faced and flustered as he rushed the timid young lady into the private dining room. Guy kept his head down to avoid further incident within the tight confines of the inn which had been built several centuries before, when men were, so it seemed, considerably smaller in stature.

* * * *

"To say this food leaves much to be desired is an understatement, but at least it will put something in your stomachs before the festivities this evening," Lady Bramley exclaimed loudly as they sat around a sunlit table in the private dining room of the inn.

When the innkeeper arrived to set a large jug of lemonade before her, she greeted him with a stern, "If you must serve a piecrust this thick and hard, you ought to provide a blacksmith's hammer to break it."

"Perhaps you would prefer bread softened in milk, your ladyship. My wife makes a good junket for the elderly and infirm."

Scandalized, she replied, "Do I look, sir, as if I eat *junket*?"

The girls all struggled not to laugh and then Georgiana managed to draw her ladyship's attention away from the inadequacies of their current repast by urging her brother to tell stories of the many strange foods he'd encountered and eaten on his travels.

Enthralled, the ladies listened to his gastronomical adventures, which included pickled sheep's ear, pig's hoof in a coconut sauce, fish eyeballs in aspic and boiled tarantula. Emma was not entirely certain these were all true stories, but he clearly enjoyed horrifying his luncheon companions. Especially Lady Bramley, who declared that his insides must be in a state as decrepit as the walls of an abandoned slaughterhouse.

To which he replied with great solemnity, "Your ladyship, when a man has had nothing to eat for three days, he will gladly chew the straw of your hat, the laces of your stays and the leather of your shoes if you let him. Indeed, I have known sailors to do just that when desperate enough. You'd be surprised at what a man's intestines can digest."

"Well then, at least you, young man, can eat this piecrust. I trust it will set you upright for a few days at least."

"Indeed, madam. This is good ballast."

Throughout their luncheon, Lady Bramley kept a stern eye on Captain Hathaway and questioned him with intensity. Sixteenth century prisoners in the Tower of London had probably faced less brutal interrogation by the warden.

From his age to his height to his habits, he was thoroughly vetted.

Thus, Emma surreptitiously learned that he was six foot two, enjoyed cricket in his spare time, had no tolerance for cabbage, despite Lady Bramley making a strong case for it, and he possessed all his teeth in their exact order. He also had five scars apparently, and a tattoo, but an indignant Lady Bramley declined to be shown their location when he cheerfully offered to display them.

"I trust you are not a drinker, Captain?"

"No more than most men. I cannot lay claim to temperance, but I seldom imbibe to excess. Especially when charged with my sister's protection."

"A gambler?"

"I confess I have never found the attraction. Perhaps I have never been rich enough."

And with every answer he gave that smile, engineered to be charming. Like the one he gave Emma earlier as they walked across the yard. Like the one he gave to anybody he caught looking at him.

Lady Bramley remained grim, unrelenting in her inquisition. "I hear there have been attachments with hussies, young man."

Emma felt a hot blush creep over her face.

"Kindly remember you are here to escort these three virtuous young ladies. Keep your mind on the task at hand, or you will answer to me and I shall scoop out your wandering eyes — and any other unsavory parts—with a rusted tea-strainer. One that is inadequately modified for the function."

He flinched and then laughed uproariously.

"You find hilarity in the pursuit of lapsed women, Captain?"

"Only in your punishment for it, madam."

"You do not deny, then, your attraction to women bereft of moral fortitude?"

"Only when it's unavoidable, it's raining and there is no other occupation at hand."

That made his inquisitor raise an eyebrow above her lorgnette and pull her lips into a tight moue.

"A jest, madam," he said, reaching for his ale.

"I should hope so," she exclaimed tautly. "I do not approve of those."

"Jests, madam, or hussies?"

Emma choked on a piece of pastry, requiring Melinda to clap her soundly on the back while Georgiana scowled at her brother and kicked him under the table.

"Both," Lady Bramley declared, lowering her lorgnette at last. "And although I am not surprised—

considering your reputation, young man— I am disappointed to find you so lacking in gravity. But your sister has a tendency to be frivolous too. I suppose it is a family trait." She sighed. "Alas, I must trust you to keep an eye on these girls, for I have much to do at Woodbyne before this evening. Men are, on the whole, unreliable, but we must make do with what can be got at short notice. And you are, apparently, *it*."

One hand to his heart, he somberly pledged, "No harm will come to any of these young ladies while they are in my charge this evening. You may rest assured of that, your ladyship. I shall fight off, single-handedly the legions of lecherous prowlers with unspeakable motives, who might come to kidnap them while they sleep. I hear the Sultan of the Ottoman Empire procures most of his harem slaves from Little Flaxhill and its nearby villages."

"You're altogether too jovial, young man."

"I suppose life has not yet trodden me down, madam. Give it time."

"Indeed. Once you are married, you'll have other things to occupy your mind and all such playful sport will be crushed out of you."

"Then I had better stay a bachelor as long as I am able." He laughed, his eyes shining, and even Lady Bramley could not resist a very slight tremor of the lip when he added, "Unless, of course, you are keen to take me on, your ladyship? I might give up my playful sports for you."

"I have better things to do with my time, wicked rogue, than see to the management of another husband. Particularly a young, disorderly, impertinent fellow. I prefer dogs. And gourds."

"Gourds?"

"I grow prize-winning marrows, Captain Hathaway. Did your sister not tell you?"

"I'm afraid Georgiana neglected to mention it, madam. I cannot think why for she knows how fond I am of marrow."

Lady Bramley waved her lorgnette. "My glasshouse produces the biggest gourds and best fruit in Mayfair. My marrows are notorious, although I must say my melons are also magnificent this year."

Emma felt it incumbent upon her to interject, "Melons are not of the gourd family, of course, but botanically of the berry genus." And then she blushed hotly again as all eyes turned to observe her.

The lady continued as if Emma had never spoken. "Everybody remarks upon the size of my melons whenever they are exhibited. My melons have, in fact, received a mention in *The Gentleman's Weekly*."

"I see," the Captain muttered, looking down and pressing his lips hard together as if he had a pain somewhere. "You must have your hands full, madam."

"Indeed. Lady Fortescue-Rumputney is lime green with envy over my success. She, of course, leaves the tending of her melons to the hands of her gardener, which is, in my opinion, a mistake."

Apparently the Captain needed something to occupy *his* hands at that moment. He reached across the table for the lemonade jug and refilled Emma's glass for her.

He had not asked her if she was thirsty, but she was. Nobody else had noticed her empty glass and she did not dare ask for another, fearing she'd perhaps been too greedy and unladylike in drinking hers already.

"I can see how you have little time for another husband, madam."

"Indeed."

"Or to take me in hand. I would be a terrible project with which to burden yourself."

"Quite," the lady replied. "I have two sons and a nephew to break of their bad habits already, and time marches on. Once beyond five and thirty, a man is wretchedly set in his ways and then one may as well give up hope. At least you have a few years yet to be cured of unacceptable practices."

He blinked innocently. "But I have no bad habits, Lady Bramley!"

"You are young, lively, pleased with yourself and handsome in an unruly way. Bad habits are inevitable. And, for pity's sake, get your hair cut. With all those wild curls you have the appearance of a gypsy. Tsk, tsk! What is the navy coming to these days?"

But Emma could see that her ladyship was on the verge of a smile, more than once, and that showed she had not taken a complete dislike to the Captain.

The fact that she had advice for him was a good sign.

"Upon your return to London, visit Truefitt and Hill on St. James Street, young man. Tell them I sent you and they will attend to you at once, even without an appointment."

"But I am on leave, madam, and when—"

"*On leave* is no cause to be lax and resort to savagery. What would become of the world if we all went about without attention to proper grooming?"

"I daresay we'd have time for more important matters."

"What could be more important, young man, than decency? Humanity has advanced, *thankfully*, to wearing clothes for bodily cover, as opposed to growing one's hair for the purpose."

He laughed again and the sound tickled Emma's insides so that she was tempted to join in.

"Miss Chance! You're breathing in that terrible, undignified way again," Lady Bramley shouted across the table. "Whatever is the matter with you?"

"Poor Emma must be exhausted after the journey," Georgiana suggested. "She's not used to traveling so far."

"I hope she's not coming down with a fever," exclaimed Melinda. "She was acting oddly earlier today and look how pink her cheeks are. She has barely eaten a morsel."

"Do you not like the pie, Emma?"

Her mind spun, words flipping out onto her tongue mechanically. "The pie is over-salted and the crust burnt. Twenty-three persons in Kent last year were seized with severe illness from pork pie poisoning."

"Poor dear!" said Georgiana. "Perhaps it's a summer cold."

"She ought to be in bed," Melinda agreed.

But Captain Hathaway took one look at her and then turned to close the wooden shutters across the window, through which hot afternoon sun had beamed down upon her throughout their meal.

At once she felt cooler and calmer. She could open her eyes without squinting. It had not occurred to her to ask if she might close the shutters, for the others seemed to enjoy the sunlight. And she hadn't wanted to move her seat for that would have made everybody stare at her and think she made an undue fuss.

He poured fresh water from the jug into her finger-bowl, dipped his clean handkerchief in it and held the damp end out to her. "For your forehead, Miss Chance," he said softly.

She swallowed and took it. "Thank...thank you, Captain. Although, *Coup de Soleil* is more speedily cured by the application of a damp cloth to the back of the neck rather than the forehead."

"Is it, by jove? Well, you apply it as you wish. I'm a simple fellow who knows little to naught. Brain of cork, that's me."

"I...I daresay it is comforting to the forehead also, sir. As you said."

He turned back to the others, beginning another conversation to distract them away from Emma, while she patted her face with the dampened handkerchief.

Her heartbeat remained rapid, not fearful or embarrassed, but excited and tentatively... happy? It was the last thing she'd expected to feel so far beyond the boundaries of her familiar world.

Captain Hathaway glanced back at her as the others talked.

Emma knew she must look a dreadful sight. Her hair clung around her face, sticking to her perspiring skin.

But he smiled. "Better now, Miss Chance?"

"Yes, Captain," she managed on a taut sigh. "Much better."

"Good." He nodded and then returned to the conversation, teasing his sister about something she'd just said.

Oh, he did not need his curls cut at all, she thought firmly, her heart thumping hard, lifting her spirits. His was the loveliest hair any man could have.

Alas, even the back of his head excited her pulse in a most unusual way. Lady Bramley would say there was no hope for her.

Suddenly she wanted to laugh, but that would make them all look at her again and comment on her red face, so she quickly resumed mopping her cheeks with the damp handkerchief. His handkerchief. It held a scent of leather— naturally— tobacco and Bay

Rum, fragrances she recognized from long ago evenings when Mrs. Lightbody had entertained gentlemen in her parlor after her pupils were abed. Emma had always been curious about those men. Occasionally she'd wondered whether one of Mrs. Lightbody's night-time visitors was her father.

But the scent on Captain Hathaway's linen handkerchief was richer and warmer than the aroma left to drift in the stale, greasy air of Mrs. Lightbody's room the morning after she'd entertained. *This* scent was still alive, fresh and bristling with vigor. And secrets.

Feeling like a trollop and a thief all rolled into one, she slyly inhaled a great greedy breath of it, holding the cloth to her nose.

But only until she felt Lady Bramley's sharp eyes upon her and feared being further chastised for breathing.

Chapter Seven

While the ladies went up to rest and prepare for the ball, Guy found himself once again cornered by Lady Bramley who, although she had called for her carriage to be brought around, delayed her departure to give him a few last warnings.

"If harm befalls any of those dear girls in this place, I shall blame you, Captain."

"Yes, your ladyship. Understood. Let me promise you *again* that I shall protect them with my life."

She sniffed. "See that you do. If disaster occurs to any one of them, there will be no excuse for you to still be living."

Guy watched her thoughtfully for a moment as she adjusted a veil over her hat and face. "You are very fond of my sister and her friends," he said. "They are indeed fortunate to have your guidance."

"Of course I am fond of them. They are, like most young girls, despicably riotous and needlessly excitable on occasion, but they have promise. I like to find pearls in my oysters and to see pretty things grow to their full potential, Captain. And I always enjoy a good challenge." She paused to adjust her gloves. "Your sister has quite brightened my summer."

"I am glad to hear it, madam. I like to know she's been useful at last. We had almost despaired of it."

"I believe her preference for descending a staircase by the banister and seat first has been nipped in the bud."

"Thank heavens. She's a little too...rounded... for that sport." He walked the lady to the door of the inn and held it for her as she stepped out into the mellowed sunlight. The air had finally cooled and softened. The birds sang with their last burst of renewed enthusiasm after the weary peak of the day and, in the west, a sleepy sun burnished the leaves of a chestnut tree as it began to sink behind the branches. A change was in the air, hinting that this would be the last fine evening of a lingering summer.

Guy had made up his mind not to ask, but suddenly he heard himself saying, "What about Miss Chance?"

"What about her, you regrettable rogue?"

"She doesn't talk much and when she does it is mostly to recite facts. Is she one of your pearls?"

"Miss Chance is extremely intelligent, which is fortunate since she lacks in beauty. She will become a governess in the near future, but for now, until I can find a suitable post— one not too far or too strange for her— she assists the teaching staff at the academy. Why do you ask?"

"Merely curious."

"Don't shrug, young man. It is not dignified. A naval captain's shoulders should remain straight, balanced and sturdy at all times, for they carry upon them the security of our great nation. Even when they are not wearing their epaulettes there is no excuse for petulant sagging. Beside, shrugging suggests the careless shedding of a drunkard's coat." As he helped her up into her open landau, she added sternly, "And do not flirt with poor Miss Chance. I know how you young men are and I suppose it amuses you to see her blush, but I won't have it. Emma Chance is not the girl for you. She is a good, quiet sort of girl."

"And I am a bad, noisy sort of man?"

"You know very well what I mean, Captain Hathaway. You are not an amiable idiot, despite the attempt to portray one. You are a thrusting young man full of ungentlemanly impatience, and Miss Chance is sheltered, untouched, an innocent. She has suffered an unfortunate start in life, with no family to support her or pay her any attention. A destitute foundling, the last thing she needs is a handsome rogue like you— temporarily bored and prone to impulsive mischief— picking her up as the mood takes you and then dropping her again. Her lot in life is grim enough without you causing her more vexation and strife."

"Cause vexation and strife, madam? I thought that was a woman's purpose, not a man's."

The lady ignored that comment. "She'd never have a moment's peace. You'd ride roughshod over her feelings. She is a gentle soul who would try to mend you."

"Am I too late for mending?"

"No. You're not ready for it. Some men never are."

"You make me sound quite hopeless, madam."

She looked at him wearily and shook her head. "You are only seven and twenty. There is a reason why dough is left to rise before it can be made into bread. There is also a reason why a firm hand is necessary to knead that dough. I daresay you have the potential to be a decent loaf. One day. At present you should be left under an oiled cheesecloth in a warm place, free of drafts. And Miss Emma Chance is just discovering her world. She must worry about herself and her future, not about helping some young man as yet unshaped and uncooked himself."

He laughed. "Would it not be better for the young lady to shape me to her specifications with her own hands?"

"That depends upon the capability and strength of the lady's hands. In the case of Miss Emma Chance, I must say no. She is not strong. Her health is frail. Her knowledge of the male animal distinctly lacking. She would have no inkling of how to manage you. I daresay that's why you took a fancy to her, you scoundrel."

Took a fancy to her? To that plain wisp? He was shocked and then amused.

Lady Bramley might have some undeniable powers of perception, but they were clearly lacking in this particular matter. She had thoroughly mistaken his simple question about that odd, fragile girl and let her imagination take flight.

"You may rest easy on that score too, your ladyship," he assured her. "This lump of unsightly, unproven dough has no plan to seduce poor Miss Chance. Or anybody at present. Besides I prefer dangerous women." He sighed as he shut the carriage door firmly behind her. "There you are, Lady Bramley, that is a vice to which I readily admit. Perilous predicaments with temptresses and vixens, who will ultimately abuse my good nature and abandon me, seem to be *my* lot in life."

She leaned toward him, squinted in an exaggerated fashion, pouted her lips and mockingly dabbed at her veiled face with a handkerchief. "Let me mop the tears from my eyes! You know nothing of difficulty. You have youth, health, wit, a promising career and a not *too* displeasing set of features— the requisite number and all apparently functional. That in itself is rare for a sailor."

"You flatter me, madam," he muttered dryly.

"Why would I? Doubtless you get flattery enough. From me you get honesty, which you need."

"So if I am not yet ready to be taken in hand by a wife, what would you advise me?"

"In five or six years, seek a wife then to keep you out of trouble. Or at least to make a semblance of it. As long as you are settled by five and thirty. If not, then you should never attempt matrimony at all. There is a narrow season of ripeness in a man. It varies, according to his character. But if you have not come to your senses by then, you may as well remain a bachelor."

"And when my dough is risen sufficiently,

madam?"

"Find an ornamental girl, one who is easily contented and not very bright. A young, unquestioning woman who can be satisfied with that handsome smile of yours and not need to dig beyond it and find what devilry lies beneath. Better she not know about that. If she can be content with your surface attractions all the better for her. She can enjoy needlework and a little dog of some sort to keep her company when you do not."

Another laugh burst out of him. "She sounds quite a prize, my future wife."

"You asked for my advice. Find a stupid woman and you'll both be happy. Somebody like Emma Chance is far too clever for you."

"I daresay you're right."

"Of course, I'm right. I always am. And get a haircut." With that she nodded to him and then raised her voice to shout, "Haste, Whitworth!", and the coachman took her away in a cloud of dust.

* * * *

The landlord's wife brought jugs of warm water to the room they shared so that the ladies could wash before they dressed. Both Georgiana and Melinda had scented soap and perfume to share with Emma, but she also had something that Lady Bramley had slipped into her hand before they went upstairs— a long, narrow box.

"'Tis only a little trinket for you to borrow this

evening, as I know you have nothing yourself," the lady had said.

"Well, open it then," exclaimed Georgiana, hands clasped as they clustered around Emma in their room above the tavern. "The suspense kills me."

So slowly she opened the box and found a simple strand of pale pink pearls inside. "Oh. It's too pretty for me."

"Nonsense! It's delicate, like you. It's quite perfect. I know she can be a terrible busybody, but that old dear has splendid taste in jewelry and knows just what suits. And she always means well, even if her methods can be heavy-handed."

"But what if I lose it?" The responsibility of looking after such a lovely object seemed onerous. Emma was still more than a little fearful of Lady Bramley— although not in the same way as she feared Mrs. Lightbody. Her apprehension in the case of the former headmistress was born of hatred and pain, but Lady Bramley engendered in her such a desire to please that she trembled at the thought of disappointing that stern but generous lady.

"You won't lose it, for you'll be with us," said Melinda, adding with her own peculiar brand of uncrushable optimism, "We won't *let* you lose it."

Georgiana pointed out that Lady Bramley might be offended if she did not wear the pearls, so really she had no choice. But it felt odd to have something that was neither Mrs. Lightbody's hard fingers, nor a collar of plain, cheap chintz around her neck.

"Your hair has gone limp since I took the papers out," Melinda exclaimed in frustration as she drew Emma back to the dresser mirror and assessed her handiwork from the night before.

"I think my head was too hot today in the carriage and at luncheon," Emma replied apologetically. "It has...wilted."

"Stop touching it! You're making it worse."

She quickly put her hands down and sighed at her reflection, while the other two girls tried twisting and twirling her hair around their fingers and combs, arguing with each other about how they might possibly improve her sad state. Melinda began pulling things off her bonnet and arranging them in Emma's hair like an eccentric crown— something that might be worn by a Lord of Misrule to preside over the Feast of Fools at Christmastide. Georgiana found a bottle of perfume with which she sprinkled the air lavishly around everybody, as if that might help.

From where she stood, Emma could see out of the casement window and down into the inn yard, where Captain Hathaway currently paced back and forth in the sunset. She was supposed to consider her reflection in the dresser mirror, of course, but there was nothing interesting to observe there.

The Captain looked sad again. When he thought nobody watched he did not bother to hide it, as he did when he felt the ladies' eyes upon him. He was being dutifully polite, naturally, keeping them amused and entertained even when he was unhappy inside.

Now that he was alone and had no need to mask his face in smiles, the bounce had quite gone out of his boots.

She sneezed suddenly, so violently that several of Melinda's hastily applied, silk ribbon bows were dislodged from her hair. Alas, despite Emma's best efforts, they were rescued and rearranged before she could step on them and put the others off the idea. Two more sneezes followed in quick succession, but fortunately she kept a kerchief to hand— Captain Hathaway's. Neither of the other girls noticed it was not hers. She held it folded away in her palm, a naughty secret, and every time she pressed it to her nose she inhaled a tiny breath of his scent. It remained faintly detectable, even through the cloud of thick perfume that Georgiana had thrown over their heads like summer rain.

"You *have* caught a cold," Melinda muttered.

"I think not," she replied. "It may be the perfume." She itched now too, but it was too late to wash and start again. The heavy scent hung in a moist cloud around them, clinging to everything they wore. Emma's nose, when she glanced in the mirror, already glowed pink.

Perfect. It matched Lady Bramley's pearls she mused dourly.

A half hour later the young ladies were all as content with their dress as they could be under the circumstances and there was no further delay. They crossed the yard to where Mr. Hathaway's carriage awaited with refreshed horses, stepping carefully around the piles of muck. Emma walked behind the others, her pace slow, wanting to let every moment sink into her skin. There was lavender growing by the brick wall — a large clump of it—and the heat of that afternoon had released a thick, warm wave of that sweet chalky scent into the air. As she walked by it, Emma could not resist letting her gloved fingers brush against those soft purple flowers and pale, blue-green stems. She brought her fingertips to her nose and smiled. That was much better than the perfume with which Georgiana had sprinkled her dress.

Then, quite suddenly, she looked up and saw that she had the Captain's attention. He was helping the others up into the carriage and had looked back to see where she was. His eyes were curious.

"Are you coming, Miss Chance?"

No, she wanted to say, *I'd rather stay here with the lavender.*

Instead, without a word, she took his hand and stepped up into the carriage, reluctantly leaving the lavender behind.

Soon the carriage was off again.

"Good god," he declared, "what is that dreadful smell?"

While Emma cringed in silent mortification, Melinda explained they'd been heavy-handed with the perfume. "I think Miss Chance got the worst of it."

The carriage windows were opened, and he leaned toward the fresh air every so often with a pained expression.

"Well, Miss Goodheart, it has not yet rained. It seems your predication was wrong."

"Not mine," she protested. "The cows predicted it. They were wrong. Perhaps they were just in a lazy mood."

It looked, in fact, to be a fine night. As the sky turned lilac, tiny stars had already begun to appear. Emma looked out to find the constellations she'd studied from her bedchamber window for so many years. In this wide open world, the stars seemed even further away from her reach.

In a few more months Andromeda and Cassiopeia would be seen at their best and brightest, but she could just make them out now. Yes, there they were, as Ptolemy had found and named them almost seventeen hundred years ago. Sagittarius the Archer would be visible clearly in the sky tonight as twilight faded.

"Do you look for the moon, Miss Chance?" the Captain asked with a benevolent smile— the sort a kindly gentleman might grant to a naive little girl in his care. "To see if it is made of cheese?"

Cheese? She was nonplussed for a moment. "Cheese, Captain, is a product made from the milk of cows, goats and other mammals. It can be preserved for some time, but I hardly think it could be—"

He chuckled, shaking his head. "Miss Chance, I refer to children's folklore."

"Oh." Of course, that is what a girl who had

never been out in the world was supposed to think. "You refer perhaps to the Proverbs of John Heywood, playwright of the Tudor era."

"Do I?" Scratching his temple, he laughed again. "If you say so, Miss Chance."

Her friends were looking out of the other window, paying no attention. Usually Emma would say nothing more, but study of the night's sky was one of her favorite subjects, and she could not resist adding, "Actually, Captain, there should be a full moon this evening. The celestial object is at its perigee, which means it is closer to earth in its orbit than at any other time of the year."

He squinted. "Indeed?"

"In some cultures, it is referred to as the Sturgeon Moon, since fish are more readily caught during this season. Perhaps you have heard it called such."

The Captain muttered something under his breath and sat back in his seat, arms folded, rather annoyed.

Emma resumed her study of the sky, satisfied that she had set him straight about cheese, the moon and the fact that she may be shy, but she was not a silly child.

During their mile and three quarter journey to Woodbyne Abbey, she soon realized that Georgiana had become strangely quiet and pensive. Apparently their friend noticed it too.

"I suppose it will be pleasant for you to see

Commander Thrasher again, Georgie," Melinda ventured. "You enjoyed your weeks at Woodbyne, I think."

"Yes." Georgiana gazed out through the opened window, a hint of blush visible on her cheek. "I enjoyed it very much."

Emma waited, expecting more, but Georgiana again seemed unusually reticent to speak. Fortunately, before the silence became a longer dangling thread, her brother picked it up. "They call him Dead Harry, you know. Because his obituary has been printed twice in the newspaper. One of the bravest men in our navy. Had a fine career until he retired a few years ago." He sounded a little excited to meet the man, his eyes warming as his thoughts perked up. "Quite a legend. Was mortally wounded at the Battle of Grand Port seven years ago and survived."

"Then it was not a *mortal* wound," said his sister, pert. "It would only be a mortal wound if it killed him, wouldn't it, Em?"

Once again she was appealed to as the arbiter of their little group. "I suppose, strictly speaking. But the word might also be used to imply life-threatening. I see naught amiss with the usage in this case, especially since we all know the subject is not deceased." She sneezed.

The Captain chuckled and felt inside his coat for something. "See. Even your clever Miss Chance agrees with me." He looked down at himself, puzzled, patting his waistcoat pocket, perhaps trying to recall where he'd mislaid the item.

Emma pressed her lips together and squeezed the folded handkerchief that she kept secreted in her palm. She felt wicked, but not at all sorry that she kept it. Now she was not only a trollop and a thief, but shameless too. In the space of less than half a day she'd fallen prey to the wicked influences of the outside world and become vain, greedy and a desperate criminal.

"Well, Harry is very much alive," Georgiana replied, "thank goodness." Then, as if she thought she might have said too much, she fell quiet again.

"And then he was shipwrecked a few years later and survived, utterly alone on an island for eight and twenty months," her brother continued. "It is a miracle he was ever found. Some say he's not the man he was before all that— he lost the will to command a battle ship— but I daresay it's inevitable that he would be changed after such an ordeal." To Emma's surprise, as she raised her eyelashes, she found him looking at her directly. "Do you not agree, Miss Chance?"

She thought for a moment, organizing her words, and then she said, "Two years and four months with only oneself for company is a very long time. A man's mind must turn inward, questioning himself and all that he knew before. When there is no other soul at hand to observe and acknowledge a man living, he will wonder about his own existence." Again she sneezed, raising her hand to her nose. "God did not want man to be alone. That is why He made woman."

He gave a curt laugh. "Sometimes I think I should like to be left alone for two years."

Emma knew just what he meant. Their gazes suddenly crossed paths and then they stopped, felt their way back through the fading dusk and met again. It was contact of only a moment, but there was understanding, amity between two private, secretive natures.

"Nonsense," his sister snapped. "You would never manage. You do not have Harry's—" she blinked, gathered a quick breath, and continued, "Commander Thrasher's incredible abilities to survive. He's a remarkable man."

His eyes gleamed as he laughed. "Sounds as if my little sister has developed a partiality for the gentleman."

In the next moment their horses were pulling the carriage around to the wide steps at the front of Woodbyne Abbey and there was no further time for teasing. Emma glanced at her friend and saw an expression of mild horror, confusion, and fear. The leader of their little group, usually so determined and bold, was suddenly rendered mute, except for a series of apparently uncontainable hiccups.

And her friends knew what that meant.

Oh, dear. It seemed Captain Hathaway was right and his sister had formed a romantic attachment to their evening's host. Emma knew she would be frantic herself if such a thing— however unlikely—

ever happened to her, so her heart went out to Georgiana.

There was not much she could say to comfort however, for while her friend dissolved into hiccups, Emma trembled with sneezes and felt the desperate urge to scratch herself where her skin itched unbearably. Only Melinda seemed unaffected and walked up the steps with her customarily careless, bounding stride, almost knocking a stone flower planter off its plinth in the process.

Chapter Eight

Woodbyne Abbey was a very old, rambling building, bits and pieces added on over the years as other parts crumbled or became too drafty to heat and make inhabitable. If one looked closely there were signs of neglect in the Abbey's not too distant past, but there were also evident, very recent attempts made to fix holes and brighten what must have been a gloomy interior. That evening, bowers of greenery and festoons of roses decorated the ceiling beams and the grand staircase. Some rose petals had fallen, littering the floor with a pattern of pinks, yellows, white and red. Every so often another petal drifted in a slow downward spin to the tiles beneath, leaving a whisper of sweet fragrance in the warm current of air.

Guy heard Miss Chance murmuring at how beautiful it was, and he remembered what Lady Bramley had said about the girl spending her entire life at the school. She could not have seen many great sights, if any. He'd heard her friends talk about how she had never been so far from "home". If that wretched ladies academy was her home, then she deserved every sympathy.

Carefully, from the corner of his eye, he looked at her. The poor thing still sneezed, although she tried valiantly, with all her energy, to smother each tiny explosion the moment it happened. Her eyes were wide, the tip of her nose glowing like a beacon at sea. She had a nervous habit of continually tucking her hair severely back, leaving her ears starkly exposed and making them appear larger than they were. Nothing about her was at all becoming. Yet he still wanted to smile when he looked at her.

Amusement? Perhaps. Especially when he thought of Lady Bramley's incredible misconception.

Pity? Possibly. She was a pathetic creature. How could one not feel sorry for her?

Curiosity? Almost certainly.

Girls like Miss Chance, as his sister had said, were a rarity in the society he generally kept. She was not flirtatious, artful or coy. There was nothing about her intended to catch a man's notice, no effort made to put up a facade.

Well, earlier there had not been.

However, now, in her ivory ball-gown, there was a glimmer of improvement. No longer hidden beneath the high collar and many hooks of that ugly spencer, her neck and shoulders were exposed and proven to be quite graceful. Her posture was less sorry and drooping. But ...what *was* she wearing in her hair? Guy strongly suspected the erratic arrangement of large bows, bird feathers and wax fruit was not Miss Chance's idea. What little he knew of her already suggested preference for a more subdued appearance. Evidence of this had come when a set of scarlet "cherries" fell to her shoulder and he watched her casually dispose of the item with a sly brush of her fingers, dropping the faux fruit to the floor of the carriage while the others were inattentive. Apparently she didn't like to hurt their feelings by refusing to let them fuss around her. She was incredibly patient.

Miss Emma Chance stood in the great hall of Woodbyne Abbey and looked around with eyes wide as a faun— or perhaps an elf of some sort would be more appropriate, with those ears. She held her arms tight to her sides, taking up as little room as possible, that reticule still clutched in both hands, her fingers rubbing back and forth in nervous agitation, showing why the colors of the embroidery were so worn and faded. Surrounded by a swirl of fashionable ball-gowns, fluttering fans and the critical glares of strangers, she looked even smaller and more delicate than she had the first time he saw her by the school railings. Almost ghostlike in her white frock.

"Miss Chance," he whispered, "if you will allow me." Swiftly, while the other two girls were distracted, he removed what remained of the ugly bows and feathered attachments from her hair, dropping them into a large, hollow urn by the wall. "That's better."

She blinked up at him in that startled way— a chick fallen from its nest and uncertain about the motives of the hand that rescued it— and then, with her face rumpled in agitation, she scratched rapidly at the side of her neck and tucked another loose lock of hair behind her ear. There went the elegant poise, he mused. A man had to be quick or else he would miss it.

The tidal flow of guests moved them forward, and suddenly they were caught again within the demanding gaze of Lady Bramley, who introduced her nephew, their host. Eager to meet Commander Thrasher, a retired, legendary hero of the Navy, Guy temporarily forgot about Miss Chance. When he next looked for her, she had been whisked away by Lady Bramley, leaving him to follow in the wake of that overbearing perfume.

* * * *

It was far more dreadful than she could have imagined. Indeed, she had not been there a half hour before it was clear to Emma that this must be The Worst Evening of her life and she should never have come. Had she known it would be quite so awful she would have feigned death itself rather than allow herself to be cajoled into attending a ball. Never again!

Having spent ten minutes being lectured to by Lady Bramley about wearing too much perfume— "less is more you know, my dear"— she stood a while by the wall, watching Melinda dance with Captain Hathaway and trying, on the good lady's advice, not to look as if she waited for a partner. But it was impossible. After all, she was at a ball. What else would she be doing there, but waiting for a partner? Waiting to have a tooth pulled?

She did not even have a book to sit with and read, or work to sew, and she supposed it would look odd if she did. Rude to her host.

The best she could hope for was a dark, sober,

quiet corner from which to watch over her friends and wait out the revelry.

But there were no dark corners. Emma was constantly in the way, obliged to move backward or forward every so often as another festive group milled by. It did not matter where she stood, for within two minutes somebody else would need to move through that exact spot of floor and apparently could not go around her.

She heard them whisper as they passed her.

"What an odd little creature!"

"One of Lady Bramley's protégées."

"Really one must admire her ladyship for so much charity work. She is truly selfless in her efforts even when they are unlikely to bear fruit."

Whatever Emma did or said, she knew it would be the wrong thing at the wrong time. Alas, she was not accustomed to standing about with naught to do, and for her there was no hope of looking decorative while she did so.

Any man who ventured in her direction, looking for a partner, was quickly put off by her sneezes, the sight of her unladylike scratching, or the pattern of ghastly red blotches that had begun to appear on her face and neck. By candlelight and at a good distance these marks were not obvious, but at closer range Emma looked, so Lady Bramley said, "like something the barn cat dragged in and played with. Twice."

Alas, there was no escape. She had no choice but to stand there, try not to be seen, and wait for her friends to exhaust themselves so that somebody would suggest it was time to leave. The time ticked so slowly by.

But then Captain Hathaway completed his set with Melinda and he politely offered Emma his hand next, pretending not to see her blotches. Across the room Georgiana watched. There was nothing to be done but accept without a fuss. She knew he felt it was his duty and his sister would be cross if he did not dance with Emma. It was an obligation then for them both.

Rather than make the time pass too slowly for him, she gathered her courage and pushed herself to make conversation. At least she had her intelligence. She need not make their dance dull for the poor fellow. But before she could speak a word, he said,

"You dance very well, Miss Chance."

"I practice a great deal."

"Miss Goodheart assured me she practices too, but I think perhaps she practiced a different dance to any I've ever known." He leaned his head slightly toward her and whispered, "My toes are not yet recovered. I hope they are still there, although they cannot be felt at present."

"What Melinda lacks in skill she makes up for with enthusiasm."

"Indeed. I can attest to the truth of that. I am not much of a dancer myself, but she certainly hastened me through it."

Emma was amused. She did not like to laugh at

other people's dancing, but Melinda would be the first to make fun of herself, and watching her rush a man through the steps was an even more extraordinary sight than when she spun around the floor in dance class, bruising other girls who got in her way. "We are not accustomed to dancing with male partners, of course, Captain. You must make allowances for us."

"You practice with each other at school?"

"Yes. Sometimes with broomsticks, rolling pins, chairs and candelabra. It's not quite the same as the real thing, but Lady Bramley says the conversation is not very different."

His eyes flared with warmth as he looked down at her and he laughed. "Well, I hope I do better than a broomstick, Miss Chance. I make no promises, but I'm game to try."

For the next few bars of music they were separated by the dance. Emma was glad of the chance to let her nerves calm, for her blood was racing through her veins as speedily and ardently as Melinda's feet had crushed their way through the previous dance. But by the time they joined hands again, she had just begun to miss his fingers and want them back.

To her surprise the conversation came much easier than she'd imagined. Perhaps because he made it so, by never being awkward himself and by treating her in a gentlemanly but friendly manner, as if they were well acquainted already. He did not talk down to her as if she was a child and that, in itself, was a rare treat. They chatted about books and music, and from that they progressed to the subject of theatre— an entertainment Emma had never experienced in real life.

"But I have read plays," she told him as they turned in the dance and rejoined hands. "Shakespeare and Marlowe. But Webster is my favorite. *The Duchess of Malfi* in particular."

"Surely not! That macabre play with corpses dug up, machinations by evil brothers, corruption and severed hands? Little Miss Chance, I am surprised at you."

He looked stern so she could not tell whether he meant to tease.

"It is such a grim play," he added, frowning. "All death and gloom, as I remember it."

"But there is hope at the end. When all is dark and so many have died, the good come together to help the orphaned son of the tragic duchess."

"They do?"

She quoted, "Let us make noble use of this great ruin and join all our force to establish this young, hopeful gentleman in's mother's right. These wretched eminent things leave no more fame behind them than should one fall in a frost, and leave his print in snow; as soon as the sun shines, it ever melts, both form and matter."

They turned again, releasing hands for the next four bars of music. Emma felt his eyes following her, studying her as if faded writing in a foreign language was marked upon her face and he tried to understand it. Such attention would usually make her hot and uncomfortable. This time it did not. He was listening to her. Really listening.

She thought it must be the new frock and Lady Bramley's pearls that gave her confidence a boost.

"You see, sir," she said once they joined hands again, "evil deeds leave nothing meaningful or useful behind. One should forget them, put them aside, for we only give them power to hurt us if we acknowledge them. Good deeds will always triumph." Emma was amazed at herself for talking to him so calmly, as if she'd known him forever. She had forgotten her itches.

"You believe that, do you, Miss Chance?" He rolled his eyes. "You may have assembled a vast deal of information from books, but I have lived longer out in the world than you, consequently I am a firm believer in vengeance. When some evil deed is committed against me I cannot simply forget it."

"I did not suggest it was *simple*, Captain Hathaway. Sometimes it is far from easy to forget and forgive a wound." She thought of Mrs. Lightbody's hard, spiteful hands and her willow switch. And of her own occasional lapses into a secret desire for violent retribution. "Vengeance might make you feel even, but I will be better than even." She raised her chin and added determinedly, "I will be better than she." And one day Lightbody— all the pain she had inflicted— would be forgotten like a footprint in melted snow.

"She?"

Emma looked up at him. "A figure of speech, Captain."

After a brief pause he said, "An eye for an eye. Is that not what the bible says, Miss Chance? I'm surprised that you, being such a good girl, don't agree with the holy book."

She wondered what made him think her "such a good girl". Of course, he did not know about those bloodthirsty imaginings with which she occasionally dispatched Mrs. Lightbody to her maker. No she was far from an angel, but she fought hard, every day, to be better. With a little chuckle, she replied, "Tell me you live your life by *every* saying in the bible, Captain, and then I might believe you are sincere in your desire to live by that one."

His eyes shone down at her. "Miss Chance! You should laugh more often."

"I should?"

"A young lady should laugh as often as possible."

"I daresay that is a very good idea, but I require something at which to laugh. I cannot laugh just for the sake of it."

"Why not? I laugh as much as I can every day. It keeps me in good health."

She studied his face thoughtfully. "Genuine laughter is caused by a complex series of muscles in the face. The Zygomaticus major and minor, which are very difficult to control. It also involves the participation of the lungs and larynx to make the proper sound. On the other hand, the smaller, Risorius muscle, which is much easier to manipulate, is often used to feign amusement. Hence, false laughter is so easy to detect, Captain."

He looked injured for a moment and then squinted, puzzled. "Do you accuse me of artifice?"

"I meant that you needn't bother with me. It must be exhausting. I thought I'd save you the trouble."

The Captain looked further confused, his mouth half open. Lady Bramley often said that this delayed closing of a man's mouth usually signified a stuck brain. The solution was to explain again what one had just said, but in the simplest terms possible.

So she said, "A man who laughs and smiles so much because he feels he ought, deceives nobody but himself."

"Perhaps I cannot deceive *you*, Miss Chance, but I doubt there are many folk who would dissect and disparage a smile so thoroughly." Again they were briefly separated in the dance. She feared she must have offended him. But when they were reunited, he said, "At least I shall know when you are genuinely amused. You're clearly not a young lady who sacrifices honesty to be polite and save a chap's feelings. I can see why Lady Bramley likes you so much. My sister did warn me that her friends would mock my efforts at charm."

"Oh, I did not realize you meant to be

charming," she replied gravely. "If you tell me next time you plan to be charming, I shall wait for it and do my best to respond accordingly."

"Miss Chance, you are a most perplexing young woman. I cannot tell whether you make a fool of me deliberately or quite by accident."

"Forgive me if I have insulted you. I merely...I do not find much to laugh at myself. I am envious of those who do." Yes, that is, perhaps, all she should have said.

He eyed her speculatively. "Ah, to see inside your head, Miss Chance. What would I find there? Rows and rows of facts, like books on a library shelf?"

"Ah, to see inside your head, Captain."

"Mine, young lady, is an open book, simply written, badly misspelled and poorly illustrated."

"I do not believe you."

Once more he looked as if she'd stabbed him in the chest with Lady Bramley's parasol.

"You only pretend to leave your pages open, Captain, but what you show to the world is a painted scene and that polite smile. Your true story you guard as well as I do my own." Had she been too frank and factual again? Probably. She had no practice at this. Broomsticks and candelabra did not hold up their side of a conversation when substituted for a dancing partner.

He shook his head, looking bewildered. "It seems Lady Bramley is right and you are too clever for me."

Since she had no idea what to say to that, Emma

fell silent again. He had talked of her to Lady Bramley? When? How? Why?

The evening, which had previously dragged slowly by, now seemed to pass far too quickly. Their dance was almost at an end.

Her itches resumed, worse than before after that very pleasant, brief respite.

Abruptly she realized that was probably why he studied her face so intently— he must be wondering at the blotches and hoping they were not the first signs of Black Death.

She imagined his cannon balls in the next letter written to a friend.

- Danced with awkward, ill-mannered, spotty girl and stabbed repeatedly by old lady with parasol.
- Narrowly escaped contagion and stampeding cows in country.
- Ate impossible piecrust.
- Long to be back at sea.
- Did not see any beautiful woman this week at all.

In no particular order of import.

Their dance over, he returned her to the corner by the punch bowl, where Lady Bramley waited with a frown pleating her brow and her lips clenched in a firm rosebud of disapproval.

Captain Hathaway cleared his throat, seemingly

embarrassed about something. Not meeting the lady's eye, he muttered, "Where on earth did my sister go?"

"I have not seen Miss Hathaway for some time. Perhaps my nephew will know where she has gone. Miss Chance, you sigh fretfully and appear limp. I suggest you sit in this chair a moment and recover. The Captain should have been more considerate and not kept you so long in the dance."

"I am perfectly alright, Lady Bramley. He did not keep me too long. I believe we danced no more than the requisite number of steps and ended with the music, did we not?" Indeed she could have danced for another hour without feeling in the least tired.

Her ladyship replied crisply, "You have a disturbing dependency upon facts, young lady."

"Surely one should depend upon facts. By their very definition they cannot be debated."

"In life, Miss Chance there are subtleties and nuances with which you are unfamiliar." And here she tossed another glare in Captain Hathaway's direction, which he tried to ignore. "A woman who relies upon facts ought to be aware that they are frequently fudged by men. She should learn to go by her instinct and her reason. You are adequately equipped with the latter but none of the former, I fear."

Emma had no idea what she'd done wrong.

At that moment, Melinda spun toward them, apparently unable to stop her course until she dropped violently into a small chair by the refreshment table. Before Lady Bramley could give over glaring at Captain Hathaway long enough to admonish the girl for her lack of grace and deportment, there was a resounding crack as the chair, unaccustomed to this abuse and possibly already mended once or twice before in its history, gave way beneath her. Melinda reached for the table cloth to stop herself from tumbling with the broken chair and, in so doing, managed to upset the punch bowl.

A wave a cold, crimson liquid splashed against Emma's front and left a gruesome looking stain on her precious ivory muslin.

She could only stand there frozen in mortification, wet and scarlet, arms out, seized by another wretched sneeze. Just in case there were not yet enough people staring at the disaster.

"Oh, Emma!" Melinda cried, along with other, more colorful expletives. "I am so sorry. What an oaf I am!"

After a moment of shocked pause, Lady Bramley seized control, taking Emma by the elbow. "Come, my dear, we had better fix you at once."

She was marched away from the scene and from Captain Hathaway with no further ado, but her tragedy was not yet complete, for as Emma struggled to keep pace with Lady Bramley's forceful stride, she raised a hand to scratch her neck, somehow caught her nervous fingers in the borrowed pearls and broke the string, sending the little pink beads in a frenzied, rattling shower all over the floor.

Chapter Nine

He had felt the harsh cut of Lady Bramley's stare as their dance ended. A flogging with a cat o' nine tails would have caressed his skin in comparison to that lady's angry regard.

Of course, she thought he'd been flirting with the girl and against her orders. But he didn't think he had. Surely not. It was merely conversation while they danced. Miss Chance was not the sort of lady he ever pursued, as he'd told her stern guardian earlier that afternoon.

Somehow, he had become drawn in— he could admit that much— but it was not *that* sort of attraction. How could it be? It was curiosity as much as anything, and bemusement. He'd never met anybody quite like her.

However, he had noticed, as they danced, that Miss Chance and her elegant shoulders were admired by several other gentlemen present. While she forgot to be bashful and became caught up in their conversation, reciting her learned facts about facial muscles— *was there any subject in which she was not annoyingly proficient?*— other men followed her with their eyes. Knowledge and her earnest desire to impart the truth somehow made her face livelier. Not beautiful in the conventional sense, but appealing.

She didn't know. Unlike most women, she had no idea of what captivated a man's attention, or when she had succeeded. Or what to do with it once she had it.

Ah yes, *that* was a subject in which she foundered. He was relieved to identify one at least.

And because she was unaware of those other admiring, wondering glances, she gave her partner her full attention without disguise, without cunning trickery. He did not have to be outrageous or dashingly witty to keep her gaze upon him. Apparently she found him interesting enough without him trying too hard. She didn't even expect him to smile at her just to be polite.

As Lady Bramley had said, Emma Chance was an innocent in so many ways. Anyone would think she'd lived in a dark box with nothing but books for company, until tonight when she was finally set free to stumble out and look around.

Now, amid flying punch and pearl beads his strange dancing partner was whisked away to be mended and, from Lady Bramley's last angry glance in his direction, Guy alone was responsible for breaking her. Even though he had not touched the punch bowl or her pearls. Nothing but her very properly gloved fingertips as they danced.

But curiously enough, it felt as if the mysterious Miss Chance had touched *him*. Somewhere deep inside, where nobody had ever ventured before.

That damnable woman, Lady Bramley, was right it seemed. Emma Chance would never be satisfied by only his cover. And he was not prepared to let anybody read beyond it. What would happen if she did? The man inside could surely only disappoint.

* * * *

From the kitchen of Woodbyne Abbey, Emma could still hear the music and merry stamping proceeding without her. Feeling subdued and deflated, her wonderful dance with Captain Hathaway now lost along with her borrowed pearls, she stood by the long table while two maids examined her gown and Lady Bramley ordered the mix of a stain-removing potion.

Melinda had been commanded not to follow them to the kitchen.

"We need no further calamity, Miss Goodheart," Lady Bramley had exclaimed. "There has been quite enough of that this evening."

As for Georgiana, she was nowhere to be found.

"Don't worry about my pearls," her ladyship said with a waft of her hand. "They can be found and mended. The muslin is of far more concern, for it is not every day you will have a new frock, Miss Chance, and you worked so hard upon it. Stains of this nature can be so very resilient."

Even Lady Bramley, who was known to storm her way through or over any obstacle, gave a rather daunted sigh as she took another look at the heinous blemish.

After shouting more instructions at the maids, she turned back to Emma and said, in a softened tone, "My dear girl, do watch what you are about with

Captain Hathaway. He is an impulsive fellow of the sort...well, I am sure you have had no experience of men in general...but, suffice to say, he is not a man to bring *you* any joy. You are a clever girl, but you are young and inexperienced in life. Do not look so alarmed, for I know you are not to blame. You are innocent. You have had nobody to educate you on this subject. For now, all I can say is that you must steer well clear of him and concentrate on your studies. That will do *you* far more benefit for the future than to nurture romantic ideas about men. And although men like the captain may be full of ideas, I can assure you their mind seldom entertains the same one twice. Or for very long."

All Emma could think about just then, however, was the shame of standing there covered in blood-red punch and not knowing what to do with herself. It was not a head to toe dousing, but it certainly felt like it. Even the music had briefly stopped. At least, under her ladyship's forbidding eye, nobody dared laugh out loud, but to be the center of attention in such a dreadful way was more than she could cope with in her current state of heightened nerves.

So all she could reply to the lady was a dejected, "Yes, madam."

What a day this had been. Her very first ride in a carriage and her very first dance with a man. Her first ball-gown, her first pearls, her first trip out of London and her first sight of a real cow. Surely nothing else could happen.

Finally, having assured herself that the maids could tackle the stain sufficiently, Lady Bramley hastened back to the ball. "My damnable nephew has disappeared too, for pity's sake. Back to his unsociable habits, no doubt. Probably barricaded in his study. Why I thought he could be relied upon to host a ball I shall never know! Thank goodness I am here to manage the business for him. All would be chaos without me. Chaos!" And she disappeared like a taffeta-clad whirlwind, leaving Emma to the care of the household servants in the kitchen.

This was, of course, a much more comfortable and familiar place for her when compared to a ballroom, so her nerves soon calmed considerably. The staff were very kind, and when an elderly fellow named Brown presented her with a cup of sweet tea she felt tears of gratitude well up in her eyes.

"Don't you fret, Miss," he said, giving her a crooked smile. "There's worse things happened to frocks in this house, but the ladies in question always survived. Come now, lass, don't you cry."

She was ashamed. Emma had never wept in her life. It had seemed to be something other young ladies did— girls who seldom felt a pain, heard an insult or suffered a disappointment and so were more deeply affected when their sheltered, cozy world of pretty things suffered a breach at its borders. She'd had no time for tears herself.

But tonight she was weak. This, of course, was the danger of having even a moment of happiness and pride in her fine new gown and borrowed pearls— the fall, when it came, was hard and swift. She should have known better. The haunting sound of Mrs. Lightbody's cruel laughter carved through her like a savage, rusty blade. *Serves you right. Who do you think you are, Cinderella?*

Now her eyes would be pink too. Why not? Complete the dreadful vision.

Emma took a deep breath, thanked the kind fellow for her cup of tea and hastily dried her lashes, blaming their unseemly dampness on a reaction to the perfume her friend had sprinkled over them all.

Glancing upward to where stamping feet now performed a lively jig, she wondered which young lady had the pleasure of Captain Hathaway's company this time. He was so wonderfully easy to talk to.

Oh, yes, she knew he was probably quite wicked, when not on his best behavior as he was tonight. She remembered his letters to Georgiana and all those hasty cannon balls reporting the start and the end of many reckless love affairs. Often within the space of a few days. A man who charmed ladies so easily would naturally use that skill as often as he could to relieve the tedium. She had witnessed it now for herself.

And Lady Bramley had no need to warn Emma about the pitfalls of attraction to such a man.

Sometimes she wished the people around her would not fuss quite so much. She might be small and scrawny in appearance, but she was not nearly so breakable as they thought. After all, Mrs. Lightbody had choked the life out of her several times— sent her into a black void of unconsciousness— but she always recovered. Her brain flickered back to light, reviving itself and restoring her breath, despite that woman's attempts to snuff it out forever.

Surely that was proof of a certain resiliency to her spirit, no matter how physically small and inconsequential her body appeared.

See, her tears were gone already. It was no more than a momentary weakness.

In any case, Lady Bramley need not be concerned that Captain Hathaway might become romantically interested in Emma. He was impulsive and enjoyed being unpredictably mischievous, but he would have to be extremely bored to attempt *her* seduction with so many other ladies at hand.

The male animal, from all that she had read, was mainly drawn to bright colors and pretty, shiny things— military uniforms would not be so decorative the higher a man climbed in rank otherwise. They liked handsome, fast horses, well-trained dogs and two kinds of women— the unquestioning, unchallenging, undemanding sort with a good dowry, or the lively, daring, adventurous type. Mrs. Lightbody used to say that men married the former and kept the latter for mistresses.

Since Emma did not fit either category, she was best suited to spinsterhood and a governess post. Lady Bramley, so it seemed, was of the same opinion.

But Captain Hathaway had danced with her and

chattered amiably out of kindness, to put her at her ease, and she would always remember that service with warm gratitude. What she felt was nothing more than that, she reassured herself with a stern sniff and a deep, steadying breath.

She looked down at the solitary pink pearl she'd managed to capture when the necklace broke. It nestled now in her white-gloved palm, a sad, lost little thing without its many sisters. A quarter of an hour ago, this pearl had been dancing with her, feeling the warmth of her skin and the rapid rhythm of the pulse in her neck. Perhaps the memory still clung to it and would be held forever within that smooth orb.

For just those few glorious moments, dancing with the handsome captain, she had allowed herself to stop worrying and counting steps. Perhaps it had shown upon her face and that was why Lady Bramley sough to warn her. But it was not the captain's fault. It was hers alone. All her doing. Or rather that of her restless, never-quite-satisfied, many-times-resurrected mind.

"Miss Chance, you ran away from me! How could you abandon me?"

Jolted out of her reverie, she spun around to find Captain Hathaway striding toward her in a purposeful fashion. She backed up to the table.

In one gloved hand he held her string of pearls. Mended. He had sought every last one that fell and then strung them back together and fixed the clasp.

"Had a devil of a time to find 'em all," he said

proudly. "Even found a few in the punch. Good thing nobody swallowed any, eh? Turn around then."

Emma stared. Behind her back, she closed her fist tightly, hiding the one pearl she had saved. He was so pleased with himself that she didn't want to point out that he hadn't found them all. "I didn't run away from you, Captain. I was taken away."

"Ah." He gestured, holding up a finger and making a little spinning motion with it. "I'll put it back for you. Where it belongs, eh?"

Was it proper? What would Lady Bramley say? Would she approve?

Most certainly not.

But Emma Chance was not a child any longer. She ought to be allowed to use her own judgment occasionally, for surely that was all part of finding maturity.

Turning her back to him, she held her breath while he returned the pearls to her throat. She felt his fingertips struggling with the clasp at her nape. Head bowed, her eyes closed, she drank in every precious, forbidden moment until she had quite forgotten there was anybody else in the kitchen. Or the world.

He swore under his breath.

"It's no good. The clasp is too dainty. I cannot manage it with these damned gloves."

Emma opened her eyes and saw the offending articles tossed to the table. In the next moment his bare thumbs brushed her skin. She caught her breath and her sight became foggy so she closed her eyes again. They were lost once more, just the two of them, in a London Particular. This time it had followed them all the way to Surrey.

An almost unbearable happiness lifted her heart and quickened the beat, as if there were little wings inside it, fluttering frantically to raise the organ up out of her body and take her spirit with it. But was it happiness or something else? She'd never known the like of it.

Captain Hathaway was almost as clumsy as Melinda would be with that tiny clasp. It took him several minutes to secure it, fumbling and cursing softly under his breath— apologizing each time he did so— and then, even when the task was done, his thumbs did not immediately leave her body. Their caress lingered lightly, but daringly, just an inch or so from the top of her spine, tracing it downward and then back to the necklace. His fingers rested shyly on her shoulders. It was no more than the passing shiver of a breeze and yet her entire body was awakened by it, her eyes wide opened again— an involuntary response to his touch. As if she was afraid of missing something in what little time they had left.

He cleared his throat quite fiercely, as if annoyed with himself. "Well, there we are. All better, Miss Chance?"

She turned to face him again, the fingers of her left hand checking the pearls and finding them all in order. All but one, of course. "Yes, sir, much better."

When he swept a fallen curl back from his brow

it stood upright in a draft of warm air, like a question mark.

"Thank you, Captain." She put both hands behind her back again. "It was very good of you to go to such trouble." He was the first man she'd ever seen, who *ought* to be untidy, she thought with a sudden, unusual burst of passionately illogical contemplation. Guy Hathaway ought to be rumpled and creased and wet with kisses— oh, she'd better stop herself. The drumbeat of her heart was too hard and lusty. She might die here and now from these violent palpitations. Her crumpled corpse would be most embarrassing for Lady Bramley.

"It was the least I could do." He smiled, but it seemed uncertain this time, wary. "For the little girl who once corrected my sums for me. And gave me a lecture on the advantage of quality over quantity, not to mention the delights of wild flowers."

Emma knew her lips had parted, but no sound came out. The vibrations of her vocal chords were stymied somewhere half way up her throat.

"That was you, was it not?" he added, eyes narrowed as he surveyed her face in quizzical amusement yet again.

She sighed, lifted her shoulders. "Yes."

"I thought so. The little girl who said she was nobody."

When had he realized? She dare not ask. It was enough that he remembered.

Suddenly he raised his hand again, his naked

141

thumb and forefinger gently touching her chin. Lifting it a half inch.

"Miss Chance, there is something I must do. Hold very still."

Still? Impossible. She was all a-quiver inside. Could he not see and feel it? It hurt to breathe and yet, at the same time, she trembled with exhilaration. Her heart's beat thumped harder and faster in her ears, a galloping horse obscuring all other sound, racing wildly with no idea of its destination. Simply running joyously and free for as long as it would be allowed. The ground shook under her feet.

"With your permission," he said. "There is a stray eyelash fallen to your cheek. Might I be trusted to deliver you of the nuisance?"

"Oh?" *Eyelash? Cheek? What things were these?* How strange those words sounded suddenly. Foreign and incomprehensible.

Apparently he took that small sound for permission. He dampened his naked fingertip with a lick of the tongue and then, slowly and carefully, he removed the tiny thing that had troubled him so.

"There. Now it won't bother you," he murmured, his voice slightly husky.

She felt her body tipping forward. Tumbling, rather. To right herself she briefly brought her hands, still clenched into fists, to his chest.

He cupped her elbows to steady her balance, and she heard a little gasp from one of the kitchen maids. Or was it her own?

Emma wanted to say so many things at that moment, but could manage none. Most of all she wanted to ask why he was sad, why the bounce went out of his boots when he thought nobody was watching. Yet she knew that if she tried to speak she would not even hear the sound of her own voice. It would come out all wrong. Foolish.

Then his touch was gone and he stepped back, looking aggrieved.

"Captain Hathaway, what are you about with Miss Chance? I thought you were looking for your sister?" Alas, Lady Bramley had returned while Emma was lost in his power, unaware of anybody or anything else in the kitchen. Coming to check upon the stain's removal, the lady had found instead another displeasing sight.

"Well, young man? Did you not mean to search for your sister?" she demanded, coming to stand between the guilty parties.

"I did, madam, but your nephew said he—"

"Then kindly leave Miss Chance to me and go...do... anything else. *Shoo*, young man." She took his gloves from the table and thrust them at him. "You are not needed here."

He gave a terse bow, spun around and walked out. But at the door he stopped and looked back. Lady Bramley, by then, was bent over Emma's stained frock again, trying to frighten it into behaving itself.

Over that well-meaning lady's head, Emma caught Captain Hathaway's sly wink and a smile that went right through her flesh to carve itself on her bones. Thus her heart lost its steady rhythm again and fell into a state of flux previously only felt by the sight of cows in a field.

And Emma Chance who had, only moments ago, come to a bleak, bereft decision about this evening, now reversed her opinion completely.

Just like so. This was the Best Evening of her Entire Life.

* * * *

On the journey back to the Black Bull, later that night, the young ladies were all subdued. In his sister's case, most unusually so. Guy still had no inkling of where she'd disappeared to for a large part of that evening, but he was certain she'd gone with Commander Thrasher, whose aunt was either refusing to accept the fact, or hoping nobody else would have noticed. There was little point lecturing his sister, for when she made up her mind on any matter there was no dissuading her. And if it was something that made her quiet for once, Guy was grateful for it. Temporarily at least. He had troubles enough of his own with which to contend and perhaps it was time some other man had the pain of keeping Georgiana out of mischief. Commander Thrasher was welcome to the post, if he thought himself prepared for it. Brave fellow.

As for Lady Bramley, she had seemed more concerned with the potential fate of Emma Chance at *his* dastardly, ungloved hands.

As if he would ever think of harming that poor little thing.

Still, he understood how it might have looked to Lady Bramley. It was understandable that she reacted the way she did. He had, perhaps, over-stepped the boundaries when he'd thought of kissing Miss Chance. But could a man truly be accused of improper behavior when it was merely in his thoughts for the fraction of a moment and never actually came to pass?

Unfortunately, Miss Chance had such a strange demeanor— it could best be described as that of a cat left out in the rain, lost and abandoned, yet still aloof and unwilling to be caught. Guy could not help wanting to comfort her, keep her somewhere dry and warm, wrap her in a blanket and feed her a saucer of cream. To tell her all would be well. To make her trust him. She needed somebody to look after her. Did she recognize that fact among the many she had at her disposal?

He doubted it. She might be fragile in appearance, but there was something strong inside her, like a wiry, twisty vine that grew determinedly. He could almost hear rain-speckled leaves rustling behind her deep sighs. She was a creature who listened and thought more than she spoke— studied and observed more than she cared to be looked at.

It was unsettling, to say the least.

Sitting across the carriage, drowning in the folds

of a large shawl that Lady Bramley had lent her, she was almost asleep now, lashes at half mast. She had not spoken a word to him since he put the pearls back around her throat— Lady Bramley made certain of it. But he'd felt her somber eyes watching him for the rest of the evening.

Now, as moon and starlight whispered over the side of her sleepy face, Guy took his turn to study *her*.

Emma Chance would say and do nothing unless she meant it. She didn't even believe in smiling just to be polite.

She was not the sort of cheerful, uncomplicated, bold girl with whom one enjoyed a simple dalliance— the "standard variety hussy" as his sister called them.

He thought of her gazing up at him in the kitchen of Woodbyne Abbey, with the tip of her nose and both her ears glowing pink in the firelight, her hair tucked back, parted sternly in the middle, her eyes huge with wonder.

Miss Chance might be intelligent, but she was only just emerging into the world. She needed help, and although *he* may not be as studiously clever as she, there were ways in which he could assist her out of her shell.

No! Not in *that* way.

He felt suddenly betaken by a different sort of desire— the wish to perform a good deed.

It was a pleasing thought: Guy Hathaway, secret benefactor of shy foundlings.

Lady Bramley thought his dough needed

proofing. Perhaps this is what she meant. He'd been a selfish man up until now, but at twenty-seven years of age it was not too late to make a change, become a sensible fellow, stop feeling sorry for himself and help a girl from whom he wanted nothing in return. Except to make her smile.

Why not? Surely stranger things had happened.

And so, a young man previously careening through his life dodging bullets and throwing himself recklessly into every fray, finally decided it was time he made improvements. It was time a boy became a man.

It was a curious sensation and he did not know what to make of it, but there it was.

Miss

Chapter Ten
1819

"Hathaway! What are you doing out here all alone?" Walter Ramsey was a well-meaning fellow, who always wanted everybody to be having as good a time as he. The more brandy he consumed the more benevolent his mood, until he was likely to burst into tears if he found anybody unhappy or unwell. An unfortunate habit for a Ship's Surgeon with a fondness for good brandy. "There are two young ladies inside whose little hearts palpitate madly with desire to meet you, Hathaway. Why do you keep them waiting. It is a cruelty unbecoming of a gentleman and a naval Captain."

He smiled. "They don't speak English, do they? And as far as I know, you speak very little Swedish."

"We school each other." His friend grinned. "It is astounding how well a pair of eyes can communicate their desires even without words."

"Just be sure, this time, that it's not simply a squint of short-sightedness that you mistake for the lady's *come-hither* wink."

"That was a miscommunication that occurred only once and you never let me forget it, Hathaway. Now come inside, man, and shake off this mournfulness."

"It is not mournful to need fresh air, Ramsey. I'll come in shortly."

"*Air?* It's damnably cold out here, Hathaway!

This is not air it's a veritable gale." Walter shivered, rubbing his shirt sleeves. "I need my blasted coat."

But Guy hadn't felt the cold wind blowing in off the sea. He was too busy watching the moon above the ship's rigging in the distance and remembering a certain small face. A warmer evening, two years ago; a set of fallen pearls; trembling fingers rubbing worn patches on an embroidered purse. An eyelash fallen to a soft cheek, tempting his intervention.

But he didn't want to share these thoughts with anybody else. Didn't want his contemplation spoiled by a bumbling intruder, however well-meaning.

With a jerk of his head toward the noise of the dockside tavern, he urged his friend, "Go back indoors and entertain your ladies. But take care, Ramsey. One of those women was last night in the company of a strapping fellow, a stowadore, twice your height and with fists the size of pumpkins. She and the Goliath appeared intimate."

"Ah, but she assured me that is all behind her. The oaf has been sent on his way."

"I see." As usual, Walter would not be told. A few years ago Guy was not so different. He knew it would do no good to waste his breath. He had never listened either.

"So come inside by the fire, join me with these darling creatures and—"

"I think not. You're in a better frame of mind for it than I."

In truth, Guy had not been in a "better frame of

mind" for some months and the company of
females— once the tried and true remedy for a glum
mood— could do nothing for him lately.

He sighed crossly, leaning against a large crate,
his arms folded. "Women. I am quite done with
them."

"What?" His friend guffawed. "Evidently you
need more rum."

"Is that what the surgeon prescribes?"

"I've not known many troubles that the good
drink cannot cure."

Ah, but Walter had very few "troubles" of any
sort in his life. As for women, he moved breezily
from one to the next, always merry, always able to
find a "darling creature" in any crowd.

In all likelihood, his "darlings" took him for
every penny, just as they once took from Guy, but
Walter didn't seem to care. As long as everybody had
a good time, the jolly fellow cared little about the cost
to himself and he had nobody for whom he need
explain his expenses. There were no lists folded up
and tucked down inside Walter's pockets, no balances
to fret over before he saw his father again. But that
was what happened, Guy supposed, when a man grew
up in a very wealthy family and had no need to pinch
pennies. Walter, the fifth son of an Earl and raised in
privilege, had no expectations put upon him, leaving
him free to do much as he pleased. His father
appeared to pay no attention to him whatsoever,
showing no objection to Walter's choice of a career,

or his endless stream of engagements to unlikely women.

Guy, on the other hand, although never poor, had not grown up with vast riches and his father still — even now—took an interest in how he spent his money and upon whom he spent it. Mr. Frederick Hathaway had always looked grim and shaken his head over his eldest son's lack of financial acumen.

When Guy was a boy, the Hathaways had lived a comfortable, simple, happy life in the country. They raised and grew their own food, and their mother, a hard-working, unfussy, loving woman, made all the clothes they wore. Their father had inherited a busy printing business from his uncle and was often away in the nearest large town of Norwich to oversee the running of it. He had also started a newspaper called the *New Gentleman's Gazette*, appealing to the interests of men like himself— the rising middle class of tradesmen and merchants. A hard-working fellow, Frederick Hathaway was much absorbed in his business, leaving the family and home life mostly to his wife. Guy's early schooling happened at the kitchen table, poring over a set of encyclopedias that their father's business printed and sold. The children played outdoors, often barefoot, and in the harvest they worked on the land alongside the men their father hired. Each night they fell into their bed, tired, happy and healthy.

At fourteen Guy went off to join the navy and so he was not present to witness, first hand, the ascent of the family's fortunes or the descent of their general happiness. But he read much from his siblings' letters.

After his mother died, everything changed. His father remarried and the demanding ambitions of his new, extremely sociable young wife brought the family to London, where Mr. Frederick Hathaway expanded his already successful printing business, and made a concerted effort to improve their status in society. The *New Gentleman's Gazette* became *The Gentleman's Weekly*, because its owner discovered that once he had reached a certain rung on the ladder it was best not to remind anybody that he was a "new" anything. Far better he pretend to have been there for centuries if he wanted to fit in.

Guy did not often visit the family's transplanted home on the hopeful edge of Mayfair, but whenever he did he observed how the strain had taken its toll on their father and in the way the family lived. He agreed with his sister Georgiana in that, oddly enough, they'd all been better off before their father found "great success" and raised the family's consequence.

What Frederick Hathaway sought from life was quite different to what his eldest son wanted and as time went on the disparity between those two objectives increased until there was no hope of bridging the space between. It saddened Guy that he could not meet his father's expectations. It seemed, in fact, as if he could not satisfy anybody at present. Not even himself.Two years ago he had begun to make changes, to put his life in better order, but tonight he felt restless, agitated, discontent. Something was still missing, and he couldn't put his finger on it.

"If you do not describe your symptoms to me," said Walter, "I cannot help you, can I? This mood hangs upon you like the stink of wet dog, Hathaway. It has done so now for months."

Symptoms? Overwhelming sadness, nostalgia for the past, impatience for the future, irritation with the present...

Not the sort of thing Walter Ramsey could fix. Certainly not anything Guy wanted to share with anybody. He was a man, for pity's sake— a naval captain. Tender feelings were for women.

But memories filled his mind like sea water leaking through an insufficiently caulked hull: the sheer happiness of splashing barefoot through mud to catch bait worms and then standing in the wooden tub later to be washed off by his mother; the "treat" of being permitted to sleep in the barn on warm summer nights— but rescued by his mother, without comment or teasing, as soon as he thought he heard a ghost; standing by the pianoforte while she played and sang for them on Sundays, her hair smelling of the afternoon sunlight and Yorkshire pudding. Finally, standing at her grave, as a young man of one and twenty, struggling to keep unmanly tears at bay while the grief of missing her last few months, although it was not his fault, pressed heavily upon him. It still did. Her illness had come suddenly and taken her before any of them had time to prepare. Guy was away at sea when he received the letter from his father, summoning him home. The weather was bad, and he had not been able to make port until the very day she died, arriving home just in time for her funeral.

The last time he saw her alive she was smiling and waving frantically by the farmhouse gate, no hint of the illness that would strike her down within a year.

All these memories flooded in tonight, ready to sink his vessel, as if the oakum had finally worn away.

He felt foolish. Did other men of almost thirty pine for their dead mothers and simpler days? No man he knew ever spoke of such matters.

After her death, his father had got on with his life, found another wife, put his head down and plowed on with it. For several years Guy had kept himself busy with work too, but smothering his grief had not lessened it. The sadness was like coins weighing down a pocket. But they were coins belonging to somebody who had asked him to keep them safe, so while he could not spend them, he was always conscious of that heaviness and afraid coins might escape through a worn hole.

These past few months he'd begun to feel that weight more than ever. Hopefully, thought Guy, this was just a phase and it would pass eventually for him too. But at this moment, what he most wanted, was to go back there, to that uncomplicated life in the Norfolk countryside, to run into the house and see his mother, with her sleeves rolled up, peeling potatoes at the kitchen table and singing to herself.

She hung upon his mind, as if she tried to tell him something. Show him something.

"A penny for 'em, Hathaway."

"For what?"

"Your thoughts, man! It's not like you to be so damned quiet."

But how could he make Walter understand? The ship's surgeon dealt with broken bones, prescribed mercury for the pox, wrenched out rotted teeth and tarred the stumps of severed limbs, but he was little help when it came to deeper matters of the heart and soul. Walter Ramsey certainly had little understanding of familial bonds as they applied to most people.

According to the few stories he told of his childhood, Walter was raised by a nanny, his mother a distant, floral-scented figure who visited the nursery rarely and certainly never darned his clothes or tested his feverish forehead with a kiss. Walter drifted along in life like a smart, fast, richly furnished clipper ship, his family somewhere on the same ocean, but not close enough to be disturbed by his wake.

Everything fell into Walter's hands without trouble and, even if it quickly tumbled out between his fingers again, he merely laughed and waited for the next good fortune and fine weather to come his way, confident that it always would. So it was for Walter with women too. He had no idea.

"The fairer sex, Ramsey," Guy muttered, leaning

against a large crate, arms folded across his chest. "You couldn't possibly comprehend my problem." It was all tangled up somehow, he mused— memories, that painful yearning for something lost in the past, families, disappointment, expectation, grief, that searching desire for...something that was no more than a blur in the corner of his eye. Caught in this vortex of thoughts and worries, he couldn't keep his head clear, couldn't see the way ahead.

No, men did not speak of these matters to each other. It simply was not the done thing.

Instead they drank rum.

Walter offered a swig from the jug, but Guy shook his head. He did not need more rum. Clearly he'd had enough.

"The fairer sex, is it, Hathaway? Well, I know 'tis not the pox in your case, so a dose of mercury and a salt bath won't help. Is it an issue with the...rampancy of the trouser beast?"

He looked askance at Walter. "There are other problems a man might possess when it comes to women."

"Really? Then explain it to me, my dear chap. I am all ears."

Guy paused, stared up at the moon, and then said, "I am drawn, constantly, to the dangerous ones. They steal from me, they lie to me and then they betray me and run off with my friends. But for the life of me, I cannot lose my wits with a good woman. I cannot let fancy happen with the sweet, kind, gentle, good woman. From them I run in all haste, and I punish myself instead by chasing the devil incarnate. Why is that, my learned friend?"

Walter chuckled drowsily. "Sounds like fear, Hathaway."

"*Fear*?" He scoffed. "I fear nothing."

"Ah, but since you know these relationships you pursue are destined to end, you know that, in effect, you are safe from commitment and a broken heart. If the young lady is bound to offend eventually, you need have no fear that you might genuinely fall in love. Not deeply and truly. The shallow passion you feel will expire in due course, when she shows the blood upon her claws— claws which have hitherto been sheathed, although you know damn-well they exist. Therefore," he burped softly, his shoulder nudging Guy's, "you have naught to fear. You know," he poked a finger into Guy's chest, "that as long as you keep choosing the wrong women, you'll soon have an excuse to end it. You call these women dangerous, but, in fact, the *right* woman— that elusive *good* woman—is the only one truly dangerous to you, Hathaway."

He thought about that for a moment and then swiftly decided the theory could not possibly be sound. The man was drunk. And the son of an earl; what did he know about real life? Besides, he had fish stew on his shirt. If he was unsteady putting things into his mouth, he probably didn't know what was coming out of it either.

"I should bleed you with leeches," Walter added. "Clearly your blood is overheated. That's why you're standing out here, man, in the blasted cold, shriveling your filberts."

"I stand out here, Ramsey, to study... the moon."

"The moon? What about it?"

"Odd to think that we're all looking up at it, wherever we are. However confined our world, we see the same moon."

"It would be even odder, dear chap, if we looked up and saw a different moon. Something square and green, perhaps."

"This time of year, in certain cultures, it's called a Sturgeon Moon."

Walter moved to scratch his unshaven cheek, but apparently couldn't find it, so he waved his fingers in the air instead. "Of course. Everybody knows that." He burped. "Enough about your wretched... emotional..." He looked as if he were about to be sick. "...agitations." He shuddered, stumbled a few steps to the left and then rolled his unsteady gaze back to where Guy still leaned. "If you're not careful you'll start writing poetry. Now, back to these lovely ladies, Hathaway! They wait! What you need is merry company. Are you coming in or not?"

Was he? What did he want? He was twenty-nine — only ten years younger than his mother was when she died — and running out of time. He was tired of the same dance, the same music, the same pouting lips and thrusting bosoms, the same cunning games and disappointments. Sick of it all, in fact. But if he confessed as much to Ramsey, the fellow would only get his jar of leeches out. And Guy did not want to think about where he would put them in this case.

"Might I remind you, Hathaway, that you escaped that wayward knife's blade two months ago. That means you are meant to live, man. God, or the devil, are not ready for you yet. You've been granted another chance, so you ought to stop being so damn moody and start enjoying life again as we always did before."

Yes, he had been lucky. The knife, thrown by an angry, drunken sailor had not been meant for him, but it spun in his direction at some point during a scuffle. Fortunately, at that moment, a little pink pearl had fallen to the boards at Guy's feet, and he bent to retrieve it. The misfired knife struck a beam where his head had previously been minding its own business, and thus he was dramatically unscathed.

"I swear it parted your hair," Walter had exclaimed at the time. "I would not be surprised if you find a severed curl upon your shoulder."

The little pink pearl, of course, was one from Miss Chance's necklace. Two years ago he had put them all back for her— or so he thought, but later he'd found one last pearl caught inside his waistcoat. He'd kept it with him ever since, planning to return it one day. He could have sent it by letter, he supposed, but for some reason he still had it about his person. Now that it had saved his life— or at the very least, his eye— the idea of parting with it was further put off.

Hmm. Miss Chance. That odd young girl whose heart one could almost see and hear beating. He'd never met another creature quite like her. Small and delicate in appearance, yet strong, unique in the way she looked at him and saw through his practiced smile.

"If you stand out here any longer, rhapsodizing about the moon, Hathaway, I shall buy you a big, frilly silk shirt, punch you in the face and send you to Italy."

"A curious prescription."

"For a curious bloody malady. Pull yourself together, man."

One day, he mused darkly, he'd have to introduce Walter Ramsey to Lady Bramley and let them advise each other.

Chapter Eleven

"Master Nicholas, pay attention!"

For the third time she stopped the lesson and now, as previously warned, she took away the marbles with which her naughty, restless student had continued to play, rolling them back and forth across his desk.

"But I *was* listening, Miss Chance!"

"No, you were not. Your cousin Charles does not feel the need to fidget, young Master Hathaway, and I am certain that if I quizzed you both on the subject of Elizabeth Tudor and Mary Queen of Scots, he would answer far more questions correctly." On rainy days, confined indoors for their lessons, her most restless pupil was more distracted than ever.

Nicholas sulked, slouching in his chair and swinging his feet. "I would rather learn about the battles of Lord Nelson. That's my favorite subject."

"Yes, but you know all about Lord Nelson already, young sir. I suspect *you* could teach *me*."

Like most boys, he threw himself whole-heartedly into subjects he enjoyed— heroic deeds, war, gruesome death and general bloodshed— but closed his ears to anything he deemed "dull", which usually meant there was a woman involved. And in the case of Lord Nelson, Nicholas had been taught every detail by his brother who, whenever he visited his family on leave, apparently received a hero's welcome from this otherwise unimpressed young man. "My brother Guy is my absolute favorite brother," he would say whenever anybody mentioned the eldest son of the house. "Wait till you see him, Miss Chance. He's the bravest captain ever. The finest fellow in his majesty's navy. All the stupid women swoon over my brother."

And Emma would reply, "Fortunately then, I am not stupid."

Today, as she confiscated his marbles, the boy complained, "I'm hungry."

Emma checked the mantle clock. "Mrs. Beddesby will come up and fetch you both when it's time for supper. You know your mama likes to keep the day in order."

"*Step*mama," the boy corrected, his foot thumping against the wall. The second Mrs. Hathaway had married his father when Nicholas was only two, but the boy was still very much aware of the fact that she was not his blood mother.

"Yes, your stepmama," she agreed, glancing at his cousin Charles, who looked down at his book and sucked his lips together. "Lucky you are to have a mother at all, Master Hathaway. We are not all so fortunate."

"You can have *her*, if you like. Welcome to her."

"That is a wicked thing to say."

"Is it?" The boy shrugged. "She'd give *me* away if she could. She don't like me any more than I like her."

"*Does not*," Emma corrected. "And do not refer to the lady of the house as *her* and *she*. You must call her Mrs. Hathaway or stepmama."

"We were happy enough before she came along, when I was the youngest. There's enough Hathaways already. She ought to stop making more."

Well, that was an idea with which Emma could not entirely disagree.

By his first wife, Frederick Hathaway had sired seven children. The two daughters, Maria and Georgiana, were now married; Edward was a vicar in Norfolk and Guy, of course, was at sea with the navy. Two further boys, Thomas and Jonathan, were away at boarding school, leaving only Nicholas, the youngest child from his first marriage, still at home.

But the house in Allerton Square remained a noisy, chaotic place, for here the second Mrs. Hathaway raised her husband's "new" family: Cassie and Isabella, four year-old twins who had less discipline than monkeys in a jungle; Alfred who, at the stout age of two and having outgrown the sweetness of infancy in his mother's eyes, was often left to fend for himself and could be found rootling like a piglet along the hallway carpet; and, finally, an ill-tempered baby who seemed to despise her mother already for having named her Frederica.

It was, perhaps, no surprise that the second Mrs. Hathaway should insist on a very regimented order to the day's proceedings, but her attempts to manage the household with timed charts and diagrams pinned to the nursery and schoolroom walls were more decorative than efficient. Their impossible success relied upon cooperation from four children under the age of five and a handful of confused, over-worked adults.

A procession of dour nannies had been hired to assist Mrs. Fanny Hathaway, but none lasted longer than a few weeks, each packing their trunk with shocking alacrity once they'd had a taste of the horrors awaiting them. Now, for inside staff, there remained only a rather harried cook who refused to come out of the kitchen— where Emma suspected she drank a great deal of trifle sherry— and a housekeeper who was obliged to do everything else, from answering the front door to wiping scuff marks off the wainscoting. As for the lady of the house, having realized her ship was sinking, Fanny Hathaway had put herself into a lifeboat, cut the rope and bobbed merrily away— leaving them all to interpret her charts as best they could. With the anarchy of so many little children running about and the adults who produced them being either absent or lost in a fog of pleasant denial, the household of HMS Hathaway barely kept its masts above water.

Nicholas did not care for his stepmother's new offspring, or for her. He quarreled with his father at every turn, and played mischievous pranks upon the remaining staff. Apparently, so Emma had heard, the young troublemaker would only pay heed to his sister Georgiana or to his eldest brother Guy. Those two he held on a marble pedestal along with Admiral Lord Nelson.

But now, under Emma's steady, determined tutelage, the boy slowly became a little less unruly. At least there were fewer screams of "wretched, impossible child" to be heard reverberating around the walls of the house.

Nicholas was short for his age, a small, fair-haired, blue-eyed angel— something he often used to his advantage, of course. It no longer worked with Emma, however, and he knew it. After two years in that schoolroom they were accustomed to each other. Miss Chance did not stand for nonsense, and she was not easily scared. He had tried his damnedest to upset the governess with frogs in her desk and beetles in her reticule, so he knew she was utterly unflappable. Eventually he gave in and put up with her.

At that moment the schoolroom door opened and the housekeeper stuck her head in. "Pardon me, Miss Chance, but Lady Thrasher is below and wanted to know if the lesson is finished? She did not want to interrupt—"

"Oh, of course." With some relief, Emma set down the book from which she'd been reading aloud. "I believe we are done for now. The attention of Master Nicholas can only be kept so long." She turned to the two boys. "You may put away your writing materials."

"Georgie is here! I hope she's brought me caramels. She knows they're my absolute favorite." Nicholas leapt from his chair and ran to the door, ducking around the other woman to dash downstairs and find his sister.

"The lessons proceed well, I hope, Miss Chance?" the housekeeper inquired wearily.

"Very well. At least, in the case of Master Charles Lennox." She smiled at the remaining boy who carefully stacked books on the shelf and tidied his pens. "Master Lennox is a prize pupil."

The boy smiled shyly and then, after a bow for Emma, hurried out after his cousin.

"He's a pleasant lad," said the housekeeper. "And surely a good influence on young Master Nicholas."

"Hmm." She smiled wryly. "We can only hope, Mrs. Beddesby."

Charles had lost his father five years ago and his mother three years after that. His uncle Frederick then took him in to live with the Hathaways in this sinking ark on Allerton Square.According to the housekeeper, when Mr. Hathaway first agreed to hiring a tutor at home for the two boys, he had planned to hire a man, but then the name of Emma Chance was brought to his attention one day.

Lady Bramley, who cast Frederick Hathaway into rigid and silent awe when she came to assess his house before allowing Emma to work there, had assured the terrified gentleman that he would find no better tutor in all London. Her ladyship had no time for the idea of male tutors being in any way superior to females, so she soon disabused Mr. Hathaway of any lingering notion in that regard.

Emma smiled to herself when she remembered

how Lady Bramley had stood in the drawing room downstairs and declared, "This house is far too full of children. I trust there are no plans to bless the world with more. Two boys is more than enough for any family. An heir and a spare. More than that is excessive, immodest and shows a distinct lack of decorum and restraint."

Only Lady Bramley could get away with such a comment. Folk were generally either too startled or too fearful to put her in her place. One day, somebody was bound to tell that woman to mind her own business, but it seemed unlikely to happen in the lady's lifetime.

A brisk, light footstep, accompanied by noisier clattering, could now be heard moving briskly along the corridor toward the schoolroom.

The housekeeper stepped aside and gave a little bob curtsey. "Your ladyship."

"Mrs. Beddesby, would you be a dear and take these boys back downstairs? I believe it's time for their supper and a bath."

"Yes, madam," replied the housekeeper, who was never asked to be a "dear" by anybody else in the house. Her thin grey eyebrows had only recently ceased to be appalled whenever Georgiana suggested it. "Come along, Masters Hathaway and Lennox, if you please."

Amid much protesting from Nicholas, she took the boys away and closed the door, leaving the two young ladies alone in the schoolroom.

Emma, as she always did now, dropped a curtsey for her friend, and Georgiana, as *she* always did, laughed and embraced her. "How many times must I tell you that's not necessary? I'm still just Georgie, you know. I married a man who calls me The Wickedest Chit quite regularly so that I never forget my humble beginnings. I have yet to be comfortable with Lady Thrasher. It sounds like a woman who provides recreational chastisement."

"But I shouldn't like to get out of the habit of greeting you properly," Emma replied. "What if I forget to do it in public? Better I maintain the practice in private."

"Dear Emma! Always so careful and studious." Georgiana pressed a quick kiss to her cheek and then took a tour of the small room. "This used to be my bedchamber, you know. I shared with my elder sister Maria. Good lord, how she hated me! But with good cause for I was a horrid girl, always stealing her belongings and getting them broken or dirty."

Emma had thought perhaps Georgiana came with news of their friend. "Have you received a letter from Melinda?" she asked hopefully.

"No. Not a word."

"Oh, dear. I confess I am greatly concerned, for when she told me her father had summoned her home she did not appear happy to go and I worried for her traveling with the mail coach. I fear it is not safe."

Georgiana smiled. "I'm certain our friend

Melinda survived the journey. If the mail coach was held up by highwaymen, you know she'd be the first to bop them over the head with something and she is an excellent shot. The robbers would soon have cause to regret their chosen profession."

But Emma could not smile. Hugging a small pile of books to her chest, she paused by the window and looked out. Even knowing their friend was brave, she still fretted on her behalf. "I do think she might have written by now. Of course, the post can be unreliable—"

"As can Melinda when it comes to keeping up with correspondence and remembering the correct address." Georgiana joined her by the window where rain, which had fallen on and off throughout the day, now renewed its feverish spittle until the pleasant view of the park in the center of the square became a smudged water-color. "Sir Ludlow Goodheart expected his only daughter to find a titled, wealthy husband by now. No doubt he called her home to find out why she remains unmarried and quite without prospects."

"But Melinda is content managing the bonnet shop for Lady Bramley."

Turning away from the window, Georgiana sighed heavily, "Sadly, Sir Ludlow is hardly likely to approve of his only daughter in trade, is he?"

"Lady Bramley says a woman should learn how to look after herself and not rely on men. She says there is no harm in a young, genteel lady of reduced circumstances owning a small, respectable shop."

"I quite agree, but it is, alas, Melinda's father who must be persuaded, and sadly fathers are not always pleased to make their daughters content. Some of them can be quite difficult. From all that I have ever heard about Sir Ludlow, he is a man entrenched in his traditions and if he wants his daughter married..." Georgiana shrugged.

"Surely Lady Bramley can appeal on Melinda's behalf." In Emma's eyes, that lady could do anything.

"I do not know that Sir Ludlow will hear her. I understand he holds women in no great estimation, especially those with opinions to express and an independent perspective."

Emma got on with tidying the schoolroom, seeking comfort in the routine of making neat rows and straightening piles. There was no point fretting over Melinda's situation until they knew the facts, and their friend was, after all, a very determined young lady, quite forceful herself when she wanted to be. However firmly her father was steeped in his traditions, Melinda was not likely to give up her dream of owning that millinery shop without a fight.

"Speaking of fathers, Em," Georgiana said suddenly. "Do you never wonder about your own?"

Emma looked up in surprise. "Of course. Occasionally. It is natural to be curious. It is logical."

"You never mention it. Would you want to know him?"

She paused, a copy of *Le Morte D'Arthur* in her

hands. Emma knew that her friends, particularly Georgiana, saw the mystery around her birth as some sort of fairytale, a fable as romantic as that of King Arthur. But it was different for the girl who lived it, far less thrilling and not at all legendary. "Perhaps I would be interested to know who he is— to stop my mind from speculating— but, if that man is still alive, I would never want to *know* him, or for him to know me."

"Why ever not?" her friend exclaimed.

"The man who accidentally sired me has never wanted to be a part of my life. If he was ever to be in it, my childhood would have been the time I needed him. Now, I am one and twenty, a grown woman. It would be too awkward and too late." She shook her head and slipped the book back onto the shelf. "Far too late for us both."

She thought of her mother too, but apparently that lady had died only days after Emma was born so there was no possibility of a meeting in that case. And since, according to Mrs. Lightbody, her mother had been unwed, a disgraced, "fallen" woman, nobody ever mentioned her to Emma. Out of politeness, she supposed, or to save their own discomfort.

Now that she was out in the world, Emma had taken to strolling though graveyards and reading the headstones, wondering if her mother was buried nearby, looking for anyone of the right age and year of death, but she never found one that quite suited. She enjoyed the peaceful walks nonetheless— a

172

luxury that still felt new to her.

"Why do you ask about my father?" she said softly, straightening the books her friend had just moved out of order.

"Oh, I simply wondered...if he was ever identified...whether you would wish to know him. To confront him for abandoning you to Mrs. Lightbody."

"I cannot think it would do either of us any good now."

"But are you happy with your life? And working as a governess, Em?" said Georgie.

"Of course." There was nothing to make her unhappy about this arrangement. Each morning she spent a few hours at the school, where she taught history and geography. Every afternoon, between the hours of two and five, she came to Allerton Square to tutor Nicholas and Charles. The salary she earned allowed her to live comfortably, even to purchase a very good winter worsted to make a warm, hooded cloak for this winter— *oh yes, must not forget to do that before the weather deteriorated.* All things considered Emma's life had turned out very well. She wanted for nothing.

Although she would never be as strong as Lady Bramley, as fearless as Melinda Goodheart, or as determined, confident and revolutionary as Georgiana, she was *herself* and getting accustomed to it. Even liking herself a little.

Emma Chance was somebody, not just a ghost chained to another person's will. She might still be finding out exactly who and what that "somebody" was, cautiously exploring her new world, but she was a fully-fleshed being now and had even begun to express her own opinions out loud. Occasionally. When there was not much chance of her voice being heard.

She often thought that her one dance in ivory muslin and pearls, two years ago, had been the start of the new and improved Emma. A girl more comfortable in her own skin and less apt to shrink from challenges that would once have frightened her. Once a girl had danced with a handsome naval captain and been drenched in punch, she could cope with almost anything.

"My father seems pleased with the way you manage Nicholas the Wretched," said Georgiana. "I told him he should raise your salary, for you are much in demand and might leave for another employer."

"Georgie!" She felt her cheeks heat up. "You are wicked! Mr. Hathaway pays me quite enough." But she was certain her friend knew all about the generous terms of her employment. There was no doubt in her mind that Georgiana was the friend who had recommended her for this post and then sent her father to seek out Lady Bramley's opinion.

"You are very good with children and they seem to like you," said Georgiana thoughtfully. "Once I have daughters of my own I shall employ your services at Woodbyne. My Harry can pay you twice as much as papa."

Whenever she thought of her friends producing children, Emma's first reaction was amazement and mild disbelief that they had ever grown up so far. This was followed by fear for their safety.

She never imagined having any children herself. Could not honestly say she yearned to be a mother the way most other women did. Just as well. Children should be born into large, merry, rowdy families where they had many folk to love them and guide them. Emma Chance, despite her good friends, was a solitary being with no parents, grandparents, uncles, aunts or cousins. She was a teacher; that was her purpose. Emma could recite mathematical tables and conjugate French verbs; she knew every king and queen of England from Egbert to George the Third; she had memorized every word written by the Cavalier Poets and could list every significant battle of the English Civil War; she possessed a stitch so neat and tiny that imps might have sewn it, and she could, if called upon to do so, construct an excellent facsimile, in paper, of the Taj Mahal. But she knew nothing of how to hold a baby or soothe a crying infant. Her own childhood and infancy had passed in equal measures of abuse and abandonment, with no example of parental love, so she felt certain there was nothing inside her that could cope with motherhood.

"But now you look sad, Em! I fear Melinda and I have neglected you! Are you sure you're content here?"

She frowned. Would folk never stop fussing? "I

am very content. You must not worry about me. You have enough to contend with."

"Indeed, Harry keeps me...busy." Georgiana swept across the room and used both hands to adjust Emma's hair, cajoling two limp locks out from behind her ears. "But I will always have time for my dear friends."

It seemed as if Georgiana was so happy in her own life at present that she felt guilt for being so and could not enjoy it until her friends were likewise settled. But Emma knew her path lay in a different direction. She'd known it for a long time and was quite prepared to make the best of it.

She took her friend's hand and squeezed it gently, before it might venture any further and disrupt the neat knot in which Emma kept her hair strictly out of her way. "I shall teach your children one day. Both yours and Melinda's. This is what I was meant to do. There is great satisfaction in knowing I have instilled a young person's mind with knowledge, and helped them to have a clearer understanding of the world. In some way I might even make a positive difference in the future, for who knows," she added brightly, "one of my pupils could become Prime Minister."

"Gracious! Let's hope it's not Nicholas or we will all be in trouble." Georgiana laughed and as she watched Emma setting a guard before the fire, she added, "I have the carriage below and can take you back to the school."

"Oh, I don't mind walking."

"But it rains!"

"You know I love the rain." And walking in it was, perhaps, her one lapse in logical sense. She did not care if she caught cold or her clothes were soaked; the freedom of being able to walk out in the rain, while everybody else ran indoors, was a treat she could never resist and worth any discomfort later. It felt as if the streets were cleared of people, just for her.

"Nonsense. You'll be swept away. I cannot allow it, for your health. You know you are not strong, dearest."

As usual, there was no arguing with Georgiana. She was just as bad as Lady Bramley when the stubborn mood took her.

But Emma wished, just once, that her friends would take her seriously when she expressed joy in the rain.

She had just reached for her pelisse from the back of a chair, when a door banging below echoed throughout the house. At this time of the afternoon Mrs. Hathaway generally took her nap before dinner, so loud noises were utterly forbidden. Apparently there was somebody below who was unaware of this rule. Or uncaring.

Deep, manly laughter wove its way up the stairs, mischievously suggesting the latter.

"Oh," said Georgiana, "I forgot to tell you, my brother is home. He called in at Woodbyne yesterday on his way here, then decided to stay with us last night so he could travel to London with me today."

"Your brother?"

"Captain Guy Hathaway on leave. He didn't tell anybody he was coming, of course. He does like to surprise us."

Buttoning her coat and half turned away, Emma took a moment to compose her face.

The only man with whom she had ever danced. The only man who had ever touched her.

More of his unbound laughter now travelled around the walls and shook the beams that held HMS Hathaway together.

"You remember my brother Guy, don't you?" said Georgiana. "He escorted us to the Woodbyne ball once."

"Oh, yes. I believe I do... remember him." Her fingers fumbled with her buttons which suddenly seemed too big for their holes.

"Well, typical of a man, he does not remember *you*, poor, dear Emma. I spent most of our journey from Woodbyne prodding his memory about that evening, but he swears he cannot remember a thing about it. Or you."

Naturally. She swiped her bonnet from the hat stand by the door with just a little too much fervor. Why on earth would such a man remember her? He led a full life of adventure, excitement and hussies. Considering the oddities of a sailor's digestion, as he described it, that stupid little pink pearl she once dropped in his pocket in hopes of prodding his memory had very likely been found, eaten and never thought of again.

Chapter Twelve

"Did you fight with Napoleon?" his brother wanted to know, pointing to the nasty bruise over his eye and the cut on his cheekbone.

Guy chuckled and scratched the side of his nose. "No. Not this time. It was a slight misunderstanding...over...ah...the price and quality of ale."

"Ale? Is there ever any question?"

"Oh, yes. Quite often."

His sister had just burst into the room behind him. "Especially if there is a woman involved," she exclaimed.

He turned to give her a dark glare and found, standing there beside his sister, Miss Emma Chance.

It was two years since he last saw her. Two years and almost three months, to be precise. Which, he knew, she would be.

Dressed in a dull brown pelisse and clutching her equally unattractive brown hat, she was evidently ready to leave his sight again and so he stared hard and greedily, before she might take flight. She looked the same, but different. He couldn't think what had changed.

Of course, she was not covered in red patches from scratching herself. Perhaps that was the difference.

"Captain Hathaway," she muttered. "I hear you are home on leave. How...how pleasant it is to see you again."

"Is it? I believe that's the first time those words have been uttered to me in this house." He grinned but she remained solemn. Of course she did. He recalled what a challenge it was to make her smile.

"I don't want a bath!" Nicholas shouted, still running around the sofa. "I'm not dirty."

Guy swiveled to watch the chase. "Well, if he's not dirty, why—"

"Our stepmother likes to keep order and it's her rule. Once a day, whether they need it or not and despite the work involved."

"Good lord." He laughed. "If only she saw us when we lived in the country. In her eyes we would have been savages."

"Master Nicholas." Miss Chance stepped forward. "Once you have taken your bath and eaten your supper, I'm sure Captain Hathaway will tell you and Master Lennox all his new stories of life at sea. You can sit down together then and hear his...exciting tales without fear of interruption."

Nicholas came to a halt and leaned against the back of the sofa. "Don't you want to hear the stories too, Miss Chance?"

"Well, I am going home now, but I will return tomorrow afternoon and you can tell them to me then. So make certain you recall every detail."

Guy put his heels together and gave the boy a playful bow. "As your stern governess says, satisfy the requirements of the second Mrs. Hathaway, young

Nick, and then you and I will have all the time we need. I shall tell you all about my black eye and my newest scars then. When the ladies cannot bother us and we shall be free to speak of anything we please without censoring our words to save their dainty blushes."

This idea pleased the boy. Anything he could learn without girls poking their noses in was well worth the trouble of a scrubbing first.

Georgiana, who never liked using a bell to summon the staff, took him out to find the housekeeper from whom he'd escaped and thus Guy was left to study the young woman standing before him in his father's parlor. The young woman he once considered kissing, because she was a sad thing and he wanted to cheer her spirits.

And why, exactly, would he assume a kiss from him should raise her spirits? He cringed inwardly at his own arrogance of two years ago.

Despite all the brown of her attire, she was not so sad and limp now. That was the difference, he realized. Part of it, in any case. The clouds of fear had gone from her eyes and where before it was an eternally rainy day, skies were now clear and calm.

He cleared his throat, looked at the door which had been left ajar, and then strolled to the mantle and back. Every step he felt her eyes upon him. Cool and composed.

"I hope managing my brother does not cause you too much consternation, Miss Chance."

"Not at all, Captain. He is a lively boy, and when interested in a subject he is insatiable. The problem lies in finding those things in which he is interested." She ventured a smile. It was warm, sincere, and lifted her features so that they fleetingly looked...pretty.

And he was so overcome in that moment he didn't know what to do. He almost dropped his hat. Moving around the sofa, he pursed his lips in a soft, casual whistle. Nonchalant. Yes, that was better. "He pays heed to you, it seems," he managed finally. *Stupid.* Why was he suddenly at a loss for conversation?

"Sometimes." She looked quizzical, plaintive. "I do my best."

"I told them you would be a good choice for the post." *Even stupider!* Damn and blast! He had not meant to say anything about it. Did not want her knowing of the part he'd played in bringing her to Allerton Square. He barely knew himself why he had recommended her to his father; why he had felt such a desire to help her. Georgiana would have teased him without mercy, had she known it was he who put Miss Chance up for the post.

Her eyes were confused, that clear day turning foggy. "*You* told them...?"

He quickly regrouped, assumed a nonchalant air with one foot on the fender, hat tucked under his arm. "On the way here from Surrey, when Georgiana mentioned that our father had hired you as governess, I thought how well you must be suited to the position."

Her right eyebrow curved upward. "Did you indeed?" There was another slight tremor around her mouth. "How clever of you to know I would be suited, considering you did not remember me at all, according to your sister."

Naturally, he'd let Georgiana think that, for his sister was a hopelessly interfering romantic and the best way to curb her festering, investigative little mind was to block it by erecting the barrier of a bad memory and a vacant stare. It had the added bonus of annoying his sister to no end. And he didn't want her sticking that freckled nose into this business. Georgiana brought calamity to any mission she undertook and from the moment she could toddle along on two feet she had wanted to be a part of anything her eldest brother had planned. Guy had soon learned not to let her know anything on his mind. At least, for as long as he could keep it from her.

He resumed his whistle, walking back the other way around the sofa, feeling Miss Emma Chance's calmly curious gaze upon his every step.

"Was it really a quarrel over the price of ale, Captain?" she asked.

"What?"

She pointed to his face.

"In actual fact—" He stopped, squared his shoulders, hat behind his back. "—I was saving a friend from a disastrous mistake with a young skirt who tried to pull the wool over his eyes, and I happened to get in the way of a fist."

"The young lady's fist?" she enquired politely.

He scowled. "No. A very large fist belonging to her lover."

"Oh, dear." She shook her head. "It is such a pity that men must resort to fighting. That they cannot discuss their problems in an orderly fashion and come to a resolution without bodily harm."

"Madam, I would have been happy to sit and discuss the matter, but since her lover did not speak a word of English, a little tete-a-tete over tea and cake would hardly have helped."

Her lips moved in the beginnings of another wry smile and then she said, "Well, at least nothing important was damaged."

"*Nothing important*?" He gestured to his face. "What's this?"

"I'm sure it does nothing to lessen your...appeal."

"Oh? Do I have one then?"

"So I understand, for some."

"Not for you?"

She stared, wide-eyed and innocent. "Some women are attracted to the image of the disreputable scoundrel and that is the impression for which you strive, is it not?"

"How lucky for you that you're not taken in then. Too sensible, eh?"

"I do find you curious study, Captain."

"*Curious study*?"

"I also find caterpillars fascinating and grub worms quite delightful," she added solemnly. "I am, in other words, not easily made queasy, or put off my supper by the unsightly."

He tossed his hat onto the sofa. "*Unsightly*? Well, of all the damned—"

"I mean to say that your face could be far worse. The wounds will heal in time. It is only a surface mark. Barely a scratch." She paused. "Like the impression I left upon you two years ago. Apparently."

Hmm. That sounded dangerously peevish for the formerly meek, patient, and bashful Miss Chance. Was she still so innocent after all?

Then she seemed to recover some of her old shyness for she flushed a little. "I did not expect you to remember me, however, so I am not surprised."

"But *you* remembered *me*?" She would not be capable of lying; he knew that about her.

"Every moment, sir." The flush deepened. "Of course, my life is much less thrilling than yours. Not much about it *is* memorable. Not in a way that makes me eager to remember it." Then she shook her head, frowning in frustration, as if she knew she'd said more than she ought.

Narrow-eyed he surveyed her thoughtfully. Before another word could be said, his sister returned, having disposed of Nicholas.

"Father has been roused from his study and will be with you forthwith," she exclaimed, slightly breathless after her exertions of wrestling their little brother into his bath. "Now I shall take Miss Chance back to the school and—"

"Miss Chance and I were just discussing *The Duchess of Malfi*," he interrupted swiftly. At once he felt that questioning gaze return to his face and knew he'd shocked her, because he *did* remember.

Don't startle Miss Chance. Ha!

"*The Duchess of Malfi?*" Georgiana muttered. "That's an odd subject."

"There is currently a performance of the play at the Theatre-Royal in Convent Garden. I thought she might like to attend. Of course, we'll need an escort to make certain it's all very proper. So I suggested you might come, sister." He turned to look at the governess. "Wouldn't want anybody to think there's something afoot, between Miss Chance and I, would we? Something... untoward."

"Nonsense, Emma is far too sensible to be drawn in by your limited charms, brother. If anybody saw her with you they'd think she lost a wager of some sort, or was being kind to you. They would never think it more than that."

"Then you needn't come. We can manage without you."

"And leave her alone to put up with your awfulness just to watch a play? Lady Bramley would be aghast. Of course, I'll come. I always love a good drama." Georgiana looked uncertainly toward her friend. "But... is Emma agreeable to the idea? I know she does not go out much and prefers her quiet evenings in."

The woman in the ugly brown coat, buttoned severely to her throat, separated her clenched lips long enough to reply, "I have never been to the theatre, as you know, but I believe I should enjoy it. I am familiar with the play."

Guy grinned— feeling rather smug. "Well, there you are then. The theatre it is. Unsightly and disreputable as I am."

"But what time and day, Captain?" Miss Chance inquired.

"Oh, I don't know. We'll decide when we come to it, eh? You know how I am. Impulsive. A wriggling grub worm in the garden of life. Never know when I might pop out of the soil to startle you."

It was surprising how much lightning could flare suddenly within eyes the color of a cool but clear October morning. "I prefer to be organized, sir. It makes life easier and less prone to accident or misunderstanding, if one knows what one is doing and when one is doing it."

"*One* doesn't have any other engagements in the evenings, does one? No prior claim upon your time to get in the way of our enjoyment?"

She chewed upon her lip and then exclaimed. "I might have." She could not say that she did, however, for that would be dishonest and Miss Chance was incapable. It was, however, most likely that she'd been warned against him by Lady Bramley, which would account for the hesitancy.

"But you're so organized and, unlike me, have such an excellent memory. You would know for sure if you have any other engagements or hindrances of which I ought to be made aware."

Georgiana had watched this exchange in some puzzlement. Now she intervened. "Stop teasing poor Miss Chance. She is not accustomed to your horrid ways. We will attend the theatre a week on Wednesday. That will give your face time to heal, because we can hardly go out in public with you looking like a dog's dinner."

"Miss Chance said it could be far worse."

"Miss Chance was being polite, as is her habit. I know you are not acquainted with many polite ladies."

He looked at the governess and winked, although it hurt. "I rather thought she took a liking to me, all bruised and mangled as I am. The quiet ones tend to be the most perverse in their preferences. And she assures me she has a fondness for pests."

"Pest is an unfair word," the young lady replied. "Every creature on earth serves its purpose."

"Even you, brother," Georgiana added sharply. Then she took her friend's arm and hurried her out of the parlor. A moment later he heard the front door shut.

He smiled, rubbing his chin. Now Miss Chance would know that he *did* remember her. He remembered everything, in fact, every detail of their conversation. And how it had felt to put those pearls around her slender neck and feel her tremble.

The moment he saw the advertisement for *The Duchess of Malfi* outside the Covent Garden Theatre that afternoon, as his sister's carriage took them by the market, he knew he'd escort her there. It was providential.

Using divine intervention as an excuse was just like using a supposedly bad memory. He had no need to explain it further, not even to himself. Most convenient.

Chapter Thirteen

His father used to be a tall, spare figure. One might even say, gaunt. But now, Frederick Hathaway was considerably rotund. Life in London, fighting for a place among the upper-crust, had, it seemed, expanded his girth, even as it decreased his patience. On this occasion Guy noticed it more than he had before. He also took note of his father's breathless wheezing and his reddened face.

"I hope you are well, sir," he said stupidly, as they faced each other in the parlor— the returning, eternally wary son and the never far-traveled, eternally disappointed father.

"As well as might be expected." His father kept looking at Guy's black eye, but he would never mention it directly. If he did, he might have to hear more about his son's private life than he cared to know. When it came to his eldest son, Frederick Hathaway had always maintained the view that he was better off not knowing. Consequently there remained between father and son a cautious distance. They might as well be two slight acquaintances that once met at a dinner party and, ever since, felt obliged to nod to each other when they crossed paths, even though names had been forgotten. "Why are *you* here?"

Guy managed a tight laugh. "Thought you might have missed me, sir."

His father grunted. "Did you indeed?" He

glanced over at the brandy decanter and flexed his stout fingers, but, for some reason, resisted the temptation. "I see."

The clock on the mantle ticked loudly, and rain spat at the windows.

Were they already in danger of running out of conversation? His father seemed distracted. He was never very interested in Guy's life, but this was a new level of indifference.

"Mrs. Hathaway is in good health, I hope, sir?"

"Ah, yes. She sends her apologies for not coming down, but she is a little tired and has gone early to her bed."

Tired was only to be expected, Guy mused, after four pregnancies in seven years of marriage— one of them resulting in the loss of the child midterm and one bringing twins into the family. He had no idea where women got the energy. It was different for men; their part was easy and over in minutes. Probably just as well or there would never be any babies born.

"We expect your brother Edward to visit any day," his father added suddenly, as if it had been preying on his mind before he entered the room. Perhaps, when he heard his son was home, he had thought of Edward first. "Have you received word from him?"

"No. Edward seldom writes to me these days. I believe he's busy with his parish."

While Guy had displeased their father by joining

the navy, Edward had also shown rebellious spirit—
although a milder one— by turning his back on
London society, returning to Norfolk, and taking up a
living there when it was offered by a distant cousin.
Their father had originally nursed higher plans for
Edward, who was considered the "clever one" in the
family, and so it annoyed him greatly when the young
man preferred the church and a small parish in the
"midst of nowhere and serving nobodies," to the
grandeur of life in London.

But despite this set-back, fair-haired, blue-eyed
Edward had eventually been forgiven. The torch of
their father's grand expectations had not yet been
wrenched from his hands, merely adjusted.

"I do hope Edward comes soon. We have not
seen him since the early summer, but he stayed with
us then for a full fortnight. It did us all a world of
good, and I believe he was most sorry to go. I
thought he would return before now."

Edward's visits, so it seemed, were looked
forward to with great anticipation and his absence
deeply lamented. It was the opposite for Guy's visits,
which, although were much less frequent, were
regarded as an inconvenience. Despite the two years
since his last return to London, he'd been left to wait
almost an hour in the parlor before his father could
be dragged away from his study. Even now, Mr.
Hathaway went to the rain-spattered window, looking
out into the grey November evening as if seeking his
other son. Or any suitable passerby that might be

summoned inside to relieve him of the tedious visitor currently at hand.

Guy cleared his throat. "I wonder, sir...my childhood possessions...some were saved for the younger boys I assume? They are somewhere in the house? Or Edward might have them?"

His father looked nonplussed.

"The things I had— books and such— when I was a boy in Norfolk," Guy explained further. "Were they kept?" Perhaps his father had thrown them all on a bonfire when they moved to London, he thought grimly.

"I know not. I suppose so." His father sighed, looking out of the window again. "Is that why you came home? Ask your sister Georgiana. She fancies herself the family historian and keeper of detritus. Never wants anything thrown out, but it must be cooed over and clutched to her heart. Any old wretched thing, moldy, flea-bitten and torn. The more so the better. She's here somewhere in the house. I just saw her."

"Yes, she took Miss Chance home."

"Who?"

"Miss Chance."

"What's that?"

"The governess."

"Oh. Yes. Her. Odd little thing she is." Another fretful sigh. "So damnably quiet I never know whether she's in the house or not. Creeps up on a fellow. Silent and stealthy as a cat."

Guy had to agree with this comparison. From the beginning of their acquaintance she had reminded him of a stray kitten with ears flat to her head and whiskers drooping. Now she had grown into a lean cat with her ears pricked and a bit more scratch to her. "The boys— Nicholas and Charles— seem to like Miss Chance."

"Do they? Yes, well Charles is a good lad. Nicholas needs a firm hand to focus his energies. Reminds me of you." And from his tone it was not a pleasant memory. "Fanny wants them away at school, out from under her feet she says, but neither boy did well as boarders so far from home."

"Yes, I know," Guy replied drily. "I received endless letters from Nick, begging me to rescue him, threatening to run off with the gypsies." That had given him the idea of persuading his father to hire Miss Chance as a tutor so Nicholas could stay at home.

His father quite suddenly seemed to have heard the rest of what Guy said earlier. Or else his favorite son remained on his mind. "Edward? Edward wouldn't have any of those toys, trifles and knick-knacks you're looking for. No, no, Edward keeps his life uncluttered and very tidy. He believes a clean, sparsely-furnished house is conducive to a clean, devout and chaste mind."

"Dear Edward." Guy smirked. "Always holier than the rest of us."

Again his father did not hear what he said. "I

have reason to suspect— perhaps I should not say. Oh, well, why not?" Turning away from the window, one hand on the buttons of his waistcoat, stomach thrust proudly forth, like that of a strutting pigeon, he said, "I suspect Edward considers matrimony at last. He hinted of it in his last letter. I shall finally have grandchildren to continue the family line."

"But my sister Maria has two children already, does she not?"

He waved a dismissive hand. "Any offspring your sisters produce will not have the Hathaway name. It is up to my sons to continue the dynasty." With a heaving sigh, he looked again at the brandy decanter and then his gaze lifted somewhat shiftily to the ceiling, before returning to Guy's face. "One of my sons, at least, ought to be able to make a good marriage."

Although this was clearly another arrow aimed at him, Guy forgave his father. He knew it was all very frustrating for Frederick Hathaway. The man had brought his family to town with the express intention of advancing their status and fortunes, to make connections with people of consequence, but his children seemed out to spoil his plans at every turn. Maria, his eldest daughter, who had once set her sights as high as a Viscount, had instead married a dour solicitor with a mumble and such a shambling walk that he seemed embarrassed by his own presence. Then Georgiana had married Commander Sir Henry Thrasher— a man who avoided society as far as he could and preferred his manor in the country to life in town.

With one son-in-law who refused to be shown off and another he did not want to exhibit, Guy's father was desperate for his remaining children to make more socially beneficial matrimonial conquests of which he might boast.

At present his hopes were on Edward, and the young man had never lacked for female admirers, all of whom were kept at arm's length. If he had thought he might hide away in his somber curate's robes, he was mistaken, for the dark primness only highlighted his angelic good looks, and all that holy righteousness increased the pounding of womanly heartbeats. Guy had once attended a Sunday service, while visiting his brother in Norfolk, and was amused to find the church crammed to overflowing with blushing, palpitating ladies dressed in their finest, almost coming to blows over who might sit in the front pews. Apparently Edward's parish included an uncommon number of unmarried women and widows, all with a great deal of feisty energy on a Sunday morning.

"Some of my sons, at least, might be relied upon to settle down," his father was saying drearily. "I do not suppose we can hope for legitimate progeny in all cases."

"Father, I know you persist in this idea that all sailors have a handful of little bastards running about, but I can assure you that none can be attributed to me. I have my faults and vices, but I'm not quite that foolish and reckless. One ride around the seven dials on a cold night is enough to show a man the human suffering wrought by careless procreation."

His father's face turned a deeper shade of port red. "No plan to settle down though, eh? Get yourself an honest woman? This time."

"An honest woman," Guy muttered. "There's a rare creature."

"Nonsense. Plenty of 'em about if you look in the right places." He eyed his son's wounded face again. "And when you stop chasing trouble."

"Ah, but trouble chases *me*. You know how I am."

"Yes, you're a hound dog chasing its own tail, boy." With another grunt, his father strode to the sideboard and clutched the decanter, as if he thought somebody might snatch it from him. Again he glanced nervously at the ceiling, before he poured two brandies. "I thought you'd grow out of that by now and this ceaseless quest for adventure. What are you? Thirty-two, thirty-three?"

Guy might have been offended. But he supposed there were a great many children now and Mr. Hathaway had too many, more important things to fill his head.

"I shall be thirty in December, sir," he said, taking the glass he was offered.

"Then it's time you found a wife. Edward is five years your junior and yet he sees no value to be had in chasing trouble. After careful consideration he is ready to settle down and marry."

"He is *two* years my junior, and as a man of the church, it would be odd indeed if he kept company with the wilder sort of female. I'm sure he'll find some poor, dutiful woman he can lecture daily, and who will manage all his very particular needs and wants without complaint. A woman to whom he can pontificate at length without her feeling the uncontrollable urge to put an apple in his mouth and roast him on a spit."

"A *poor* woman?" His father had picked up only those words and mistook their meaning in this instance. He seldom did listen to much his eldest son said, and then picked at and reshuffled the words to find something with which he could disagree. "No, no. There are many wealthy, well-connected widows in his parish and the Earl of Cottingham, who resides nearby, has several daughters of marriageable age."

"Father, I admire your ambition, but I think you aim too high." Guy was amused. "Even for Edward, the golden boy, an earl's daughter is a stretch."

"But the family is fond of Edward and has him up at the great house often for dinner."

"I expect he tastes well enough if properly cooked and seasoned. Otherwise I imagine him to be a tough, tasteless chew."

His expression unmoved, Mr. Hathaway replied dourly, "Edward is a mature and responsible young man. He does not find himself awakening in the early hours, naked in a Spanish port town with an aching head, a tattoo and a wife whose name he does not remember."

Whenever father and son were together, the subject of Guy's unfortunate and brief marriage to a Flamenco dancer in Cadiz when he was nineteen always managed to rear its head eventually.

"Edward has been mature and responsible since the nursery," Guy exclaimed. "He was an old man at ten. A curmudgeonly old man with the face of an Archangel."

"Better an old man at ten, than a boy still at thirty."

Guy swigged a mouthful of brandy and relished the fierce burn in his throat.

"Sooner or later," his father added, "a man has to stop running and keep still. It's time you became an adult and did your duty for the next generation. I do not expect much from you now, but—" Again the brisk up and down assessment, coming to a halt on Guy's bruised face. "Surely even you can find some *decent* woman to marry. Perhaps then, when you come ashore, your first order of business won't be a dockside tavern brawl."

"I was caught up in a disagreement between a friend of mine and a large, angry fellow who would cheerfully have crushed his skull with one fist. It wasn't deliberate."

"Yes, as I recall, that affair in Spain was another of your spur-of-the-moment and costly impulses."

"That was ten, almost eleven years ago, sir. Must the event forever be revisited?"

"You were fortunate— as were we all— that the woman was proven to have another husband still breathing and the marriage could be annulled. If not for that we would all still be living with the consequences of your mistake, young man!"

Guy drained his snifter.

"That would have been something to explain to the neighbors," his father went on. "Now at least it's only a bruised and beaten face that must be explained. Oh, I'm sure they all saw the state of you when you arrived in your sister's carriage."

"Why not put an article in your paper, sir, in case anybody missed it? Disappointing son returns home. Still disappoints."

"You seem to think the disappointment is my fault. Not yours."

"Remind your neighbors that I'm a sailor. We do tend not to remain in pristine condition. I'm sure they'll understand." He managed another tight smile.

But his father had never been impressed by a son in the navy— even a Captain. He might print the brave exploits of seafaring heroes in his paper for the enjoyment of his readers and subscribers, but for his own son he'd wanted something different. Guy had never been entirely sure what it was his father had expected of him. He simply knew he'd failed to meet those expectations at every turn. And at some point it became easier to continue as he'd begun, rather than try to repair their relationship or seek that elusive seal of approval.

Guy had known, from an early age, that he wanted to go to sea. When he was a boy he found a miniature portrait his mother kept in a locket, along with a curl of sandy hair. She had told him it belonged to her younger brother who died at sea, fighting in the navy. As a little boy, Guy heard such love and admiration in his mother's voice when she spoke of the man in the portrait that he had wanted to follow those footsteps. He was convinced at once that there could be no pursuit more worthy, no career path more bravely marched. At fourteen he left for Portsmouth, and every time he went home after that he felt the distance growing between himself and his father, while the attachment to his mother was stronger, quietly understanding, sharing his love for adventure— although she had known little in her own life— always ready to hear and be amazed by his stories. Even when he ran out of things to tell her, she prompted him to make up more stories, her eyes alight with curiosity and admiration. And yearning. Somehow this connection he had to one parent irritated the other all the more.

"How long do you plan to stay in London?" his father muttered, returning to the brandy decanter, his tone dreary.

Guy exhaled a sigh. "Oh, only a week or so. I must report to the ship in the new year and I'll be at sea by March. Don't worry. I shan't get in anybody's way or embarrass you. Too much."

"Good. See that you don't. Pity you can't get yourself a half-way decent, respectable wife, but I suppose we might as well give up on that idea."

And then, in that moment, as Guy watched his father turn away yet again, those slumped, weary shoulders bent over the decanter, he felt the sudden urge to light the fuse of a gunpowder barrel. He'd always been the mischievous son and on this day, with rain rattling the windows like battle drums and his father being so ambivalent to see him, he wanted to wake the whole house, the entire square, out of its pompous complacency. Give them all something new to talk about.

Suddenly his thoughts spun and careened, bouncing in all directions. Like the pearls of a broken necklace.

But the thought was not nearly so impulsive as it might seem, for he'd been mulling her over now for some time. He simply hadn't realized that he was serious about it, until now. Or rather, a few moments ago, when he saw her standing in the doorway with her hair tucked unflatteringly behind her ears again. He had not even realized exactly what brought him home to Allerton Square until the moment he watched that tentative smile lift the corner of her lips.

When she compared him to a grub worm and called him unsightly he knew, finally, what had been brewing all this time inside his restlessness.

It was a curious sensation and he did not know

what to make of it, but there it was.

Chapter Fourteen

That evening, Emma sat by her fire, supper on a tray across her knees, and ate with a very healthy appetite. She was generally what Lady Bramley disapprovingly called a "nervous" eater, but tonight she was ravenous and finished her bowl of soup before she knew she'd begun or tasted any. It was shock, she supposed, at seeing him again so suddenly. There had been no warning of Captain Hathaway's possible return. Not even a hint of his ship making anchor.

For two years her ears and eyes had been attentive to every little clue about the absent eldest son of the house, so Emma was sure she would know, and have time to prepare herself, the moment he was expected. But once again he took her by surprise.

He liked being unpredictable; she knew that. Two years ago, as they rode to Surrey in his father's carriage, his eyes had lit up with mischief when he teased her, "*Anything can happen on a journey into the countryside, Miss Chance. Who knows what excitement lurks in wait for us?*"

This afternoon, having crept up on her again, he took advantage of her scattered nerves by abruptly suggesting they attend a play. She should not get too excited, for later he might forget he ever mentioned it. Something more interesting and entertaining could arise in the meantime and put *The Duchess of Malfi* and her torments out of his mind. Lady Bramley said men like the captain seldom had the same idea twice.

And this particular idea must have come to him when he saw her, since he had told his sister that he did not remember anything about Emma Chance. Perhaps the sight of her plain face had jogged his memory. At least her mostly inadequate features were good for something then, she mused.

Setting her tray aside, she paced a while, rubbing her fingertips on the lace cuff of her sleeve. It was not wise to get out of one's routine, and attending a play at the theatre-royal was certainly a new experience for her. With a man, no less. Well...and his sister. Georgiana would be with them, so it was all quite innocent. Lady Bramley could not object.

Or could she?

Emma paused to stir up the fire and then continued her restless patrol of the small room, listening to the rain that still drummed at the windows with half-hearted gusts of enthusiasm.

She stopped and looked up at the paler space on the wallpaper, where Mrs. Lightbody's portrait once smirked down from an ornately carved frame. The angry lady had taken the painting and frame with her, when she departed the place under the stern eye of two men sent by Lady Bramley to see her out. Now there was simply the clean rectangle left where pipe, cigar, candle and coal smoke had yet to make their stain. Lady Bramley kept asking her what she meant to put there— suggesting various biblical inscriptions sewn on canvas— but Emma could not decide how to cover the mark, or whether she should. It reminded her of that breath of hope once given to her by a certain young naval lieutenant leaning against the wall outside. A patch of fresh air through the cloying fog. A window of light into the future.

Perhaps she would just leave it as it was. After all, it was her choice entirely now to do with it exactly as she pleased.

When Lady Bramley became "temporary" headmistress of the academy she had decided not to use her predecessor's study. Instead she allowed Emma to use it as her own private sitting room. Her ladyship spent every evening in her own grand house, several streets away, and did not require a room for herself at the school. Nor did she show her face at the establishment every day, for she was busy with many charitable pursuits. The daily running of the school— supervising mealtimes, ordering provisions, fixing gutters and mediating between quarrelsome young ladies— was left mostly to Emma, and Mr. and Mrs. Bishop, a cheerful couple who lived in the house, maintained the building and cooked for the school. There was also a housemaid, Annie, who came in every morning, and two full-time teachers found by Lady Bramley: Miss Pegg, who taught needlework, art and French; and Miss Gunderson, who taught mathematics and science— two new subjects at the school. Lady Bramley herself tutored the students in dancing, music, manners and deportment, but she occasionally appeared without warning to inspect the classrooms as other teachers worked. And, of course, to "assist" with the lesson, wherever she felt her expertise was needed.

In the evenings, after the students had retired to their rooms, the house was mostly quiet— not in the sinister, watchful way it had been in Mrs. Lightbody's day, but in a contented, happy manner. Occasional giggles filtered down the stairs to Emma's little parlor and sometimes one of the other teachers, or Mrs. Bishop would knock on her door to discuss the day's events. Other than that, she was left alone to spend her evenings in any fashion she chose, here in this room which was now her pleasant sanctuary.

Emma smiled when she thought of how infuriated Mrs. Lightbody would be if she knew her study had been given to Chance the Ingrate. That would be the final indignity, the straw that broke the camel's back.

On usual evenings, Emma sat by her fire and sewed, read, or prepared for the next few days of lessons. Tonight however, none of these actions could keep her feet from circling, her mind from rustling its pages restlessly.

She was appalled that the return of one man should cause such a disturbance to her routine. But he was not just any man, was he? Guy Hathaway was her dragon prince.

Emma went to her desk, opened the top draw, reached into the back of it, and drew out a neatly folded square of linen. Pressing it to her nose she inhaled deeply and sighed.

She had never laundered his handkerchief, fearing to lose the precious scent.

Often she let her mind wander back in time to the ball at Woodbyne Abbey and the journey home to London the next morning. Emma had not slept well at the inn that night after the ball, for she was still too full of excitement, reliving her moment with the captain, over and over again. The following morning he had been rather quiet, but still kind and solicitous at breakfast. They were all in a subdued mood, actually, nobody having much to say. It had been much cooler that day, autumn making itself felt with a sharp bite, but Emma was glad of it. She might have melted had the summer loitered any longer. Oh, but their return journey to London had passed so swiftly and in the carriage he had not said another word directly to her. Nothing meaningful, in any case, just polite mutterings.

She had longed for him to look at her again— properly look, as he did in the kitchen of Woodbyne Abbey. Yet on their way back to London he had been very careful not to do so.

It was all exceedingly stupid to want his attention— what could she possibly do with it? — but she could not help herself. Sometimes, she supposed, logic simply took flight. When it came to her feelings for the dragon prince there was no reason. She was no better than those tittering fifteen and sixteen year old girls in the rooms above. Addled, that's what she was. A seething mess of silly, unhinged impulses.

But she had just turned one and twenty. As Lady Bramley had been heard to say whenever she saw a mature lady dressed in a style deemed too young and frivolous, "A woman should know her age and embrace it with pride."

Once Georgiana had asked, "Should we not try to stay young, madam?"

To which the lady replied, "Youth is effortless because those who possess it are quite unaware of its value. That is the very point. Anybody who tries too hard to regain youth completely misunderstands the matter and always appears more advanced in age than they truly are. Good health, good humor and good sense are the way to a well-led life and should be the aspirations of us all. No amount of carmine rouge will help the soul."

Emma always paid close attention to her ladyship's lessons and she felt certain that her soul was improving every day. She wanted to look back on her life in her last years and be able to say that it was "well-led". That unhappy beginning would never be forgotten, but it would be overcome in time, those grim days outnumbered eventually by far many more memories of good years. It was up to her to make it so. Several folk had helped her this far, but it was in her hands now. She could not rely on her friends forever, but must go boldly into the world. And she must not be distracted by idle, impossibly romantic thoughts, for that only led to vanity and envy, amongst other sinful leanings. Look what happened last time she got carried away in the captain's presence— a dress was ruined, a necklace broken and a young gentleman shouted at needlessly by Lady Bramley.

But she sometimes thought a little carmine rouge in one's life wouldn't go amiss.

While Lady Bramley was one of those handsome women who could afford to sneer at cosmetic enhancement, they were not all so fortunate.

In another attempt to put her mind in better order, Emma sat at her desk and inspected the day's post. Left on the blotter by Mrs. Bishop, it was full of the usual— inquiries from parents eager to find a place for their girls, bills, pamphlets about miracle tooth powder...and a letter addressed to E. Chance.

She opened it quickly, wondering if it might be word at last from Melinda, for the handwriting was familiar.

Come to 22 Woolpack Buildings, Millers Square, Lisson Grove. Urgent. I have news you might find lucrative. Don't forget what you owe me. Noon tomorrow.

JL

So that was why she recognized the messy writing. Emma could even hear the woman's voice as she read the words on the paper.

It was more than two years since anybody had heard from Julia Lightbody. Wherever she'd gone when she left the school was unknown. After such a dismissal, surely most women would slink away and try to reinvent themselves somewhere new.

But she should have known Mrs. Lightbody was not the sort to fade away, or forgive a debt. She still seemed to think that raising a child in misery was a service for which she ought to be compensated. That woman had no shame and no pity for others.

As Georgiana had always said, it was a mystery how Mrs. Lightbody ever became headmistress. "It must have been a clerical error of some sort. Or blackmail."

Emma tended to agree with the latter idea. Somebody somewhere had the influence to get her into that school, but whoever it was, they had not been powerful enough to keep her there once the forceful and fearless Lady Bramley began making a stir and asking pertinent questions. Emma had always suspected that she would return one day to wreck vengeance on "The Ladies Most Unlikely", whom she blamed for getting her dismissed.

Two years ago, when she was still haunted by that woman, Emma would have burned the note immediately. But she was no longer fearful of facing Julia Lightbody. Just as her dread of cows had been consigned to the childish past, so must that woman. The heinous monster must be slain— mentally— to put history behind her once and for all.

* * * *

The next morning, when Emma walked into her parlor another surprise awaited.

"They were delivered this morning, Miss Chance, when it was barely dawn out. Annie had just got up to light the stove, when a boy came to the door. Frightened the life out of her."

A tower of encyclopedias sat upon her desk in order from A to Z. They were clearly of a good age, the gilt lettering on the covers quite worn, the pages dog-eared. Clearly they were once well-read and much-loved.

"But who are they from? Was there no note?"

"None, Miss Chance. The boy brought them in a barrow, huffing and puffing. Had no breath left to say anything and took off again before Annie could stop him by the ear. I thought it must be a donation from somebody, Miss. A bequest left for the school."

"Yes, I see." Emma picked up the top book and looked through it. "These will certainly be put to good use by our students." And then inside the back cover she found a scribbled line of faded ink.

To G. Hathaway on his birthday 1797.

It was a very generous gift for the school, but why would he not save the encyclopedias for his little brothers? Perhaps his sister had persuaded him to donate them.

She ran a fingertip over his name and felt that skip of excitement in her heart. The captain was back in London. Close by. So close she could almost feel his breath upon the back of her neck and had to put her hand up suddenly to check that her hair was not teased out of its knot by his venturesome fingertips. Really, she should not be so wound up about his return. Before she knew it he'd be gone back to sea and she'd be weeping again like an idiot, she mused darkly.

He was taking her to the theatre, but only as his sister's little friend— a creature to be pitied. It was a kindness on his part, nothing more. As for Emma, she was still exploring and discovering her new world and a trip to the theatre would be a part of that study. There, that was everything in its neat place and carefully explained. Nothing romantic about it.

It was highly unlikely that she would see much of him apart from that event. In the afternoons, when she tutored the boys at Allerton Square she might catch a glimpse or hear him somewhere in the house, but there would be no reason for them to cross paths while she was there. He must have much to do, many sociable friends to do it all with. Emma was merely his sister's plain little friend, a governess hired by his father.

She had tried, yesterday, to show him that she was more than that now, but alas he still seemed to be laughing at her. Then, naturally, in her nervousness she'd gone and said the wrong thing again, chattering on about insects. When she thought back to their conversation she had no idea how she came to mention grubs and caterpillars. Oh, yes she did! She realized now that she had tried to explain that ugly things didn't frighten her, which is why his bruised face had not seemed so serious or bothersome an injury.

"I am, in other words, not easily made queasy, or put off my supper by the unsightly."

"Unsightly? Well, of all the damned—"

Emma raised a hand to her head and bit her lip. She would not blame him if he never looked at her again. Yet he had invited her to the theatre.

And now he sent her encyclopedias. It seemed to her significant. Of what, she had no idea.

"Miss Chance, you look flushed. Are you feverish? Perhaps a nice buttered kipper for your breakfast? Do sit down and I'll get you a cup of hot tea."

"Mrs. Bishop, just because I have a slight color in my face for a change does not mean I am sick. Whatever you all think, I am not an invalid who must be coddled!" And then, grieved by her harsh tone, she softened it immediately. "Forgive me, dear Mrs. Bishop. Good sleep evaded me last night. All I truly need is a walk in fresh air."

"Well...if you must, but it looks to be a chilly day, Miss, so you wrap up warm, won't you? Can't have you catching cold."

Cold? That was quite impossible. She might, however, explode in flames.

This was what happened, she thought crossly, when one lay awake all night thinking about a man. Lady Bramley had been quite right to warn her. But then, that lady was always right.

* * * *

While it was a cool, overcast day, the promise of rain sitting heavy in the low clouds— the sort of threat that trapped most folk indoors— Emma was glad she had errands to keep her busy and give her cause to be outside. After lessons that morning, the first item on her list was a trip to the haberdasher to purchase that worsted she needed for her winter cloak.

Just as she was leaving the house, two students of the school wanted to come with her so she was delayed while they fussed over their bonnets, reticules and muffs. Finally the little group was ready and they set off for the brisk walk to Regent Street.

But as they hurried along, her two young companions arguing about the material they planned to buy, Emma suddenly saw Captain Hathaway crossing the road ahead of them. He was alone, focused on the ground under his feet as he strode along purposefully. His coat flapped open, even on that cold day, giving him the appearance of a great black crow bearing down upon her. Nobody dared tell *him* to button it against the cold, she mused. But then, he was hardly a wisp of a thing. He was solid, full of vitality— overflowing with it, one might even say. Sometimes, as she had observed before, when the bounce went out of his stride and he thought nobody watched, he bristled with a darkly brooding energy.

From this distance it was difficult to ascertain his mood. Handsomely agitated would, perhaps, be the best way to describe his appearance. As far as she could see he wore no cravat or waistcoat and this neglect, coupled with the open coat, suggested dressing in haste before he left his father's house. Some folk turned to watch him in the street, a few gathering their children to their skirts, as if only a madman would be out on such a cold, wet day in an undressed state. He seemed perfectly unconscious of the dangerous impression he made on that very proper street.

Emma briefly pondered the idea of crossing the street to avoid him, but why would she do such a thing? There was no need to let him know that he had such a strange effect upon her logical mind. They were acquainted through Georgiana and in another week they planned to attend the theatre together. He had donated a set of lovely encyclopedias. So one should be civil. Nothing foolish in it. In fact, it would be foolish *not* to acknowledge that she'd seen him.

Oh, sometimes she wished she could stop her mind from thinking...

It was too late to change course, in any case, for he had seen her now and his pace slowed.

"Miss Chance." He stopped and raised a hand, presumably to sweep off his hat, until he remembered he did not wear one that morning. Perhaps that same absent-mindedness that sometimes affected his father had taken hold of him too, she mused. "Are you on your way to Allerton Square already? I can escort you."

Trying very hard not to look at his broad neck, exposed to the cold air so casually, Emma explained that she had a task to fulfill at the haberdasher and when he heard this, rather than take his leave and walk on to his own business, he turned to join her. She had no choice but to introduce the two students by her side, who finally ceased arguing over fabric and gazed admiringly up at the Captain in his rather delectable disarray.

Lady Bramley would say he should cut his hair, but Emma saw absolutely nothing amiss with those rambling dark curls.

He put his hand up to them again now, as if her expression had suggested something amiss.

Emma hastily remembered her manners. "This is Miss Fortescue-Rumputney and Miss Patchett, two pupils of the Particular Establishment for the Advantage of Respectable Ladies."

With a quick bow he greeted the girls. "Delighted to make the acquaintance."

"Oh, Captain," exclaimed Abigail Patchett, who was not known for her restraint. "Whatever happened to your face? It's black and blue!"

Before Emma could intervene, he answered, "It is the fashion you know, to have one's face colored thus. Like a peacock showing its tail, the brighter the color the finer the specimen." He grinned mischievously. Of course, he was perfectly at his ease. The art of flirting came naturally to him.

The girls exchanged glances and giggles that bubbled along like silky ribbons in a warm breeze. Emma had never been a giggler. She tried once and her friends looked at her so oddly that she never dared again.

"Captain Hathaway was involved in an argument," she said firmly, "but perhaps the less said about it the better."

He added with unlikely solemnity, "Indeed! Let it serve as a cautionary warning to young girls, to stay away from sailors and port-side taverns. A fact of which the eminently sensible Miss Chance is already aware."

The four of them walked along the pavement and Emma, after struggling a moment for something to say, thanked him for the donation of encyclopedias.

"I remember how you like your facts, Miss Chance," he replied smugly. "I thought you would make good use of them."

"I'm sure the students will. It was a generous thought. Did your younger brothers not want them?"

He laughed. "You know how Nicholas is. He's only interested in books about the navy. The other two think they are men already and can be told nothing. Besides, they want everything new. Young men today, tsk tsk."

"But you might have a son of your own one day."

"Good god!" His eyes glistened down at her in an odd way—as if he shared with her a naughty secret. "There's a thought to make a man feel old." He held open the door of the haberdashery while the ladies passed through. The other customers inside looked over at once to admire the tall fellow and take note of who he was with. As Emma knew they would, every eye looked surprised to see a rather nondescript, dowdy woman in his handsome, distinctive company.

It felt very strange to have him there by her side. To be the focus of so much curiosity from other women, who barely even noticed her on other occasions. She had expected him to take his leave once they had entered the premises, for there could be little in the place to keep his interest. But he stayed with her and began to whistle, much to the clear astonishment of other customers. His wounded face did nothing to detract from his good looks and only drew more salacious curiosity. When Emma looked at him today she barely noticed the awful bruise at first, too distracted by his beautiful, darkly exotic eyes and sensual lips, but now she realized what his sister meant by waiting until his face healed before they might go out in public.

"Did you have nothing else to do this morning,

Captain?" she murmured.

He looked surprised. "I was on my way to see you." Although he did not add an "of course" she sensed there was one. She simply could not imagine why.

"You were?" she asked somberly. Had she forgotten something that she was supposed to know? Immediately she imagined the worst. "Did your father send you with a message? Are the boys ill? Is something amiss at home? Is it Georgiana?"

"No to all the above." He scratched his chin. "You know, Miss Chance, why I was on my way to see you. You keep me in suspense deliberately."

How extraordinary. It must be one of his merry japes, she thought. So she decided to be brave and answer in a similar tone. "Was nobody else you knew at home this morning? Surely all the entertainments of London are not closed today."

Now his brow wrinkled and he laughed again. "That must be it. I was bored. I was out for a thoughtful stroll and before I knew it, my boots were walking in your direction. There can be no other explanation, can there?" He stole a quick glance at the two young girls walking with them, and then looked at her again, his eyes gleaming with a meaningful sort of mischief. It was as if he thought she was in on the joke with him, but Emma was utterly confused.

"A...a thoughtful stroll?"

"Yes." He ran a hand over his unshaven cheek. "Believe as you will or won't, but I'm a very meditative chap. I suppose my sister has told you the opposite and that I never think."

"Actually your sister is very proud and has always spoken of you in such glowing terms that there is an air of the implausible to her stories. But she never mentioned you as being a man who enjoys contemplative strolls."

"I daresay there is a vast deal about me that Georgiana doesn't know. As you once pointed out to me, Miss Chance, the book I keep open is only for show. The real man is a private fellow. Even my family do not know everything there is to know about me."

Then why was he telling *her* this suddenly? He must truly be bored.

As far as she remembered it, Captain Hathaway had not liked it before when she suggested he hid his true self behind a false exterior. Now he admitted it and looked very pleased with himself for doing so. Almost as if he expected her to pin a medal on his greatcoat.

Clearly she was missing something.

Lady Bramley was right and she knew *nothing* about men like him. There was no entry in the encyclopedia marked "Capt. Guy Hathaway of His Majesty's Navy." She only wished there were and then she could pore over it at her leisure. Every evening alone in her parlor. In secret.

At a loss to understand his sudden companionship, Emma decided to concentrate on her sensible worsted wool. Perhaps he would go away and then people would stop looking at them.

The Bounce in the Captain's Boots

Chapter Fifteen

Guy followed her around the shop, hands behind his back, nodding politely to a few folk who glanced their way as they passed.

"What is it we seek, Miss Chance?" he asked, having watched her examine a number of increasingly ugly fabrics.

"*I* am seeking worsted for a new winter cloak, Captain. Please do not feel that you are obliged to follow me about." She stopped and looked over her shoulder, her small face grim. "I am quite capable of looking after myself and do not require an escort at the haberdasher's. Or has your sister told *you* that I am so weak and sickly that I can't be trusted out alone? That I need a sentinel?"

He caught just a slight twinkle of wry amusement before she turned away again to run her hand over a sample of rough grey worsted wool. That brief hint of humor was enough to quicken his pulse. Odd how she need do so very little with her lips and it made him feel honored. He had the sneaking suspicion that Miss Emma Chance, despite her downtrodden demeanor, was quite capable of getting her own way whenever she wanted it. If she wanted it badly enough.

The only question remained: was she aware of that power?

He probably ought to hope that she was not, he mused. It could be dangerous for him if she was.

Beside her the two younger girls waited impatiently, occasionally rolling their eyes at each other, clearly having no interest in dull, practical worsted and anxious to explore the other prettier offerings.

"Aha!" He pointed across the shop, "I see some exquisite apricot satin and gold gauze over there. And lace. Machine made, but affordable. I often think there is nothing more suited to a youthful complexion in the evening than apricot satin with a hint of gold laid over it, especially this time of year when the candles are lit earlier."

At once they applied to Miss Chance for her approval and then hurried off to inspect these treasures.

She looked at him. "Another surprise, Captain. You not only indulge in contemplative strolls, but you are also an expert in fabrics?"

Ah, she was becoming confident with her sense of humor. That too was new.

"Not in fabrics." He lowered his voice to a whisper. "I am an expert in distracting young ladies."

"Not a very challenging sport." She smiled. "I'm afraid they seldom concentrate on anything for very long."

He stared at her lips until she looked uneasy and turned back to the wares displayed on the counter.

"I wanted to give you my opinion on the worsted, Miss Chance. And I wanted to do so out of your students' hearing."

"Your opinion?"

"It is grim and unflattering." He took it away from her and tossed it along the counter out of her reach. "Time to stop hiding. What we need is crimson velvet."

"*We?*" She looked as if he'd suggested silk rosettes on her garters. "Captain, I—"

"Velvet, if you please," he said loudly to the shopkeeper. "Your finest branched velvet in crimson. None of this riff-raff. And rose silk in a similar quantity for the lining."

As the shopkeeper hurried to comply, looking happy at the prospect of a more handsome sale than previously expected, she stared at Guy, her face growing paler by the moment.

"What is it, Miss Chance?" he drawled. "You're breathing in that terrible way. Has Lady Bramley not warned you about it?"

"*Rose silk?*" She finally exhaled the words, puffing them out under duress. "For a cloak lining? And crimson velvet? I would be a laughing stock. What practical use would such materials be to me? I'm a governess not a....a..."

"Standard variety hussy?" he inquired politely.

"Precisely, Captain. I know you enjoy your jests, like your sister, but this is quite enough. Kindly pass me that worsted."

"It's horrendous."

"It is perfectly appropriate and more than adequate for a serviceable winter cloak."

"I cannot allow it. Put your hand down. You're not having it."

"*You* cannot allow it?" she exclaimed.

He stared down at her, bemused. "I would rather have my eyes poked out on toasting forks than see you in it."

"Well, goodness gracious, you don't have to look at me. Nobody does."

He laughed, casually leaning one arm on the counter. "That would be a bit of a rum do. Not looking at the woman I mean to marry. Probably most eccentric and unwise, don't you think?"

Whatever she had been about to say next was cut off as her teeth came down on her tongue and caused a dreadful, unbecoming wince of her features.

"Ah, here comes the velvet. Yes, that's much better. Puts a bit of color into your cheeks. Although when you're sucking them inward like that it looks as if you just swallowed something unpleasant in the grog." Guy took her arm and led her away from the shopkeeper to hold the material up to her face in the light of the window.

As soon as they had gone far enough to be out of anybody's hearing, she pulled away. "Have you parted from your proper mind?" She stopped, gathered a breath and whispered, "I'm sure you find this a most amusing ruse, Captain, and I am familiar with your sister's sense of humor also, but I would rather not be the subject of your mockery. Kindly allow me to proceed with my shopping unhindered." It had not escaped his notice that she kept looking at his throat, as if she suddenly dare not raise her gaze higher.

"Mockery? How have I mocked you? It is an awkward business, I confess, but since you have no parent to ask, I do not know how else to go about it. I thought the encyclopedias would be a beginning. It seemed respectable, sensible and a most appropriate gift considering your love of facts. I knew the poor reception that would greet hothouse flowers."

"If you would be so kind, Captain, as to cease talking. I have the most abominable headache suddenly, and your words appear quite devoid of sense. I'm sure it must be a confusion on my own part." She looked around nervously, her hands reaching to take the velvet from him.

"Well, who am I supposed to ask then, if not you directly? You have nobody, do you? No family. Are you not a foundling?"

She closed her eyes briefly and clawed the bolt of material to her bosom.

"I do not know how else to put it," he added in a whisper. "I did not think you would appreciate me asking my sister to speak to you on my behalf. You're too straightforward for that nonsense, and I do not like entrusting my words to others. Especially not to Georgiana, a young woman with great capacity for chaos. My leave is not long and by the new year I shall be back at sea. I must make the most of every day if I am to pay court to you. I know this may seem a trifle hasty, Miss Chance, but when an idea comes upon me—"

"I think it is something heavy that has come upon you, Captain," she replied gravely. "Specifically upon your head and with some force. Perhaps you were more wounded in that brawl than you thought. You ought to see a physician."

Impatient he tried to take her hand, but she kept both gripped to the velvet, looking around the shop in alarm. "You told me before, madam, that I must apprise you of my intentions when I mean to be charming. Apparently you were afraid you might miss it, or had little faith in my abilities. So now you are duly warned. Prepare to be charmed."

She merely stared at him, aghast.

"A man must marry eventually, if he can," Guy continued, "and I know you need somebody to look after you, Miss Chance. Somebody to put a roof over your head and save you from a lonely life of hardship and toil. You have nothing of your own, Lady Bramley told me. I thought you would leap at the opportunity of rescue."

Her lips parted and then clamped shut again.

"I can give you a comfortable home— when I find one that suits— and I can provide you with a reasonable allocation of pin money. My career has been profitable, and I have made some attempt to save coin." He paused and smiled. "Especially since a certain fog-dwelling creature once advised me to restrain my spending."

Her eyes were very large and very round. A black

cat startled by sudden light in a previously dark room could not have looked more alarmed, more poised to scratch. He was certain the tips of her ears must be red, but at present they were hidden by her bonnet.

"You can see the match would have its advantages for you," he added. "Why would you not think it a very sound idea, Miss Chance? You're practical."

"Practical?" she murmured.

"I am the brother of your good friend, I can protect you, and I shan't bother you much for I will often be away at sea. You did not strike me as the fanciful and romantic sort, but clever enough to know when an arrangement would be to your advantage and convenient."

"Convenient?" He couldn't quite make out her expression.

"Surely you do not want to be a governess all your life." He paused. "You look offended."

"I do not know what I am, Captain, except exceedingly confused. I feel as if I have opened a novel and found the end of the story printed at the beginning. The pages are littered with corpses and people dangling from cliffs, and I don't know any of the characters."

"Forgive me. I thought you would understand when you received the encyclopedias. I thought you clever enough to understand my meaning and realize my intention."

"We assumed the books were a donation for the

school. Why would we think otherwise?"

"Did the messenger lad who brought the books not give you my note?"

She shook her head, lips tight.

"Damn the lad! My note asked if I might call upon you this morning."

Her expression now changed from shocked to scandalized and back to puzzled. And lost. Utterly lost. She was really rather sweet when she looked thus, he mused warmly. Still small and scrabbly, but engaging.

"I gave you an hour or so to consider all the advantages before I made my way to see you. And then, there you were, in the street, heading toward me. You seemed in a fair mood, so I thought the forecast must be favorable for me. I supposed you were on your way to throw yourself into my arms." With a sniff, chin up, he added, "I cannot see any reason why you would not." Then he grinned at her appalled face. When one headed into the storm, he'd always thought it best to push onward with brazen audacity and laugh at the thunder, to scare it back from whence it came.

For a long moment she said nothing, but clutched that velvet as if it were a raft bobbing on the ocean, the only thing left from a violent shipwreck.

"What's wrong, Miss Chance, you are being very quiet. More so than ever."

She swallowed visibly and then looked up from under her lashes. "I am aware of the fact that I often say the wrong thing at the wrong time. So I am trying to compose my sentences and find the right thing to say, without causing offence. I don't want to call you a grub worm again, for instance. You do realize, I hope, that I was making a point about your face and why it didn't upset me or repulse me as much as it might have. Oh, you see, it always comes out wrong and I—"

"I see you are plagued by demons of doubt. Tell me what they are and I shall vanquish them all, one by one."

After another steadying breath, she said solemnly, "I hardly know where to begin."

The buoyancy he'd previously felt diminished somewhat.

"Captain Hathaway, I ...have never had plans to be anything other than a governess. It is everything I have worked for. All that I ever expected."

"Plans can be changed. I change mine all the time."

"Yes. And I fear you will change this one too before long. Then where shall I be?"

"No indeed. My mind is made up."

She groaned under her breath. "Why are you doing this to me?"

"I am in need of a wife to settle me, Miss Chance. It is time I found a *good* woman for once. In fact, my ship's surgeon has prescribed that very thing to heave me out of this bleak mood into which he finds me sunk of late."

"A good woman?" She gave a pained little smile and squinted cautiously up from under her lashes. "And you think that is me? Oh, dear."

"I know it is."

"We shared one dance and some hours in a carriage two years ago. I think I might safely say you know very little about me. I have my share of sins, the same as anybody. You would be surprised, I'm sure, and alarmed by the wicked thoughts I have at times."

"Interesting." He grinned. "I shall enjoy discovering all these sinful thoughts of yours."

"You should not say such things," she murmured, her eyes downcast.

"Would you put that velvet aside and let me take your hand?"

"Good lord, no! We are in a public place," she whispered urgently. "I fear we have already caused a shocking scene by talking together like this. So...intimately."

When she took a step to move around him, he stood in her way, determined. "Miss Chance, do you believe in ghosts?"

She sighed wearily, eyeing him as if he were an annoying child dragging on her skirt in the street. "Ghosts?"

"Spiritual intervention?"

"I have made no study on the subject. Why?"

"Because I believe I received a message from beyond the grave." Taking the pink pearl from his pocket, he showed it to her, opening his gloved fingers slowly. "Some months ago, this fell out of my pocket and as I ducked to retrieve it, a carelessly tossed knife's blade narrowly missed my skull. Now, if that is not a message from the beyond, I do not know what is. If not for this, that knife would have been the end of me, and you would never have laid eyes on this splendid form ever again. What do you say to that then, Miss Clever Puss?"

She looked at the pearl and then her gaze lifted to his face again. This time her eyes were gently amused. "Captain, I am sorry to disappoint you, but *I* left that pearl in your waistcoat pocket. So it was a matter of terrestrial intervention, I'm afraid."

"*You* did?" He closed his fingers around the pearl again, before she could take it from him. "Why?"

She blinked, took one of those heaving breaths and rubbed her fingertips against the crimson velvet in her arms. "Thinking you might see it and remember me, I suppose." Then she added hastily, "But my point is that there is a logical explanation for most things we might be tempted to claim as—"

"Miss Chance, you saved my life." He felt another grin impulsively taking over his face as he slipped the pearl away again in his pocket. "I am now obliged to look after you for the rest of yours. It is a fact more certain than ever now."

"*Obliged?*" Her gaze flashed up at his face. "This marriage you seek would be practical, convenient and now an obligation too?"

"I think it's a law somewhere. A statute. One

must marry a woman who saves one's life." He whistled briefly and then added, "Must be one of those facts you missed."

"So it would seem," she replied drily.

"Miss Chance, I do not like to raise this subject of your poverty, but you force me. Think of your plight if you do not marry. The world is littered with sad spinsters who gave up their one chance out of fear or pride and now sit in dimly lit corners, stabbing themselves with needles because they cannot afford the candles to see properly when they sew."

"Pray, do not concern yourself about my candles. After twenty-one years with very little, I am exceedingly frugal and well-practiced in the art of economy. I'm sure I'll never use more than I can afford."

"Another reason to accept me, madam, for I am a hopeless spendthrift— as you know. I need your prudence to keep me from ruin."

Her eyes shone up at him with knowing amusement. "I thought you just said your career has been profitable and that you have saved enough now for your own home?"

He frowned. "Look benevolently upon me to save my health, then, for who knows what might befall my wretched carcass if I don't find a good wife now? Will you send me back to sea with no reason to return again? It is *you*, madam, who ought to pity *me*."

She looked at him steadily for a moment and then said, "Captain, you have a very full and merry life. I've seen your letters. A good wife— as you call her— would surely only get in your way."

"That was my past. When a man confronts his end, as I did when that blade parted this fine head of hair, he begins to see what is important in life. What he has overlooked in his haste."

"Are you sure that knife missed your brain entirely? It didn't skim the bone and break a little off into the soft part?"

"I have no soft parts. But that is a conversation for another time." He winked. "When we are alone and have advanced in our courtship."

"I—" Suddenly, looking through the bow window behind him, her expression changed yet again. "As delightfully discombobulated as this conversation has been, Captain, I suggest you make yourself scarce."

"Scarce? Why?" He'd never made himself scarce in his life.

At that moment the bell above the door jangled behind him and a loud voice called out, "Don't lag, Filkins, and for pity's sake look where you're walking today in the street. We don't want a repeat of that episode when something very unpleasant was brought in onto my carpet and you tried to blame my darling little Horatio!"

He knew that voice, of course. It was unmistakable above the general rumble of voices in the shop.

Miss Chance was looking up at him, one eyebrow

arched in amusement. "You still have time to get away. You have your back to her. She hasn't seen either of us yet."

"Why on earth should I flee like a cowardly thief in the night, Miss Chance? You do not think very highly of me, it seems, madam!"

"Do be rational, sir. Any moment now she'll see me and then she'll want to know who I am talking to. Then I fear you will need genuine supernatural intervention to save you from her inquisition." With a degree of drollery, she added, "You do remember *her*, I'm sure."

Guy squared his shoulders and put on his most nonchalant face. "Good. Her arrival is timely. I suppose she is the nearest thing you have to a guardian, so perhaps I ought to get her permission in any case."

Now the second eyebrow joined the first, making the top curves of two question marks. "Really? You *are* brave, Captain."

"Victory! I have impressed you at last." He would have turned then to face the lady, but Miss Chance caught his arm and prevented it. They both looked down at her small gloved fingers on his coat sleeve.

"Now is not the time, Captain. What do you suppose she will think of you so casually attired, no hat, and with a face like a rotten potato?"

"Madam, you have a talent for insult."

"And you have one for mischief."

Behind him the voice boomed out again, "*Filkins!*

You're stepping on my gown, man! Get out of the way. In fact, stand outside and wait for me. You're cluttering up the place in here. The premises are not overly large. Nonsense! It's only a little rain and you can stand under the awning. It will keep you dry when the wind doesn't blow it about. Serve you right, for forgetting to bring my darling Horatio's little ball to the park with us."

Every other conversation in the shop had faded to a distracted murmur as folk slyly observed the new arrival, but only in the very British way of pretending not to notice. A little dog growled. Guy heard the rustling of curtseying skirts.

"Now, now, darling Horatio," Lady Bramley cooed in a most unlikely manner. "We don't want to bite anybody today. Unless we must."

He looked down at Miss Chance.

Her expression genuinely concerned now, she mouthed the word, "Go."

"So you will consider it?" he whispered. "Tell me I am not making an utter imbecile of myself and I'll believe you. At this moment I need the reassurance."

"*You* need reassurance?"

"Yes," he said simply. "Is that so hard to believe?"

There was a brief pause while she looked down at his boots, then back to the base of his throat. "And then you'll go?"

"Yes. I shall be..." he winced, "gentlemanly patient as long as I can."

"Very well." She put her head down, adding in a whisper little more than a sigh of anxious breath, "You are not an utter imbecile, Captain." A smile, fretful and wispy, crossed her lips and then was gone as she examined the velvet in her arms. "This *practical* arrangement you offer me, and all those reasons why you offer it, will receive due consideration."

He wanted to lift her face in his hands and kiss her. There and then.

But, of course, he could not.

Miss Chance was right; now was not the time or place to face Lady Bramley.Caution and discretion— two things he'd never granted much credence before— must rule the day if this fledgling romance was to stand a chance. Without a doubt, everybody who knew her would advise her against it, and nobody who knew Guy would take his intentions seriously.

"Say nothing to my sister, I beg you," he whispered. "She would be intolerable, if she heard."

His intended fiancée looked askance. "I certainly have no desire for anybody to know."

He was not sure what to make of that comment, but Lady Bramley's steps advanced and there was no further time for discussion. Ducking around a mannequin, Guy slipped out through the side door of the shop.

As he'd said to Miss Chance, he did not really know how to go about this and had leapt in with both boots. Other women were easier to seduce. But how did one court a woman so different to any he'd known before? A woman who would not fall for what his sister termed his "limited charms"?

With knowledge, he'd thought. Thus the encyclopedias.

She had admitted that she put that pearl in his pocket so that he would remember their first meeting. That, he supposed, was a good sign. Promising. Enough to make him forge ahead.

Well, he'd try his damnedest to allay her fears and prove to the doubting kitten that he could and would take care of her. That this was not another reckless fancy. There remained the distressing matter of her intelligence and that ability to see through his smile, but whatever Lady Bramley thought, Guy Hathaway was willing to face a woman who challenged his mind.

Emma Chance, when she dared look at him at all, made him feel as if he was the only man in the room. The only man in the world. And for her, that was what he wanted to be.

It was shocking how certain he was of her place in his life. It had been coming on slowly over the past few years while they were apart, but seeing her again had made it clear and simple and definite. At least, in *his* mind.

Chapter Sixteen

"Some of us might be daring enough to ride down a banister, but most prefer the steadier progress of steps to arrive at our destination with a little bit of dignity."

Emma Chance had said that once to her friends, when they were caught in some misdemeanor. Today the words came back to her quite suddenly and made her smile. Apparently, Captain Hathaway, like his sister, preferred unconventional methods and paths to arrive at his destination. In the process, he too knocked everybody off their feet.

Could he be genuine in this pursuit? What she knew of him told her that although he liked to tease, he would not intentionally be cruel. But that was all she had time to think before Lady Bramley bore down upon her.

Her would-be suitor had escaped by the shadow of a curly hair's breadth.

"Miss Chance, there you are! And in that thin pelisse on such a cold, damp day! I just called in at the school and Mrs. Bishop informed me of where I might find—" The lady's eyes alighted on the bolt of cloth in Emma's arms. "*Scarlet velvet?* What could be the meaning of this, young lady?"

"Actually, your ladyship..." she faltered, "I believe it is crimson."

"Whatever the official name, it is hardly a color I would expect to find *you* admiring. Unless, of course, you have suddenly decided to take up a life upon the stage, Miss Chance."

What Emma really wanted at that moment was to be alone and get her thoughts in proper order, but there was no possibility of that just yet. Lady Bramley was before her, dog under one arm, and lorgnette raised in her other hand. The lady would know at once if there was anything amiss. Not only did that eye-glass magnify her vision, it seemed to have far-seeing abilities that reached through muslin and bone.

"I thought we had discussed a sturdy, warm, hard-wearing worsted wool for your winter cloak, Miss Chance." The little dog under her arm let out a sinister growl. As if it knew she'd been up to no good.

"Yes, of course, Lady Bramley. I merely wanted to look at this color in the light of the window."

"Well, now you have looked at it, you had better give it back, before it is marked and must be paid for. Whatever next? Rings on your fingers and bells on your toes? A tambourine to dance among the gypsies?"

Clearly the lady was in a good mood and eager to make quips. She would not have been so, had she noticed Captain Hathaway in deep conversation with her protégée. After the ball at Woodbyne two years ago, Emma had received a long lecture about the horrors of losing one's heart— and more— to an unpredictable, too-handsome, too sociable, irresponsible young man. The untamable, forbidden dragon prince.

Now, under Lady Bramley's critical eye, Emma

took the bolt of objectionable crimson back to the counter and resumed her intended purchase of the grey worsted. Although she could never have imagined herself in such a bright color as that velvet, she did feel rather deflated as she watched it being returned to the shelf, out of her reach.

She shot a sideways glance at Lady Bramley and wondered what would happen if she suddenly told her, *A man has just announced that he plans to pay court to me, madam. And you'll never guess who.*

Instead she said, "You were looking for me this morning, your ladyship?" She kept her face calm somehow, while her insides spun in mad circles.

"Indeed. Now, my dear, you must tell me." She put her hand on Emma's arm. "Has there been no word from Miss Goodheart? I confess I become most concerned about her extended absence. When she left London, I was led to assume she would be gone for no more than a week or so. I shall have to find somebody to manage the shop if she is gone much longer, for I shall be spending the month of December in the country."

"I have had no letter, madam, and neither has Georgiana. We too are worried. Perhaps her father is ill and needs her. He might want her to stay for the Yuletide season."

Lady Bramley sniffed, as if no man's needs could be greater than hers. "Then I shall write at once to her father and ascertain the matter."

"I think that would be an excellent idea, your

ladyship."

"Now, to the matter of my trip into the country." She paused to look over some samples offered by the shopkeeper and then shook her head briskly. "I have been invited to spend Christmas with my eldest son, Sir Mandrake, at the estate in Shropshire."

"How lovely, your ladyship."

"And I have decided to take you with me as my companion, Miss Chance. There is no need for you to be anxious, my dear, for it will be an intimate company over the season, nothing grand." Before Emma could say anything, the lady continued, "I shall speak to your employer in Allerton Square and let him know that they must do without you for a month. I'm quite certain your pupils will manage."

"But...what about the school, your ladyship?"

"All students will be going home for Christmas this year, which is fortunate, and the Bishops will be in residence should anything arise."

But Emma had looked forward to a peaceful celebration, with a beautiful goose and plum pudding cooked by Mrs. Bishop, card games by candlelight in her sitting room, holly on her mantle and the scent of clove-spiked oranges. She had even politely declined an invitation to Woodbyne, because she thought it would be pleasant for the Thrashers to have their own company without her in the way— she had too often been a guest there as it was and feared becoming too dependent on her friends for company, when they surely had far more entertaining prospects.

In truth, she rather liked the rebellious idea of a few days when she might do as *she* pleased for once, not have to rise and dress for breakfast at a certain hour, or worry about housemaids giggling over the poor quality of her patched petticoats when unpacking her trunk. In her little sitting room she did not have to be at all sociable if she did not feel inclined, and guests came at *her* bidding.

Now, it seemed, that quiet pleasure was to be taken away from her. The fact that Emma might have her own plans did not occur to the lady.

"Do not look glum, my dear! Yes, there is much to organize, but plenty of time to do so and you have me to help, of course. In Shropshire you will not need much in the way of new wardrobe, although perhaps two fresh day gowns and one for evening. Something simple, whatever time allows. Perhaps an old dress can be made over with new trimming. That will be the quickest solution. We will not leave until the beginning of December, so you have a full fortnight yet, and nobody will expect much of you in Shropshire. You do not ride, do you, my dear? No. In that case, there will be no need for anything too smart." Looking over the fabrics and fans on display, Lady Bramley's instruction drifted onward about the requirements of a month in the country at Christmas, while Emma's thoughts returned to Captain Hathaway's extraordinary request.

"In the meantime, I expect a houseguest here for a few days," her ladyship was saying. "But he should not inconvenience me for long. His mama is an old friend of the family and she wrote to ask me if I might take him in while he's in London. It seems he needs guarding to some degree— like most young men— and his mama thinks me the best person to take charge of him. But once he has gone again, the house will be shut up and we shall travel to Shropshire."

The two girls who had walked to the haberdashery with Emma now returned to the counter and wanted to know where the captain had gone.

Lady Bramley paused her critical examination of silk ribbons to raise that lorgnette again in Emma's direction. "Captain? What Captain?"

"Lady Thrasher's brother, Captain Hathaway," Emma explained. "We encountered him in the street."

"Hathaway? That saucy scoundrel? Back in London, is he? I wonder why I did not know this."

"I believe it is an unplanned visit, madam. He only arrived yesterday afternoon."

The lady's perusal swept her swiftly. "Of course, a spur-of-the-moment idea, no doubt. These young men are unreliable at best. One can certainly never set a clock by their antics. But it is a pity he is gone again. I should like to see how he has turned out."

"I did not find him much changed." But then she had never seen anything wrong with him. Unlike Lady Bramley, who seemed to think that although he had a certain charm, he was a fellow to be kept at prodding length with her parasol.

"The Captain had a black eye," Abigail Patchett exclaimed. "It was most gruesome."

"*A black eye?*" Her ladyship blanched, and the little dog nestled under her arm gave a gruff bark. "It is as well I did not encounter him then." She glowered at Emma. "And what did he have to say to *you*?"

Oh. Where to begin? "Very little. He was in haste to go about his business."

"Hmph." The lady shook her head briskly and then resumed her discussion with the shop-keeper. Short of time herself and with much, apparently, to be done, she had no further words to spare for naval captains of a mischievous bent and wicked sense of humor.

With her own purchase packaged and tucked under her arm, Emma was eager to be alone with her thoughts and try to make sense of them. But there was no opportunity at present. She could not afford for Lady Bramley to see her distracted or there would be more searching questions asked and she did not feel up to answering them.

Chapter Seventeen

Emma stepped down from the Hackney carriage and looked about with some trepidation. Twenty years ago, Lisson Grove had been a rural area, popular with painters and composers who enjoyed being close to London's entertainments and yet far enough away not to have them intrude on the open fields of countryside. But the arrival of the Regent's Canal had caused an increase in the less well-heeled, more transient population, bringing with it prostitution, drunkenness and crime. Today she found the air in this part of Lisson Grove, before it led into the Edgeware Road, thick with wet and rotting things, sewage and coal dust.

A tribe of shoeless children with sooty faces and ragged clothes tumbled about in abundance. Some of them, seeing this respectably dressed young woman climbing out of a Hackney carriage, ran up to beg for food and pennies. She had none of the former with her and only a few of the latter, but a handful were dispensed to help find her way to Woolpack Buildings, a grimy, greasy pile of bricks, boarded windows and rusted iron work on the corner of Millers Square by the canal. Laundry hung from ropes strung from one window to another, dripping onto the flagstones, gaining a new layer of dirt from the same air that slowly dried it. The adults she passed watched her warily, their eyes staring out of dirty faces; their clothing stank of gin and cheap beer.

This, of course, was the sort of place in which she might live now, if fate had not taken another turn.

"Will you wait for me, please?" she asked the driver.

Fortunately she knew him, for she often rode in his carriage to and from the Hathaway's house. "Of course I will." But he looked concerned. "A young lady like you shouldn't be here alone, Miss."

"It's quite alright. I'm visiting a...an elderly acquaintance. A sickly widow in need of company. I shan't be long. It's good of you to wait."

Briefly she regretted coming alone. But then she squared her shoulders and quickened her step. The demon known as Julie Lightbody must be faced and put behind her if Emma truly meant to move forward with her life. And she wanted nobody else involved or contaminated by that woman's foul aura. She had been exposed to it before and was now immune, so she would manage this business on her own. It was, she felt, part of her discovery and emboldening, for she could not rely on her friends for everything.

So Emma passed through a brick arch into the square, crossed the dimpled, wet paving stones, skirted puddles of mud, ducked beneath the flags of laundry, and found steps to the second floor of the building. There she walked along the covered passage until she came to the door marked with a sloppily chalked "22".

Before she could knock, the door swung open and there stood the old headmistress.

"I knew it was you. Recognized that wretched, timid footstep." The woman paused, her mean gaze scratching up and down, from Emma's walking boots to her bonnet and back again. "Think you're special now, don't you? All grown up and under that meddling old cow, Bramley's thumb. Looks as if she's fattening you up for slaughter."

"Mrs. Lightbody, I came here today only to mark a final full stop on the story that was my past. I find it necessary for my peace of mind. After today I hope you and I need never revisit that history."

"Do you indeed? Well, you haven't even heard yet what I have to tell you. Best come in." She stood aside, holding the door open.

Emma stepped over the threshold into a narrow hallway with peeling walls, and then into a small, dank room with rough curtains at the window, a stained, moth-holed cloth upon the table, and an oil lamp with a glass chimney that needed cleaning. There, against the wall, rested that old portrait which once hung in the headmistress' parlor back at the school. It had not been hung here, but merely leaned in wait. A monster lurking, its face half in shadow.

She hesitantly raised a hand to her throat, recalling all the times this woman, in one of her rages, had tried to throttle the breath out of her. But it was over now. Over. Emma was no longer a timid child, and she was stronger than she looked.

"This is only temporary lodgings, Chance, so you needn't turn your nose up." The woman followed her into the room. "I just came back to London, but I shall soon find a better place."

On the mantle, above the cold hearth, there was a man's pipe. So Lightbody did not live here alone. No doubt she had found somebody to use for as long as she might get away with it. Beside the fireplace there was a hook in the wall and a sooty, iron poker hanging from it.

Emma stretched her fingers, thinking how easy it would be to grab that poker and swing it. The woman who had made her youth a misery would never expect it, never see it coming. Not from meek, frail Emma Chance.

She turned away from the temptation. "You asked for me to come here, madam. I believe there is something you had to tell me?"

It would not be an apology; of that she was sure.

Mrs. Lightbody went to a simple wooden box on the table and opened it. The contents were a muddle of shining, winking trinkets— bracelets, rings, beads and combs, the sort of items a magpie or jackdaw might steal for their nest. The trophies of a thief, thought Emma. But among these pretty things there sat a bundle of aged letters. Mrs. Lightbody took them out and tossed them down on that frayed cloth. "These are from your father. I've kept them for years. He doesn't know I have them."

Emma stared at the yellowed paper. She felt ill, dizzy.

"Oh, they're not written to me," the woman

clarified. "He sent them to your mother, back when love was in the air. Or so that silly girl thought."

"You...have letters that belonged to my mother?"

"They came into my hands when she died. Like you did." Lightbody gave a cold laugh and took a half-empty bottle of gin from the mantle. "Looks like you need a sip, Chance."

"No. Thank you. I'd rather not."

"Suit yourself." The woman poured a generous amount into a half-filled, chipped teacup. "Go on. Don't you want to look at them, then? They won't bite."

But Emma couldn't move. She looked at the old headmistress, who now sat at her crooked table and drank her chin. Surrounded by the gaudy knick-knacks that once crowded her parlor at the school, Julia Lightbody looked smaller now, older and wearier. Even meaner, perhaps, but in a gaunt, hungry way she'd never been before, when she could still take for granted her cozy nest at the center of a vile web. Since she was dismissed from her post at the school, her descent, it seemed, was rapid. Her clothes were faded, tattered and dirty at the edges, less filled-out than they used to be. Her wig was slightly off kilter and looked in need of a rinse. Despite all this, it was impossible to feel pity for that woman.

Disgust, however, came in great waves.

"How?" Emma managed on a tight breath.

"How what, girl? Spit it out."

"How did these personal letters belonging to my

mother come into *your* hands?"

"She and I once worked in the same house, years ago. Didn't Miss Sharp-Mouth tell you that by now?" She coughed, and it rattled in her chest. "When your mother died the rest of us girls in the house went through her things to see what we could make use of. Some took the feathers and the jewelry. But I knew what was more valuable in her case. Your mother didn't have much taste for expensive jewelry. She had something else worth taking." She tapped the side of her brow with one finger. "I knew what would stand me in good stead later. So I took these letters. He came looking for them, of course. I told him I'd burned them, so he owed me a favor." She chuckled croakily. "But what he saw me burning was something else. Some other man's letters."

"What do you mean...you worked in the same house?" Emma was confused, wondering what Georgiana knew and why she had not told her.

"House of Pleasures in Bethnal Green. *A bawdy house*." The woman let out a harsh caw of spiteful laughter. "That's where you were born, Chance. Your mother ended up there when her family disowned her and that's where *he*," she jerked her head at the letters, "became acquainted with her. He never wanted her to have you. Tried to make her be rid of you, but she would have none of it. Stupid. And look where that got her in the end. Lost everything just to give you life."

Emma finally stretched her fingers and reached

for one of the letters. But they froze, curled up again, and withdrew. She couldn't look. She thought of her conversation with Georgiana yesterday and realized now, as the moment of discovery beckoned with a sly finger, that she did *not* want to know who her father was. Just as meeting him would do no good, knowing his name would be just as useless and might even be harmful to her.

Had her friend attempted the subject because she knew his name and felt the burden of that secret pressing upon her?

"Why do you show these to me now, madam?" she murmured. "After all these years."

"I need money, don't I? Thanks to you and your wretched friends I'm out of a post."

"It was not *our* doing, madam," Emma replied steadily. "You lost your post due to your own behavior."

"Oh, your Miss Sharp-Mouth knows what she did and what she stole from me. You ask her how she schemed against me."

"Do you refer to Georgiana, Lady Thrasher?"

"Ha!" The woman snorted, grabbed her wig with one hand and made an effort to tug it straight, which only resulted in the tightly-curled monstrosity leaning left instead of right. Wigs had been out of fashion as long as beauty spots, but Julia Lightbody still sported both, lost in a past era— one in which she was young and, according to her portrait, had possessed some gaudy beauty. "Ah yes. Lady Thrasher. That's what she calls herself now, isn't it? Lady indeed. I daresay she schemed herself into the commander's bed. Some say he's not all there in the head and here's your proof for you. For all her airs and graces, she's nothing more than a jumped-up newspaperman's daughter who married well."

Emma said nothing, her revulsion mounting, her skin itching. Waiting for her chance to leave, she hesitated, sensing there was something important she had yet to learn here.

The light in the room was cold and grey, shifting across the other woman's face whenever a draft touched the thin, frayed curtains at the window. By turns her features were sunk in shadow and then exposed to stark daylight that made her flinch as if it might burn her skin. Her cup was soon emptied and refilled with pure gin.

"And now your father," she nodded at the letters again, "has decided he can't help me out anymore. After I took you in and raised you—*you*, his unwanted, bastard brat left with me like abandoned baggage. I kept his dirty secret for twenty-one years, now he wants to distance himself from me." She burped without the slightest sign of shame or hint of apology. No doubt she thought "Chance" unworthy of any good manners. "Perhaps he thinks you're dead and gone. Perhaps he thinks I've got no proof you're his by-blow." Her shoulders lifted in a quick shrug. "Or else he's just an idiot who underestimates me. In any case, he thinks he's safe, because I'm disgraced and sent off. Thinks it's his word against mine now, he can just turn his back on me after all these years and forget. But I've got these." She tapped the letters with her finger and gave a smug chuckle. "Insurance."

"I see. And now you mean to use his letters to my mother for your own benefit somehow."

"That's right. I'm going to get a good pension out of that man. He can't just turn me out like an unwanted cat, not until he's paid me handsomely."

Emma took a step back when she saw that familiar flame of viciousness in the other woman's eyes. "You must do as you wish. It is naught to do with me now."

Mrs. Lightbody almost choked on her gin. She slammed the saucer-less cup down, spilling some on the cloth, proving how the archipelago of stains got there. "You'll help me, if you know what's good for you, Chance. It'll double the price for the letters, if we go to him together. If he sees how you've grown up, he'll have to put his hands in his pockets, won't he? He can't have you coming out of the woodwork. If you do as I say, we can take him for plenty between the two of us."

"Why on earth would I want to do that?"

"Can't rely on ol' Bramley's benevolence for the rest of your life, girl. What will you do when she loses interest and finds another worthy cause for her charity? Because she will, eventually. Your blessed father owes me. He owes us both. Play your cards right, Chance, and he can get you a better post, something more profitable."

Emma moved toward the door. "I want no part of this, madam," she said firmly, trying to quell the sick feeling in her stomach. "I never wanted to know my father, and I have no desire to meet him now. For any purpose. Certainly not for bribery and extortion."

"Don't tell me you're happy, dancing about like a loose-limbed marionette for that old bitch Bramley. Hoping for a handout there, eh?" She paused, screwing up her face as she considered the possibilities. "Well, she has no daughters, only sons who do nothing for her, so I suppose..." Those hard, cruel little eyes watered as she swallowed another burp. "But no. She might like to imagine herself the mother hen for now, but you'll never get anything out of her beyond a few pennies. Her sons will drain her of every penny. Mark my words, that fine lady will soon move on to other projects and drop you like the drip you are. You might have a head full of clever bits and pieces, Chance, but you have no inkling about that lot at the top and how to use an opportunity to get what you want. Folk like us have to scheme and lie to get ahead in this world. We have to pull strings and sneak in the back door. I'm surprised your friend, Miss Hoity Sharp-Mouth, hasn't taught you that. Lady Thrasher, indeed!"

"Madam, although I have been made to feel ashamed of my existence for most of my life, I know that I am not a criminal. So I will not participate in your schemes. I have no interest in using other folk's misfortunes for my own advantage."

The woman sneered into her cup. "Then you'll always finish last, Chance."

"Better that than know I have not led a good life. I will take my leave of you, madam, for the last time."

But she was only two steps to the door, when Lightbody choked out angrily, "You can't turn your back on me either, girl. I'm not done with you yet."

"Yes, I can and yes, you are done, madam. I am not your servant."

"You owe me for keeping you off the streets and out of the gutters."

"I am not and never was indebted to you." She kept her voice calm, despite the rising nausea in her belly. "My father paid a fee for me to stay at the school, although whether he meant to pay for my education or merely to reimburse you for your silence, I do not know. The fact is that you were never inconvenienced or put out of pocket. If anything, you gained by having my labor at your disposal. Nobody questioned you for more than fifteen years, and I did not know I had any right to speak up for myself. But I am not afraid now, madam. I came here only to say a proper goodbye at last and sever, forever, whatever hold you might think you still possess over me."

"Oh, I see you've found your tongue to talk back to me. Got that from your friends, no doubt."

"Good day to you, madam. We have no further business between us."

"But we've got the past, haven't we, eh?"

Emma raise a gloved hand to her throat and then quickly straightened the collar of her pelisse. "I leave the past here with you and your conscience. I have no more to say about it."

With Lightbody's scornful laughter ringing in her ears, she walked out of the room. "I tried to give you a hand up, girl, and that's the thanks I get." That voice followed her to the front door."There's no helping some folk. You always were an ingrate."

Help, like "charity", apparently meant something different to Julia Lightbody.

Out in the rain again, Emma walked swiftly to the waiting Hackney and the kindly driver who waited for her. Her hands shook, but the sick taste subsided.

It was over. The past would not haunt her again. She had seen her cruel tormenter, hopefully, for the last time— seen her shrunken, powerless *and* powderless, her wig adrift, her fingernails stained and chipped like her teacup. Pathetic, tawdry, and broken.

But Emma had a life now, things to look forward to and people who cared about her.

Emma Chance was somebody.

She'd once said to Captain Hathaway that she did not seek vengeance against her enemies, but that was not entirely true. Yes, she occasionally had bloodthirsty thoughts; she was far from perfect, but her vengeance would be the better, happy life she led in her future, leaving those who once hurt her far behind in the misery of their own making.

Chapter Eighteen

When Guy returned to his father's house, he found the place in some excitement over another visitor. His first thought, when he heard the merry ruckus, was that the favored son, Edward, must have arrived. Moments later, however, he opened the drawing room door to find Walter Ramsey regaling a portion of the Hathaway family with some yarn about fighting two-headed monsters that lived under the sea. Even the second Mrs. Hathaway had descended the stairs to enjoy Walter's story and Mr. Hathaway stood by the mantle, surprisingly attentive. Although the couple listened to their guest, neither of them gave any attention to the two year-old boy who climbed upon him continually, intent on putting something in his ear.

"You did not tell us you had such an entertaining friend," his stepmother exclaimed, turning to look at Guy from her chaise, her expression accusatory.

"Madam, I did not know my friend was so entertaining," he replied wryly. "But I'm glad you find him so." He might have pointed out that she and his father never asked anything about his life in the navy or his friends, but he did not. He also might have reminded them that this was a story he himself had told in this very room, to an audience of blank stares. Walter had merely borrowed his story and apparently told it with greater aplomb. Or perhaps it was simply because he was not Guy— not the family disappointment.

Of course, the second Mrs. Hathaway had a great interest in medicine and new cures, for she frequently found herself too ill to get out of bed, so a ship's surgeon was welcomed with open arms.

Walter explained, "My mother insisted I pay a visit to an ancient friend of the family while I was on leave. Apparently the old dear is in want of company and mama thought I might cheer her spirits, so I promised I would. I was on my way there when, realizing you lived in this part of Town, I decided to call in. Only to find that you, Hathaway, have taken to morning strolls— of all unlikely pastimes."

He wondered why that was such a surprise to everybody. It was not as if he'd ever been the sort to lay abed long after cock crow, but for some reason people took one look at him and assumed he lived a life of debauchery.

Mrs. Hathaway now invited Walter to join them for dinner, but he could not accept for that evening because he was expected at the Mayfair house of his hostess. "In fact, I must make my way there now, for she will be waiting and woe betide me if I am too late."

"Then you must come another day, as soon as you can," the lady of the house assured him with a condescending bow of her head. "We are always in want of *good* society."

Walter agreed to come and dine in a day or two and Guy walked him to the front door.

"I have worried about you, Hathaway. When we parted company you were in a strange melancholy. I felt it incumbent upon me to see how you fair."

"That was good of you, but unnecessary. As you see, I am still standing."

"Yet, what is this business about morning strolls? Another phase of your desperate malaise, perhaps. I came in the nick of time to rescue you."

Guy knew exactly what his friend would consider rescue, so he replied hastily, "I do not require your intervention, Ramsey. A man simply needs the occasional morning exercise to clear his head. Indeed, you might find it does you the world of good to get some fresh air with a brisk walk. As a medical man, surely, you ought to recommend the practice."

Walter eyed him curiously. "I am glad to see your spirits revived considerably, Hathaway. Indeed, there is a *new* gleam in your eye, stronger than ever. Where did you go this morning? Your stepmama said you were gone before she rose from her bed. Even in the rain. And now you return at noon."

"It was not early when I left. It might have seemed so to my stepmother, who has assumed the habits of a grand lady of leisure and rarely comes down before eleven, but the hour *was* civilized, I assure you. In any case, I've never been one to sit about with nothing to do. I love the rain. And if you knew my father's wife a little better, you would know why leaving the house before she is up and about has its advantages. Besides," he laughed uneasily, "you

263

know me. I like to be unpredictable. Keep folk on their toes by varying my routine."

"You do protest too much, Hathaway. What are you up to?" Walter paused, grinning. "'Tis a woman, is it not? That would account for your much improved mood."

Guy put his arm around the shorter fellow's shoulders and amiably assured him that he would be the *last* to know. "Because you cannot keep a secret, Ramsey."

"Why must it be kept a secret? She is married already? Or there is some other matter—family disapproval perhaps?"

"Come, time is pressing, Ramsey. Are you not expected at the house of this ancient family friend who is desirous of your company? Don't keep the old dear waiting."

Walter grimaced at the reminder. "You must promise to visit me there, Hathaway. I do not know how often I'll be able to get away without some reasonable excuse that passes muster with Lady Bramley. She can be...difficult. And her own sons neglect her dreadfully, so she will put all her attention into me while I am in Town, I fear." He gave a deep sigh. "She is a lonely widow, in want of companionship."

"Bramley?" Guy sputtered. "*Lady Bramley?* That remarkable warship of a woman? *Lonely?*"

Walter's eyes narrowed. "Widow of Sir Melchior Bramley, mother of the current Baronet Sir

Mandrake. Resides in Hanover Square when in Town and has the largest glasshouse built in London. Why?"

Now he laughed. "Life never ceases to amaze me. But I know that lady...that is to say, we have met."

"Then you can visit me there. Come and rescue me, if you have any pity in your soul."

"I suppose I might." But he rubbed his chest with the knuckles of one hand, hoping to loosen the knot that formed there whenever he considered what that woman would have to say about his intentions for Miss Chance. He'd have to get a few things done first— including a haircut.

Walter stepped down into the street and then turned back to face his friend. "I thought you had sisters, Hathaway. I was hoping to meet them. Thought they might enliven my stay in London."

"Poor Ramsey. For two of them you are, alas, too late. They are both married."

"What of the others. Are there none unspoken for?"

"A pair of twins actually."

"Twins?" Walter perked up.

"Who, I have no doubt, would very much like to be taken out and about."

"Would they indeed?" He rubbed his hands together. "Splendid!"

"But you must take the nanny too."

Walter's face fell speedily, as only his— too often a gullible victim of his friend's mischief and never learning the lesson— ever could. "The nanny?"

"The twins are not yet five."

The other man creaked and groaned, like a ship dying at sea. "Then I shall be at the mercy of Lady Bramley's matchmaking attempts while I remain in her house."

"It might be a good idea for you to abstain from romantic attachment for a while, don't you think?" Guy gestured to his own bruised face. "At least give me a chance to heal, before I must come to your rescue yet again."

That was another reason, of course, to delay his appearance before Lady Bramley. She was hardly likely to believe his dough was sufficiently risen if she saw his black and blue eye. Or, as Miss Chance put it, a face like a rotten potato.

* * * *

Nicholas Hathaway's excitement was just as boundless on that days that followed as it had been the moment his eldest brother returned on leave. Waiting for the boy's enthusiasm to wear itself out was a fruitless task, and Charles Lennox was no less thrilled to have a brave sea captain in the house, although his natural shyness made him more reserved in showing it. To be honest, Emma didn't mind at all when, occasionally, their lesson transgressed into the amusing world of "tales my brother told me."

Captain Hathaway was out and about during the day, apparently in the company of a friend who was also in Town on leave, so although there were signs of him about the house— a muddy boot print on the staircase, a pair of gloves thrown down on the narrow console by the door, sailboats he made of folded paper for the boys to show off— she had no sightings of the man himself. Any anecdote about his adventures, therefore, was more than welcome. She yearned to hear his name mentioned, to learn a little more about him with each story, and by hearing it from Nicholas— who could not be silenced even if one tried— she didn't have to ask anybody or risk exposing her secret fancy.

There was little that could be done about anything as "wretched" as a mathematics lesson unless she adapted it to involve sailing somehow.

Toward the end of her lesson on that Saturday, Emma decided to combine the mathematics with geometry, history, *and* astronomy by focusing the lesson on Edmund Gunter and his adaption of a quadrant to determine latitude at sea. She thought she was doing rather well, until Captain Hathaway burst into the schoolroom, unannounced, and declared, "Well, this is a rather dry subject, Miss Chance! I've been listening at the door, and it almost put me to sleep. 'Twas fortunate I still had my riding boots on to keep me upright."

The boys laughed— even Charles, who looked rather sorry to be doing so, but couldn't help himself.

Ever since her visit to Mrs. Lightbody in Lisson Grove, Emma had been in a strange temper, cheerful and yet in no mood to suffer fools. She had spent every waking moment wondering if the Captain had come to his senses by now, fretting that she could become just another cannon ball in his next letter.

• While bored on rainy day, proposed marriage to pale shrimp.

• Regained sanity when the sun shone again.

Closing her book with a snap, she exclaimed, "I would have imagined you, of all people, to appreciate the subject of navigation at sea, Captain. Would you not be lost without these methods?"

"But all this reading of facts, Miss Chance, will result in a stoop, wrinkles and strained vision. I cannot allow it." He walked up and took the book from her hands, his fingers slyly brushing hers. "Practice is much more enjoyable than theory. And more memorable."

"For you, perhaps, Captain." She quickly put her hands behind her back for her fingers throbbed from that slight caress. "We do not all learn and retain in the same manner."

"'Tis true, my good woman. I never thrived in a schoolroom, but learned through experience." He propped his backside on the edge of his little brother's desk and flicked idly though the book he'd taken from her. Back to front. "Sometimes we have to feel and taste and see for ourselves. You must put your theory into practice."

"As I said, we all have different methods of learning. Did you want something, Captain?" She took the book away from him and he looked at her, specifically at her mouth.

"Yes, Miss Chance. I do want something."

Had she smiled at him? She hoped not for he needed no encouragement, not with the boys watching every move, listening to every word. "We are, as you observe," she added, "in the midst of a lesson."

"Oh." His eyes widened in the pretense of innocence. "Do I disrupt—"

"Yes."

"Then please do go on. Don't mind me. My needs...can wait."

She waited, but he made no move to leave. Instead he assumed a face of patient attention, one finger to his chin, one leg raised to rest his ankle across his knee. Like a mischievous pixie perched on a toadstool. Of course, she knew what he was up to. He wanted to see her blush and become utterly and totally adrift.

It was easy for him to put her in that state, for his own amusement, it seemed. To see what she would do about it.

Although she had always been capable of seeing through his charming smile to the sadness beneath, Emma still had difficulty knowing when he teased and when he was serious.

"Captain Hathaway, your presence distracts my

pupils. I fear they find you far more interesting than they do me."

He grinned slowly. "But I do not distract the teacher, surely. She is far too serious."

"Go on, Miss Chance," Nicholas exclaimed. "Let 'im stay."

Guy swiveled to address his little brother. "I shall stay only if you promise to pay heed to your governess. I do not want to make her angry with me. I have cause to need her on my side."

She tried not to look at him, fearing that any glance in his direction might only advance his mischief. But they both had rather a habit of letting their eyes meet and Emma found it very challenging to pull her gaze away from that strong tug once it began.

"Why do you need *her* on your side, brother?" The idea of that tall, brave hero needing any female was, of course, confusing for the naughty lad.

"Because Miss Chance is exceedingly clever and sensible. Mark me, young Nick, it is never a good thing to make an enemy of an intelligent woman. She is the most valuable asset a man can have, *if* she is his friend."

The boy absorbed all this thoughtfully, as did his cousin Charles. "I don't want a girl for a friend," Nicholas eventually muttered.

"One day you shall. Now, pay heed. Let stern Miss Chance get on with the lesson, before she gets even angrier with us. See— the steam coming out of

270

her ears?" And he resumed his pixie-like pose upon the desk.

So she reopened her book, found her place, and read on, but before too long she saw the Captain sway a little and try to hide a yawn.

"Sir, we bore you. Don't let us interfere with *your* day."

He leapt down from the desk, clapped his hands together and exclaimed, "What we need is a trip outdoors to a lake— or better yet the seaside— to put all this into practice! Of course," he must have seen her doubtful expression, "now is not the season for it. The pleasure parks are shut up again until May and the coast will be cold and windblown, but we shall make a plan of it for when I am next on leave. Then I can show you how a ship's speed is measured by use of knots on a rope and a sand glass. And Miss...this lady...will demonstrate how to use a quadrant." He smirked. "We shall see then if she knows how to put her lectures and facts into useful practice. For I've known many book-learned fellows lose their gumption at sea."

Why did he say "this lady" in such a tone? This lady. *This lady.* It felt as if he'd unbuttoned her frock. She had never thought of herself as a lady. An ingrate child, a foggy spirit of nothingness, a blushing girl who always said and did the wrong thing, and then a somber governess who lived her life by careful, tidy routine. But never a lady. Flustered, she quickly set her book down before she dropped it on his foot.

271

"Oh, yes, let's!" cried Nicholas. "Let's go to the seaside, Miss Chance!"

"The seaside?" The door had opened at that moment to admit Mrs. Hathaway. "I must say that sounds tremendous fun! I should like a little sea-bathing. It is so beneficial for one's health, I hear."

Immediately all eagerness for the trip was severely dampened. Nicholas dropped back to his seat and gave a low groan.

Emma curtseyed for her employer's wife, but the lady had no interest in her. "I wondered where you had gone, Guy, for Mrs. Beddesby heard you come in and she did not expect you home until dinner. Did that young lady you chase after let you down already?"

"Madam." He stood from the desk. "I was out with Walter Ramsey, and his company is best enjoyed in small doses." Here he shot Emma a quick, sideways glance. "Hence I returned early to the house after our ride in the park. There is no *other* lady involved."

"You sly thing! Of course there is a lady. I do not know why you are so reticent to confess it this time." She reached up and slapped his shoulder playfully, tittering in a foolish way. "'Tis not like you to be bashful about your amorous conquests."

The second Mrs. Hathaway was, in actual fact, only a year or so older than her eldest stepson, and apparently he brought out the coquettish girl in her. While Emma watched in morbid fascination, her employer's wife flapped her lashes and made a display of herself that was reminiscent of bacon, bubbling, crackling and drooling in hot fat.

"Now I find you wasting the governess' time here in the school room of all places." She drummed Guy's shoulder lightly with her fingers and simpered, "Do come downstairs, for I am in want of a partner for baccarat and your papa refuses to play. He says he has work to do. This rain is so dreary, and one can find nothing to amuse on such a day. I am tired of solitaire. Come and save me from ennui do!"

He could not refuse such an impassioned plea, of course. With a quick bow for Emma and a hand out to ruffle each boy's head, he followed his stepmother from the room. As the door closed behind him, Emma felt her shoulders sag. It was as if he took all the light with him.

The lesson proceeded, but nobody cared much for it now. Not even the teacher who had entirely lost her place.

* * * *

Returning to the school that evening, Emma found a package awaiting her. She took it into her little sitting room and unwrapped it by the fire. It was six yards of deep, midnight blue velvet and the same amount of satin in lilac, shot through with tiny bluebells. With it was a note.

This will not offend my eyes and it will bring out the color in your own. Take pity on me.

Yours Hopefully, GH

She realized that this was a compromise between the somber shades she thought appropriate and the confidently bright colors he preferred for her intended cloak. At least it wasn't crimson. It was, in fact, quite lovely. But a young, unwed woman should never accept a gift from a bachelor unless there was a formal engagement. They did not have that, did they? She had only promised to consider, because it seemed far too strange and sudden. Out of thin air he had decided to court her. If she was a reckless woman she would leap at her opportunity, but as she had once said to her friends, she was no rider of banisters and preferred the steadier progress of sure-footed steps.

She had to be certain of her footing. And his.

The Captain's gift of velvet suggested that he had not changed his mind since their conversation at the haberdasher's, although he might still let her down, his attention seized by something or somebody else. He wouldn't hurt her deliberately, but such a man could surely take his pick from many beautiful, vivacious, and wealthy young ladies, and she would not want him to one day find himself stuck in a promise with her. A promise made out of pity.

Prudence would not let her leap in with both feet, but she could not return to him the gift of midnight blue velvet any more than she could demand that he go back in time and untouch her neck and shoulders. Even before that, eight years ago, she had known that he was the only man in the world for her. He was the only man in the fog. It was she and him. She would always think well of him. Fondly, secretly and from a cautious distance.

But she had never expected him to think of her. Not in this way.

Chapter Nineteen

Whenever Georgiana was in Town on a Sunday afternoon, she came for tea in Emma's little parlor. It was always an occasion of mixed emotion, for while they both had good memories of their friendship forged in that school, there were also more than a few less savory memories— mostly Emma's— combined with the bittersweet evidence of time passing so swiftly when they talked of their new lives. The "Ladies Most Unlikely" were getting older; life for all of them was changing. They could not stay girls forever, and their adventures were no longer confined to their imaginations.

But seated together by the fire with a tray of tea and Mrs. Bishop's wonderful bakewell tart, they had the chance to relive a little of the old days— the happier parts— to gossip about past pupils they both remembered, and to keep each other abreast of new developments. Georgiana, naturally, was the one who had far more going on in her world. Usually.

On this Sunday, however, Emma had much to share. Not that she could tell all of it, for she'd been sworn to secrecy by Captain Hathaway. The matter of Mrs. Lightbody, on the other hand, must be told.

"Emma Chance! Why would you go to Lisson Grove all alone to see that wretched woman? Have you taken leave of your generally sound senses?" Georgiana demanded in astonishment. "Anything might have happened to you! You must not go there again."

"Don't fret, Georgie, I am no longer afraid of her."

"But Lisson Grove, particularly that part of it, is not a safe place for a young lady to venture alone these days."

Emma sighed. "The people who live there are no different to me. They have been less fortunate, and that is all. I too am poor. I merely have a cleaner face and good friends on my side."

"And a naive soul! Dear Emma, do not let her take advantage of your kind nature."

"Oh, I did not feel pity for her and I refused to take part in her scheme."

"What scheme?"

So Emma explained about the letters in Mrs. Lightbody's possession and then she added carefully, "Did you know that my mother once worked in a house in Bethnal Green? She seemed surprised that you had not told me of it."

Her friend licked her lips and peered shyly through lowered black lashes, looking guilty. "I had heard...something. But...I did not know—"

"Is that why you raised the subject of my father? You tried to find a way to tell me?"

Georgiana looked at her empty plate and then set it on the tray. Fingers knitted together, she got up and paced around her chair. "I have tried for some time to tell you what I knew. But you never mentioned your parents or seemed to have any desire to know about them and, when I first came upon the information, I did not know if I *ought* to tell you."

Emma sat very still and straight in her chair, curled her fingers around Captain Hathaway's handkerchief, and asked softly, "Does anybody else know?"

"Only me. Somehow I have kept it to myself this long."

After a moment to straighten her thoughts, Emma said firmly, "I don't want to know *his* name. I have no interest in him. But I...I would like to know about my mother. Whatever it is, please tell me." It hurt to breathe suddenly. She did not want to dissolve into tears, but the need was thick and heavy inside her, the weight of it almost too much to bear. After she left Mrs. Lightbody's lodgings in Lisson Grove it had occurred to her— too late, of course— that if she had read one of those letters in the woman's possession she could have learned her mother's name. At the time she'd been too flustered, too sick to think of it and in haste to leave.

Slowly her friend began to explain. "Some years ago, when I was punished and made to clean Lightbody's study, I found a book. It seemed to be a diary of sorts, covered in dust and cobwebs because it had fallen down the back of her bookshelf and been forgotten there. I knew it was not hers for the handwriting was neat and studied; nothing like her careless scrawl. Inside the book, its owner had written certain facts about gentlemen she...knew. Customers,

I suppose they would be."

Emma swallowed and looked down at her fists, but she said nothing and let her friend continue.

"There was an entry about a baby born against the wishes and efforts of its father. A baby born to one of the women who worked in the same house. The mother had died soon after giving birth and the child was passed off, by its father, into the hands of a woman who said she would raise it *out of sight*." Georgiana paused, shuddered visibly and then turned and walked back to the fire, where she rubbed her arms and warmed her hands. "Identities were hidden, marked only with initials on the page, but I had already formed suspicions about a connection between Lightbody and...your father, and his initials matched those given for the man who so callously abandoned his lover and child. When Lightbody found the book missing, she confronted me at Woodbyne and accused me of stealing it— which I suppose was true, although it was not her property in the first place." Georgiana took a breath and then added, "In her fury, Lightbody admitted to me that...this man I believed to be your father...was enraged with her for losing the book. It was clear that he had much to hide and she had been using the book, probably for her own evil advantage against him. But with the book gone she had lost much of the power she held over him and, of course, over other men mentioned in its pages. I refused to give it back to her and then Lady Bramley walked in on the conversation and Lightbody swiftly departed, empty-handed." She took a deep breath and dropped back into her chair, reaching for her tea at the same time. "And if you truly want to know nothing about your father I can say no more than that, or it will all spill out. As my brother would say, *you know how I am*. It has taken me all my willpower to keep the secret as long as I have."

For a while there was silence, except for the chortling, wheezing coals in the fire and the soft, nervous rattling of her friend's cup against its saucer.

Finally Emma looked up again. "And my mother?"

"Whoever penned the diary commented that she was a gentle soul, *too delicate and good for this life*."

"And she died because she had me?" The question caught half way up her throat, as if Mrs. Lightbody's rough hands had choked it there.

"According to the diary I found she died of pleurisy, Em. I'm sorry. Although, now you know you were not to blame." Georgiana frowned. "If that was indeed the terrible thought under which you've lived all these years. I wish I had known what you were thinking and then I might have spared you that agony at least."

Her mind flicked quickly through stored facts.

Pleurisy: An inflammation of the lung, caused by pneumonia and other diseases.

Her mother had been sick then and it was not childbirth that killed her. Not directly.

"The only other thing I can tell you is that her name began with a 'Y'. That was the initial."

A 'Y'. Her mother's name began with a 'Y'. An uncommon name then. She was glad of it. Piece by piece the picture continued to be filled in, but it might never be complete. Her mother might never be more than a shadow, another London Particular.

One day, perhaps, she would want to know who *he* was, but she was not yet brave enough for that. She had come a long way in the past few years, but she still had more distance to cross before she felt capable of confronting the man who had caused her to be born. Indeed, she might never reach that point in her emancipation.

* * * *

That night, before she went to bed, Emma opened her cabinet, took out the little hand mirror Georgiana had once bought her, and, for the first time in a long while, examined her face. It was still as plain as she remembered it. Her mother must have been prettier— enough to be envied by Julia Lightbody, for the pea-green tone in the old woman's voice was unmistakable when she spoke of that "silly girl".

Perhaps she could try a little rouge and some lip balm. She might thin her brows a little— not too much. And her hair! But what was to be done with her limp, colorless locks?

Oh, what did it matter? She put down the mirror,

cross with herself.

Captain Hathaway didn't seem to care what she looked like.

On the other hand, his reasons for proposing marriage had all been practical, all about saving her from poverty and himself from too much frivolity. Was it too much to ask that he look at her one day and think of her in less...functional terms? Could she not try to be decorative too, so that he was not embarrassed to have her on his arm the way he had been once before, when he walked into the Black Bull with her on Lady Bramley's orders? Well did she remember how he bent his head, flushed with apparent mortification, as he raced her into the private dining room, out of sight.

She raised the little mirror again and reassessed the hopelessness of her face. She might appeal to Georgiana for help, but she must be guarded. The Captain had asked her to say nothing about their conversation to his sister. He was right, of course, it was all much too early for her friends to know, for once they did they would crowd her, make a fuss, try to shelter her. The tender shoots of this strange, unexpected courtship needed a chance to grow without intervention— however well-meaning.

But she had nobody else to help. There were several young girls at the school who would leap at the chance to lend their "talents", for they frequently lamented Emma's lack of sartorial elegance, as if it was a misfortune equal to a severed limb. She'd heard them extolling the virtues of pimpernel water for the complexion and grated horseradish in sour milk to reduce freckles. They quarreled voraciously over which was better: 'Royal Tincture of Peach Kernels' or 'Liquid Bloom of Roses'. They pored over recipes for various unguents and creams, even when they were supposed to be studying their books. Apparently there was nothing they would not try if it promised infinite youth and the beauty of Cleopatra.

Emma could only imagine how she would look, however, if she threw caution to the wind and gave those young girls free rein.

She wanted Captain Hathaway to admire and, perhaps, to be surprised, but she didn't want to frighten him.

So, the next day she braved the apothecary with Georgiana, who seemed surprised to be asked, but delighted to help. They came away with an array of liquids and powders, and later that day Georgiana took a pair of tweezers to her eyebrows. Ten painful minutes later Emma had two neatly, nonchalantly curved brown lines.

"Much better," her friend announced, holding the hand mirror so that her subject could assess the final result. "See how it opens your eyes and makes them larger?"

It looked like her, but different. Not so perplexed or annoyed. Softer. Even— dare she think it— more feminine.

Next, Georgiana dabbed her lips lightly with

balm that tasted of honey and gave her mouth a faint rose pink color. She pressed a little powder over Emma's nose and forehead, and then lent her the use of curling tongs for her hair. Until then she had only used papers at night to try and entice a curl into her limp locks, but Georgiana now swore by tongs to achieve a better, long-lasting ringlet. Alas, although this method worked without incident on her own, lush dark waves, the tongs became distinctly uncooperative when put to use in Emma's sad lengths.

Two singed half-spirals later and the heated tongs were abandoned.

"I fear I must resolve myself to a flat head," she muttered."Perhaps, in time, it will become the fashion and then you will all envy me."

"Of course," said Georgiana in her kindly "you-poor-dear" tone. After a pause she added, "But what, pray tell, has induced this sudden interest in fashion and your appearance? You've never been one to bother much, Em."

She replied hastily. "Lady Bramley prods me to do so, and she is taking me with her to Shropshire for Christmas, to her son, Sir Mandrake Bramley's estate. I suppose I ought to make myself presentable, while we are there... for her sake."

"Oh," said her friend, having surprisingly little else to say on the matter.

Emma had broken out of her usual strict spending rules and purchased two, frivolous new ribbons for her hair — one dark sapphire and the other ruby. For a woman who generally used plain pins this was an extravagance that would necessitate wearing them sparingly, with great distance between, so as not to encourage comment. She had seen a sketch in a ladies magazine, in which the ribbons were used in a supposedly Grecian style. For evenings. Foolish, really, for there was nothing in the least Greek or goddess-like about Emma Chance.

But she purchased them all the same.

Now she was ready for her outing to the theatre with Captain Hathaway. Or as ready as she would ever be.

* * * *

"Edward, my boy! Here you are at last. We expected you every day for the past week, but I suppose you have many who rely upon you in that parish and could not get away sooner. At least you are here now. Come! Come in, dear boy, and greet your brothers and sisters. Sherry! You will have a sherry, will you not? I know you do not imbibe strong drink, but surely a sherry..."

With his brother's arrival, Guy observed an immediate and dramatic change in their father's demeanor, but he could not even be annoyed by it this time. He had too much else on his mind. Even Georgiana had noticed he was unusually quiet.

"Are you sure you're not ill, brother?"

"Quite the opposite. Why?"

"You seem...withdrawn."

"How so?"

"Yesterday you sat in the drawing room for half an hour, looking out of the window, with nothing to say. Even when I teased Edward, you did not participate. I heard you tell your friend Mr. Ramsey that you could not join him for cards at his club on Friday and again this evening. I saw you standing in the garden yesterday smiling at a dandelion for a quarter of an hour. You've been so quiet, staying in for dinner, being polite and awfully obliging to stepmama, helping with the little ones instead of stirring them up and inciting riots..."

"Perhaps I am too old now for teasing Edward, inciting riots and going out every evening," he replied. "Have *you* no other tasks to keep you busy? Does the commander not want you back at Woodbyne by now?"

"My darling Harry is at work on his latest experiment and, I'm sure, is grateful to have me gone for a few days. He does like to have, what he calls, space in which to think. Apparently I often make it impossible for him to think. As if I chatter incessantly."

"Fancy that!"

"In any case, I wrote to tell him of our theatre plans, so he won't expect me back until the end of the week." She looked at him, her head tilted, lips pursed. "But it is all so strange."

"Is it? Hmm." He reached for a newspaper.

"What is?"

"That two people I thought I knew so very well have both begun to act oddly of late. Most unlike themselves."

Guy opened the paper and shook it briskly. "Then perhaps you did not know these people so well as you thought." And he proceeded to whistle, thereby ending the conversation.

The Hathaway house was, at that time, almost at full capacity with only two of the younger boys away at school. The lady of the house spent much of the day hiding in her room, and when Frederick Hathaway was home from his office, he took refuge in his study at the end of the hall. The children were mostly left to the management of household staff and, of course, the governess, Miss Chance.

Guy did his best not to get in her way— to be a patient gentleman, as he'd promised — but passing the schoolroom door he was always tempted to look in. If he did not, she might easily sneak in and out of the house in her silent way and he would miss her completely.

One afternoon she left a scarf on the console table in the hall, and Guy would have bundled it hastily in his fist and taken it to his room with the mischievous greed of a magpie, had Edward and Georgiana not come out of the parlor at that moment.

"Oh, that's Emma's. She must have dropped it," his sister exclaimed.

And Edward immediately swept up one end of it. "I shall take it to her."

"I'm sure that's not necessary. She'll be down soon, and she will see it there before she leaves."

"There are too many children with sticky, wayward fingers in this house," Edward snapped, his eyes fixed upon Guy's knuckles. "We don't want it spoiled or stolen, or used for some foolish game."

Guy had the other end in his fingers and feared the scarf would be pulled out of shape or torn if he gripped it any tighter. So he relinquished his half rather than let it be damaged.

In the evenings, when Mr. and Mrs. Hathaway emerged to be sociable, the family conversation generally revolved around Edward, who was not naturally talkative and had to be poked and prodded to get any information out of him. He had, apparently, laid some heavy hints of his matrimonial plans in letters to their father, but in person he could not be drawn into the subject; instead he hedged around it nervously. Guy wondered if his brother's plans had changed— perhaps his suit had been rejected— but apart from that he was not terribly interested in whom Edward meant to marry. It could have no bearing on his own life.

Or so he imagined.

On the following Monday evening, when Walter Ramsey came to dine, Edward was finally forced out of his secretive corner when Georgiana, in the midst of the first course, casually mentioned their forthcoming trip to the theatre.

"Pardon me," the prim fellow exclaimed, setting down his soup spoon. "Did you say that you and *Guy* mean to take Miss Chance to the Theatre-Royal?"

"You make it sound as if I could have no interest in the theatre," Guy remarked with a chuckle.

"It is not your unexpected interest in the theatre that troubles me."

"Oh? Then what, brother?"

Edward dabbed his lips with a napkin, glanced furtively around the table and replied in a low voice, "I had planned to invite Miss Chance to the theatre myself to see *The Duchess of Malfi*. Although I do not entirely approve the subject matter for a young lady's viewing, I know it is a favorite of hers."

Guy was familiar with that expression on his brother's face. It was the same look Edward used to give when he hid a battalion of tin soldiers in a box under his arm and pretended it was empty, just to keep anybody else from playing with them.

Ah, he should have known.

"But that is the very play *we* are to see," Georgiana cried. "What a coincidence that we all thought of it. I don't suppose it will matter if you come too. Will it, Guy?"

He suddenly lost interest in dinner and reached for more wine instead.

"There is room for four in papa's carriage," she added.

What could he say? Of course he did not want

his brother tagging along too, but how could he admit this without exposing his own interest in the governess? He had sought to keep the romantic aspect to himself until both he and Emma were in definite agreement, and he still had only a whispered promise from her to consider his suit. And that might have emerged from her lips purely because she wanted to save him from Lady Bramley's inquisition.

It had been his hope that their evening at the theatre would bring them closer, give him an opportunity to remove her doubts. Some of them, at least.

Over the brim of his wineglass, he caught Edward's slyly annoyed, sideways glance.

Well, that made both of them, he thought grimly.

Apparently he and Edward had more in common than he'd realized— not only did they both have an eye on the same woman this time, but they also sought to keep it secret for as long as possible. He had his reasons, but what were Edward's?

And then another terrible thought followed that one. Had Edward made a declaration to Emma Chance already on one of his previous visits and sworn her to secrecy?

"The theatre? Wednesday you say?" Walter abruptly joined in, belatedly paying attention to their conversation from the other end of the table where he had been subjected to the second Mrs. Hathaway's whining about her many and varied illnesses for the past quarter hour. "Oh, do say you have room for two more. My hostess insists upon me taking a Miss Godfrey out for an airing, and this sounds a most painless way to do it. I would die of boredom without the additional company. And if you can abide our presence in your merry group, I do believe Lady Bramley will happily lend us her box at the theatre. Let that be my contribution to the evening."

His sister replied immediately that she thought this a very good idea and she could see no reason why the party could not be expanded to six, especially since Walter Ramsey said he could borrow a curricle in which to transport the unfortunate and unsuspecting Miss Godfrey.

"I'm sure Guy can have no objection," said Georgiana brightly. "As he always says, *the more the merrier.*"

Guy drained his glass, looked at the empty crystal and contemplated the pleasant noise it would make when it hit the wallpaper.

This, he mused darkly, is what happened when he tried to do things properly and follow the rules. He should simply have swept Miss Chance up over his shoulder and ridden off with her to Gretna Green. To hell with the "gentlemanly patience" and anybody's approval.

But he'd wanted so badly to do this the right way. No more reckless decisions and foolish mistakes that he later regretted. He must try to be patient and hold his temper. Must, with gritted teeth, *try*.

So he carefully set the glass down and hoped

nobody had seen his hand shake with the effort of restraint.

After dinner, Edward approached him. "Miss Chance is surely too decent a woman to be of interest to you, brother."

"Is she? Do you know so much about her?"

"I know that she is entirely suitable for a curate's wife. And what do you know of her?"

But he did not want to share anything that he knew about Emma Chance. This time he too would jealously guard his box of tin soldiers. Guy would have shrugged, but then remembered Lady Bramley's comment

A naval captain's shoulders should remain straight, balanced and sturdy at all times, for they carry upon them the security of our great nation.

"I will not let you toy with her," said Edward, his eyes heavy with disapproval— much like their father's. "Have you no other prey with which to pass your time on leave?"

"Dear Ed," he smiled politely, "always worried about my entertainment."

"Somebody ought to be concerned, before you drag the family name into further scandal." His gaze brushed over Guy's eye which, although better than it had been, still showed signs of a less than gentlemanly encounter. "Old habits die hard, I see."

His brother, of course, tried to prick his temper, but Guy was determined to remain calm. "We cannot all be as holy as you. Thankfully. But I can assure you

I have no ill intentions toward Miss Chance." He smirked. "Only wicked ones that would benefit both she and I." Yes, indeed, he mused, old habits did die hard and teasing Edward was too easy. He'd resisted thus far today, but the man had followed him into the hall, buzzing about his head like a damned fly. And one could only put up with that for so long without swatting at the nuisance.

"I see." Edward's eyes darkened. "Well, it may have escaped your notice, but Miss Chance is a woman who wears all her clothes in public."

"But not always in private, I trust."

Edward closed his eyelids slowly and shook his head. His hairline was receding, Guy noted with some satisfaction. "Her virtuous innocence alone makes her unsuited companionship for you, but I suppose that also makes her a challenge you cannot resist."

"Yes, I suppose that's it. That must be her only attraction. You are always right, Ed, of course."

"Miss Chance is a woman of intelligence— a quiet, somber, chaste, hard-working, unfussy, plain-living sort, who will make an excellent, frugal wife for a man of the church."

"She might not appreciate your desire to give her a hard-working, plain-living life. Perhaps she's had enough of that."

"Do you honestly think she would prefer marriage to an unpredictable scoundrel who is at sea more than he is home? A man who thinks a church is the place to sleep off the effects of too much liquor and that a chancel rail is not for solemn prayer but for scraping mud off his boots? Loudly."

"I fell asleep *once* in your church. And drink was not to blame, it was your damnably tedious sermon. And if there is something at a convenient height upon which to rest my heels for three lingering hours, you can be sure I'll make use of it."

"It was one hour."

"It felt like six bloody days. Even God took his rest on the seventh."

"I'm surprised you know so much about that."

"No doubt he fell asleep too once he heard you droning on like a rusty mill wheel."

"The fact of the matter is this— Miss Chance is far more suited to my life than yours."

"But since you always have to be right, Ed, how will you tolerate a woman who knows more than you?"

"Whatever do you two debate with such intensity?" Georgiana exclaimed as she came upon them in the hall. "I have seldom seen you both in conversation so deep and low. What secrets do you try to hide from me? I demand that you tell. Are you discussing what to buy your favorite sister as a Yuletide gift?"

Edward replied gravely, as if he spoke from his pulpit. "I merely expressed astonishment that our brother should be so bored here in London that he would seek out the company of Miss Chance. Surely he has *other* women to entertain him. As far as I recall, there is usually an excess of easy females about, whenever he is on leave."

Georgiana laughed merrily. "Oh good lord! Poor Edward. You do have what is commonly termed the wrong end of the stick. Guy has no interest of that sort in my friend. He was merely escorting us to the theatre as a gallant favor. If he has led you to think otherwise, I fear he has teased you again." She shot Guy a sly glance. "It seems he has not outgrown that pastime after all."

Edward's eyes narrowed as he looked at Guy. It was clear he wanted to believe it was all a jest, but something stopped him from being entirely convinced. His lips tightened and he raised a hand to smooth back his thinning hair. "For Miss Chance's sake, I do hope he toys with me. Not with her. *I* am accustomed to it. *I* know that almost everything he says and does is meaningless frivolity, and after so many years *I* cannot be hurt by it."

Guy laughed loudly and thrust open the door to the drawing room in search of libation. He did not often drink to excess, whatever his brother thought, but sometimes the occasion warranted an oiling and loosening of over-wound parts. He found this particularly true on his visits home to Allerton Square.

Chapter Twenty

She had almost fallen asleep over her sewing. In that strange state of twilight, not quite lost in her dreams, and yet not wide awake and sensible, she heard a sound at her window. Was it more rain?

There it was again.

Yawning, she shook her head, set down her sewing and went to look out.

It was dark, but down below in the back yard by the water pump, she could see a figure. Tall and broad of shoulder. He lifted a swaying lantern to show his face.

Oh, was she dreaming after all? Emma waited a moment to ascertain her state because she did occasionally have very vivid dreams, but now he prepared to throw another handful of gravel at her window, so she hastily opened it, fearing he would wake the house.

"What are you doing, sir?" she exclaimed on a taut breath. He must have climbed that wall, high and slippery as it was. The dogs in the brewery yard across the street made a great barking ruckus.

"I came to see you, Emma." He stumbled a little on the cobbles.

The sound of her first name on his lips lifted her out of that sleepiness and made her heart beat faster. "It couldn't wait until daylight, Captain?" What if somebody saw him there?

"No. Can't wait."

Something was wrong. Was he ill?

Emma quickly threw a knitted shawl over her shoulders, took a lamp and hurried downstairs, through the servants' passage to the kitchen. He was at the door by then, lantern swaying violently from one hand. Her fingers trembling, she let him in.

"What is—"

He almost crushed her as he fell forward, tripping over the step. With difficulty she got him into a wooden chair by the range, set his lantern beside her lamp on the table and assessed the damage.

To her relief he looked healthy and in one piece, although hatless and soaked to the skin. For one dreadful moment she thought there had been another fight of some sort. But this was not the case. In the next breath, her relief changed to annoyance.

"Captain Hathaway, are you in your cups?"

"I am indeed, madam," he muttered unapologetically, arms falling over the sides of the chair, one boot stretched out. "And I felt the uncommon urge to seek you out before daylight returns me to reason and sobriety again."

She folded her arms, tucking her shawl more tightly around her body. "I left my warm parlor for a man who is drunk."

"It would seem so." Head resting on the back of the chair, he looked up at her. "I saw the light at a window and guessed it would be yours."

"Then you're fortunate it was no other window at which you threw your stones. You might have roused

Mr. and Mrs. Bishop, and they would be less forgiving."

He reached for her hand, trying to pry it from her crossed arms. "Bishop be damned."

"Hush." Emma resisted his attempt and took herself away to close the kitchen door. "You need bread and cheese, Captain. I have read it is beneficial when one is intoxicated."

"I do not presently wish to be rendered sober, Emma my sweet. What I wish is for you to sit with me." He patted his thigh.

"You may not wish to be sensible, but one of us must." She returned to where he sprawled. "What if somebody hears and comes down to the kitchen? We have some barley water in the pantry. Wait here while I—"

Once again he reached for her hand, and this time he caught it. "Be still, if you please. The walls sway enough as it is. You promised to consider my suit. So now what say you?"

That is what he came to ask, in the middle of the night?

But Emma had planned to give him her answer when they went to the theatre, when she was in her prettiest frock and her new velvet cloak. When everything was just right. Not like this, while he was inebriated and they might be discovered, sneaking around in the night like fugitives. He might always be impulsive and imprudent, but she could never be anything but circumspect and wary.

Beneath his open coat his shirt was wet, almost transparent. He wore no waistcoat. He must have left his father's house in careless haste again. His bare fingers, clasped tightly around her own, were warm, so strong that she was surprised he did not crush her bones.

"What do you suppose Lady Bramley would say if she saw you here now?" Emma gasped, shaking her head.

"Surely, even that fearsome fire-ship has suffered the throes of passion at least once in her life."

She tried not to laugh, out of respect for the lady.

"Besides, how else can I come upon you alone?" he added, his voice cracking a little as he tried to speak quietly and with what, she suspected, was his attempt at tenderness. "We barely have the chance to speak."

"Wednesday, at the theatre, I will give you my answer."

"I must wait two further days?" He groaned, tugging her hand to his lips. "Tell me now, Emma. Relieve me of my misery."

Nobody, she supposed, had ever made him wait for anything before. Opening her eyes wide, she said,"If I accept you now, you will stop trying so hard to be a gentleman, won't you?"

A line appeared between his brows. His lips wavered.

"But if I refuse you now, you may sulk and not take me to the theatre. Then I shall miss the play."

He glowered up at her.

"You said you would be patient and gentlemanly," she reminded him. "All possibilities considered, it would seem to my advantage to wait until Wednesday, when I have had my evening at the theatre, as promised, and it cannot be taken away from me."

He blinked slowly. "You possess a cunning and mercenary logic, madam." With a drift of smoke and in a shower of sparks, she thought the dragon prince was about to bite her knuckles.

"I am only teasing you," she whispered, breathless. "My turn, for once."

In the next moment, he had pulled her down into his lap and secured one arm around her waist. "I did not take you for the teasing sort. For that you must be punished, Miss Chance." But when he kissed her it felt like no punishment she'd ever suffered.

What a strange thing it was — to press one's lips to those of another. How was such a gesture ever stumbled upon between two human beings?

Her inquiring mind struggled to make sense of it and then crumbled, giving up on finding any answer. It was very pleasant and that was all that mattered in that moment.

The prickles of his unshaven cheek chafed a little, but the softness of his dark, damp curls under her shyly venturing fingers more than made up for that. She did not even mind the brandy on his lips. Perhaps it made her slightly drunk too, she mused. It certainly made her bold.

He kissed her chin and then the side of her neck, before growling suddenly, "There is no other man, is there, Emma?"

She was puzzled.

He tipped back a little to look at her. "Well? Is there some other man I must fight for your hand?"

Emma smoothed the curls away from his temple to look at the remains of his bruise and the scar on his cheekbone. "Have you not done enough fighting?"

"Answer my question, madam. I must know the obstacles before me."

"What other man could there possibly be?"

His eyes widened and then he exhaled a low chuckle, shaking his head. "Most other women would be coy in answer to that question. You are too sweetly inexperienced. And tonight I am sincerely grateful for it."

"Why would I let you think there was any other man?" And who on earth, she mused, would believe it?

"It may be difficult for you to comprehend, but some ladies like to make their lovers jealous."

"That would be unkind. Why would I do such a thing to a man that I—" Emma got up quickly, before she said too much, and before his lips could find their way under the collar of her chemisette. "Captain Hathaway, do let me find you something refreshing."

"You, my sweet Emma, are refreshment

enough."

She felt decidedly rumpled and knew her hair was loosened from its knot. If anybody came down, they would see her flushed cheeks. Her solution was to be very formal. Put everything back in its neat place. "I will find you some supper before you go home. I cannot put you back out into the street until you are steadier in your boots."

"'Tis just rain," he replied nonchalantly.

Something she had so often said.

But that rain drummed harder now at the door, blown horizontally by a vicious winter wind. Even Emma would not want to be out in it tonight. Before he might decide to leave again— and she certainly would not be able to stop that strong man if he made up his mind to go—she quickly assembled a tray of bread, cheese, and cold kidney pie from the pantry. Then she poured him a large glass of barley water.

"How well you look after me, Miss Chance," he exclaimed, smiling drowsily and looking remarkably, roguishly handsome.

Why would she not look after him, as he once did for her? But apparently he did not remember. She thought of his handkerchief still folded and kept in her possession.

"Somebody must take care of you, Captain."

His smile drooped. "Not many would trouble themselves." With slow fingers he scratched his cheek and surveyed this hasty repast she set before him. "Not since my mother..."

Her heart pinched as she remembered his sadness all those years ago, when he was on his way to his mother's funeral. "Yes. But you still have your father and a large family. A very large family. I...I have none."

At that he gave a gruff chortle. "You may be better off, Emma. Just because a man has a family, it does not mean he is loved by it."

"Nonsense! What of your brothers? To them you are a larger than life hero."

"They're children still. What do they know? My life is not nearly so exciting as they imagine it. Half the stories I tell are fabricated." He shot her a dark look. "Surely *you* know that, Miss Clever Puss."

"They still entertain. And your sister, Georgiana, adores you. She was always so proud of your letters from sea."

He sighed. "Georgiana and I share a bond in humor. Edward and Maria never had the humility to suffer being laughed at. They were always too serious and proud."

"And your father cares about you, of course."

Now he scowled, threw down a crust of bread and leaned back, making the chair groan. "My father? What can you possibly know about that relationship, madam? It's certainly nothing you could have read about in a book. Father and son have seldom had so little in common."

Startled by his sudden anger she fell silent.

Emma knew Mr. Frederick Hathaway was a man

burdened with the pressures of his work and many responsibilities, but she did not think him a deliberately unkind, unfeeling gentleman. Frequently she'd seen his expression fraught with concern about anything from a colicky baby to the impending death of King George. With so many worries on his mind, he could surely be forgiven the occasional absent-minded "*Tut-tut, what?*" when he almost ran into her in the passage and forgot her name.

"Edward was always his favorite," Guy snapped. "Me he could do without. Smug, superior Edward could do very little wrong. Ed the trustworthy and responsible. Ed the chaste." He raised his eyelids only half way and peered at her through the black lashes. "No doubt you like him too. Everybody does."

"Don't you?"

"He's an unremitting prig, who thinks himself better than the rest of us. He and I will never see eye-to-eye."

"But he is your brother."

"For what that's worth. Never does anything but criticize and turn his bloody nose up."

She watched him eat, her hands on the table, fingers pressed together. "I see you are at that stage of drunkenness when you feel dreadfully sorry for yourself."

He snorted. "Don't tell me you researched that subject too?"

"Lady Bramley has a son, Maxwell— her youngest. He makes for fascinating study in the matter of alcohol and its effects on the mind and body. I have only met him a few times, but he is seldom sober and always veering between ebullience and depression. Her ladyship is quite at the end of her tether."

Guy licked his long fingers and tore off another hunk of bread. "Hard to imagine that lady ever gives up on a cause."

After a moment, she said, "I daresay your brother Edward is envious of you."

"Envious?" he scoffed. "Have you had so many conversations with my brother? You know him so well already?" He sat up straighter, his eyes focused on her face. "I did not know you and he were so well acquainted."

She frowned. "We are not. But I have met him a few times, whenever he came to Allerton Square to see your father. I have worked there two years, you know."

"And what has he said to you on these visits? Of what did you talk?"

"I do not remember. The weather I suppose. The stars—"

"The *stars*?"

"Edward and I share an interest in astrology."

"Aha! So that's it! He crept in and wooed you with astrology, behind my back!"

She was amused. "Wooed me? I hope that was never his plan, Captain, for his sake. If it was I fear it went completely over my head."

He pouted for a moment, studying her face.

"And I said he must be envious of you because you are all that he is not."

The angles of his face softened and he looked less sulky. He sniffed and rubbed his thighs. "Such as? Tell me what I am then."

"You are handsome, adventurous and bold. Successful in your career. It cannot have been easy to live in your shadow."

He sat back and stared at her.

"I would not want to be anybody's favorite in a family," she added. "Even if it is not true, as long as the perception is there, all other siblings must be resentful to some degree. And for the favorite themselves, held up to be admired, there is a greater distance to fall."

Slowly he resumed chewing. Then he reached for his glass and took a gulp. "You mean to say I can only rise in my father's estimation."

"Better that than the reverse." She brushed his crumbs into her cupped hand and sighed. "Sometimes when a person is at their lowest it is easier to look up and see a break in the clouds. But if you are already up there, how can you see it? I often think how hard it must be for those folk born with everything in their favor, for they have no idea how to help themselves, or how to manage without when bad weather strikes. As you said, Edward lacks the humility to laugh at himself. He never had the chance to learn for he was never allowed to fail. Not by his father, nor himself.

You and Georgiana, on the other hand, have learned the art of rebounding when you fall, because you've had practice."

As she got up from the table, he caught a pleat of her frock and held her still. "You are quite remarkable," he said, sounding bewildered. "Thank you for trying to cheer me. Why do you bother?"

"I wanted to put the bounce back in your boots," she said simply.

He swallowed, his fingers tightening on her skirt as he looked up at her, his eyes wondering and searching. Finally he said, "You're a good woman, Emma Chance. You ought to run like hell from me."

"I thought you meant to save me from a spinster's lonely poverty."

Now he frowned, confused. "Perhaps I should run away from you," he muttered. "I never wanted to be trapped with one woman until you looked at me with those damnable eyes. Somehow," he pulled on her skirt, "you befuddled me."

She was amused. "Let me go then. Go away and stop bothering me. Run. Run far away. Save yourself before it's too late."

"I can't. I'm too intoxicated."

She resisted the temptation to laugh and touch his hair, to kiss him again. Instead she went to the door for a blast of cooling air and tossed the crumbs out into the yard. In winter, the birds needed crumbs all the more. Mrs. Lightbody used to shout at her for feeding the birds, for she said it only attracted rats to the house. Emma did it anyway. Rats had as much right to be there as anybody, she thought.

"They spread disease," the old headmistress used to spit and fume.

And you spread misery, but we have to feed you, Emma would think in reply.

These days she was getting brave enough that she would say it out loud.

Besides, she'd always felt empathy with the poor, reviled rats who did not ask to be born into this world and could not help their appearance.

The wind and rain were far worse now, whipped up into an icy storm. She shut the door again and wondered what she was going to do about Captain Hathaway. He could hardly stay in the house with all these young ladies under the same roof, entrusted to her care— what would folk think if they found out? On the other hand, she could not put him out in this weather to find his way back through the streets. He had come all that way on foot and they had no carriage or horse to take him back again. The man was not dressed for winter weather either.

For now he tucked into his impromptu repast and looked at her with warm gratitude. And something else for which she had no name. It made her feel like a shiny, ripened apple upon which he had his eye. A part of her wanted to fall from her branch and into his hands, but another part wanted to cling there, uncertain of his bite.

All she knew for sure was that she must keep

him talking as long as possible, because when he was silent and looking at her she felt devilishly tempted. When he studied her in that darkly sensuous way his eyes spoke their own language and it was not one a virtuous girl ought to understand. Lady Bramley would say his eyes asked for trouble and, undoubtedly, they generally got what they wanted.

She returned to the table. "Tell me about the places you've been."

His brows lifted. "Too many."

"Tell me. I have been nowhere."

"If you share my supper." Guy took a slice of cheese and held it out for her. "I'll tell you about the Caribbean islands."

"Where coconuts grow?" She'd tasted some once in a cake at Lady Bramley's house and thought it must come from paradise.

"Correct."

Now that she dared look into his eyes for longer periods without looking away, Emma had begun to find herself uncomfortably warm, her throat dry and a heaviness in her blood for which she had no explanation. Clutching at threads of sanity, she murmured, "A coconut, you know, is not actually from the nut family. It is a drupe. Like an olive."

"Fascinating. Between my experience and your facts, we can go far together." He had almost winked, but his eyelids were too drowsy. "Tell me where you would like to go, Emma, and I shall take you there. Anywhere you want."

"Anywhere?"

He slapped his hands down hard on his thighs, possibly to wake himself. "Anywhere."

She licked her lips. "One day, I would like to find my mother's grave."

He looked askance. "I was thinking Italy, Portugal, Jamaica—"

"You did say anywhere *I* wanted."

With a heavy sigh, he looked at her, his hands still resting on his thighs. "Very well, if that's your choice. Do you know where she is buried?"

Emma shook her head. He might as well know the unfortunate truth about her, she supposed. If he did not already. "My mother died very soon after I was born, in a house of ill-repute in Bethnal Green."

He squinted. "Ah."

"That is all I know about her. Other than the fact that her name began with a 'Y'." She paused, swallowed nervously. "I will understand completely if you wish to withdraw the offer you made to me, in light of this information."

"Why would I do that?"

"A girl born in such a place and with no father willing to claim her? I am hardly a matrimonial prize, Captain."

He looked at her for a long moment and then chuckled low. "Then we make a perfect pair. For who else would take me?" His large fingers enclosed hers and that tight knot rested on the table between them.

"Nonsense. Many women would, to be sure."

"But they wouldn't put the bounce back in my boots the way you do, Emma."

Whenever he said her name like that she felt a little bird fluttering in her heart, as if it were caged there. But to ask him the question that preyed upon her mind would be clumsy, greedy, foolish. When he was ready, he would tell her. If he ever was. It still felt too unlikely.

"So does that mean you'll take me?" he added.

"I shall give you my answer on Wednesday at the theatre, as I told you already."

"You're a stubborn woman. You keep me on tenterhooks deliberately. Merciless Miss Chance!"

"If I was truly merciless I would have left you out in the hail. Instead I let you into this warm kitchen and fed you."

"Hmph." Now he examined the remnants of pie before him. "What is this anyway?" he muttered. "I thought it was steak and kidney pie."

"It is," she replied solemnly, "but without the steak."

His eyebrow quirked as he glanced up at her again, tongue pressed into his cheek.

"We cannot all afford steak in our pie, Captain. Some of us must budget. Besides, Lady Bramley says too much red meat is bad for the blood of young ladies, for it will make them over-heated and restless."

Guy shook his head and chuckled sleepily again. "We can't have that, can we?"

"Certainly not. We have the physical health and

moral well-being of these young ladies to cons—"

"Then you had better not go within a mile of a brothel, had you? See? Thank goodness I was here to stop you." He leaned over and kissed her.

"Aren't you supposed to ask before you do that, Captain?"

"I'm afraid I haven't the time, because it might take you as long to answer me in that case, as it does for you to answer that other damned question of mine."

"Clearly you eat too much red meat."

"And you don't eat enough. First order of business, when we are married, is to feed you steak and plenty of it. But for now," he wiped his free fingers on his shirt, his other hand still holding hers, "I suppose we must be content with only half of a steak and kidney pie."

Emma had never eaten steak in her life. There were a lot of things she'd never tasted, seen and done. He, naturally, had done it all.

As he finished his supper, Guy told her stories of white sand islands, dancing natives, and strange fruits that made a man see hallucinations if he ate the wrong part. He told her of foreign lands where the blistering heat could bake a man's skin dark brown in a few hours, and of frozen plains of unblemished white, in lands where a ship could be frozen in place for months and where a man had better get a taste for fried blubber and sea urchin or else starve.

Emma watched his face as he talked and she was

amazed at how far she had come— to sit here like this and converse with her dragon prince, without fear or nervousness. To let him grip her bare hand so firmly, his darker fingers entwined with hers. She was quite at home in his presence. He made it so, as he did when they danced together two years ago.

But even so, she could not say she was entirely at her "ease". There was nothing calm about her pulse and something churned within. Something new. A naughty, fire-breathing beast that lived within her own sinews and flesh.

How warm and full of vitality he was. It was almost overwhelming for her.

And, most extraordinary of all, her mind was empty of rustling pages, none of her facts seemed important at that moment. They were silent, resting at ease. There was nothing to think about; nothing to do but feel.

Eventually, Emma had to request that he release her hand so that she could fetch more food from the pantry— he had an astonishing appetite— but when she returned to the table, she found his head and arms slumped upon it, and gentle snores reverberating around the kitchen.

She fetched some blankets and a pillow then woke him gently.

He would have to go in Mr. Bishop's store shed across the yard.

"I suppose I must," he groaned, gripping her face in his hands. "I can expect no better comfort tonight, can I?" There was just a slight, winsome lift to the question, suggesting it was not rhetorical.

Emma replied firmly. "No, Captain, I fear you cannot. But the store shed is well-roofed and dry. Mr. Bishop takes very good care of his tools."

"Bishop be damned," he grumbled.

With his tall weight leaning on her, she managed to get him outside, across the wet yard and into the small, but cozy, storage shed.

Before she left him there with a lantern, he gripped her hand again and said, "Next time you and I share a supper, Clever Puss, we'll share a bed too. And we'll not leave it again for five days."

"I know you are still inebriated, Captain, and so I must excuse your impertinence, but it is not proper to mention the marriage bed. Nor does it sound very practical to laze in it for five days. Won't you be hungry?"

He grinned slowly and in a manner that she could only term as demonically. "Ravenous," he whispered. "There shall be no part of you left that I have not nibbled upon."

She could hardly bring herself to think of it. Oh, who was she trying to fool? It was on her mind all too often. She had overcome a fear of cows and Mrs. Lightbody. Surely she might overcome this too.

But was it fear, or something else that fizzed and sputtered inside her when she looked at his teeth and imagined them softly grazing her bare skin?

He laughed softly, as if he read all that on her

face. "Kiss me once more before you abandon me to this dreadful place of cobwebs and discarded paraphernalia."

So she did. It would have been a quick, gentle peck, but one hand cupped the back of her head, his other her cheek, and he seized her lips again in a slow, deep, extraordinary kiss that left her claimed, her decks breached, sails overtaken. As if she was bounty captured at sea.

Another low groan shattered her heart's beat. Somehow his kiss reached inside her and took possession of her soul, in the same way his sad sigh once drew her to listen through a wall and a fog.

"I'm not certain how much longer I can be patient and gentlemanly," he murmured, his breath warming her knuckles as he drew her hand to his mouth.

"I daresay you need practice at it."

"My less polite parts might seize up if they are not soon put to good use, Emma. Do you see how hungry I am?"

But she would not look. "Abstinence, I understand, is hard for a man."

"At present I find it intolerably, achingly... hard." And then the tip of his tongue swept across her palm and she felt her heart pick up that too-rapid pace again.

How had this handsome man ever fallen into her hands? By what unlikely stroke of luck had he ever noticed her? She caught herself waiting for a pinch to wake her.

When he looked up at Emma, the lantern light flickered in his eyes and then turned to hot smoke. "Will you leave me here alone, Clever Puss?" There was such yearning in his voice that a weaker woman might have relented. As, according to rumor, many women had before her.

She replied softly. "You are not alone. The spiders will keep you company."

He groaned and swept fingers back through his rain-dampened black curls. Something else at which she could not look.

"Besides, this is where we keep all the best tools, and their parts, until they *can* be put to good use."

With that she left him in the shed, satisfied that he would be warm and dry there.

Another Best Night of her Life, she mused.

But only so far. Because she knew now that there would be more. Many more.

Chapter Twenty-One

The next morning Emma woke late for the first time in her twenty-one years, probably because she did not fall asleep until the small hours. She had no lessons that morning, but usually she would still be up to help around the house. When she entered the kitchen to warn the Bishops about their overnight visitor encamped in the tool shed, she was alarmed to see Lady Bramley, in full sail, advising the cook on a "proper" way to make scones.

Her heart in her mouth, Emma went to the door, pretending to look out at the weather. A hasty scan of the yard showed nothing amiss. Mr. Bishop's storage shed was shut up, no sign of last night's visitor.

"Now, Miss Chance," her ladyship called out, "I hope you dress warmly for the theatre tomorrow."

Emma shut the door. "The...the theatre?"

"Yes, my dear, I hear you are going out to see a play. You did not think to tell me?"

"Oh." She took a deep breath. "I was going to mention it today." How had her ladyship found out? Emma studied the good lady's face and found it devoid of anger. In fact it was amiable. "You do not mind that I go?" she asked tentatively.

Lady Bramley's brows arched high. "Why would I mind, my dear girl? It is time you had some enjoyment."

Her heart swelled with relief and happiness. She had not expected the lady to be so agreeable about an evening in Captain Hathaway's company, but her demeanor this morning was good-humored and generous.

"I shall lend you my second best muff. The boy will bring it round tomorrow morning."

"Thank you, Lady Bramley," Emma managed, trying to restrain her smile before it took over her entire face. "I am very grateful. I was not certain you would think it appropriate."

"Why ever not, my dear? There are seldom riots at the theatre these days, and there can be nothing amiss with the company of a respectable country curate. Especially with his married sister as a chaperone."

"A country curate, madam?"

"That is Mr. Edward Hathaway's profession, is it not?"

"Well, yes, but—"

"And it is to be a moderate-sized party of young people. I understand Captain Hathaway will also be in attendance with his sister, so if any riot *should* break out, I am certain you will all be well protected. He might not have much to recommend him, but by all accounts the young man knows how to handle himself in a ruckus of that nature. At least we can let him be useful for something. Even brawn and a hot-temper has its place. His presence will keep undesirables at bay, as anybody of criminal intent will think better of trying their luck while he is one of your party."

Emma opened her mouth to speak, but no sound emerged.

"All considered, I can find nothing to which I might object about the evening. No, indeed, and it will be a chance for my houseguest to get out for the evening. I confess he can be most tiresome to watch over and now he has something to do."

Emma was utterly lost. "Your houseguest?"

Lady Bramley examined the crust on the bottom of a scone. "Mr. Ramsey will be with your party tomorrow evening. It is he who told me of it yesterday when he returned from dining with the Hathaways. He has been anxious to find entertainment for Miss Godfrey, and this little trip to the theatre, suggested by Lady Thrasher, will be an excellent outing."

Having no idea who Miss Godfrey might be and only faint memory of her ladyship having a houseguest, Emma wondered whether there had been some confusion on Lady Bramley's part.

Last night Guy had said nothing to her about anybody else joining their party. But he was, of course, in his cups when he stumbled to her door.

And Lady Bramley was not a person who might be confused very often. She was clear-headed, nononsense, and generally pressed a person for so many details that there could be no mistake made on her part when she repeated them.

So it must be assumed that Edward Hathaway was attending the theatre too. Is that what initiated the Captain's surprise late night visit and the ire against his brother?

Emma's spirits were severely deflated now that she knew their party had grown to a possible six. Who knew, perhaps there were more by now. Why not invite the entire square, she thought crossly. Bring the hurdy-gurdy man from the corner. Might as well.

"Oh, Miss Chance," said the cook suddenly, "Mr. Bishop found that stray you put in the shed for shelter last night. He wanted you to know he made sure it ate breakfast before it departed."

"He...he did? Oh, good. Thank you."

"It was a bleak night for a stray tom-cat to be out." Mrs. Bishop gave her a wry look. "Wonder how he wandered into our yard. Must have come over the wall."

"Yes, I think so."

"He had a healthy appetite by the looks of my pantry this morning."

Before Emma could reply, Lady Bramley began a lecture on the feeding of strays. "Plain bread and milk is all one should give. A bland diet helps balance the digestive system, and anything richer is likely to make the creature sick. Strays scavenge all day long, poor things, and one does them no favors by over-indulging their stomachs with fancy food. Was it a very little creature, Miss Chance? I do so hate to see them out in the rain and cold. I would take them all in if I could."

Emma managed a smile and a grateful look for

Mrs. Bishop over the other lady's head. "This one was a fair size, your ladyship. I have no doubt he does well enough for himself."

"A handsome fellow too," the cook added wryly. "With a twinkle in his eye."

"Indeed? Hopefully, somebody is looking after him then," said Lady Bramley with a sigh. "I, for one, would much rather have the companionship of an animal, than a man." She twisted around in her chair and raised that ever-present lorgnette to study Emma through it. "If I were you, young lady, I would give that stray a home if he comes back again and proves himself to be not completely feral. We shall give him a flea bath and I daresay, he will be pleasant company for you in the evenings."

"Yes, madam, I believe you are right."

"Of course, my dear, I always am."

* * * *

The promise Wednesday evening once held in store for them was now severely depleted. Guy, his sister and his brother traveled in their father's carriage to fetch Miss Chance from the school, while Walter Ramsey and Miss Godfrey made their way to Covent Garden in a curricle borrowed from Lady Bramley, who was clearly eager to get her guest out of the house.

Any chance of an intimate whisper or a private glance to go unnoticed was all gone. To make matters worse for Guy, his sister, having apparently decided that Edward would be a perfect match for her friend, made certain they sat together in the carriage and then in the box at the theatre.

"I think Miss Chance is fond of Edward," she whispered in Guy's ear as they waited for the play to begin. "And she certainly enlivens his expression, do you not think?"

He growled in response, "Edward's expression could not be enlivened if he were to be chased by an irate bull."

"Oh, Guy!" She chortled softly. "What has he done to annoy you now?"

"Me? I am in a perfectly civil mood. I simply see nothing to be gained by pushing him at Miss Chance."

"*Nothing to be gained?* How can you say that? I would love to have Emma as a sister. She is so steady, selfless and kind; I think she would make a perfect wife for our brother, and we all know he seeks one."

He sank into his seat and scowled. In front, to his left sat Edward and Miss Chance. Tonight, for once, she did not have her hair tucked behind her ears, but had made it curl in soft waves which, in the amber kiss of gaslight, shone gold whenever she tilted her head.

On their journey to the theatre she had worn a hooded cloak made from the velvet Guy had chosen, but before they sat in the box she had removed it to reveal a pale blue muslin gown beneath— simple and elegant. She seemed more delicate than ever and yet not in a brittle, feeble way. Delicate like a priceless bone china ornament, gilded with a soft brush of liquid gold. Exquisite, sought after treasure.

Well, he might not have her beside him, but from behind he could watch the curve where that slender neck met her shoulder. He could admire that slope of soft skin, study it at his leisure, and nobody would even know where he looked, as long as he kept his head resting on one hand, his eyes half-closed. His sister thought he'd fallen asleep, but the truth was far from it.

On his other side sat Walter and poor Miss Godfrey, who looked as happy to be in his company as he said he was to have her there. The young lady was very tall and narrow, her lips constantly working themselves together into a tight bow that suggested nerves, irritation or the smothered urge to laugh. Her eyes darted from side to side and whenever Walter ventured a remark they rolled all the way over in the opposite direction from where he sat on her left, as if he was too foolish even to be acknowledged with a look.

"Are you familiar with *The Duchess of Malfi*, Miss Godfrey?" Walter inquired dully.

"No. Is she an acquaintance of yours?"

Walter frowned. "That is the name of the play, madam."

"Oh."

"John Webster is the playwright."

"Is he, indeed? I'm sure I never heard of the

fellow." And she worked her lips disapprovingly. "I prefer a good comedy. A juggler or an acrobat."

"Well, I am sure we shall enjoy lighter fare in the afterpiece."

That, as far as Guy could tell, was the sum total of their conversation for some time. Walter leaned closer to Guy and whispered, "Miss Godfrey does not get to the theatre very often. She is very grateful to me for bringing her out."

Miss Godfrey gave a low huff.

"Yes. So I see." Guy smirked. "The lady seems... thrilled."

"And why would she not be? My company is always much in demand when in London."

Abruptly Miss Godfrey leaned around him to look at Guy and exclaimed, "What happened to your eye then, Captain?"

It was no longer a vivid black and blue, but a slight discoloration remained, along with a little grazing at the temple and a scar on the cheekbone where his opponent's ring had cut into his skin. "A little misunderstanding, Miss Godfrey."

She looked smug, her lips gathered up like a drawstring purse.

Walter cleared his throat and whispered, "I told her it was an altercation over your woman."

"*What?*"

"Oh, Mr. Ramsey told me all about you and your wicked ways, Captain," the lady hissed, her eyes sliding back and forth. "How you cannot stay away from danger and lose your heart to all the wrong women. You're lucky you have him to look after you."

"Miss Godfrey, I can assure you—"

Georgiana nudged him with her foot. "Shh! The play is starting."

He stared ahead to see Edward leaning closer to Miss Chance and whispering in her ear. It felt very hot in that theatre box suddenly.

A soft curl meandered shyly down the back of her neck, tempting his fingers. He did not care for her attention to be stolen away by Edward and he was very glad that he had kissed her last night. Hopefully, she would remember that now, as he did, and the memory would distract her from his brother. It was worth a cold, uncomfortable few hours in the store shed to plant himself firmly in her mind, squeezing in between all those learned facts.

His gaze narrowed upon her spine and he imagined slowly working his way down it with his lips. He could almost taste her skin on his tongue. Last night it was sweet, redolent of sugared almonds. And Guy had a very definite sweet tooth, or so he had very recently discovered.

Don't startle Miss Chance. Hmm. She would be startled very pleasantly when he finally had her to himself and she was Mrs. Hathaway. He intended to startle her frequently, to make her laugh and sigh and cry out with excitement.

But as he watched the two people in front of him

he realized that Edward's hair was not thinning after all, just very pale gold. It was, in fact, quite lustrous and smooth. Edward was not only the brother with all the brains, but all the good looks too. It was most unjust.

He scowled and sank further in his seat, arms folded over his chest. A clergyman. What use was that hair to a clergyman? Why didn't Edward find a wife from among all those blushing hopefuls that filled his pews back in Norfolk? What about one of those earl's daughters? As Guy had said to his father, such a conquest was surely beyond the reach of a country clergyman, but stranger matches had happened and Edward was very...."pretty". Really, he ought to be encouraged to aim as high as he could. And leave Miss Chance alone.

"What's amiss with you?" Georgiana whispered. "You look as if you're plotting Edward's demise."

"I merely wonder when he means to go back to his parish. Surely this is an important time of year for a clergyman."

"It is. Whatever brought him to London must be exceedingly urgent." Georgiana looked very smug.

Guy ground his jaw and then rubbed it with one hand to release the tension. "I pray that whatever takes him back again will be equally urgent. And swift. I wonder how they can manage without him. Does he have no sickly parishioner on their deathbed? No weeping widow in desperate need of his pastoral care?"

His sister leaned closer to whisper. "Oddly enough he said the same to me of you today. Wanted to know why you had none of your standard variety hussies eager for your companionship these days, and that he hoped you would soon be going back to sea."

"And what did you tell him?"

"That you must both be gracious and courteous to each another and entrust that the better man shall win. Because my friend has excellent taste and will make her choice wisely."

He looked at her. She grinned.

"Poor, dear Guy. Did you think you could keep it from me? Or that she could?"

"Better man be damned," he growled.

"Don't be a sour loser."

Loser? Ha! He had no intention of losing Emma Chance to anybody. She damn well needed him. Who else could make her a better husband and look after her as he could?

* * * *

Edward was being very solicitous, offering his arm before anybody else might, and insisting she take a chair in the very front of Lady Bramley's box. He worried whether she was too hot or too cold, whether she could see all of the stage, and whether she would like refreshment. And just as it was whenever anybody fussed too much around her, Emma found it stifling. On top of her disappointment at being separated from Guy, it was doubly irritating to have her every sigh questioned and her every twitch assumed to signify some dissatisfaction with her surroundings. But she remained polite. It was, after all, hardly Edward's fault that his elder brother had all her attention even when he was not beside her, and she did feel sympathy for Edward. As she'd said to Guy last night, it cannot have been easy to grow up in *his* shadow.

Although she tried to pay attention to the play, there was far too much going on in her real life tonight. Far too much to explore with all her senses.

The theatre had only been fitted with gaslight in the past few years— a development of which Lady Bramley had not approved, "We shall all be blown to pieces in an explosion, no doubt!"—and Emma, bathed in that bright, unnatural light, felt herself to be a tiny bead in a great golden crown. Looking out over the edge of the box, she admired all the glittering jewelry around the theatre, all the exquisitely attired members of the "beau monde" who came to see and be seen. Feathers nodded and fans wafted. Some of the ladies in other boxes looked very highly painted— more so than the actors below. Low conversation and gusts of laughter trickled from box to box, even when a character on the stage was being brutally murdered, for very few members of that noisy and restless audience were interested in the play, it seemed. Far below, in the notorious "pit", a particularly rowdy segment of the audience coughed and jeered and even threw nuts at the stage throughout the performance.

As her gaze traveled over the seats in the auditorium, faces turned upward toward her like flowers seeking the sun, and Emma knew they must wonder who she was. The plain girl with the blue ribbon in her hair and no jewelry, sitting among the grand folk. Surely they must be thinking that she didn't belong there.

At one point Emma was quite certain she felt Guy's gaze on her shoulders, so she turned her head to look behind. He smiled slowly, sensuously.

"Ham, Miss Chance," Edward blurted in her ear, snatching her attention back to him.

"Ham?"

"Might I fetch you some?"

"Well, no I—"

"Or a cold chop, perhaps? Some wine? A pasty? I hear they are very good here."

She swallowed a chuckle. "No, thank you, Mr. Hathaway. I am not hun—."

"We shall be seated here for some hours. I would not want you to fade away."

"Please get something for yourself. Do not worr—"

"A blanket? Let me get you one for your shoulders."

"I am not in the least col—"

"If anything on the stage should upset you, Miss Chance, merely say the word and I shall escort you out."

"I am familiar with the—"

"The plot is of a gruesome, bloodthirsty bent, I fear. You may find the action too much for your genteel sensibilities."

She licked her lips, leaned closer to him and whispered, "To be honest, I have something of a bloodthirsty and gruesome bent myself. Don't tell anybody."

This comment he finally did hear and let her finish. Clearly shaken by her calm confession, he sat back in his seat and remained quiet for some time.

Emma exhaled a soft sigh of relief and returned her attention to the play.

It was not long however, before she was distracted again, this time by the snippets of whispered conversation occurring on her right, where Mr. Walter Ramsey sat with Miss Godfrey.

"I have always done what I can to keep him out of trouble, but Guy Hathaway is a hot-head, a fool when it comes to the female gender. He will not be told. Thus I am ever stepping in to save his posterior in a brawl. My reputation is such that other men put down their fists and retreat rather than face me."

"Perhaps they don't want to hurt you."

"They fear for themselves, Miss Godfrey," he answered in a condescending tone, "not for me."

"Is it only the men that back away?" the young lady inquired archly.

"The ladies tend to flock around me, but I do not like to bask in glory."

"You are the very epitome of modest and

retiring, sir."

Her dry wit apparently went over Mr. Ramsey's head. "It has always fallen to my duty to rescue others. They rely upon me so, for I am the one with the level-head. I am the one they come to in greatest times of need. Of course, a ship's surgeon— a man of medicine— is often called upon to save life and limb."

"You must be busy, sir. Rescuing and saving all over the place."

"Oh, but I always have time for a young lady such as yourself."

"What would I need *you* for?"

Emma, still unintentionally eavesdropping, struggled not to chuckle.

Mr. Ramsey blustered onward valiantly. "Well...should there be any rioting for instance. Or some ruffian try to snatch your reticule in the street outside."

"What could you do about it? Play dead would be your best option, from the look of you."

"I should chase the fellow down and give him a piece of my mind."

"Can you spare any?"

There was a pause and then the fellow forced a laugh. "How amusing you are, Miss Godfrey. Delightfully...*piquant*."

Later Emma heard him say to Captain Hathaway, "I believe Miss Godfrey is smitten with me. Is she not hilarious? I declare I have never met such a lively, witty creature. I am on the way to being thoroughly enchanted with the little minx."

To which Guy replied, "Then I would take the lady's advice and feign death if I were you. It might be easiest. For all of us."

* * * *

At the end of the performance, after a light-hearted pantomime that finished the evening, their party stepped out through the tall columns at the front of the theatre and stood waiting for the carriages.

Pushing his way through the crush of people on the steps, Guy managed to grasp Emma's arm while nobody was looking. Edward had bossily taken command of finding the coachman and Walter was too busy making a fool of himself with Miss Godfrey. Georgiana had seen somebody she recognized and gone to poke her nose into their business. They were, thus, alone in the midst of that crowd.

"I regret that the evening did not turn out quite as I had hoped," he murmured.

She looked up at him, her eyes shining in the shadow of her velvet hood. "On the contrary, I enjoyed every minute. Thank you for thinking of the play and inviting me."

"But we did not sit together."

Head tilted, she whispered, "Did it really matter?" He could hear a shy smile in her voice, although he could not see her mouth. "We were together nonetheless. I felt it. Did you not?"

He cleared his throat. "Yes."

They were connected somehow, he mused. It was as if a gossamer thread linked him to her and vice versa. Even from the very beginning. Nobody else could see those lines, but they both felt the gentle tug.

A sly warmth stole its way through Guy's body and lifted his mood. That thread, he knew, would always be there now. They did not have to hold hands and sit together to acknowledge that bond. How extraordinary that he should feel this for a woman so very different to any he had ever pursued before. With her he was...at home.

And then a startling thought came to him. Was he in love with Miss Chance?

It was a curious sensation, and he did not know what to make of it, but there it was.

At first he had seen marriage as an end to a means, a convenient solution for both of them. He wanted to help her and it was time he settled down. That was what he had told himself from the beginning. But could it be possible that there was more to his proposal? Much more?

Her hood had tipped slightly back, revealing a gleam of fair hair in the lamplight. The color was much richer tonight and her eyes, usually cool morning grey, were different too. They were darker, filled with their own luxurious blue velvet.

Once, he had been drawn to her mind. Curious, intrigued he had taken a second look at a girl he would probably not otherwise have noticed. But the attraction had grown. Now it was physical too. He wanted this woman and not just to save her from poverty. The gallant knight had wicked, lustful thoughts about her too. It could no longer be denied or disguised as something innocent and practical. She was everything he needed, all tied up in those strange, somber eyes that saw directly through him.

Guy Hathaway was terrified suddenly by the thought of losing her.

What about that thread? Well, nobody else saw it, did they? The thread could be trampled, snapped, broken by any clumsy fool who got in their way.

There was not a moment to lose.

Suddenly feeling very serious and somber, he took her hand. "Whatever you've been told about me, I am not a bad man, Emma. I may not be as pious as Edward, but I am not *all* mischief."

She looked up at him again, stars reflected in her wide eyes. "Thank you for clarifying, but it really wasn't necessary. I seldom believe everything I hear, and I prefer facts to supposition."

"Yes," he exclaimed, gripping her hand tighter. "I know."

"And not everybody is good, just as they are not all bad."

"Yes."

"Well, there you are then."

In his peripheral vision he could see Edward coming back toward them, ducking his head against the first spatter of rain. There was not a moment to lose.

"Miss Chance," he blurted. "Will you do me the honor of becoming my wife?"

He did not care if anybody heard, but there was too much noise in any case and nobody paid the two of them any attention.

"Captain Hathaway, I ...I shall. As long as Lady Bramley gives us her blessing."

His fingers tightened around hers and his pulse quickened. He could scarce believe it. She had accepted him. With one condition. One large condition.

"I know we do not officially require her ladyship's blessing," she added. "But I should like it very much, all the same. Her opinion means much to me."

He nodded slowly. Guy had not forgotten the prominent role Lady Bramley took in the lives of his sister and her friends. Whether it was official or not, she saw herself as Emma Chance's guardian and caretaker— and apparently the young lady saw her the same way. It would be disrespectful to overlook, or treat lightly, the role Lady Bramley had assumed.

In truth he would rather face a court martial than another inquisition from that redoubtable lady, but confessing so would make him appear weak in Emma's eyes.

So, he must take the bull by the horns. Miss Chance wanted it so and therefore she would have it.

Chapter Twenty-Two

The following morning, as he passed his father's study, Guy heard raised voices through the door.

"Miss Chance? *Miss Chance,* the ruddy governess? Certainly not, Edward. I expect great things of you, and there are far better prospects out there than *Miss Chance.*"

"But sir, I believe she would make a good wife for a clergyman. She is virtuous, modest and exceedingly frugal. I—"

"What about one of those earl's daughters?" His father sounded almost desperate. "Do they not invite you to dine up at Cottingham Hall frequently?"

"Not with any intention of that sort. Usually I am invited merely to fill a seat and the earl likes to tell me what he thinks the subject of the next Sunday sermon ought to be. I hardly think I would be deemed good enough for one of his daughters."

"Nonsense! One of the younger girls surely could do worse than you for a husband. When there are so many daughters in the family a father is often eager to get them quickly settled and at the least trouble or expense to himself. You haven't tried to put yourself forward enough, I expect." Their father's unrealistic expectations continued unabated. Nobody could tell him that his favorite son wasn't good enough for an aristocrat's daughter. "And now I find you have been wasting time, dwelling on that pale little nobody."

"But I would much rather marry a young lady

who was not raised in luxury. Miss Chance would make a more suitable bride. She would be appreciative of the life I can give her."

In other words, thought Guy, Edward wouldn't have to try too hard or put himself out. His life would not change for Emma.

"Miss bloody Chance is out of the question. And if you keep harping on about it, I shall dismiss her from this house." There was silence for a moment and then Mr. Hathaway, having regained his breath and lowered his pitch, added, "You disappoint me, Edward. The girl has nothing. She's not even much to look at."

"A clergyman is better off with a wife who is plain and humble, sir. His congregation would approve such a choice, whereas a bride of great beauty and fashion would only elicit envy and other unpleasantness."

Guy frowned at the door, amazed that his brother thought her plain.

Emma Chance was surely the most beautiful creature in the world. Were Edward's eyes closed?

"I cannot allow it," their father replied, huffing and puffing like a kettle on the fire. "I refuse to see you throw away your chance of betterment. To take Miss Chance as a wife would, in fact, be a step down. Three steps down. Good God, boy, so far down I can no longer reach to raise you up. I gave in to you years ago when you chose the church for a living. I will not give in this time. You are the son for whom I have hope, Edward. You have the manners, the looks *and* the brains. Don't let me down by throwing all that away on a girl with no dowry and no prospects. If you insist on this madness, you needn't think I shall help you financially. If you cannot help yourself, I can no longer help you either. I shall leave you nothing in my will. In fact," he roared, "I shall never again mention you as my son."

Again there was silence. Finally he heard Edward exclaim, "I am sorry it comes to this, but I must follow my instinct, sir."

Guy ducked hastily behind the hat stand as his brother came out, slamming the door and striding off in a most unholy huff.

* * * *

"Captain Hathaway! This is a surprise. I was not expecting a visit from *you* this morning." Lady Bramley swept across the drawing room to inspect him. "Mr. Ramsey tells me it was a most enjoyable evening at the theatre."

"Yes, your ladyship, it was very good of you to lend us your box for the event.""Well," she waved her lorgnette, "I do not use it much myself these days, and I thought you young people might as well enjoy it."

Guy had removed his hat and now struggled with what to do with it. She did not invite him to sit, but stared steadily and said, "I wonder what can have brought *you* to see me so early. And, if I am not

338

mistaken, with your hair trimmed."

Had she expected his brother Edward instead? He tried a smile, which was not reflected on her expression. But her eyes glittered with a slight amusement. Or was it scorn? Better press on with it. "Lady Bramley, I come to you for the purpose of securing your approval. I have asked Emma Chance for her hand in marriage."

She blinked. Twice. "Emma? Emma Chance? For *you?* I think not, young man. Whatever can have induced you? Is this one of your jests?"

"Your ladyship, I recall the conversation we had two years ago—"

"And well do I, Captain! I told you then that she is not the girl for you, nor you the man for her."

"I have changed since then, your ladyship. I believe I can make Miss Chance happy."

Shaking her head, she walked to the mantle and rang the bell in the wall. Guy feared he was about to be dismissed already.

"Madam, I have only the very best interest in Miss Chance's future. I know you think I had a wild youth—"

"Captain Hathway." Spinning to face him, hands clasped before her, she spoke in that same booming, self-assured voice with which he'd heard her address servants and an inn-keeper. "I am certain that this fancy, however it has come into your head, will swiftly be erased from it to make room for another before too long. But I cannot allow poor Miss Chance to become attached, to believe you can offer her any stability. I have heard all about you, sir, and about your many affairs. My houseguest, Mr. Walter Ramsey, is acquainted with you, is he not?"

"Walter." He sighed and looked down at his hat. "Yes." He'd heard his friend boasting to Miss Godfrey yesterday evening, but had dismissed it as Walter's usual bluster. It had not occurred to him that the fool might also be saying the same to his hostess.

"He has regaled me with stories of the many duels and brawls from which he has been obliged to save you over the years. While I was aware of those rumors of your wicked behavior, long before Walter confirmed them, I had not heard until now of your Spanish wife, Captain Hathaway."

He groaned softly. "Your ladyship, I entreat you to consider, I was a boy of nineteen. And the marriage was annulled when she was found to have another husband still living."

"Nevertheless, these things leave a stain not easily erased, Captain. Walter seemed to think it a most amusing story— he could barely keep to his chair as he told it— but I fail to see the hilarity."

"Did you never make a mistake, madam, when you were young?"

"Certainly not. I was raised to know my duty, to hold my reputation as if it were made of crystal. I always considered my family's honor in any undertaking. I see you smirk at that. Yes, I may have walked a path you see as narrow and unadventurous,

340

but it was straight and steady, with nothing I might later regret."

"Then I wish I could have been like you, madam. Alas, I had different experiences in my life."

The door opened, and a mournful-looking butler entered. "Madam?"

"Ah, yes, Filkins, do bring a tray of tea. And Mr. Ramsey is leaving tomorrow, so I shall begin closing up the house. You may instruct the maids to get out the dustcovers and begin packing. And do not forget my darling Horatio's winter things for the country. Do not toss them into a box the way you generally do. Pack with care."

"Yes, madam." He turned slowly and walked out.

"You are going away, Lady Bramley?"

"Yes, to visit my son in Shropshire for the Christmas season. So, as you see, I have much to do. You are returning to sea soon, are you not?"

"I am. I had hoped to marry Miss Chance before I leave again."

"But your courtship has endured only a matter of days. No wonder she mentioned none of this to me."

"It was at her insistence that I came here for your blessing, madam." Anxiety tightened cruelly in his chest. "Unless she has your approval, I fear she will not accept me. It was her one condition."

Lady Bramley looked smug as she lowered herself to a chair. "She is a good girl, as I told you before. Miss Chance is sensible and knows what is best for her. She also knows my judgment to be sound."

"Of all this I am aware. And I beg you, madam, not to dismiss my suit so hastily. I know her happiness and security is your concern. But can it not be my concern also? Is it so impossible for you to believe that this young lady and her goodness might be capable of making me a better man?"

She let her lorgnette fall to her lap. "Very well. Plead your case if you must, Captain. You have until my cup of tea is drunk, and then I really must get on with my day."

So, he had wedged his virtual foot in the door and prevented her from closing her mind completely. Or else she simply wanted to see him beg for her own entertainment, he mused darkly.

The door opened to readmit Filkins and the tea tray.

"Do sit down, Captain. You may as well, now that you're here. A man pacing about in a room makes it dreadfully untidy."

He promptly sat. "Your ladyship, I have saved a considerable amount of—"

"Pray, do not lower the tone immediately by mentioning finances, Captain. It is impolite. I shall assume that part of it. Even you would not be so reckless as to consider a wife if you had nothing with which to feed, clothe and house her."

"Indeed." He took a deep breath and tried to settle his nerves. "It is my intention to lease a house on the Norfolk coast. I grew up in that county and have always thought I would return one day. I believe Miss Chance would like it there very much."

"Miss Chance is accustomed to Town."

"But she can become accustomed to the country. She seems keen to explore the world a little more than she has up until now. Books are all well and good, but they cannot win out over experience."

"What of her work? She enjoys it immensely and yet she must give that up if she is to marry."

"But why?" He began a shrug and then, remembering how she disliked the gesture, stalled the movement in the nick of time. "I have never seen the necessity for a lady to give up her passion when she marries. If she desires to continue, why should she not take in pupils even after we are married? Mrs. Hathaway might be a governess just as well as Miss Chance."

"That is an extraordinary view, young man. One might even say, revolutionary."

"I want my wife to be happy and fulfilled. Besides, when I am away at sea she will need occupation to keep her content. Otherwise," he grinned, "she might miss me too greatly."

"And what of you, Captain? Do you see yourself putting aside all other attachments and devoting yourself to one lady for the remainder of your days?"

"I do. I will."

"You answer with great confidence, young man."

"Because I know what I want and what I need."

"Hmph." She considered him over her teacup.

"You are a devilish charmer, sir. When you wish to get your own way, you know how to say the right things to a lady. And I am no exception, it seems. But Miss Chance is too young. This...courtship...has been too swift."

"Madam, it has taken me two years to come to this decision."

"Then should not Miss Emma Chance be given the same time to come to hers?"

His heart sank. "*Two years?*"

"She may feel pressured into accepting you, Captain. Unlike you, she has not long been out in the world and has yet to see all the choices she might have. I cannot put my blessing behind this hasty match. But if you can prove your commitment by waiting another two years, and Miss Chance has had no change of heart in the meantime, *then* you shall have my approval."

He stared, felt the world falling away, crumbling under his boots like soft chalk at a cliff's edge.

"The truth is, young man, I do not dislike you. I find you amusing company. But there have been too many misjudgments in your past, two many of those *mistakes,* as you call them. And Miss Chance is very dear to me. I have come to see her almost as my own daughter. In fact, I am willing to give her a dowry if she does choose to marry. But I do not want her to become another of your *mistakes.*"

"I don't care about a dowry. Indeed, my father is likely to strike me out of his will when he learns whom I've chosen to marry. And I care just as little about that."

"Will he?" She frowned. "How do you know this? You have spoken to your father in this matter?"

"No, but my brother Edward has and was told that if he pursued the idea of marrying Miss Chance he would no longer have a father."

"I see." Her face was grim for a moment. "Then your brother the clergyman does have his sights set on Emma too, as I suspected. He would make for her a more suitable husband."

"He's not in love with her."

"And you are?"

He took a deep breath. "Yes."

Lady Bramley stirred her tea and looked thoughtful. "And you are not concerned by your father's threat of disownment?"

"I don't care if he does. I want Emma Chance, and I mean to have her."

"That is a bold statement of defiance, Captain. Reckless."

"I have never had the burden of being my father's favorite son." He smiled wryly. "There are, after all, advantages to being the scapegrace. As Miss Chance has said, I can only go up in everybody's estimation, can I not? It's certainly not possible to get any lower in my father's assessment."

She seemed about to smile, but curbed it, shaking her head. "You may not think you care about your father's good will or a dowry, but you should, young man. You should. Being swept up in romance is all well and good, until you run out of coal and you cannot afford medicine for the baby. Then you will find your love makes a thin blanket and an even thinner soup. I am aware that you have enjoyed success in your career, that it has been profitable. Oh yes," her eyes twinkled, "I know a vast deal about you, young sir. Your sister is an unbridled chatterbox and even more informative than Walter Ramsey. But Miss Chance should not be made to feel like a beggar, who comes to the marriage with nothing. That would make her your possession, not your wife."

But to wait two years. It felt like a lifetime.

"You may court Miss Chance. To that I give my blessing. But until I am satisfied that brawling and naked Spanish ladies are out of your life for good I cannot give my support to marriage. Of course, neither you nor Emma are required to have my blessing to do as you please, and your willingness to come here and ask me shows that you have good intentions at heart, Captain Hathaway. That, however, is my decision. For now."

He blew out a slow breath. "I see."

"I hope that you do." She sniffed, one eyebrow arched. "And I am pleased that you did heed my advice to you two years ago. That hair looks much better, Captain. Quite respectable at last. Now, if only the rest of you can follow suit."

* * * *

346

When Emma heard Lady Bramley's judgment she felt her heart slow, a cool veil falling over it like a dustsheet.

Two years. In two years he might well change his mind, fall in love with a beautiful woman of sophistication and fashion, then forget Emma entirely. But then, that was probably exactly what her ladyship expected to happen, and she meant to save Emma from the heartache while she could.

"As she acknowledged, we do not *officially* need her blessing," said Guy, his eyes dark and more than a little angry.

"But what of your father? He will not approve either, will he?"

He scowled. "Why not? What does that matter to us?"

Emma licked her lips and wound her hands together. Although she stood by the fire in her parlor, she was cold, felt a brisk, unsettling draft blowing through. "Your brother Edward paid me a visit this morning."

Guy stood before her in silent but palpable fury, grinding his jaw.

"I must admit, although Edward paid me a great deal of attention last night, I had no inkling of his intention. Until this morning I thought him merely polite toward me, so the news that he'd actually considered marriage came as a great surprise." She had not intended to tell Guy about the strange visit from Edward. But she would have to now to explain how she knew of his father's opinion of her. "And in the process of letting his intentions be known, he told me everything Mr. Hathaway said about me."

"Damn him! Whatever my father has to say, Emma, means nothing to me."

His declaration brought tears to her eyes, but she refused to succumb and held them back as best she could. In truth, hearing how little Mr. Frederick Hathaway thought of her had been very hurtful. She was good enough to tutor his little boy and his ward, but she was not good enough to marry into the family. All those times when she ran into him in the passage and he did not know her name, she had put it down to the gentleman having too many names to remember. He was a very busy man, always at work. Yes, she had made excuses for his rudeness. Had even felt sympathy for him.

But now she knew that in his eyes she was no more than a servant. A nameless one.

"I would never want to come between father and son," she said sadly. "The guilt would be too much and eventually you would resent me, even if you think now that you would not."

"My father and I have never been close, Emma. I do not *care* what he thinks! I am not Edward who cowers before him. Do not be afraid of my father's bluster."

She walked to where he stood and took one of his hands in both of hers. "I am not afraid for myself, but I am concerned that we have too much against us.

Lady Bramley—"

"Likes me. The old lady confessed it. Even she could not deny it finally."

"Of course. Who would not like you?" And she smiled, feeling that dampness still hovering under her lashes. Two handsome Hathaway men vying for her hand. It made her want to laugh, even through her heart's pain. "But I do not want to give the lady any cause to *dis*like you. Guy, she has been so good to me, has given me so much— not just material things, but advice and courage. She has set me an example that I try my hardest to follow. Her approval means more to me than I can express."

"And what of me? Where do your feelings for me stand in all this?"

Emma swallowed, her throat tight, her heart aching. "I believe you are the kindest, dearest man I ever met. I have never known what love is, apart from that of friendship, but I believe I am in love with you."

His face relaxed, his eyes warmed. He brought her hands to his lips. "Then marry me now. The doubters be damned."

"If I am in love, will I not still be in love two years from now?"

Somehow she must try to improve his father's opinion of her, just as he must persuade Lady Bramley of his reformation. Perhaps he did not understand everything that lady had done for her or how ungrateful it would make her feel if she turned her back on that noble advice now.

He looked down, his mouth tight, jaw twitching angrily. "Would you have made Edward wait two years? Bramley thinks he's perfect for you."

She put her finger under his chin and raised it. "I told Edward I could never marry him. I thanked him very politely, but explained it was out of the question for me because my heart belongs to another."

His eyes narrowed.

"And when I told him where I was born, the circumstances of my birth and my mother's misfortunes, I believe he was rather relived that I had rejected his offer. Although he did his best to hide it, I could see he was shocked. I suppose, until today, he had merely thought me orphaned. At the very least he thought me respectable. But, as I explained to him, a woman born in a bawdy house is hardly a suitable curate's wife."

"But Bramley—"

"Knows nothing of where I was born or who my parents were. She knows I am the natural daughter of a gentleman who wishes to remain anonymous. That is all."

He brushed a lock of hair from her temple. "You should not be ashamed of where you were born or how. It is not in your power to change that. It was not your fault."

"No, but I can change how people see me now. I can prove that I am somebody. As you once told me that I am." She rose up on tiptoe and pressed her lips gently to his. "You made me believe it," she added softly. "You were the first who ever saw me. Even in the fog."

He managed an unsteady smile and looked young suddenly, a boy struggling to do the proper thing. From the pocket of his waistcoat he took a slender gold ring, in the center of which he had set the pink pearl Emma once lost from her borrowed necklace. "I had this made for you. Wear it every day, please, madam, so I know you do not forget me."

Her hand trembled as she held it out so that he could slip the ring onto her finger. Tears now filled her eyes too quickly, and she could not fight them back. Her vision blurred as if she sank underwater.

"But what do *you* have to make certain you remember me?"

In reply he swept her up in an embrace that took all the breath from her body and left her floating a few inches off the ground. He saved her from drowning. With his kiss he emptied her and filled her again and again, promising her more than she'd ever thought possible for her future.

Those next two years would pass at a glacial pace, she thought, suddenly tempted to marry him here and now. Why shouldn't she?

But no. Her good sense reined her in. She did not want to strain his relationship with his father, nor did she want him to earn Lady Bramley's wrath. He was a man intent on improving himself, and she wanted to show her strength and capabilities to the world. A hasty elopement would be no way to go about it, for either of them.

Chapter Twenty-Three

Walter came to Allerton Square later that morning in great distress.

"I didn't realize, old chap! How could I have known that you had an eye on that little governess? You should have said! This is what comes of keeping secrets from your best friend." He paused and looked sheepish. "I *am* still your friend... I hope."

With a groan Guy was forced to concede that Walter could not have known the damage he did with his tales for Lady Bramley— stories that had been rearranged to make Walter look better in the eyes of his hostess, and cause her to write a favorable report back to his mother.

"I was not even aware of any connection between the old lady and Miss Chance. I had no inkling of that guardianship for she was never mentioned to me. You know I would not bring you harm for anything, Hathaway."

"It doesn't matter now."

"But the young lady—"

"I'm sure she will recover, Ramsey. We both shall." He sighed heavily and rubbed his chest, casting a pained glance upward. "Somehow life must go on despite this disappointment you have caused us."

Guy would, naturally, use it for every favor he could entice out of the sorrowful Walter. He had to be paid back somehow, didn't he?

* * * *

He discovered that his brother had made amends with their father. Of course he had. Despite that earlier claim of being willing to disregard any threat of his father's, when push came to shove he did not want to risk losing his portion of the family fortune. Apparently even a clergyman could be mercenary without disturbing the balance of his halo. He made certain to use Miss Chance's rejection to his own advantage, by pretending that it was his decision to give her up.

While Guy pretended to read the paper at breakfast and the ladies had not yet come down, he heard his brother mutter, "Ultimately, father, I found the young lady lacking certain...qualities a curate's wife ought to have."

"Then we are finished with this business?" he heard his father reply gruffly. "And the governess is forgotten?"

"Yes, father."

"Well, thank Christ for that! Good god, son, you almost gave me an attack of the heart!"

"Don't take the lord's name in vain, father." Back to prim holiness again. Of course, Edward never ventured far off that path.

Guy peered over the top of his paper. "Hmm? What's that about the governess?"

"Your brother had taken a fancy to the idea of marrying her. I talked him out of it." His father bit into a slice of toast and chewed contentedly.

"Did you? *You* talked him out of it. Couldn't have been a very certain and decided fancy then."

"Edward knows he's destined for better. I knew he'd come around."

Guy folded the newspaper and looked at his brother across the table. Edward pulled a brattish face— the sort he always used and which their father failed to notice.

"So Miss Chance gets to keep her post then. That's fortunate. I thought you'd end up getting her dismissed, Ed."

"As long as she does the job she's paid for, she can stay," said their father, scraping butter across another slice of crisp toast and turning his gaze to the paper Guy had set down. "The quiet ones! Tsk tsk. They do have to be watched, it seems. I had no idea it was going on under my nose."

"Perhaps Guy ought to be warned too, father."

"Guy?" Their father sputtered, spraying crumbs. "He doesn't want a wife. Isn't fit for one either. He'd certainly never look at that pale, scrawny creature, not for any purpose."

"I thought you wanted me to find a decent bride, father?" Guy was amused. "It's never too late. I might yet surprise you."

His father, not looking up from the paper, huffed scornfully, "Indeed."

"If Ed's decided against the governess, I suppose she's free to think of somebody else." He grinned at his brother. "After all, very little is expected of me. I ought to be grateful for what I can get. Even that sad bit of a girl."

"Yes, son, very amusing. You and your sister Georgiana love your pranks and always did. Two peas in a pod."

And Edward added his sixpenny-worth. "The day you finally marry is the day hell will freeze over."

Leaning across the table, Guy whispered, "Then I'd advise you, little brother, to invest in some thick, woolen unmentionables."

* * * *

Emma, at that moment, was packing her own unmentionables, slowly and with great care as always. That afternoon, Lady Bramley's carriage would call for her and then she would be off to Shropshire for Christmas. She would not see Guy Hathaway again until he was next on leave.

But she had his ring and the little pearl set into it.

Every so often she stopped what she was doing to admire it and feel that silly flutter in her heart.

Even in her most vivid dreams, she'd never thought this would happen to her. Dead bodies and people falling over cliffs, yes; falling in love, no.

A sudden ringing at the front door bell broke into her pleasant thoughts. The Bishops were both out, stocking up on provisions for their own Christmas feast, so she went to answer it herself. Was it Guy come back again to kiss her? They had said goodbye yesterday, but coming back again for more was the sort of thing he would do. He was, of course, terribly impatient and reckless still, despite his claim to have changed.

Because he was at the forefront of Emma's mind he seemed to be the only possible visitor at that early hour.

Smiling, she opened the door.

Woman

Chapter Twenty-Four
1822
Norfolk

She looked out through the kitchen window, dried her hands on a cloth and puffed a strand of hair from her face. The sun was bright in her eyes, barely a cloud in the sky. Thirty yards from the window there was an oak tree, now in full, rustling green glory, and under it, in that leafy shade, sat a man in a wicker chaise, a wide-brimmed hat over his bent head, a walking cane resting against the chair.

Every day, while the weather was still fine, he sat out there watching the birds and periodically cursing at the bees. If it was chilly, he kept a blanket over his knees. He did not like the outdoors much, or so he said, but he was getting accustomed to it. Occasionally she read the newspaper to him, for he liked to keep up with the comings and goings of London society. As long as it was nothing about him. If it was, she carefully read around it.

"Chance," he shouted suddenly from the chaise. "Where's my wine?"

The position of the sun had told him it was after noon, and his thirst was prompt, as always.

Emma took a tray out to him as she did every day, a wine decanter and single glass balanced upon it. And with it his medicine— the elixir that he'd been told would cure him, but only seemed to give headaches and long bouts of sleeplessness.

As he heard her soft footfall approach through the long glass, and he put out his trembling hand, reaching for it, she saw the sores on his skin. On a bad day they oozed and wept; on a good day they were merely grotesque blisters and scabs. He didn't like her to look at them, so she never made comment.

What could she say, in any case? He did not want pity.

Wardlaw Fairbanks stricken with illness, his body weakened, had looked to the daughter he never wanted, precisely because he knew he would get no pity from her, feigned or otherwise.

* * * *

"So you are the girl they most amusingly named Chance," he'd said, staring at her with dull eyes.

"*Emma* Chance."

"You don't look quite as I imagined."

It must have been disappointing for him, she thought. He was a tall, slender, very elegant gentleman, fashionably dressed. And this man standing on her doorstep claimed to be her father.

Two and a half years ago, as she prepared to leave London with Lady Bramley, he had turned up at the school on a cool, crisp winter morning, to accuse her of villainy.

"Now you think to insidiously work your way into my life, and my purse, along with Julia Lightbody."

"Sir, I have no part in her scheme. She and I are

not in league whatever she might have told you."

He laughed without mirth. "You expect me to believe that you want nothing from me?"

"I did not even know who my father was, sir, until you came to my door."

Drawing back slightly, he took her in again with a slow, methodical, languid gaze. "I, girl, am the Viscount Fairbanks."

"Well, I know that now, of course. But had you not come here, you could have kept your secret. I would have been none the wiser and could have continued in ignorance."

She knew the name Lord Fairbanks. Everybody in London knew it. There was a time when he could make or ruin a person with one word or one look. Due to outrageous gambling and drinking habits, his fortunes and his looks had diminished in recent years. He had become something of a lampoon and, because of the fickle world of fashion, fewer sycophants hung on his every word. It was said, however, that he still bought his shirts abroad— or had them laundered there, she couldn't recall which— and he held court every day at a table in the window of his club, where people stopped in the street outside to look at him.

Emma had always thought how awful that must be, but the Viscount Fairbanks never altered this habit so apparently he liked being gawped at.

"I am soon to be married, and I do not want anything to get in my way. Do you understand me, girl?"

Now she remembered reading of Lord Fairbanks engagement to Lady Louisa Carnforth, daughter of a duke. It would be the wedding of the century, so people said. Fairbanks had avoided marriage all these years, and seemed to be the perennial bachelor. But at the advanced age of forty-two he had finally succumbed to the business of marriage. People speculated on the reason: Perhaps he needed "retirement" from his old ways now his exalted position at the top of the heap had waned; or he needed his legitimate heir before it was too late.; or he needed the influx of coin from his bride's dowry. Nobody was naive enough to think he'd fall in love with anything other than his own reflection.

By all reports the duke's daughter, his fiancée, was very young, virginal, sheltered, and really another creature to be pitied as she was led to the slaughter in an arranged marriage with an older man. Not, by any means, an uncommon occurrence, but no less likely to make any reasonable person's skin feel as if it leapt off their body.

So this was the very moment for Julia Lightbody to put her extortion scheme into motion. He wouldn't want an illegitimate daughter or any of that unsavory past brought out into the open and displayed before his new father-in-law. Clearly he thought Emma so stupid that he felt the need to come to her and explain in person.

Utterly unnecessary.

"Once again, sir, I want nothing from you. Whatever Mrs. Lightbody might have told you, my connection with her was forced upon me from birth, but I do not participate in her crimes. She wanted to tell me your identity, and I declined to know it."

"So you do not demand money from me? Or anything else?"

"Certainly not." She had added with great feeling, "I wish you had never come here."

The aging peacock walked around her, casting a critical eye over her parlor, swinging his decorative walking cane. "A teacher," he sneered. "Of all things I might have produced." Coming to a sharp halt, he looked at her again. "When you were born, I did not think you would live long. Nobody did." It was said so calmly, almost bemused by the happenstance of her survival. "And here you are."

Emma said nothing, wishing only that he would leave and she could continue her packing.

"You are not what she described," he said.

"She?"

"Our shared acquaintance."

She could well imagine how Mrs. Lightbody had described her to the Viscount. Not that she cared what that woman said.

"You are very like your mother," he added suddenly, one finger to his lips as he considered her through those hard eyes. "But perhaps our mutual friend does not remember."

Unable to resist, she replied, "I am surprised you

do, sir."

He looked away with a sigh and stared at the clean patch on her wallpaper. "Yvette too was pale and delicate, like china. Very fine china."

Yvette. The breath caught in her throat. "It is an unusual name."

"French. Yvette Beaulieu. A sweet thing but so easily broken. I, of course, was a young man then. The world was my oyster, as they say. We would have made a fine couple." And then he laughed coldly. "Were she not a penniless whore."

"Well, even if I look like her, I am not fragile and delicate, sir. I am not breakable."

His gaze returned to her. "So I see. There's a fire in your eyes, Chance. A very hot fire that spits and flickers. Something else our friend neglected to mention too."

"She is no friend of mine. And I am getting on with my life without you, so you need not have come here. I will never intrude upon you, and I would thank you to stay away from me."

Emma did not know whether it was the unexpected spirit he found in her that day, or some other reason that drew him back eventually, but apparently he stored her away in his thoughts after that visit and, later, when he was sick and quietly desperate for a safe haven away from the gossips, he sought her out again.

This time he found her in Norfolk, in the house Guy had purchased before they married— yes, we will get to that in good time, dear reader, but let us dispose of Lord Fairbanks first. He promises not to trouble us for long.

"I shall not trouble you for long," he'd said when she found him on her doorstep again. Despite the span of more than two years between visits, he acted as if he had seen her yesterday. As if she should not be shocked to see him again, and this time so far from his usual haunts in Town. "I require a sanctuary in which to convalesce, and my sources informed me you had come here. The sea air, so I am told, can be beneficial to the sick. Yes, this place suits me very well."

She could have said he was not welcome, turned her back and shut him out. Heaven knew he deserved it.

But there was a reason why Emma agreed to let him stay at the house.

Not long after his first visit to her, she had discovered, with help from Georgiana, who used the resources of her father's newspaper, that a young woman named Yvette Beaulieu had died in Bethnal Green in November 1798. Her body had been reclaimed by a brother who buried her at a church called All Hallows. There were many churches by that name in London, but after a search of several weeks, Emma and Georgiana had located the gravestone at last. Inadvertently, therefore, Wardlaw Fairbanks solved a mystery that had plagued his daughter for as long as she could remember. Now she could visit her mother's grave whenever she wished and whisper her questions. Sometimes she imagined she heard answers.

And that was not all. Emma had found flowers on her mother's grave. Each time she went, the flowers were fresh and beautiful. Somebody loved her mother still, even after all those years and although she did not know who it might be, it cheered Emma's heart to know this simple fact. For a long time she had imagined her mother lying cold and lonely in some dark, dank place. But it was not like that at all. Yvette was at peace and remembered.

Georgiana had suggested they try to find any surviving members of the Beaulieu family, but there were none in the area. There was not even any further trace of the brother who had made certain she received a decent burial.

Nevertheless the discovery had, in a way, given Emma a family and it had soothed some of that churning dissatisfaction that once made her feel so disconnected with life.

So when Lord Fairbanks stumbled all the way to Norfolk to find her, she could not shut the door in his face. Sometimes she thought herself betaken with madness to let him into her life— Guy certainly did when she wrote to let him know.

"I do not like that man taking advantage of your kindness and goodness," he'd written. But he did not forbid her from giving the Viscount shelter, and he had every right to do so.

It was not the first time Fairbanks had suffered from this disease and thought himself cured, apparently. He understood nothing of an infection lying dormant for years, and saw no reason why he could not regain his health. After all, he paid for the very finest physicians and the latest medicines they produced.

"All I need is time and a quiet place while I recover my vitality," he'd said. "This will do me very well. It is rustic, but surely the very last place anybody would think to find me." His vanity would not allow him to stay in London, of course, looking the way he did, covered in scars and ulcers that no amount of powder could cover, patches of lost hair, and a swollen, puffy face. He was physically tired too, even if his brain would not let him sleep. His limbs weakened, and he bumped into things around the house, which is why he so often spent his day outdoors and seated under the tree. He knew where he was then, could enjoy the birdsong, and the brightness of the sun told him the time if he needed to know it.

They did not have any conversations about the past.

* * * *

Emma stood by the wicker chaise while he drank his "miracle" potion and then she passed him the wine glass to help hide the taste of it. He almost missed his lip with the edge of the glass and his hand shook worse than before, his wrist seemingly too limp to hold the bones up today.

"I daresay my lady wife is enjoying the grouse season," he muttered. "There has been no word, has there?" His wife was the only person he'd informed of his whereabouts while he hid in the country.

"No, sir. Perhaps you would like to send her a letter today? I can get my writing things, and you can dictate."

"Certainly not. She will know it is not my hand, and she will think I am worse."

You are, she wanted to say. Each day he declined steadily, but refused to see it.

As for his "lady wife", that young girl had penned only two letters since he arrived in Norfolk four months ago. After that, complaining of boredom, she had gone off to a house-party in the north country and he'd not heard a word since.

Their marriage had taken place in the spring of 1820, once a suitable mourning period for the death of King George had been observed. As far as Emma could make out, the Viscount had not lived under the same roof as his young wife for more than a few weeks and had continued his dissolute ways about town. Not that his wife seemed to mind. She too went her own way, perhaps less virginal and naive than she'd appeared, and relieved to get out from under her stern father's roof.

"August will soon be over," Fairbanks exhaled the words in a series of sighs that stopped short of contentment and, if he had any greater strength, would have suggested impatience. "In another month I shall return to Mayfair. I am feeling much improved today."

Emma adjusted the blanket over his knees and went back into the house, leaving him with his wine and false hope.

The flint cottage with brick-bordered windows and door, had a small farm attached, a few acres of land, stables and a paddock. Although the Viscount called it "rustic", Emma considered the house quite grand. It had five bedrooms in all.

"Who is going to fill all these rooms?" she'd said to Guy once.

Standing behind Emma, he'd enclosed her in his arms and laughed. "Perhaps we'll take in lodgers."

Of course, Viscount Fairbanks was not the lodger he'd had in mind at the time.

The house was decorated in a comfortable manner, with some pieces Guy brought home from his travels and others to which Emma had taken a fancy when she saw them in King's Lynn or Fakenham on market day. It was not a palace, by any means, but it was a real home. Her own at last. From the first moment Guy took her there she knew it was perfect for them.

A pleasant village crouched behind hedges, elms and poplar trees, just a short walk down the lane, and if she felt the desire to stretch her legs farther, or take the pony and trap, Emma could visit the coast at

Hamberton for the afternoon. There was a time when she would have been terrified at the prospect of going so far alone. The sight of the vast churning sea itself and those colorful, layered cliffs would have bewildered her senses. But she was no longer fearful of falling off the edge without walls to hold her in. Day by day she grew stronger and braver, taking in great gusty breaths of that fresh air.

Three times a week she took in pupils, who sat in her parlor, in various degrees of attentiveness, and mostly just wanted to play with the pair of noisy cockatiels Guy had brought her, "For when I am not here to annoy you, dearest."

Her husband never came home on leave empty-handed and he took great pleasure in surprising her with the oddest, most impractical presents. When she told him that his greatest gift to her was simply to bring himself home safe and sound, and that was all she wanted, Emma was not being entirely romantic, but considerably practical.

Still, despite this gentle plea, he went on filling the house with eccentric trophies from his adventures.

He would not be home again until Christmas. It felt so far away.

While the sun was high and she could use that light, thereby saving on the expense of candles, she sat down by her bright kitchen window and wrote to Guy, as she did once a week without fail whenever they were apart. As she had done since he went back to his ship in 1819, leaving her with that little pink pearl ring. And a promise.

Chapter Twenty-Five
January 1820

"Still reading that long letter from your little governess, eh?" Walter exclaimed. "It never ceases to amuse me, that fond, silly look you get on your ugly face. What can the lady possibly say that makes you so happily enthralled?"

"My dear fellow, I could never explain it to you."

"She is still in Shropshire, is she not? With Lady Bramley."

Guy nodded, turning the paper to read on. Her descriptions of Lady Bramley's son and the other people she met in the country were so vivid that he could picture them exactly and laugh at all their foibles, just as she did in her wry, quiet way. "She is very proud of the fact that she walked by an entire herd of cows yesterday," he muttered.

Walter tried to look over his shoulder. "Cows? What is so significant about that?"

"See? That's why I cannot explain it to you. If you knew her, you'd know why it's funny. You don't know Emma as I do."

"Oh, lord." Walter rolled his eyes. "You *are* in love, my poor dear fellow."

Love. It was a curious sensation and he did not know what to make of it, but there it was.

Of course, now he felt the pressure of making his own letters just as interesting. Otherwise she might grow bored with him and fall out of this strange love.

"Strange" because he didn't really know what she saw in him. He had never lacked for confidence before, but then his affairs with ladies had always taken place within sight and had never been left in purgatory for two years. They had, in fact, seldom outlasted two months.

But this was a woman he had to woo while he was apart from her. Somehow he had to stay in her mind and her heart, and he really didn't know if he could keep that clever woman interested for so long. With such a quiet, reserved female one seldom knew what went on in her mind.

"I suppose you worry she might turn some other fellow's head while in Shropshire at the Bramley estate," Walter offered helpfully.

Guy frowned and looked up from his letter again. "Thank you, friend, for bringing *that* idea to the forefront of my mind."

"Well, she caught your attention, did she not? And your brother's. It seems likely some other chap might be similarly enchanted."

"Miss Emma Chance does not go about willy nilly enchanting random men."

Walter shrugged. "She might not be aware that she's doing it. The good one's don't."

"Indeed," he snapped, folding his letter and slipping it inside his waistcoat.

"Look at that delightful minx Miss Godfrey, for instance. She assures me she has not deliberately set her nets for me. In fact she teasingly declares she cannot stand the very sight of me, and yet I am on the way to being thoroughly smitten."

"My sympathy lies with Miss Godfrey."

"Odd, isn't it?" Walter mused. "Here we are, once two determined bachelors and now considering the ball and chain."

"Really? You are? Does not Miss Godfrey have to agree before you organize a barrel of ale for the wedding breakfast?"

"Oh she will agree. Eventually. All ladies play coy at first, 'tis a well known fact."

Guy laughed. Couldn't help it. He never could be angry with Walter for long. The man was simply too hopeless.

* * * *

His first set of cannon balls made her smile.

•Cut hair again. Lady B will be pleased.

•Had cold for three days. Sheer force of will to kiss you again pulled me through.

•Think I might purchase a monkey. Better company than Walter.

•New ship barely seaworthy, so insisting all crew can swim. Superstition be damned.

•Nicholas wrote to complain you've been gone too long.

But his last cannon ball in that first letter swept her smile away.

• Ship sets sail March 21st, weather permitting.

It was different now, of course. When she used to read his letters over his sister's shoulder, years before, she did not know what he looked like and could not picture him writing those messy words. Now she could.

Now he was the dearest thing in the world to her. And she was terrified. Sometimes, on dark days, she thought her fear was the reason why she made him wait two years and didn't marry him immediately. Her love for him was too much, too overwhelming.

He had terrible handwriting. Yet, somehow, that made it more lovely, because the reader got the sense of the effort taken. It was not all smoothly flowing curls and tails, and cleverly composed sentences. One never knew what the next cannon ball would say or from which direction it might be fired. Much like the man himself.

Shropshire with Lady Bramley had been an interesting exercise. Her son, Sir Mandrake, was very pleased with himself and very fond of pontificating at length on many subjects. His favorite topic was government and his seat in the House of Lords. He was the only person Emma had ever seen capable of silencing his mother, but that was only after both their voices had been raised in concert for a considerable time.

The manor house was a fearsomely turreted

monstrosity and one could spend an entire day walking around inside without ever running into anybody— only occasionally colliding with a grim and watchful suit of armor poised by an archway with shield, pole-axe or halberd at the ready. Emma had conversations with a few of them over the course of her stay and found them considerably more intelligent than the master of the estate.

Much to his mother's despair, Sir Mandrake also liked to discuss the monetary value of objects around the house. It was most improper and always made Lady Bramley flinch, but anything that was admired out loud by one of his guests, whether it be a painting or a salt cellar, was instantly labeled with what it had cost to purchase and what it would be worth to replace.

Emma amused herself by adding the ongoing sum in her mind.

During their stay in the country, she forced herself to be more outgoing, wanting to show Lady Bramley how much she'd improved and matured. When anything strange was put before her at dinner, she was willing to try it and she even managed, one evening, to regale the gathered guests with an amusing anecdote about the time she and her two friends had caused havoc at one of her ladyship's garden parties. It was a tale that Georgiana could have told much better, but since nobody there had heard it before, they all enjoyed it very much. Even Lady Bramley was obliged to laugh at the massacre to one of her prize-winning marrows.

Time, of course, had healed the sting of that terrible tragedy.

"That was how we three Ladies Most Unlikely came to the notice of her ladyship," Emma explained. "She took us under her wing, intent on improving our behavior."

"And it seems," Lady Bramley added proudly, "I have performed miracles."

There was a time when Emma Chance would never have spoken out loud in company, but once she had begun it became easier. Her fondness for Lady Bramley and her desire to please made her braver and less reserved.

But although at least one gentlemen guest that Christmas had tried to flirt with her, Emma remained true to her Captain. No other man would ever claim her heart the way he did. The longer they were apart, forced to wait, the more she was certain of it.

Yes, she loved him and she was no longer afraid to love.

When she returned to London with Lady Bramley, they discovered that Melinda had finally escaped her father's house, was still unmarried, and happier than ever. There was a new gleam in her eye, but she had surprisingly little to tell of her sojourn into Buckinghamshire, other than a brief explanation of how she had made the acquaintance of a genteel young lady who, being deaf since birth, required a companion to live with her. Melinda intended still to manage the hat shop "Desperate Bonnets" in Mayfair, although she would now live in the fashionable but quiet area of Bloomsbury, amid the pretty green gardens that could almost make a person forget they were in London.

"It's all exceedingly proper," Melinda assured them. In such an urgent, red-faced way that suggested something the very opposite was afoot.

It seemed the Ladies Most Unlikely were stretching their wings and flying off in different directions. But they would always remain close friends, their bond too firm and dear to be broken.

* * * *

When Emma returned to her governess post in Allerton Square she was startled — and gratified— by the warm welcome she received from young Masters Nicholas and Charles. Apparently she had been much missed.

"It has been so very dull here," Nicholas complained. "Guy went back to sea, and Edward won't push over an earl's daughter."

"Oh?"

"I heard him arguing with papa about it. *You needn't think I'm pushing myself at an earl's daughter*, he said, and then he went off back to Norfolk in a huff."

"I see. You really shouldn't eavesdrop, you know, Nicholas. It is not polite. And there is always the danger that one might misunderstand what one hears."

"It's hard not to eavesdrop in a house so crowded, Miss Chance."

And now, she soon learned, the second Mrs. Hathaway had defied Lady Bramley's advice and was, once again, in an "interesting condition."

HMS Hathaway would surely sink with the addition of one more baby. Emma was quite unable to stop herself from looking at the befuddled, busy Mr. Hathaway and his drooping, ever-ailing wife and wondering how on earth they managed it.

At midnight on January 29th of that year, the tolling of St Paul's great bell announced the death of King George to the populace of London. The people immediately fell into deep mourning for, even though his son had served as regent for the past decade, the king was still their longest reigning monarch and much beloved. Haberdashers sold out of black crepe and even the newspapers sported black borders.

But eventually spring came again and chased away the grim months of grief.

Emma did what she could to ease Mrs. Hathaway's lot by taking the twins, along with Alfred and baby Frederica out to the park as often as possible in fine weather, allowing them to run up and down with kites, daisy chains and paper birds until they wore themselves out.

The Hathaways filled their childrens' nursery with expensive toys, especially anything the lady of the house heard of being popular among the fashionable set, yet these objects were soon broken or abandoned— usually left scattered in the corridor for somebody to trip over. Mr. Hathaway was often the victim and could frequently be heard shouting that, "Children, in my day and age, were to be seen and not heard. There was no such thing as a fashionable toy, for pity's sake. We were not cosseted and drooled over and given every little thing our hearts desired. And we damn-well survived."

In Emma's view any amusement that cost nothing was priceless. An imagination could not be broken or left on the carpet to cause an accident. Nor did it have to be tidied away at the end of an afternoon. So she taught Cassie and Bella how to find shapes in the clouds and make stories from them, something she had often liked to do when, as a child with no toys at her disposal, it had been one of her favorite entertainments. She taught the children how to make games for themselves and how to observe the world around them.

The HMS Hathaway, although not much quieter, soon became a more civilized vessel with fewer monkeys climbing the rigging.

"Miss Chance, you are indispensable," said the second Mrs. Hathaway, wilting in chair beside her dressing room fire, one limp hand pressed to her brow. "I do hope you will never leave us. We missed you at Christmas."

And at the lady's insistence one rainy day, Emma organized Mr. Hathaway's study in a more efficient manner. When his wife proudly announced what she had done, the man could be heard popping and spitting like pinecones on a fire.

"Tut-tut, what?" he mumbled. "What the devil—?

Poor Emma was mortified, since she had not realized this was a project undertaken by his wife without his knowledge. But eventually his anger reduced to a smolder and more than once she heard him exclaim in surprise that he was able to find something for which he had looked no more than two minutes. He gave her no direct thanks, but did manage to nod to her in a genial manner one afternoon in the hall, when he saw her putting on her hat and coat.

"Miss Chase," he muttered. "Off home, eh?"

"Yes, sir," she replied, deciding not to correct him. After all, "Chase" was close enough and a marked improvement on nothing at all.

* * * *

The storm raged, pushing the ship into a savage pitch and yaw from bow to stern. An ominous grinding creak stretched the length of the vessel and threatened to tear the planks apart. Fortunately they had a full hold and that weight would help maintain some stability and ought to prevent rolling, but the sea was fierce, the wind brutal. He couldn't remember a storm this wild, not in his fifteen years at sea. Mother Nature was never predictable.

The prow, being the sturdiest part of the ship,

was directed into the oncoming, crashing waves, and he tried to keep the ship angled to the wind. There had been no time to put storm sails up, so they must do their best with none. Shouting against the wind, a stout rope around his waist, Captain Hathaway ordered the back sails taken down first to prevent a deadly sideways slew and then had the lower courses furled. Finally the fore top sail and jib had to be adjusted. Rain lashing his face, he watched his men valiantly working on that slippery yardarm, wrestling with heavy water-logged canvas, so many feet above the pounding, roaring sea. The deck rocked and rumbled under his boots. He hoped those damn barrels in the hold were well tied in. And through it all, even with a watery death nipping at his rudder, Guy Hathaway felt that hearty thrill pumping his blood, giving him what he needed to push ahead and fight.

He had never been one to back down in a fight and now he had even less cause to do so, because in calmer waters someone waited for him, trusting that he would return. He'd promised and she needed him. As he needed her.

* * * *

He came home in late summer of that year, and this time he made his way to see Emma first at the school, but on his way through the streets he suddenly caught sight of her walking along on the other side of the road, her step purposeful, her mind apparently far away. He quickly crossed the street and followed her, mischievously taking pleasure in being covert. A few moments later she lead him through the doors of a circulating library.

There she conferred with a clerk and then waited in the reading room while the books she sought were collected. Guy moved stealthily around the room, watching as she perused various newspapers and magazines, paying no attention to anybody else there.

How lovely she was, he thought with a sudden surge of overflowing pride that she would be his wife soon. He wanted everybody there to know it and could only imagine her expression if he suddenly shouted it out to the occupants of the quiet library. He could swing from that chandelier above her head and declare his love for her in tuneless song. Sweep her up and run off with her. There was a day, some years ago, when he would have done exactly that and caused a scandal.

But no, it was her idea that they wait. She tortured him. And he was supposed to be a grown-up these days.

Eventually the clerk returned with her selections and she took a chair by a table to look them over. Her head bent gracefully over the pages, her gloved hands carefully turning the pages as if they were precious documents. He watched as she licked her lips and smiled.

Unable to bear the distance any longer, he strode up behind her and whispered, "Aha! here I find you indulging in naughty books, Miss Chance!"

She jumped a few inches and would have slammed the book shut, had he not put his hand down on the page and prevented it. On a gust of breath, like a guilty soul with a well-rehearsed alibi, she exclaimed, "It is quite proper. Lady Bramley pays a guinea a year to belong to the library and she lets me use her subscription." Only then did she seem to come to her senses and see that it was Guy. Her fogged gaze cleared and she put one hand on the crown of her hat, as if he might have knocked it off her head.

"What do we have here then the moment my back is turned? Clearly you're up to something illicit. Tsk, tsk! Don't novels encourage idleness and corrupt morals, young lady? I'm surprised your guardian approves. I've heard it said that a man might as well turn his daughter loose in Covent Garden as trust her mind to a circulating library."

Emma flushed, but could not keep the delighted gleam out of her eyes. "What are you doing here, Captain?"

"That's not a very civil way to greet one's fiancé."

"I meant here in this library." She smiled shyly. "I would not expect to see you in such a place."

"Why not? I do read, you know. I am not merely a handsome face."

"Hush! You're too loud."

Before she could move away, he pulled out a chair and sat next to her. He'd seen her try to hide the books, so now he was doubly curious. "Let me see what keeps your interest so thoroughly, Emma."

"I would rather not."

"Why? What subversive literature is my future wife devouring with that smile on her face? I believe I have a right to know."

Still she resisted, but he tugged the first book from under her hands and turned it over, much to her evident embarrassment.

"English Housewifery Exemplified," he read the title in a bemused tone, while she fidgeted with her hat brim and her gloves. "Useful for mistresses of families, higher and lower women servants, and confined to things useful, substantial and calculated for the preservation of health and measures of frugality. Good lord, that's a mouthful!"

She cast her eyes down. "There is much about being a wife I need to learn. I must study."

Guy grasped her fingers, speechless for a moment, astonished and pleased that she would go to so much effort. "I'm not certain you can learn it all from books," he managed finally, wishing they were alone and he could kiss her. "Indeed, I know much of it will come from practice and practical experience. For us both." And he looked forward to that practical experience very much. He tenderly rubbed his thumb against her pulse, under her glove.

Her lashes lifted slowly and he was caressed by the warm blue of her gentle, wondering, loving regard. No other woman had ever looked at him the way she did with such honesty and straightforward devotion. She looked different again today, he marveled. Her smile was wider and less wary now that it flared properly into life. Her eyes were a soft, dewy shade of blue and her hair was no longer scraped sternly back behind her ears, but waved softly around her face under the straw brim of her hat.

"I also have a book with excellent directions for cookery," she murmured.

He leaned a little closer. "You needn't worry about getting anything wrong for me. You couldn't possibly be anything other than right for me. In every way."

Eyes wide, she studied his mouth. "I suppose you already know how to do everything."

"Whatever experience I have had, none of it will compare to you, Emma Chance. With you I am starting from new again. Do you think I would wait two years for any other woman? It is physically hurting." Which was ridiculous, of course. But honest. He was only a man and had needs like any other. She may as well know his weaknesses. She was one of them now. The greatest, it seemed.

"I am sorry you're in pain," she said somberly.

And then he laughed because she looked so forlorn and yet beautiful in her simple straw poke bonnet with a light flush still tinting her cheeks and her eyes full of sympathy for his predicament.

"It will pass," he promised her softly, "once you are mine at last. I have much to look forward to."

"But I am yours now," she replied.

"I mean, completely. In every way."

"In every way?" She blinked. "Oh." He felt her pulse quicken to a very lively, coltish skip.

"Precisely," he whispered, pressing more firmly with the pad of his thumb and stroking that charming quiver.

"I wish you had not crept up on me," she exclaimed, seeking an excuse perhaps for her reckless pulse. "I am all discombobulated."

"Good," he replied. "Now you know how I feel every time I look at you, Emma."

A few moments later he was obliged to stand hastily when Lady Bramley's voice was heard booming through the vestibule.

"I am shopping with her ladyship today." Emma sighed.

He swore under his breath, but she smiled. "I am grateful that she keeps me busy so I do not spend every hour dreaming of you and moping, Guy Hathaway. I would be a wretched creature if not for her companionship."

When Lady Bramley saw him standing there she came over immediately. "Captain Hathaway you are home on leave again?"

He was extremely glad that he'd got his hair cut again before he saw her. "I am, your ladyship. I trust you are in good health?"

"As well as might be expected." She looked him up and down through her lorgnette. "You certainly look to be bursting with it yourself, young man. And for once tidily dressed."

Guy bowed. "I will entrust Miss Chance to your able guidance madam, as I have some errands myself this morning." With that he departed before she could question him further or turn her critical eye on Emma's blushes.

* * * *

It was Mrs. Bishop who opened the door the next day. "Miss Chance," she called out with a wry smile, "that handsome stray tom cat is back again and looks in need of a good meal and a warm fire."

Emma, in an apron covered in floor, took him into her parlor at once, as if he was a parcel for which she'd been waiting and wanting nobody else to see. She literally took him by the cuffs of his coat and dragged him behind the door.

"Have a care, Miss Chance," he exclaimed, "people might think there is something untoward between us."

"But I could not inspect you at the library yesterday and now I must make certain you still have all your parts. I have a vested interest in your health, now," she said solemnly. "I don't want you damaged, Captain."

He laughed at that. And then, having wrung her hands together she abruptly threw them around his neck, launched herself into his arms and kissed him.

Guy was reminded of that storm that surprised

his crew at sea a few months earlier. This one was more likely to knock him off his feet.

"I'm learning how to make apple pie, but Mrs. Bishop is teaching me. She says cooking isn't something you can learn from a book. Like you, she is a believer in hands-on experience."

"She sounds very wise, and I shall look forward to tasting all your delights, however you learn them." He licked the end of her nose where he'd found a little dob of butter and sugar. "Hmm. That has whet my appetite."

"Be careful or I'll get pastry on you."

"Good." The soft muslin of her gown slipped under his palms as he pulled her closer still and kissed the side of her neck. "Cover me in it."

The stormy seas were calmer now. The stars came out, and moonlight gently tickled the rippling waves.

"I want to show you something," he whispered against her cheek, holding her tightly to his chest, inhaling the scent of apples and cinnamon in her hair. "Come with me now."

She did not even ask where to. For once she threw caution to the wind. "Yes."

* * * *

That was the first time he brought her to the cottage. Lady Bramley had to come too, of course, to chaperone. He was on his best behavior and the journey was long, requiring two overnight stays, one in a coaching inn that barely met her ladyship's standards, and one at the country manor house of her friend Lady Fortescue-Rumputney.

When they finally arrived at their destination, he took them through a field of lavender to where they came upon a low, flint-stone wall and a simple wooden gate. Through that he took them along a path overgrown with herbaceous borders that, having been left to their own devices for some years, strayed across the stone and gravel in bulging ferns and arching grasses. Finally there was the home he had purchased.

"You have brought yourself a considerable amount of work, young man," Lady Bramley announced, having looked the place over through her lorgnette. "The roof must be replaced, the floors above stairs are terribly uneven, the leaded-windows fit very badly— which will cost you a fortune in winter coal— and I have no doubt there are jackdaws nesting in that chimney."

But as a soft breeze blew the fragrance of lavender through the open front door, Emma came to his rescue. With tears in her eyes, her reticule clasped tightly in both hands, she said softly but firmly, "I adore it, Captain. It is perfection."

And he had to curb the instinct to gather her up in his arms again.

Lady Bramley looked a little taken aback. "But it will be so much trouble to put together."

"Yes, I know it will be hard work," said Emma

earnestly, "but the best, most worthwhile things are, surely you would agree? The Captain and I can make it beautiful together. We can make it ours. I can see it now, as it will be when we've put it back as it should be. Can you not see it? I can sew curtains for this window and put a little table here to write in the sun. Over here a sofa for two and a fender, and a comfortable wingback chair, of course, for you, your ladyship, when you are so good as to visit. I shall even put a little basket here by the fire for the darling little Horatio to nap in, when he is done chasing rabbits in the garden." She paused, her eyes large and shining. "Remember when you first looked at Georgiana, Melinda and me, Lady Bramley? I'm sure you saw a house just as decrepit and in need of repair, but you accepted the challenge, undaunted."

"Well," the lady exclaimed after a moment's stunned pause, "I have never heard you speak so certainly of anything, Miss Emma Chance. It seems your mind is made up."

It was a good thing his future bride liked the cottage, Guy thought with an inward sigh of relief. Would have been most awkward if she didn't and it was already his. But he'd known, from the first moment he walked through that lavender and over the threshold, that this was the place for them. It was an instinct she too had felt, it seemed. The excitement in her voice was unmistakable and gratifying.

He saw her working her fingers against her skirt and bringing them to her nose to smell the scent of swaying lavender stalks that had brushed her gown as they walked through. Their eyes met and she smiled.

It was a magical place and he'd found it for her, because this is where she should be. Where they both belonged.

Chapter Twenty-Six

"You did what?" His father's eyes almost popped out of his head.

"I purchased a house. A cottage in Norfolk. Not far from the coast."

Frederick Hathaway swiped off his spectacles and fell back in his chair. "You did not think to ask my advice in this undertaking?"

"I am one and thirty, father. It is time I made my own financial decisions. I mean to make a life for myself, something more than the navy. Something to come home to." They both knew this house in Allerton Square had never been Guy's home and his father could not even pretend that it was.

"I hope you have not bankrupted yourself, young man."

Guy smiled. "No. I have saved well these past ten years. "

His father looked skeptical. "Well enough to buy a house?"

"It's not a grand manor, just a cottage with a paddock and some acres of fertile land to grow anything we want."

"We?"

"Yes." Guy cleared his throat. "That's the other thing, sir. I'm taking Miss Chance with me."

"*Miss Chance?*"

"We are engaged to be married, sir. We've been engaged almost a year and next summer— unless she changes her mind— we intend to marry."

"Just a minute, boy. The quiet *governess?* The same one your brother thought he wanted? That creature?"

"Her name is Emma."

His father stared and then put down his spectacles. "And I suppose this idea came to you because you know I will object. You want to be contrary again. You want my attention. You want me to shout and rail and tear my hair out. Then you will quietly laugh and say it was a jest."

"Sir, forgive me, but I do not come here for your approval." He tried not to smile too much as he saw his father's face grow redder. "I came merely to let you know of my plans. I thought it would be the polite thing to do."

A large fist came down on the desk blotter. "You will not marry this...woman—"

"Emma."

"She is a nobody with nothing to her name. I forbid it."

"It's too late, sir. You must do as you think necessary, but my course is set."

His father's lips shook as a low whimper slid between them and his eyes rolled from side to side, looking for anything to clutch at in his fury.

"You said you wished I would find a decent woman and settle down," said Guy calmly. "And I have."

"The idea, you fool boy, was to find a decent woman with a dowry and connections. The Chance woman is a foundling and, according to Edward, was born in a bawdy house!"

"But she has come here every day, sir, to teach your son and your ward."

"Yes, she has done well to get herself an education, but she is no more than a paid servant of the household. You are the eldest son of the house. It is no better than if you announced your plan to marry a housemaid!"

Now Guy began to get angry. "Emma has, so I understand, taken on many other duties too and managed the little ones for your wife without complaint. I think she has become decidedly more to this household, and to Nicholas and Charles, than a servant, sir! She certainly is to me!"

His father got up and walked around his chair. It was as if he had to move or else explode.

Guy took a deep breath. "Are you no longer in favor of other folk striving to better themselves, sir? There was a time, before my mother died and you moved the family to London, when you were a gentleman farmer with a little printing business on the side, and you started a newspaper. *The New Gentleman's Weekly.* Is that not what you called it back then? A beacon for the modern, industrial age?"

Frederick Hathaway kept his back to his eldest son, but his head bent forward slightly on that thick, stubborn neck.

"Those were happy days, sir. When you were a champion for those striving to better their lives. Now having made your own life so much grander, you look down on somebody like Emma Chance, who only works hard to lift herself up, as you have done. In fact, she does not even want all this. She simply wants a happy life such as we used to have. And I yearn for that too."

"A happy life," his father muttered. "One cannot go back to the past. Do you think I do not wish..." His words trailed off into a deep sigh.

Guy waited a moment but nothing else was forthcoming, so finally he said, "I have thought often of my mother lately. I know, in my heart, that she would adore Emma. She would have no objection and would support us in any way that she could. I feel it as strongly as if she stood behind me and whispered in my ear. Almost as if she put us together somehow."

At last his father turned and looked at him again, his eyes heavy and sad. "You were always her favorite. I do not know how she let you go away to sea. I felt for sure she would make you stay. A boy of fourteen, marching off to Portsmouth. Not listening to me then, either. That hasn't changed."

"I've had a successful, profitable career, father. Nothing to be ashamed of."

His father's grey brows wriggled in confusion. "Ashamed?"

"That is what you have always felt, is it not? You didn't plan for a son in the navy. For some reason it was not good enough."

Frederick Hathaway flopped into his chair again,

took out a kerchief and wiped it over the furrows of his brow. "Do you think I wanted you to go off to sea so young? Not knowing if you would ever return?" He shook his head, blew his nose soundly and stuffed the kerchief back in his pocket. "Yes, your behavior, at times, has caused me more than a few shudders, young man. But I didn't want you to join the navy, because I...I didn't want you to be killed. Did that never occur to you? I wanted a safe profession for you. I thought you might have followed in my footsteps, but when you showed no inclination for the business and chose the navy, I set my hopes on Edward." He paused, heaved his shoulders in a shrug that would have received a stern lecture from Lady Bramley, and then continued, "It puzzled me that you could be so sure and courageous at the age of fourteen. I was never so brave as you. You wouldn't get me on a ship for twenty thousand pounds. I am a coward. Seeing you run off so merrily to get yourself shot and drowned...well, it made me ashamed of myself. Your mother was so proud of you, and all *I* could do was print stories of battle victories and naval heroes. I decided I had better prepare myself for hearing you were dead one day." He frowned. "I shut a door on you, I suppose, afraid of what might happen and how the duty of telling your mother would fall to me."

Guy sat still for a long time, letting his father's confession slowly sink in. It was true; he knew it. His father was embarrassed and he was only ever embarrassed when forced to admit a weakness.

"I do not know what has become of my children. Nothing I planned for them has come to pass. Has ever a parent been more superfluous in the raising of his sons and daughters?"

"Perhaps you would be better off not making plans," Guy replied wryly. "You might be surprised at how well we can work things out for ourselves. But I wouldn't call you superfluous, sir. After all, you taught us all to be stubborn, to fight for what we wanted. You raised independent, fiery-tempered children who know what they want and never back down from a fight."

His father squinted and then exhaled a gusty laugh. "I did, didn't I, by God!"

"Don't use the lord's name in vain, father. Edward wouldn't be best pleased."

"Hmph. That's another thing that puzzles me. How the Devil did *he* become so pious?"

Guy, having no answer for that, could only laugh.

"So," said his father finally, "you are set upon this girl?"

"*Woman,* father. Emma. And yes, I am more set on having her than I have ever been set on anything. She makes me..." he smiled slowly, "happy."

"You are willing to marry a woman, knowing nothing of her family."

"Why not?" He arched an eyebrow. "She's willing to marry me and she knows everything about our family."

* * * *

After that, whenever he was home on leave, Guy spent weeks working on the cottage. Walter Ramsey volunteered to help, although he was not much use with a hammer and more likely to hit his fingers. Or Guy's.

One day Edward found the time to inspect his brother's future home. He traveled on the mail coach and arrived without warning, to find Walter and Guy sprawled in the long grass with two jugs of cider, admiring the sunset.

"I must say, I expected something a little less...infested with wildlife."

"I've always liked animals," Guy replied smugly. "Are we not supposed to love all God's creatures?"

"So Miss Chance has accepted you, has she? I suspected she might be unstable. And here is the proof."

"It would seem so. A strong streak of madness runs through her blood."

Edward nodded and stood in the long grass, assessing the view on all sides. Gentle wind ruffled his golden head of hair. "Well, I wish you luck with the place. I daresay you'll make silk from a pig's ear. You always do."

Guy, leaning back on both elbows, squinted against the sunset. "Do I?"

"Of course. That's what makes you so damnably irritating. Some of us must work so hard, and you just breeze along carelessly."

Breeze along? Edward had no idea about his life, it seemed. But then, perhaps neither of them knew of the other's struggles. They were always so busy putting up their weapons. He remembered what Emma had said once,

"Edward lacks the humility to laugh at himself. He never had the chance to learn for he was never allowed to fail. Not by his father, nor himself. You and Georgiana, on the other hand, have learned the art of rebounding when you fall, because you've had practice."

Guy decided he could afford to feel pity for his brother now. After all, he had Emma— the cleverest woman in the world— and Edward didn't yet know what he needed.

"Come, Edward," he said. "Sit with us and share our cider. You must be thirsty after that long journey." It was impressive, actually, that his brother had come so far to see him. Of course, it was likely that he wanted to be nosy and preach, but today Guy was happy enough to give his brother the benefit of the doubt.

And Edward, it seemed, was in the mood, for once, to imbibe strong drink.

There in the long grass, with lavender soft in the air, they could put their swords aside at last.

* * * *

Emma Chance and Captain Guy Hathaway were finally married on Friday, August the 17th in the year

400

1821. There was a small announcement in *The Gentleman's Weekly*— Frederick Hathaway thought it only proper for his naval hero son's nuptials to be publicly acknowledged. Besides there were several important guests in attendance, including Lady Bramley of Hanover Square; Commander Sir Henry Thrasher and Lady Thrasher of Woodbyne Abbey, along with their baby son who gurgled loudly throughout the service and threw a rattle at the groom's head; Mr. Walter Ramsey, fifth son of the Earl of Charlecot and his soon-to-be-although-she-didn't-know-it-yet fiancée, Miss Godfrey, youngest daughter of Sir Roderick Godfrey; and Miss Melinda Goodheart, only daughter of Sir Ludlow Goodheart, who was accompanied by her friend, Lady Clara Beauspur, and a rather nondescript fellow who introduced himself as "Caulfield", in a tone that could best be described as "brusque" and not particularly conducive to further conversation. Further guests included, Mr. and Mrs. Bishop; Mrs. Beddesby; Miss Pegg, Miss Gunderson and a vast array of excited young ladies in their best bonnets.

Few weddings could boast such a varied assortment of guests, but for Emma and Guy it was only fitting.

Even I was there, although they didn't see my shadow.

After the service, a wedding feast was held in the superb garden of Lady Bramley's town house. And not a single marrow was harmed.

* * * *

They spent their wedding night at the inn on the road out of London.

At last, after that busy day and almost two years of waiting, they were alone together. The world finally stopped spinning.

He took Emma's hand, stripped off her glove and placed her palm against his heart. "Do you feel how hard it beats?"

She nodded. The rhythm shook through his firm chest with a pounding, thrusting energy. But tonight her own was no less excited.

"I am glad we waited," he said huskily. "I never thought I would say that. Good God, over the past few years I have endured agony, not to mention a considerable amount of animosity toward Lady Bramley." He gave her a quick grin. "But now we made it this far and it feels so much more special. As it should be. Perhaps that old dear was right after all."

Emma smiled. "She always is."

* * * *

He made love to her so slowly that she forgot such silly, meaningless things as time, or such practical considerations as how tired they would be in the morning when they had farther yet to travel. Nothing mattered but the two of them in that large, four-poster bed.

She had never imagined it could be quite so wonderful and now she understood the gleam in

402

Georgiana's eye. Now Emma shared that secret. She too was a bold adventurer at last.

With daring fingers she explored those dark curls and eyelashes that had always drawn her imagination to hot, sandy desert landscapes and turned him, in her mind's eye, into a conquering, brooding Sheik in wind-blown white robes. Why she ever thought a Sheik would have curly hair she had no idea. But hers did.

"Emma," he whispered, his voice catching in the desert heat. "I love you."

She arched happily and contentedly beneath his long, powerful body, and she very nearly purred. "When did you know it? Just now?"

He chuckled. "No. I fell in love with you when we were far apart and I didn't even know it was happening." Then he devoured her lips again, hungrily, as if he had not already taken his fill of her, and she began to think her dragon prince would never be sated.

But Emma Chance was a woman at last. He made her one officially.

She had a husband, a home, and a life of simple joy.

Sometimes, she worried that it was all too happy. Naturally there would be rainy days, but at least they both loved the rain.

* * * *

No hands had ever touched him as hers did. That

too was new for him. With her fingertips brushing so
tenderly across his skin, her eyes wide-open and
smoky with that shy desire. Almost as if she feared to
look, but had to do so, just the same. And little by
little that shyness fell away, as they found the
closeness and deepest intimacy a man and woman
could share.

He was feeling quite poetic. His ship's surgeon
would despair of him, buy him a frilly shirt and send
him to Italy, he mused.

"But when did you fall in love with me?' he
demanded of his bride as she lay pleasantly rumpled
and warm in his arms, her soft, jonquil locks spread
over his chest.

"I did not," came the drowsy reply.

His heart stopped for a beat. How strange it was
that this small, quiet creature should be capable of
conducting swift and merciless changes in the rhythm
of his pulse.

But then she raised her head and he saw that she
was smiling. "I did not have to fall, because I was
always there in love with you. I think I was born that
way."

"Really?"

She nodded and rested her chin on his chest. "I
was simply waiting for you in the fog. And finally you
came."

Guy combed his fingers through her hair and
thought again of his mother, the heavy sadness he'd
felt at her death. Today he still missed her, but the

404

pain was softened and he had much to look forward to now. He had finally pulled his own life out of a hole and into the light.

How strange it was that he should have first encountered Emma Chance on the very day his mother died. And how glad he was that their paths collided.

As he'd said to Emma, love came to him when he was far apart from her. It took him by surprise. He was not looking for it, did not even know he wanted it, but her spirit crossed the ocean to haunt him with her sad eyes and trembling, gasping breaths. Telling him she needed him to save her, when, in actual fact, it was quite the other way about.

It was a curious sensation and he did not know what to make of it, but there it was.

* * * *

When they finally arrived at their cottage, man and wife at last, a wicker hamper awaited them.

"From Lady Bramley," Emma exclaimed, reading the little note attached. "She was anxious we would not have eaten sensibly on our journey. Young lovers never do, she says."

The hamper was filled with many luxuries from "Fortnum and Mason" and a few things from the lady's own orchards and hothouses. There was even a tablecloth, candles and silverware. It was a very civilized picnic, as only Lady Bramley's attention to detail could make it.

But her head would very likely have spun like a whirligig to see how the young couple enjoyed it later, on the floor by their fire, in a state of wicked undress, curled up in each other's arms on that very same, no-longer-quite-so-respectable white linen tablecloth. The hallowed halls of Fortnum and Mason had probably never seen the like or even imagined what might be done with their very proper, royal-warranted strawberry jam, fresh-churned butter and crumpets.

"I shall never eat supper at a boring old table again," Guy whispered, feeling remarkably warm and relaxed, as they watched the smoldering fire and sipped their excellent champagne. "It tastes so much better nibbled directly from my delectable wife's charming little belly. Particularly when she is giggling and unable to lay still."

"That's all very well, my dear, but what if we have guests?"

"I see your point. We'll be on our best behavior on those occasions. And only naughty when we're alone."

He sincerely hoped they would be alone together most often.

Chapter Twenty-Seven
Norfolk, 1822

"Do not send my body back to London, Chance."

It was October. The leaves outside her window had rusted and begun to drift down onto the wicker chaise.

Until then she had never once heard Lord Fairbanks suggest that he knew he was dying. "I beg your pardon, sir?"

"There is nobody who waits for me there. My lady wife is long gone, and my father, the Earl, gave up on me many years ago." He leaned toward. "My father told me once that he intended to live forever, just to prevent me from inheriting the earldom. What do you think of that, girl?"

"I think it's dreadful. I'm sorry."

"Pish! I don't want your pity, Chance!" he said crossly. "I am telling you the facts of the matter."

Yes, she understood, being fond of facts herself, and knowing how they could form a protective shield around one's feelings. But they were all only human, even if they wished they were not.

"I rely upon you to be practical," he added. "I knew, when I met you, that you stood for no nonsense. That you would never weep and be foolish." With unsteady fingers he felt the rings with which he kept his knuckles decorated, even as his skin covered with peeling scabs. "In London they are all scavengers. They will come and take anything they can, before my body is cold. Particularly...*her*."

"Sir?"

He snarled, "Our mutual acquaintance."

"Surely she would have no chance to—"

"That creature can trick her way into anything. She slyly insinuates herself like the serpent in Eden, spreads lies and feeds poison into ears. I made the mistake once of letting her in to my life and then I could never quite get her out of it again. You were wise, at least, and escaped from her sly, winding, choke-hold."

Quite literally, she mused darkly.

Emma rubbed her arms, for it was getting colder, the sky greyer. "I realized, when I was young, that she must have secrets in her possession. She used them to blackmail people in society. Yourself included, I suppose."

"Oh, yes, she knew every sin I'd ever committed. But I must confess, in the early days I used her too. I took advantage of the stories with which she came to me. Indiscretions, adulteries, young virgins suddenly caught *enceinte,* grand debts, suicides, mischief and theft. She had it all at her fingertips and often she shared it with me. But," again he fidgeted with his rings, "when she turned her poison fangs in my direction, I realized my mistake. Too late. I was no innocent, and no doubt you will say I got what I deserved."

Emma was silent.

"Well..." he huffed, "when I was at my height I did not concern myself."

Perhaps he expected her to ask "With what?" But she didn't.

"I sent her packing that last time she came to me, wheedling for money and favors, threatening to expose my bastard child to the world. Mark my words, she will come to find me again and take her pound of flesh."

She nodded slowly. "Then if you do not want to go back to London—?"

"If I could be buried at sea, I would." He snorted with amusement. "Let her dive in and drown trying to get at me. But no..." he paused, sighed. "There is a little church overlooking the sea. A place called Hamberton. Only a few miles down the road. I saw it as the carriage brought me here. That is where you can put me."

"Very well. If that is your wish."

He waved her off in his usual way, but as she turned away he said, "Your mother would have liked it here, but she remains at the churchyard of All Hallows. It was the best I could do for her at the time."

Emma paused. "They said her brother reclaimed her body and had her buried there after she died."

The viscount snorted with dour amusement. "There was no brother, Chance. That was me."

"*You?*"

"That surprises you, does it? Yes, no doubt. It rather surprised me too, at the time. I was beset by a sudden desire to *do* something, and that has seldom occurred in my life. I have done, on the whole, as little as possible."

A chilly wind rustled the leaves overhead and a handful scattered onto the man that sat there. He made no move to brush them off.

"It's getting cold," she managed, struggling to keep the emotion out of her voice. "You ought to sit indoors."

"Why? Because I might catch my death of cold?" he drawled sarcastically.

Since there was nothing else to say she went back to the house and left him sitting there. When it grew dark he would call out for her help to get inside, but for now he did not want to move. It seemed as if he wanted to let all the leaves fall upon him. She looked back and saw him staring up into the malting branches, transfixed as if they spoke to him. His vision was so bad now she suspected he couldn't clearly see the leaves and could only feel them when they fell, touching his arms and legs.

Perhaps he knew he was fading and falling with them. Perhaps he guessed that once the last leaf fell he would breathe his last. He waited for it the way a person sleeping under a leaky roof would anticipate the next drip.

* * * *

Years later, whenever she thought back to his last months in her custody, Emma liked to think that Wardlaw Fairbanks came there, not just for somewhere out of London in which to "recuperate", but because he'd had that last thing to tell her. Not being the syrupy, gushing type, he had to let it out as if he barely meant to say it, as if it were nothing more than a whisper on the autumn wind. But he had wanted her to know that however brief his association with her mother, he had done what he could for her in the end. And he came to Norfolk in some attempt to make amends with that confession.

That was what Emma liked to imagine, in any case. Guy said she was getting sentimental.

"That's what happens to expectant women," he told her.

She looked at him in shock. "How the devil did you know?" She'd only just discovered it herself and, with her customary caution, hadn't planned to tell him until she was well along and there could be no disappointment.

"My darling Emma, I watched my mother proceed with six pregnancies after I was born. I think I know something of the matter."

He took delight in finding any subject about which he knew more than his wife, and which had nothing to do with sailing.

Immediately after the death of her father, Emma donned mourning black. Fairbanks would not have expected it, but she felt it only right.

"You gave him more in his last months than he gave you your entire life," Guy muttered, befuddled by her ability to forgive.

"But it's not what we don't do that matters. It's what we do."

To her surprise he left a short will, written out in a shaky hand during his final days. In it he bequeathed to her his rings as "payment for the inconvenience" of taking him in.

Emma, who had expected nothing, bit back silly tears and reminded herself of the facts. The bequest was a practical gesture, not an emotional one. He never wanted her pity or affection— never sought it. He paid her with those rings, because he thought she had provided a service and that was the fee, the compensation for her time.

At the funeral there was only herself and Guy. Lord Fairbanks had wanted nobody else notified except his young wife, who failed to appear. Of course, women rarely attended funerals, but Emma felt it necessary for herself to be there. Guy had nothing but a barely-stifled disdain for the dead man and it would not be right to leave him at the graveside as the sole mourner.

It rained on that day— a gentle, warm mist that was almost invisible and hovered rather than fell. As the vicar droned on, something made Emma look up through her black, net veil and that was when she saw a figure standing by the churchyard wall, also in black, her hard, mean little eyes fixed upon the scene at the grave.

Just as Fairbanks had said, she came for her pound of flesh.

Guy would have chased her off with a riding crop, but Emma pressed a hand on his arm and whispered, "I'll manage this. I'm not a child any longer."

He could not argue with that, of course.

"I will be rid of her," she said calmly, "once and for all."

So she walked across the churchyard to where Julia Lightbody stood watching and greeted her coolly. "Is there some reason why you came all this way, madam?"

"He would have wanted me here."

"I think not."

"What do you know of it? He was a stranger to you and you to him. As far as I recall, that's how you both wanted it."

Emma could hear Guy approaching from behind, reluctant to leave her alone with the woman. "How did you know where to find Lord Fairbanks?"

"That stupid little girl he married, of course. The chit couldn't keep a secret to save her life. I came here, Mrs. Hathaway, for what I'm owed."

"My father is dead, madam. You can threaten him no more with harm to his reputation or ugly gossip. He is beyond your reach."

The woman sneered as rain dampened the black ruffle around her bonnet. "But he promised me those rings."

"What rings?"

"From his fingers, of course, you daft wench. Promised them to me long ago when we were lovers, before your wretched mother came along and turned his head away from me. Oh, then I wasn't good enough for him anymore. But she's dead and so now is he. Those rings come to me. Like he promised." Her eyes were bulging and red-rimmed, as if she had shed actual tears.

Emma doubted they were tears for anybody but herself.

"I'm owed," Lightbody added, her shrill voice scratching across Emma's nerves. "I suppose you've got them, have you? Oh yes, you always were a rotten little schemer and opportunist. I daresay you took them off his fingers as he lay dying. They're far too valuable for you to have buried them in the ground along with him."

She thought for a moment, looking into that greedy woman's trembling face, and then she said, "Yes, I have them." If she'd lied and said they were still on her father's corpse, would the despicable woman come back by moonlight to dig him up? Her eyes did have an unhinged wildness about them. Too much gin, perhaps.

"They were meant to come to me! He promised. Swore to me! If you don't give them to me, Chance, I'll spoil things for your friends."

"Madam, I do not—"

"Goodheart, by the way, is living in sin with that dour-faced fellow who claims to be her companion's brother. Oh, yes, I know what they're up to. Shameful goings-on in that Bloomsbury house. What do you suppose old Bramley will have to say about that? And Lady Thrasher has a husband who's stark raving mad. Wanders about at night naked as the day he was born. Secrets. I know them all. So you'd best give me those rings, Chance. Or else."

Trophies, Emma thought, remembering the box she once saw in that mercenary woman's possession. As her father had said, Lightbody was a scavenger. Unconscionable.

Again there was a pause while Emma considered. The wind was picking up. Clouds swirled above them. A storm threatened.

She sensed her husband's bristling impatience and knew he would soon draw nearer to intervene. For now he was doing as she'd asked, and he was never one to fuss unduly, but now that she was expecting his child he had a tendency to treat her at times as if she might break.

So Emma lowered her voice. "I cannot give them to you now, as you see, my husband observes us. But I will bring my father's rings to you." With one careful hand she smoothed the black fur collar of her coat. "I can bring them to the cliffs along the coast this afternoon. There is a path cut out and I go there often alone so my husband will not suspect. And then you must be gone from our lives, madam. Forever."

"The cliffs? Not good weather for walking out, is it?"

"I don't mind the rain and never did."

The woman looked skeptical, but she was desperate. And more than a little drunk. "Very well. Have it your way. You bring those rings and then we'll be even."

Even? Emma smiled. "Yes. Then we'll be even."

* * * *

"Where are you going?" he demanded, when she asked to borrow the pony and cart and suggested he wait for her at the church. "You shouldn't go off without me."

"I do when you're at sea, Guy."

"But I'm here now and you're—" Oh, he knew that look on her face by now, so he shut his lips and contented himself with a scowl.

"I am not weak, sickly, fragile or a child," she said crisply. "I'm a married woman in full health and wits. I am quite capable of going out for some fresh sea air by myself."

He shook his head. "Sometimes I wish you were still meek and afraid of me."

She laughed softly. "I was never afraid of you, Guy Hathaway." And she leaned over to kiss his troubled brow. "I was only afraid of what I might do to you one day."

Before she could leave his side, he gripped her hand and drew it to his lips, kissing her little pearl

416

ring. "But now I must wait for you to come back. Wondering where you are and worrying."

"What do you suppose *I* do, when you are away at sea?"

To that he could not reply.

"I am your loving wife," she reassured him firmly, "and in six months I shall be a mother. But in addition to all this, there is one other thing I am."

"Stubborn?"

She didn't answer. He would find out.

Warrior

Chapter Twenty-Eight

The wind do puff and blow up 'ere

So there she was, on the cliffs at Hamberton.

When she arranged to meet Mrs. Lightbody there, she'd thought about all those old daydreams. A quick little push would do it. The woman was never a steady walker and the gin she consumed daily made her a liability to herself.

Emma knew, of course, the extraordinary strength of the wind in that spot. She pictured the fall, that black bonnet slipping free as the woman screamed into the roaring air. If anybody heard her cries for help they would simply dismiss it as another howl of the wind.

On a particularly blustery day, like this one, when a brooding sky of livid clouds brought about that sinister, jaundiced light, not many would bravely venture closer to the edge and investigate the source of that sound.

But by the time she had left her pony tethered in a sheltered spot and then made her way up the steep cliff path, Emma Hathaway realized that nature had done her work for her. The crumbled chalk edge was evidence, along with a torn ruffle of black lace waving frantically.

Whether Emma would actually have gone through with it, even she didn't know just then. Sometimes a person couldn't know what they were capable of until the moment was upon them. But exhilaration surely raced through her veins as she looked over the edge and saw that woman clinging to a few dry tufts of rough grass. Her mind echoed with the many times she'd felt those hard fingers around her slender throat, squeezing until her ears rang and she sank into a dark cloud. How many times had that woman almost killed her?

Now the world was turned upside down and she who had previously been down-trodden stood high above. When Lightbody looked up and saw her there, panic flooded that cruel face even as all color left it. Greed and spite had brought that woman here, that sense of entitlement with which she had plowed her way through life had sent her to this edge and over it. All for a few rings.

Or was it more than that the woman had wanted from Emma? Now they would never know.

How odd, thought Emma, that she'd had this dream so many times and now, here she was, no longer asleep, but wide awake. She felt the rain on her face, tasted it on her lips.

Vengeance. Her friends would never blame her. Nobody here would even identify the woman when she was found.

She took a deep breath, closed her eyes.

Five years ago she had danced for the first time with Captain Guy Hathaway and they had talked then of revenge against ones enemies. Clearly she remembered every word of what she'd said then.

Evil deeds leave nothing meaningful or useful behind... we only give them power to hurt us if we acknowledge them. Good deeds will always triumph. Vengeance might make you feel even, but I will be better than even. I will be better than she.

And she knew it was not what one didn't do, but what one did that mattered. Those last months tending her father had taught her that.

So the Warrior Woman previously known as Emma Chance, opened her eyes, reached down, grasped her old tormentor by the stout wrists and dragged her to safety.

That wailing wind tore across the cliffs, rain soaking the two breathless, black-clad figures.

A moment later, Guy came running, having followed his wife on a borrowed horse.

Her face and hands scraped and bloodied, her gown torn, wig lost, arrogance punctured, Julia Lightbody scrambled away from them both, as Guy quickly pulled his wife out of the wind.

* * * *

After her brush with savage death that day, Mrs. Lightbody was never quite the same again. She swore she had seen the devil in "Chance's" eyes on that cliff and it scared her to such an extent that she never went near her again— or that was the reason she used— but the woman's life was shortened by poor health, her decline was rapid and she was not to see another summer in any case.

Even Guy was a little afraid of his wife when he

saw the strength with which she'd pulled her old enemy to safety.

"Why did you do it?" he demanded. "I could have lost you over that cliff, Emma."

"If I had let her fall I would never be free of her. The moment would have haunted me for the rest of my days. I saved her life, to free mine."

The dream never came to her again. Whenever she went for a stroll along that cliff path she stopped to look at the crumbled place which is all that remained of Julia Lightbody and she smiled. The lady was lucky she came by when she did and not a moment later. How ironic that the woman once gave her the name of "Chance".

Not that she could have predicted it; she never had much imagination.

* * * *

Emma Hathaway stood at her window making pastry, watching her husband dancing with the baby under the oak tree. Sun glittered down onto their heads as a sweet breeze moved the leaves and the baby reached up a pudgy arm, fingers trying to grasp at the swaying, whispering colors. His father whistled and the baby cooed along with the tune.

Happiness filled her heart as she watched the two beings she loved most in the world, cavorting about in the shifting shade. A cup of tea sat getting cold on the window sill. Guy was oblivious to the time while enjoying himself— but she'd known that since their wedding night. There he was now, dropping his tools and finding something else to distract him. As if he had nothing else to do! He was supposed to be pruning the tree, she mused.

A sweeping, feathery breath of lavender came in through the window and tickled her nose. Later she would pick some to make soap.

There were three pigs, two horses, half a dozen chickens and a cow to feed, and soon the baby would need his supper. The list of things to do rolled on through her practical mind, but it trickled to a slow halt as she watched her husband making the baby laugh. Captain Hathaway smiled a great deal now, even when he didn't know anybody was watching.

It was her greatest satisfaction to know that she was responsible for putting that bounce back in the Captain's boots.

Epilogue

The five bedrooms of that cottage were soon filled. With Emma's agreement, his brother Nicholas and his cousin Charles Lennox came to live with them, relieving some of the strain on the Hathaways in Allerton Square. The boys came to view Emma as their own sister and she soon learned that being part of a family can have its ups and its downs. But she loved them all and would never want to go back to being solitary Emma Chance.

As Guy had promised them long ago, they all went out in a boat one day so that he could show Nicholas and Charles how to use a quadrant and find their direction at sea. While the boys were preoccupied that day, Emma drew a little leather purse of rings out of her coat pocket and, with a silent prayer on her lips, she emptied the contents into the waves. It had taken her a while to decide what to do with her father's bequest and in the end she thought this would be the best way to put his spirit— and her own— at rest. One day, perhaps, a lucky fisherman would find the treasure and make good use of it. She liked that idea. For her it would have been too much; she had never wanted riches, just a home and a family, both of which she now had.

She had found where she belonged and with whom. It was all any human being could ever want.

And as for Captain Guy Hathaway, I was content

at last to see him well settled and happy. I might have left him in body long since, but I never left him in his heart. From the moment he was born it was my task to look after him and that didn't end when I was no longer visible in his eyes. Love never does end, you know.

Some people don't believe in ghosts or spiritual intervention. My daughter-in-law never did— she's the practical sort— but when I leave her little bunches of lavender on the window sill she wonders now.

And I like to see her puzzled surprise.

I suppose my son got his sense of mischief from me.

COMING SOON

The Mutinous Contemplations of
Gemma Groot
An Unlikely Romance

Also from Jayne Fresina and TEP:

Souls Dryft

The Taming of the Tudor Male Series

Seducing the Beast

Once A Rogue

The Savage and the Stiff Upper Lip

The Deverells

True Story

Storm

Chasing Raven

Ransom Redeemed

Damon Undone

Ladies Most Unlikely

The Trouble with His Lordship's Trousers

The Danger in Desperate Bonnets

The Bounce in the Captain's Boots

A Private Collection

Last Rake Standing

The Peculiar Folly of Long Legged Meg

ABOUT THE AUTHOR

Jayne Fresina sprouted up in England, the youngest in a family of four daughters. Entertained by her father's colorful tales of growing up in the countryside, and surrounded by opinionated sisters - all with far more exciting lives than hers - she's always had inspiration for her beleaguered heroes and unstoppable heroines.

Website at:
jaynefresinaromanceauthor.blogspot.com

Twisted E Publishing, LLC
www.twistedepublishing.com

49084352R00256

Made in the USA
Middletown, DE
05 October 2017